FOR HEAVEN'S SAKE, Marry the Man

Patty Campbell

FOR HEAVEN'S SAKE, MARRY THE MAN
Copyright © 2022 by Patty Campbell

ISBN: 978-1-955784-65-8

Published by Satin Romance
An Imprint of Melange Books, LLC
White Bear Lake, MN 55110
www.satinromance.com

Names, characters, and incidents depicted in this book are products of the author's imagination or are used fictitiously. Any resemblance to actual events, locales, organizations, or persons, living or dead, is entirely coincidental and beyond the intent of the author or the publisher. No part of this book may be reproduced or transmitted in any form or by any means, electronic or mechanical, including photocopying, recording, or by any information storage and retrieval system, without permission in writing from the publisher except for the use of brief quotations in a book review or scholarly journal.

Published in the United States of America.

Cover Design by Caroline Andrus

This Book is dedicated to my wonderful senior writers of Simi Valley

Tricia Randell - Deep thinking philosopher
Rudy Uribe - Master of the short story
Roy Seeger - A wealth of entertaining life stories
Bernie Chin - Math whiz and budding romance writer
Bruce Sackett - Former Bad Boy musician with stories to prove it
Bo Schwetz - Southern Gentleman with a taste for dark, anti-heroes
Maureen Brown - Spiritual Poet

Prologue

MATHEW

There are angels, and then there are Angels with a capital A. I am of the former category, a garden variety guardian angel to be precise. Truly. It will be several millennia before I reach the Seraphim level—if ever. First, I'd have to be elevated from angel to Angel, an unlikely scenario based on the way things are going.

I am aware that some humans don't believe we exist, but that's not my problem. The Kavanaugh family is my problem.

Here I am on the carpet again, even though it feels more like a bed of nails. How this project got so out of hand is the question I keep asking myself, just as my immediate supervisor is presently asking.

"Well, Matthew, it seems we have another difficulty with the Kavanaugh assignment. Please explain yourself."

She's a capital A. She is imperious when she takes such a tone with me, but who's to blame?

I've been on assignment for the Kavanaugh family since, well, forever. I thought that after all this time I could predict where I'd be needed, what had to be done, and then do it. But, Caroline Clayton wasn't in the equation until recently.

Every hint I drop, every nudge, every dream, every subliminal suggestion has flopped. I must change my tactics. It requires showing up in person, not that I haven't done it before. The director doesn't like us to resort to such tactics, and I'm way over my quota of personal appearances.

In fact, I've been put on notice that I may have to go back for more training if I don't accomplish this job in a timely, uncomplicated, and efficient manner. Timely, uncomplicated, and efficient are not my strong suits. I have until the earthly Christmas celebration to get it done.

It's not that the Kavanaughs are a particularly difficult assignment. Daniel Kavanaugh has seldom been a problem. He's usually responsive to my influence, but this time he's dragging his feet. It's not like him.

Daniel and his love interest, Caroline Clayton, are resisting their destiny. It should have been a slam dunk. *I love sports metaphors.* They're crazy about each other and have been a couple for almost three years. Caroline has decided she will never marry and will never have children. Oh, dear. Two strikes and you're out. *There I go again.*

Daniel is biding his time. He understood early in their relationship that he intended to marry Caroline, but he's reluctant to press the issue for fear she'll bolt. Perceptive young man, my Daniel.

For you to fully appreciate what I'm faced with, I should let you inside Caroline's head. Usually this would not be permitted, but I can't see any harm in it. Perhaps you can help me with a few new ideas. Get the old wheels turning, as it were.

Caroline is my challenge. Like it or not, she will need my help and support in the coming days. This woman is going to cause me to get a demotion. I just know it. Although now that I think of it, one can't go any lower on the angel ladder. I'd have to go back to my beginning and start over, be born again. Once is enough, trust me on that.

My deadline is nearing. I can hear those silly jingle bells already.

CHAPTER 1

Caroline

It all started with Matthew. I didn't know his last name, just Matthew. I didn't know if he had a last name, and I didn't know if Matthew was even his first name. I called him Matt, and he didn't like it much. I could tell because I saw him wince a little when I said it.

I'd had a rotten day at work and was sitting in the little bar on the ground floor of my office building, having a scotch and soda, while listening to a mindless loop of Christmas music. Ack!

"Jeez, Jimmy. Why am I hearing Christmas music? We just got past Halloween."

"I got no control over it, Caroline. Sorry."

I loved my job and I didn't usually sit in bars and drink alone. I seldom drank, but in my present mood, I wasn't ready to go to Danny's and spoil his mood, too. I refused to simmer in my car waiting for it to pass. That was when I met Matt. He'd been sitting at a booth in the far corner before he walked over and sat next to me.

Oh, sheesh! Just what I need after the day I've had. Some desperado who wants to hit on me.

"Hi," he said.

"Hi." *Go away, Buster. I'm not interested.*

"It's a bummer, isn't it?"

"What is?" *Why am I answering this jerk?*

"Life. May I buy you a drink?"

"No, thanks, I have a drink." *Goodbye.*

"Mind if I buy myself one?"

"Why would I?" I looked at his face. Jeez, he had such a sweet smile, almost angelic. I couldn't help myself. I smiled.

"You have a lovely smile."

Oh boy, here it comes. "Thanks." I stopped smiling, looked into my glass, then out the window. I watched traffic and tried to concentrate on the various noises in the bar.

"Does that make you uncomfortable? A compliment? It wasn't intended to."

"Look, I don't know you, and frankly..."

"Matthew. I'm Matthew. Nice to meet you. Now, you know me." He smiled that sweet smile again. "You're Caroline."

"How do you know my name?" *Why was I still sitting there? I should get up and leave.*

"We have a mutual friend," he went on. "I've met you before, don't you remember?" He waved a hand. "That's okay. I seem to have one of those faces people forget. Don't be embarrassed. It happens all the time."

"Look, Matt..." I used my coldest, end-of-the-flirtation voice. He didn't have 'one of those faces.' I would have remembered if I'd met him. "I don't think we've ever met, and I don't think we have a mutual friend. I'm in a crappy mood, and I think you should go find someone else to hit on, okay?" *I can be really mean when the occasion calls for it.*

"Hey, I'm sorry. No problem." He smiled, picked up his wine, and went back to the booth.

Why am I such a complete bitch sometimes? Why do I feel like I'd just kicked a puppy? I breathed a big sigh, picked up my drink and purse, and walked over to his booth.

"Look, I'm sorry. May I sit down?" I slid onto the bench opposite him, not waiting for permission. "I've had a really lousy day, and, just so you know, I have a boyfriend. I'm not in here drinking alone so I can get myself picked up."

"Caroline, I wasn't trying to pick you up. You looked as if you could use a friend, that's all. Don't worry about it. It's okay."

There was that sweet smile again. For the first time, I took close notice of his eyes. They were a clear, pale aqua. When I looked into them, it was as if I could see for miles, but see what? I didn't know.

They were very compelling, unusual eyes. That's all. For reasons I couldn't explain, I felt comfortable with him. I smiled back.

"That's better," he said. "Why don't you tell me about your bad day?"

I had no intention of discussing my problems with a stranger. I didn't discuss my problems with anyone, period. Whatever it was, I could handle it, but I began to get a strange, uncomfortable sensation. To my everlasting shock, I started to cry.

"That bad, huh?" He handed me a beautiful white handkerchief that smelled like a breeze off a spring meadow.

Mute, I nodded. I was so shocked at my tears I couldn't have blown on my bangs if my hair was on fire. I sat there crying into that handkerchief and for some reason I wasn't embarrassed that he was there. Truthfully, having him there was a comfort to me when I hadn't realized I needed comforting. All I thought I needed was a drink to brace myself before going home or to Dan's place.

Home. What a laugh. My apartment was beautiful, tasteful, and expensive, but home? Just thinking of how much it was *not* a home made me cry again just when I thought I was about finished. Cry. Crap! I never cry. It's such a stupid indulgence and a total waste of time.

"My life is a mess," I finally managed.

"Why?" He tilted his head to the side and waited for my answer.

"For starters, I could get canned from the job I love. I dunno. Maybe I'll quit. My bastard boss is looking for any excuse to fire me."

"No. Why?"

"He wants me to relocate to Seattle, and I told him to go screw himself. Seems I'm often shooting off my mouth lately."

"Oops."

"Yeah, oops." I sighed deeply and shook my head. "I think he's looking to replace me with the little bimbo he hired and is probably sleeping with."

"Mmm." He put his fingers to his lips, a thoughtful expression on his—now that I really looked—handsome face. "Perhaps you should talk it over with Daniel."

"I've thought about talking to Dan about it, but I can't. I mean, I, uh, I've always given him the impression that I can handle any problems that come up on the job. I don't want him to think I'm a helpless crybaby."

I leaned onto my elbows and rubbed my temples. The after-work crowd was thinning out in the lobby bar.

"Let me guess. Daniel thinks you're Superwoman?"

"Yes, well, that's the way I've always acted. Sometimes, I really do some stupid things." I folded my arms and put my head down. I was hoping I'd sink into a hole.

His fingers patted my hair lightly. It was a sympathetic pat. It didn't offend me. I sighed.

I rolled my head back and forth on my arms. "Seems all I can think about lately is the sorry state of my love life, my job, my parents, my future."

He shifted when I looked at him and jiggled the ice cubes in his glass. "That's not good."

Who puts ice in their wine?

"No kidding, I feel like hey, I'm smart. I'm successful, for crying out loud. I should know what direction I want to take, what I want."

He raised his eyebrows and tilted his head. "What do you want?" His eyes squinched up, making him resemble a big question mark.

"I thought I had what I wanted, and when I got it, I could only think it must have been something else I wanted."

"Mmm." Matthew signaled the bartender to bring another round.

I was doubtful, but he smiled and patted my hand in a reassuring way. "It's okay." He smiled. "Looks like you need it. You can always call Daniel to come and fetch you if you don't think it's wise to drive."

I could feel my forehead wrinkling because I couldn't remember mentioning Danny by name. I must have. How else would Matthew know?

I nodded. "Thanks." I asked myself again why I was sitting there with him. I didn't know him. He could be a serial rapist for all I knew. Yeah, he could be, but not likely. I'd take my chances. I raised my new drink and sipped at it, enjoying the feel of the cold, damp glass.

"Better?"

I couldn't help it. I smiled again. "Yeah, I guess." I did feel better. I wasn't sure if it was the scotch or Matthew, but I definitely felt better.

We sat and talked some more. Actually, I did the talking. He was a great listener. Lousy at giving advice though, because his only comments when I asked his opinion were answers like: "Is that what you want?" or "Would you be happy with that?" or "Could you have done it differently?" Two hours passed before I knew it.

Matthew leaned back against the padded backrest. "Maybe you should be getting home." His voice was quiet, soothing. "From what you've said, tomorrow could be an important day of decision for you."

He gazed at me with those aqua blue eyes of his. Such eyes, I wanted to sink right into them like a warm blanket. Every time I looked at him, I relaxed more. The tension that had been in the back of my neck for a week was gone. What was it about him, anyway? All he'd done was listen to me.

"Matt." I noticed the little wince. "Matthew, sorry. Thanks for acting as my crying towel. I haven't cried since I was in junior high. I must have been saving it for you." I laughed self-consciously. "You're right, I should go. Danny will be worried."

I stood, and he did, too, and extended his hand.

"I've enjoyed talking with you, Caroline. Would you like me to walk you to your car?"

"No, the garage is secured. I'll be fine." I took his hand and felt currents running right up my arm into my shoulders. My head cleared, and the effect of the scotch disappeared. It was unnerving, and I didn't hang on long either.

"Have a safe drive home." He winked at me and left the bar, giving me a little wave as he went out the door.

I stood, wondering what had happened. I'd spent more than two hours with a stranger. Oh, well, okay. He introduced himself and said we'd met before, but I didn't remember, so maybe he wasn't a stranger. It didn't matter anyway. It was just that I was still puzzled about why I'd poured my heart out to him and cried like a baby, for God's sake.

∼

When I got to Daniel's apartment, he was working at his computer, probably preparing a brief or whatever it is that contract lawyers do when they sit at their computers, pecking away for hours. He glanced over his shoulder. "Hi. I didn't know you were going to be late tonight."

It wouldn't cause my teeth to fall out if I apologized. "Sorry, I should have called. I wasn't planning on being late. It just happened."

I knew I should have asked him right then if he could be interrupted, so we could talk. Instead, I kept right on going. I'm hopeless.

He continued to stare at that screen. Dan had great concentration. "Hope you've had dinner," he said without turning. "I fixed myself something."

I'm not sure if I was angry at myself or Danny, but I couldn't keep the nasty tone out of my voice. "Jeez, Danny, this place is a pigsty. Don't you ever pick up anything?" I mumbled more complaints on my way to his bedroom.

He called after my retreating back, "If you'd move in with me, you'd only have one apartment to clean."

His good-humored banter annoyed me further. "Don't start."

I was pulling off my clothes before I got through his bedroom door. I hung my clothes in his closet and put on a big, furry, red bathrobe I keep there and a pair of comfy old slippers that I absolutely love, and then headed for the kitchen.

I navigated through an obstacle course of discarded running shoes and newspapers in his cozy–meaning small–apartment and wondered how come such a neat, clean guy could be such a lousy housekeeper.

"Dan?" I called out. "I'm going to fix myself something to eat. Do you want some coffee?"

"Sure, Care," he said absently. "Coffee would be great. Call me when it's ready."

I hate it when he calls me Care. I guess that's why Matthew winced every time I called him Matt.

I got the coffee pot going, opened the refrigerator, and took out two eggs and the tub of soft butter. I really hated scrambled eggs, but that's all I could think of fixing. I had to eat something.

While I cooked, I asked myself questions. Why didn't I quit and look for another job? Why didn't I go spend some time with my parents at their villa on the Italian Riviera? They kept inviting me, and I kept telling them I couldn't take time off work. Well, that one I could answer. I didn't like spending time with them. Maybe I should break up with Danny and take the transfer to Seattle. Why couldn't I come to a decision? I should talk to Dan. Why didn't I?

"Dan, coffee's ready. There or here?" I carried my plate to his tiny bistro table.

"I'll come there." He sauntered in and sat at the table across from me. He leaned back, stretching, and ran his hands through his hair. He's one good-looking son-of-a-gun. I wish I wasn't in love with him. Well, maybe not. I don't know what the heck I wish.

Danny's great in bed, and we have a good time together. But we've always had this unspoken understanding that we're not in love, just happy lust. We've been a couple for almost three years. He does some kind of specialized, big company, big celebrity, high tech contract law or something. Jeez, I am interested, but I don't understand most of it.

He gave me a sympathetic look over the rim of his coffee cup. "You look frazzled, babe."

I hate it even more when he calls me babe than I do when he calls me Care. He'd probably stop doing it if I ever bothered to tell him I didn't like it. Why was I so afraid to open up to him? What would he do, bite me?

I chewed a mouthful of eggs. They didn't taste bad. "Yeah, I had a super crappy day, and I'm going to take a nice, warm bubble bath when I finish eating."

I studied him as he drank his coffee. He was a bigger, handsomer version of his dad, Liam. Dan's hair was curlier, and he had more of it. His dad and four older brothers are tall, blue-eyed, and gorgeous. Danny, the baby of the litter, was the best looking one in the bunch.

I asked him, "You have much more work to do tonight?"

"Nope, I can wrap it up any time. Why? You want me to crawl into that bubble bath with you?" He flashed that sexy smile of his, the one that always gave me little twitches you-know-where.

"I was thinking about it." Some good, hot sex might be good for what ailed me. I picked up my empty plate and stood. "Okay, I've thought about it. Why don't you shut down your computer and clean the bathtub while I clean this kitchen? Then we can go in search of paradise."

He laughed, stood, and set his cup on the counter. He gave me a little bite on the neck. "You're funny, and I love that you're always my ready-when-you-are girl."

Our *relationship* worked for both of us, kept us at home. What complicated things was me being stupid in love with him. That definitely put a pothole in my smooth little road.

Later, just before we fell asleep, I asked him, "Hey, Danny, do you know a guy named Matthew?"

"No, babe." He gave me a little nip on the earlobe. "Why?"

We were both naked, and he had one arm across me. I was sort of melted across his chest and belly. I like it there. God, he always smelled so good.

"I ran into this guy today, Matthew. He said he'd met me before and knew who you were."

He mumbled sleepily, "Whatziz last name? I don't recall anybody named Matthew. I'm usually pretty good with names."

"I don't know. It doesn't matter. Go to sleep," I murmured the words against his neck. I really did intend to discuss things with Dan, but he was almost out, his breathing slow and rhythmic.

I sighed. Tomorrow—I'll tell him my troubles tomorrow.

CHAPTER 2

Caroline

The next morning, I definitely felt better. Anytime I could watch Daniel's naked butt while he shaved put me in a good mood. I had to resist bending down to take a bite out of it. Not that I hadn't tried before. All I got for my efforts was a pinch on the bottom.

Danny and I looked good together. I'd be lying if I said we weren't initially attracted to each other by our looks. We were, but there was more to it than that. Dan's IQ is off the charts. I know it seems hard to believe because of what I've already said, but the sexiest thing about him was his brain.

I was twenty-seven when we met and had been in love once before. Nothing ever came of it. Actually, what came of it was the guy jilted me. By the time Dan and I met, we'd both been through the romance wars. I'd decided that love was a cruel joke, so I'd quit looking for it. Two hours after we met, we were on his bed, breathing very hard.

That's all we both wanted at the time. I ended up falling in love with Dan, and it scared the heck out of me. I didn't want to be in love. My brain didn't work right when I was in love. Almost everyone I've ever loved ended up letting me down. It's too darn painful, and I didn't want to do that anymore.

Truthfully, Danny and I avoided the subject of love. No strings, no complications. He had his place. I had mine. That was our arrangement.

Well, time was wasting. I thought I'd better get my rear in gear, or

I'd be late for work. I didn't need to give that obnoxious boss of mine any more reasons to dislike me. Hell, he only disliked me because I gave him the brush-off.

I worked for the largest commercial design firm in L.A., Leebow Elvey Honnet, as a graphic artist and interior designer. I specialized in executive suite design, and I was good at it. I also enjoyed my job when I could keep the boss off my back. I'd be on the fast track to a vice presidency of the division if he wasn't getting in my way. It also wouldn't hurt if I quit doing things that provoked him. I really must apologize for what I said and quit being such a smartass.

When I got to work, I discovered he was off sick. Too bad, I'd apologize tomorrow. I thought I might get some new design work done. That depended on if I could find enough scut work to keep the little airhead he hired out of my face. She was a doozie, poor kid. Long on boobs and short on brains. I decided I would try not to be such a bitch and go easy on her. I didn't know why she liked me, but she did. I could be nice to her if I really tried. Anyway, she wasn't so bad, kinda cute, too. Her name was Tiffany. Gag! One thing I could thank my parents for was not sticking me with some cutsie, trendy name.

I brought coffee over to the worktable for both of us and nearly shocked the daylights out of her. She gave me a big, grateful smile, which made me feel like the witch that I tend to be sometimes.

"Thank you, Caroline, for the coffee. That's so nice."

"Sheesh, it's only coffee, I thought I'd be civil for a change. I'm in a good mood because the boss won't be in today."

"Nice, isn't it?" She looked around to make sure we were alone. "I know I shouldn't say anything, but he gets on my nerves. I secretly call him Old Hot Pants." She whispered, even though only the two of us were in the room at the time.

My eyebrows shot up, and I laughed at her remark. "That's funny. I call him Old Smoking Crotch."

She opened her mouth, and her eyes sparkled with amusement. All of a sudden, I felt something akin to respect for her. Oh, my God! We had something in common, and all the time I thought she liked his *attentions*.

"You know, Tiffany, I think I owe you an apology. I don't know for sure where the idea came from, but I thought you and he were uh...you know."

"Oh, please!" The look on her face was a combination of surprise and disgust. Her blush was deep pink, and the freckles on her nose glowed like they were on fire. "That man makes me crazy. You'd think with all the awareness about sexual harassment in the workplace, he'd know better. The only reason I haven't reported him is because I don't want to come across as a whiner."

I have to say I looked at her in a different light. I was embarrassed I'd judged her on my thoughtless perceptions and her name. Every now and then, I'm aware of what a shallow, self-centered twit I could be. I'd probably like myself better if I had more of her upbeat, happy attitude.

Taking the coffee cups, I backed from the table. "I'll be right back."

She looked mystified. Her eyes grew really big, and for the first time, I noticed they were dark russet brown. What a dynamite combination with her short mop of curly blonde hair.

I walked to the break room, did a U-turn, and went back to the worktable.

"Hi, Tiffany, how are you today? Let me introduce myself." I set the coffee cups on the table and extended my hand. "I'm Caroline Clayton, the lead designer here. It looks like we'll be working together today." She took my hand, and a quirky little smile trembled at the corners of her mouth. I went on, "I'd like to get acquainted. I've been looking forward to working with you."

She played out the little scene with me. "Tiffany Gaines, so nice to meet you, Caroline. I'd love to know you better. I hope we can be friends."

A warm smile, accompanied by genuine intelligence, beamed from her face. Why hadn't I noticed before? I didn't know. She took a sip of the coffee and tried to suppress another smile.

I shook my head. "Do you have any idea how stupid I feel? All this time we could have been working together, and I've been acting the self-involved prima donna." I shook my head and wondered about myself. Again.

"It's okay. I know you're super busy all the time, and the boss doesn't help matters, does he? He's the embodiment of the—I hesitate to use the expression—Peter Principal."

I laughed and almost choked on my coffee. "Somehow I had the idea he was singling me out for his particular brand of charm. I guess I should have been paying more attention. Sorry."

She waved away my apology. "I'd love to help on some of your projects. I think you have great ideas." She sounded earnest. "I hate to admit it, but I sneak a peek at what you're working on, when you're not around." She looked as if she were ten years old and had just confessed to wearing Mommy's makeup and high heels. "I was afraid you'd catch me at it one day."

I wagged my finger under her nose. "Sneaking a peek, huh? For shame."

Her sigh was dramatic and exaggerated. "I feel so relieved now that I've confessed."

We both chuckled again and took a swallow of coffee.

The large, open workroom buzzed with the activity of early morning arrivals. "Okay, Miss Nosey, where should we begin?"

"How about the Wilshire Bank project?"

"Good choice."

At lunchtime, I ran down to the bar to buy a Coke to go with the sandwich I forgot to bring to work. No wonder I had a skinny bum.

Guess who was sitting there in a booth in the corner? Right, Matthew. I spotted him as I turned to leave, and he smiled the pound puppy *adopt me* smile and waved.

I turned to the bartender. "Who *is* that guy, Jimmy? And how long has he been sitting there?"

Jimmy used to work in our mailroom before he found out there was a lot more money to be made bartending. He looked across the room and shrugged. "I don't know. I didn't see him come in. I never saw him before."

"Come on, Jimmy. I sat with him for two hours last night after work. Don't you remember?" The drink was freezing my fingers, dripping on my shoe.

He chuckled. "If you sat with him for two hours, why are you asking me who he is? I remember you were in here, but sorry, I don't remember him."

"Forget it, okay?" I waved to Matthew and high-tailed it out of there. Tiffany and I were making real progress, and I wanted to get back to my drafting board.

When I left work that evening Matthew was strolling along the sidewalk in front of the building. He spotted me as I drove by and waved. He was getting on my nerves. Who was the guy? He couldn't be

Danny's friend. Dan hadn't heard of him. Tomorrow I was going to ask Jimmy if he would keep an eye out for him and let me know if he showed up again.

∼

When I got to my apartment, Daniel wasn't there. He'd left a big note on the mirror in the entry. He'd gone to an unplanned business dinner, and he'd be back around ten. He was good about calling or leaving a note. It pissed me off because it reminded me that I was an inconsiderate little turd. I never left notes and usually forgot to call. It's a wonder he put up with me.

Probably, what it meant was his parents did a better job bringing up five boys than mine did bringing up one girl. You probably have to be around once in a while to do any quality parenting. Am I bitter? You bet. Hey, I love my parents. They trained me well. Look, I turned out to be just as selfish and self-centered as they are. They did a service to mankind when they stopped with one child, me.

My contribution to the betterment of the world was that I don't want, or plan to have any children. *Yeah, yeah, there must be something wrong with me. So, shoot me. I know myself, right?* Did I want some poor, unsuspecting infant to pop into those bright lights and find out I was its mother? I don't think so.

After hanging my coat and dropping my portfolio, I called Chinese-We-Deliver and headed for the shower. Their ten-minute-guaranteed delivery usually took at least forty-five. I'd have more than enough time to shower and pull on my terry bathrobe and bunny slippers before they got there.

The kid who delivered the food was a skinny, pimply redhead. He couldn't take his eyes off my chest. I didn't think there was a single Chinese person in that entire restaurant. The food was okay. It would sustain life.

I was halfway through my latest romance novel—yes, I loved romance novels—when I heard Danny's key in the lock. He strolled in wearing a big grin. I knew that look. Everything had gone his way.

"Hi, babe. I smell Chinese. Guess that means you remembered to eat."

He kissed me. I pulled him down for another. He was a great kisser.

"How was your meeting? You look like the cat that ate the canary." I couldn't resist answering his smile.

"Great. We nailed the contract and secured a client we've been after for years. They didn't know what hit 'em. My presentation left them speechless." Danny shuffled through my CD rack. "Wanna dance?" He popped a CD into my stereo. He loved to dance when feeling triumphant.

"Sure." He's a good dancer, too. Not many of them around anymore. He grabbed me and danced me around my living room, cleverly avoiding the furniture. I loved his arms around me.

"Hope that was a good cigar," I said. "Every inch of you smells like a barnyard."

"Yeah, sexy, isn't it?" he said with a chuckle, while getting a big woody. "Know what I want to do?" He dipped me way back, Valentino style.

I tingled all over. "Hmm, let me guess. No, I can't think of anything. I give up," I said in a voice I thought sounded coy.

"You know how this old robe of yours turns me on, babe." He pulled me closer and breathed in my ear.

"Yeah, right." I unbuttoned his shirt. "Do one thing for me, okay? Brush your teeth. A little Havana goes a long way."

He laughed and took my hand and led the way to the bedroom. All in all, it was a pretty good day. I'd talk to him about my problems tomorrow.

~

The next morning, I walked into the office to find Tiffany leaning over my table, studying the suite design I'd been working on the afternoon before. I could hear The Jerk talking on the phone from his office with who I assumed was a customer. He was using his soothing, professional voice. It was similar to his I'm God's gift voice, the one he used when he thought he was too irresistible. Must be some kind of trouble, I thought.

"Find a problem, Tiffany?" I asked as I walked to the table.

She jumped. "Oh, no, hi, I was wondering if you'd let me work on this one with you. It's so interesting, the configuration of the space, I mean. Like these windows over here." She pointed to the floor plan.

Hey, I'm thinking, this kid had a brain.

"Sure. Why don't you make another copy of the print and rough sketch your ideas? We can both work on it."

The expression on her face was pathetic. She looked as if she'd won the lottery. Like I said before, I was wrong about her. She was okay.

Mister Thinks He's Big came out of his office wearing his serious-supervisor face. He marched to my desk, and I had an excuse to ignore him because I was busy changing out of my flat shoes and putting away my carry bag. Finally, I looked up. There was no sense in pushing it. I still owed him an apology.

"We have a problem, Clayton." He was in the habit of using my last name when he planned to discuss business. My first name was reserved for mash moments.

My hair prickled. "What problem?" I wondered if I was about to get canned.

"I just got a call from the Harrison Publishing job site in Seattle. They've run into a predicament with the contractor who's doing the renovations of the old building. They have to completely change the floor plan of the executive offices."

"Meaning?"

"Meaning, you have to get your ass up there, and find out what in hell is going on, and how much we're going to have to change the design." He added, "The custom furniture has already been ordered."

"Why me?" I knew the answer. He hated to travel, and his missus didn't trust him out of the city. Wonder why?

"Because you did the initial design, and they want to work with you on the re-do." The only thing he didn't add–to his credit–was duh.

I refused to give in without a token fight. "Can't the architect just send us the blueprints? I can work from that. I'd rather not go to Seattle in the fall. The weather can turn stinky in a minute, and I hate hotel rooms."

"Look, Clayton," he huffed. "I'm not asking you. I'm telling you. Have Russell make hotel and flight reservations and go on home and pack. She can call you at home and leave the information. I don't want an unhappy customer on our hands. This contract is big money. We can't afford to lose it now."

"Okay, okay," I conceded. "Give me a few minutes. I want to call Danny and let him know." I was getting better, wasn't I? "Then I need to get Tiffany started on the Markham design." I gave him a sour smile, and he probably felt like the conquering hero. He couldn't get me into bed, but he could tell me what to do as far as the company was concerned. Damn.

~

"Knight Kristensen, how may I help you?"

"May I speak to Daniel Kavanaugh please?"

"I'll see if Mr. Kavanaugh is in. May I tell him who is calling?"

I didn't recognize the voice. "Ms. Clayton."

"Hi, Caroline, this is Billie. Danny said he was not to be disturbed but let me check. I'm sure he'll want to take your call."

She put me on hold. I listened to Aaron Neville, not the kind of music you expect when you call a big law firm.

"Hi, babe. What's up?"

I pictured him sitting at his desk, shirtsleeves rolled up, tie thrown over the top of the file cabinet, and piles of files all over the desktop. Men in suits are sexy. Danny in a suit is very sexy, or out of a suit, for that matter.

"I have to leave town for a couple of days, Dan. A customer in Seattle has a problem and wants me to consult. I'm calling because I'm leaving in a couple of hours."

"Seattle! The weather up there's been a sumbitch all week."

"Yeah, I know. Nothing I can do about it though."

"When you gonna be back, babe?"

"I'll call you tonight or in the morning. I hope I can wrap it up with a single overnight." I was going to miss the big hunk.

"I'll miss you, Caroline." He whispered, "Know what I mean, babe? Hurry back."

"Bye, Danny."

He'd miss me. That was kinda nice. It suddenly struck me that we'd never been separated more than a night since we'd been together. He's traveled, and I've traveled, but it was usually there and back in the same day.

"Miss you, too," I add, and it didn't even break my teeth to say it. Wonders never cease.

When I got to the Los Angeles Airport, I checked in and took my boarding pass, then realized that I hadn't had any lunch. Not wanting to depend on the Cordon Bleu peanut service on the flight. I spotted a fast-food place and bought a ham and cheese and coffee, then sat down to eat. I took out my novel and opened it.

"Caroline. How nice to see you," a voice at my elbow said.

I looked up. Matthew stood there holding a tray. I was so surprised to see him I didn't say anything, just sat there with a stupid look on my face, my mouth full. He pulled out the chair across from me. "Mind if I join you?"

I swallowed. "Matt?" He grimaced when I said it. "Sorry...Matthew, what are you doing here?" I asked, but when he set the tray down, I could see a boarding pass under his coffee cup.

"I'm going out of town on business for a couple of days. You?"

"Same here."

"Good book?"

"Yes. I read lots of her stuff. Good travel reading." I closed the book and stuffed it into my briefcase.

"I enjoy her, too." His eyebrows danced.

I was barely able to keep a straight face. "You read romance novels?"

"Sure, big, macho man that I am. I'm not embarrassed to admit it, I enjoy them. They always have happy endings. I like happy endings. Don't you?"

There was his sweet smile again. I grinned back. I had to agree. "Yeah, I guess. If you have to have an ending, why not a happy one?"

"Personally, I prefer beginnings." He took a big bite out of his hamburger. "Want some fries?" He pushed the tray in my direction.

His bottomless aqua blues were sucking me in again. I cleared my throat. What was it about his eyes, anyway?

"Sure, I love fries." I shrugged as I stuffed a couple into my mouth.

"Don't want to go, huh?" He took a big swig of his soft drink.

"What?" I mumbled through my mouthful of fries.

"I can tell from your face that you don't want to go on this trip. Problem?"

When did I become so transparent? I'd always prided myself in being the inscrutable ice queen. "No...uh...yes. Yeah, I'd rather not go, but I have no choice. One of our customers ran into a construction problem, and I have to go work on a redesign. It's a drag to have to go back and do something over, especially when I was so happy with the first results. The customer was, too."

"The weather in Seattle is lousy this week. I don't envy you," he said, shaking his head, then took another big swallow of his drink. I'd never seen a man enjoy a simple hamburger, Coke, and fries so much.

"How did you know I was going to Seattle?" I asked, and not too nicely. "I didn't say I was going to Seattle."

"That could be a problem." He chuckled. "That's what it says on your boarding pass." He pointed to the card on my tray.

I actually blushed. "Oh." The last time I blushed was when I lost the bottom of my bikini while paddling in the ocean at Malibu. I was five at the time. "Matthew, why is it that everywhere I turn, you seem to be there?"

"Just your good fortune, I guess. Life's full of coincidences. I could ask you the same thing."

He laughed and took another big bite of his burger. The way he was going at it, you'd have thought he hadn't had a hamburger in a hundred years.

I had to concede. "Yeah, I guess it works both ways, lucky me. Where are you going?" I pushed the remains of my ham and cheese away.

"Portland. In fact, we're on the same flight, I think. I get off at Portland, and you stay on until Seattle. Alaska flight 1267. Right?" He tilted his head and studied my boarding pass.

"Right, well...uh...business?" *Tell me, is this scary or what?*

He nodded. "Yes, I'll be there one day. How about you?" He wiped his mouth and said, "Good burger."

"Just till tomorrow, I hope." I studied him thoughtfully. "What do you do anyway, Matt?" Oops, there was the wince again.

"I'm what you could call a motivational or inspirational speaker." He wiped the last of the burger off his lips, then took another swallow of Coke. "I travel a lot."

"Does that bother the wife and kids?" My sneaky way of finding out more about the guy I seemed destined to bump into all the time.

"No wife. No kids."

"Oh." Now that I had that information, what was I going to do with it?

His eyebrows raised in curiosity. "How about Daniel? Does he mind when you're away on business?"

I wondered if Danny would really miss me. "Nah, he won't even notice I'm gone." I took another swallow of coffee, put the cup next to what was left of my ham and cheese, and dropped my paper napkin on top.

"He'll miss you. I know I would." He winked.

"You're not hitting on me, are you, Matt?"

Matthew flashed his sweet smile, his eyes devoid of any come-hither look. He didn't say anything, and to my everlasting mortification, I blushed again.

"Sorry," I apologized. "I'm so used to guys trying to make a move on me that after a while I start letting my imagination run amok." I closed my eyes and shook my head.

"No offense taken, but I still think Daniel will miss you."

"He said he would when I called him. Come to think of it, that really surprised me. That he'd say that, I mean. It's out of character for him, you know?"

I was blabbering. Was the guy practicing hypnosis or something? What was it about him that when I talked to him, I told him stuff I didn't intend to?

I took a breath. "You're not a priest or something, are you?"

"No." He laughed and shook his head. "I told you what I do."

"Yeah, sorry. I don't think I got enough sleep last night."

"Will you miss Daniel?"

"Yes," I said. I wanted to shut up, so I sipped my now cold coffee and vowed to keep my trap shut about my personal life. *That's none of your business, Matthew Whatever.*

"There's no shame in that, you know. It's natural to miss your significant other when you're separated. I miss the ones I'm close to when I have to be away."

I protested, "I'm not ashamed, for God's sake! It's that I...I never realized I would miss him; and I never said it out loud before. I probably shocked the hell out of Dan. Why am I telling you this? You make me crazy, you know? Excuse me. I'm going to visit the ladies room."

I picked up my stuff and left in such a hurry that I tripped on somebody's flight bag and nearly fell flat on my face.

The hubbub of the airport increased in size and volume as departing passengers gathered at the various gates for the crush of numerous afternoon flights. I visited the women's room, and then found a quiet corner at the departure gate across from mine in attempt to shield myself from Matthew and the world at large.

I didn't see him anywhere in the boarding lounge. I sat and took out my book, but my concentration wandered. After a few minutes, they called my flight. I boarded the aircraft and took my seat next to the window. I couldn't help myself; I craned my neck, looking around to see if Matt was onboard.

Just before they buttoned up, Matthew came down the aisle and took the seat next to me. By then, I knew that I was in the Twilight Zone. There are coincidences, and there are coincidences.

I glared when he sat down. "Did you ask for that seat?" I shot at him angrily.

"No, did you ask for that one?" he said, the picture of innocence.

"God!" I put on my sunglasses, slammed the window shade down, and rolled up my jacket to put under my neck. Then I turned as far away from him as I could. "Don't talk to me. I'm going to try and sleep."

"Sweet dreams." He chuckled, making me want to turn around and pop him.

The next thing I knew, my ears were popping. We were losing altitude. My wakeup call. We'd land soon. I no more than sat upright than the captain came on the loudspeaker. Why are those things always cranked up to heavy metal concert sound and right over my head? He said we'd be landing in a few minutes, fasten your seat belts, put all tray tables and seat backs in the fully locked and upright position, yada, yada, yada.

I glanced over at Matthew and watched him arrange his papers and close his laptop. He looked at me and winked. "You'll be rid of me soon. Have a nice nap?"

I quickly covered an unexpected yawn. "Yeah." I hadn't dreamt. That was unusual for me. My mind is usually grinding away, awake or asleep. Sometimes I'm more tired when I wake up than when I went to sleep. I was puzzled and pleased that I felt so refreshed.

"We seem to be on time, so if things go smoothly, I should have time to visit with an old friend of mine before I check into my hotel," he said. "I travel so much I know people everywhere, it seems. It's nice to keep in touch."

I shrugged. "I don't know anybody in Seattle except my customers. I'll check in to my room and get room service. I don't like finding a place to eat and sitting there alone." I surprised myself with that confession.

If Matt was not a priest, why was I always confessing to him? He looked at me with those wonderful, incredible bottomless eyes and smiled.

"What?" I asked.

"Nothing. You look sweet and unguarded. It's very attractive. I like your smile."

My back stiffened, and I scowled at him.

"Now settle down. I'm not hitting on you, and I have no ulterior motive. Can't someone give you an innocent compliment without you dragging out your big guns?"

I decided the best thing was to shut up. Every time I opened my mouth around him, I lost control over what I said. Maybe I was on my way to a nervous breakdown. Nah, I didn't have time, but I hoped he would stay in Portland for a long time.

Once the plane landed and they turned off the seat belt light, he stood and pulled his jacket out of the overhead. Briefcase in hand, he stood in the aisle with all the other passengers, who could barely wait to get in line, so that they could stand there twiddling their thumbs until disembarkation started. They reminded me of L.A. drivers who speed between signals so they don't miss any red lights. Personally, I get a lot of enjoyment of adhering to the speed limit, then sailing right past them at the next intersection.

He leaned toward me. "Hope your project isn't too complicated. I know you want to get back home in a hurry," he said, smiling down.

I involuntarily nodded my agreement. "Yeah." Well, dammed if I didn't think of where Danny was, as home. When had that happened?

He extended his hand, and I reached to shake it. "Call Daniel tonight. I bet he has some news he'd like to share with you," he whispered. Then he moved toward the front of the aircraft.

"Wha...?" My voice trailed after his retreating back. Call Daniel? He had some news.

CHAPTER 3

Matthew

Lake Sherwood Country Club in the rolling hills of Thousand Oaks is right up there among the world's best. I hadn't looked forward to a day of golf so much since I played Old St. Andrews with Jamie Kavanaugh, one bitterly cold and windy morning back in 1862. The view there had been of the North Sea, not the rolling hills of sunny Southern California.

I looked out on long fairways lined with ancient California live oak, starkly beautiful hills cloaked in rocks and chaparral, dotted with homes of the rich and famous. This job had its advantages. My status didn't require me to forgo *all* earthly pleasures.

I hung around the pro shop, browsing through gloves and golf balls, the holiday gift suggestions. The club pro, Jack, was the starter this afternoon. He reviewed his lists and checked his watch to see that everything was moving along on schedule. Jack, an old friend of Daniel's, was a good-looking man in his early thirties.

Daniel and his father, Liam, approached from the parking lot, right on time. They hailed Daniel's boss, Bill Knight, on the practice green. He'd arrived at the club ahead of them.

Daniel bears a strong resemblance to his robustly healthy father, broad shoulders and flat belly. Athletes to the core.

I made my cell phone ring and held a brief conversation with myself as the men approached the door. Right before they entered, I walked over to Jack through the aisles between racks of clothing and equipment. "Darn it! My partner called and said he had car trouble and won't be able to get here for our round. Is there any chance of getting me into a foursome in the next hour or so?"

"I don't know, Mr. Angeli. I have the Kavanaugh threesome starting in a few minutes. Maybe they wouldn't mind a fourth. Here they are now. I'll introduce you."

"Morning, Jack," Daniel said. "We're all here and raring to go. I told Dad and Bill to take the padlocks off their wallets. I feel lucky today." He shoved his hands into his pockets and rocked back on his heels, clearly enjoying himself.

"Hey, Danny. How's it goin'?" Jack smiled in greeting. "How are you today, Mr. Kavanaugh, Mr. Knight?"

"We're ready to teach this young smart-aleck a lesson in the finer points of golf," Liam answered.

"Yes indeed," echoed Bill dryly, "and a lesson in humility."

"Then you'd better pray for rain," Danny said, and playfully punched his dad's shoulder.

"We'll just see about that," Liam said. "You're not the first duck I've heard quacking."

Jack tipped his head in my direction. "Mr. Angeli's partner couldn't show up for their game, how about if he joins you? Then you can triple-team Danny."

Bill extended his hand to me. "We don't need any help putting this young pup in his place, but we'd be happy to have you join us. Bill Knight's the name."

"Matthew Angeli." I shook hands with Bill and then Liam, enjoying tremendously the physical contact, after so many years of behind-the-scenes work.

"Happy to have you join us," he said graciously. "Liam Kavanaugh."

Daniel offered his hand. "Dan Kavanaugh."

"Dan Kavanaugh...Daniel Kavanaugh," I feigned confusion. "I think I'm acquainted with your young lady. By any chance is her name Caroline?" Sometimes in order to get the job done, it is necessary to tell small lies. It's a case of the end justifying the means. Heaven knows I don't take any enjoyment in it. Oops, there goes one of those fibs now.

"Yes, Caroline Clayton," Daniel answered with raised eyebrows. "How do you know her?"

I detected some wariness and perhaps a touch of jealousy in his voice. I could almost feel the hair pricking up on the back of his neck.

"We met at a social gathering some time back." *More lies.* "You were there also, but I didn't have the pleasure of meeting you then," *I fibbed some more.* "I bumped into Caroline again a few days ago at her office building. We spoke for a time after she got off work." *The truth.*

Daniel flashed a brief, less than friendly glance my way. "Oh, yeah, I remember her saying something about it. She asked if I knew you."

"It is a small world, isn't it?" Quickly changing the subject, I added, "I'd love to join you, if that's okay." With gracious smiles they nodded.

"You're up, gentlemen," Jack said. "Have a good game."

"See you later, Jack," Daniel called out as we walked to the door. "I'll buy you a beer with my winnings."

Liam pounded him on the back. "Quack, quack, quack."

"Oh, Dan," Jack called out. When Daniel turned around, Jack pointed to the "No Gambling" sign and winked. Small sins add to the pleasures of human life.

We picked up our clubs and headed to the first tee, pulling our handcarts along the walkway. Modern generation golf shoes are silent on the pavement. I missed the familiar old clicking sound. Glancing heavenward, I reminded The Director that I had to play well enough to keep up with these hotshots.

Daniel noticed me looking up and followed my gaze. "Looks like we're in for perfect golf weather today, doesn't it?" He pulled off his sweater as we walked.

"Yes, it sure is beautiful," I gazed into the blue.

Dan attempted more friendly behavior after his initial frostiness. "What's your handicap?" He rolled up the sweater and stuffed it into his golf bag.

"I play in the high seventies, low eighties."

"Hey, that's great." His grin was sincere.

"Yes, if it gets any hotter than that, I don't enjoy the game."

He groaned and flashed a tight-lipped smile. "I can't believe I walked right into that old one."

I raised my right hand. "I promise no more old, bad jokes."

The three men chuckled. I hoped they weren't just being polite. I told myself to behave. After all, I was there to work.

Daniel took a coin from his pocket, and we flipped to see who would be first off the tee. "You have the honors, Dad. Get ready to lose big."

"That'll be enough out of you," Liam warned. He leaned down, carefully placed his tee and lined up his shot. He hit a perfect drive, right down the center of the fairway. He gave Daniel a that'll-show-you grin.

"Not bad, not bad for an old man."

Daniel lined up his shot and hit his own perfect drive. I admired his beautiful follow-through.

"That's the way it's going to be, I see," Bill observed. "Looks like war, Matthew." He winked and drove the ball a very respectable distance.

I took my place at the tee. "Here goes nothing," I said on my back swing and was delighted when I looked to see my ball fly straight and true. I murmured a silent prayer of thanks.

The play progressed smoothly for the first five holes. I enjoyed myself and felt a little cocky about how well I was doing, when I was reminded by Headquarters that I was there to work. The message was conveyed to me by way of a sharp slice that took me directly into the middle of a large water hazard. Pride goeth before a fall.

"Ooh...too bad," Daniel said. "I've been in the drink here many times. Bad luck."

His statement was sympathetic, but the tiniest bit insincere. What had I done to irritate him so?

"I hope you didn't jinx me." Bill said, lining up his shot.

"I'll pray for you," I joked and decided to quit fooling around and get busy with why I came there.

"So, Bill," I said as we took the long fairway walk to his second shot, my third. "It strikes me odd that the son of your best friend is working for you instead of his dad."

Liam and Daniel were on the other side of the fairway looking for a lost ball. Believe me, I had nothing to do with it.

"Yes," he chuckled. "Lee wasn't too happy with me when I took Dan on as a law clerk after he graduated some years back now."

"He's an asset to your firm, then?" I tried to appear nonchalant, gazing around the fairway, tightening my glove.

"Oh, yes. He's bright, an innovative thinker. Boy has a promising future. We're lucky to have him as our lead contract lawyer."

I stood at my ball and studied the terrain. "Is it likely, do you think, that he'll leave you one day in favor of working at his family firm?"

Bill pondered the possibility. "We have a lot invested in Daniel. I'd be disappointed if he made that decision. He's on track for a partnership." He took a step back. "I'd aim right for that eucalyptus tree on the left of the fairway. There's a sand trap on the right side."

"Ah." I paused and followed his pointing finger with my eyes. "It would be a shame if Dan decided to make the move, not knowing your plans for his future at your firm."

I was careful not to lean hard on the subject. Whatever Bill decided, he had to think it was all his idea. He wrinkled his brow and nodded as he considered the matter. I thought it was clever of me to plant the little worry worm.

My fairway shot was respectable. Bill's had a hook, and I could tell he'd lost some of his concentration. We went off to the left of the fairway, looking for his ball.

"Damned if you haven't got me thinking, Matthew." He took time and care to line up his pitch. "I've taken a lot for granted with young Dan."

I let the idea simmer. "I'll go look over this putting surface," I said. "Looks tricky."

"That's a good idea. It has more twists and turns than a pole dancer. We can even the score on this hole if we're lucky."

I didn't ask Bill how he was familiar with pole dancers.

The Kavanaughs joined us. Daniel stuffed his scorecard in his back pocket. He knelt to study his position, placed a marker, and picked up his ball. He tended the pin for me.

"Take your best shot, Angeli. This is where I start to leave the rest of you in my wake."

"In that case," I answered, lining up my shot carefully, "I'm going to sink this one."

"That's the ticket," Bill said. "You show him."

"Watch and learn," I said with audacity.

It was at least thirty feet to the pin, down and across a wicked green. I closed my eyes and prayed. Now, I, of all people, know that prayers should not be wasted on such frivolities as golf shots, but I was feeling very human at that moment. I gently tapped the ball and held my breath.

We watched, speechless, as my ball rolled and swerved toward the pin, speeding as it skidded downhill. Daniel yanked the flag stick out in the nick of time. The ball dropped in with a satisfying *boink*. For a second, I didn't react. Then, I let out a whoop that might have been heard all the way back to the clubhouse. The others joined me in celebratory laughter. Disturbed birds squawked and screeched their annoyance.

"What an unbelievable shot," Daniel said.

"I can't take all the credit. Somebody up there must like me."

"Put in a good word for me while you're at it," Bill said.

"No problem, Bill. I'll do my best." I hoped I still had some influence with The Boss.

Just as Liam went into his back swing at the eighteenth tee, Bill said, "Oh, by the way, Lee, did I mention that George and I have decided to offer Daniel a full partnership at Knight Kristensen?"

Liam's driver came down hard and took a deep divot, knocking the ball no more than twenty feet. He turned and glared at Bill, his face white.

Bill ducked his head. "Oh, bad luck," he mumbled. "I'm sorry, my friend."

"What?" Liam asked, his expression a study in shock.

"Bad luck," Bill repeated.

"Not that, you sneaky bastard. You know what I'm talking about."

"The partnership?" Bill asked innocently.

"Yes, goddammit, the partnership. You picked a fine time to announce it." He turned to Daniel. "Why didn't you tell me about this?"

Up to this point, none of us had looked at Daniel for his reaction. His mouth was agape with the beginnings of a foolish grin, and his eyes were wide beneath the shady half-moon shadow of his golf cap.

"Well?" Liam asked again.

"I didn't know about it, and I still don't believe it. Are you serious, Bill?"

"Never more so, my boy. Congratulations." He reached over to shake Dan's hand. "We know your value at Knight Kristensen. It will be burnished further when we add Kavanaugh to the name. Now, should we give Lee a Mulligan?"

"No way. A shot's a shot in my book. Move over Dad, I believe it's my turn."

"Spoken like a true lawyer," Liam grumbled, then smiled. "If I'd known this crooked shylock was going to pull that, I'd have stolen you away from him long ago."

"Too late now, my friend," said Bill with a deeply satisfied chuckle. Bill glanced my way with a surreptitious wink.

Hopefully, the revelation of the big promotion during the golf game will speed up the marriage game. We shall see what unfolds.

CHAPTER 4

Caroline

Still thinking of Matthew's comment about Daniel and good news, I checked into the Water's Edge. I sat on the side of my bed and dialed the phone. I'd almost given up when Daniel answered, sounding out of breath.

"Hi, Danny." Tears pushed out from the back of my eyes. I wanted his arms around me, but I'd have to settle for his voice. I was losing my grip on reality. There's no other explanation. Jeez, maybe I was going through an early, real early, mid-life crisis or something.

"Care, I'm so glad you called. I have great news. I'm busting with it!"

News? The hair on the back of my neck prickled.

"What, Dan? What is it?" If I'd shut up, he'd tell me, but I was astonished because of what Matthew had said.

"I'm going to be full partner! Partner, do you believe it, babe?" He was jubilant. "I'm so excited I want to reach in this phone, grab you and pull you right through the speaker. Care, I want to hug you so hard I crack your ribs." He laughed. "I can't shut up. Knight Kristensen Kavanaugh. How does it sound?"

I had to laugh. "Danny, you're babbling." I'd never heard him so happy. "It sounds like the KKK to me."

"You would come up with that." He took a deep breath. "I'm so excited I can't help myself."

"Danny, honey, that's just great. I'm so happy. Congratulations. I'm really proud of you!" I could picture that killer smile of his, and I was getting turned on. "I wish we were together to celebrate."

"You won't have long to wait. What's the name of your hotel?"

I heard drawers opening and closing. "I'm at the Water's Edge. What are you talking about?" I was completely baffled.

"I'm packing as we speak, babe. I'm taking the rest of the week off, and we're going to have a little vacation. When you leave the hotel to go to your jobsite tomorrow, leave a key to your room for me at the front desk. Otherwise, I'll have to use all my manly charm to sweettalk the girls at the hotel to let me in."

My head spun. "Daniel Kavanaugh, I'm here on business, not vacation."

"I know you. You'll make quick work of that job. Call your boss and tell him you'll be back Monday."

"I can't do that. He'd like nothing more than an excuse to bad mouth me with the brass. He's such a jerk he'd love to torpedo me."

"I'm coming up, babe," he stated flatly. "Figure something out. I'll see you tomorrow." He disconnected, and I stared at my cellphone.

Stunned, I sat there. What was happening to my life? How was I supposed to deal with this stuff? I'd go to the bar and get tipsy, but no thanks. It would be just my luck to find Matthew sitting there. My elevator wasn't going to the top floor. Okay, I needed to take a few deep breaths and think.

I punched the number for room service and pulled off my clothes. I wished I could put on my fuzzy old, red robe then lie down on the bed in the fetal position. I hadn't gone that far off the deep end, yet. I turned on the TV, washed my face, and got comfortable in my pajamas and travel robe. I'll do a Scarlet O'Hara—think about it when I got back to Tara.

The waiter arrived with my dinner. He pushed the cart into the room and walked over to pull open the drapes.

"Do you mind?" he asked. "I don't want you to miss this magnificent sunset. No sense in having this great ocean view room without getting what you paid for." He turned and set my table.

I strolled to the window, peered out, and drew in my breath. It was a wowser. All red and purple and the water in Puget Sound shimmering melted gold. "It really is wonderful, isn't it?" Gosh, I hoped it would look like this when Danny got here.

The waiter handed me a glass of wine. "Compliments of the hotel. It's a local vintner. I hope you enjoy it."

I mumbled, "Thanks." Maybe, I thought, maybe I was in a time warp or something. You know, like Dorothy or Alice?

"Bon appétit," he said with a slight bow as I handed back the check. "Have a good night. Weather report for tomorrow is looking good."

∽

I walked into the offices of my customer the next morning, looked for the project coordinator scheduled to meet me on the second floor. I was directed to the elevators. The place looked terrific, the work done so far, spectacular in the beautiful old building. They'd done as much as possible to preserve all the original marble, brass, tiles, and murals.

The elevators were straight out of a 1930's movie. The open cages and those accordion folding doors with brass trim. The crank handle had been replaced with a modern button panel, but it was done so cleverly that it didn't detract in any way from the charm of the original equipment. These were my kind of people. The old stuff has so much character. I love it.

Peter Langley, the architect, was conferring with the owner of the building when I reached the construction office. They looked up as I entered and gestured for me to join them at the work table. The blueprints were stacked all over the top, and the architect leafed through the big pile to find the executive suite.

"Ah, here we are, Ms. Clayton. Have a look at this."

He plopped his pencil down on the print. I could immediately see the changes in the room configuration.

"What happened here?" I studied the placement of the walls and windows. Substantial changes had taken place since I'd done the design of the individual suites and reception area.

"Let's look at the original print, and you can see what we're dealing with." He rooted for the old print. "Here we are. This wall, which we removed in the original design, had to be restored. It's a major weight-bearing factor in the overall design of the building. To compensate, we've pushed out this area over here." He pointed to the new drawings. "And added this corner window. This will affect the area that was originally designated as the reference library."

I studied the new drawings and knew I had to do a major redesign. "Could you provide me with a place to work? I have my final design in my briefcase and all the furniture and fixture specs. This is going to take a while."

"Sure thing, I've cleared that entire area in the alcove back there." He pointed to a large temporary table built-from-a-door resting on a couple of tall sawhorses. "Let us know if you need anything."

I carried my stuff to the alcove and went to work. As I studied the new configuration, it dawned on me that it was considerably more interesting than the original space. After a couple of hours, I determined that everything we'd custom ordered could be adapted to the new floor plan. We only had to change a couple of the stock items. The more I worked on it, the more I liked it. It would be a whole lot more attractive than the original, not that the original wasn't good. It was. I don't do shoddy work.

"Clayton!" a voice called out, making me jump.

"Yes, what?" I looked up from the blueprints. Langley gestured to me.

"Come with us. We're going to catch some lunch. It's almost one o'clock."

"Gosh, I lost track of time." I picked up my coat and purse. "I'm starved." I walked over to the two men. "Where are we going?"

"Just a few blocks down the street. There's a great fish place over by Pike Place Market. Do you like fish?"

∽

By five-thirty that afternoon, it started to rain again. My design complete, I was satisfied with the results. I spent about a half hour going over the details with Peter Langley and the project manager. They were pleased with my changes.

I used their phone to call my office and left a message for The Lecher, telling him where I could be reached, and that I'd be back Monday morning. I didn't mention that I'd already finished the redesign job. I'd fight that battle when I returned to L.A.

∽

Squishing across the lobby of the Water's Edge in my soaked shoes, I was about to step onto the elevator when the concierge called my name. I turned around as she started toward me, carrying a large florist's box.

"Mr. Kavanaugh asked me to give you these. There's a note attached." She handed me the flowers and the card. "Have a lovely evening, Ms. Clayton." She smiled like a conspirator.

For a couple of minutes, I stood there like a dodo. Then I tore open the card. There was a key card inside and a note from Danny that I should go to suite twenty-four-seventy. I opened the box and saw that it was filled with long-stemmed yellow roses and white freesia—my favorite flowers. I couldn't believe it. How could Daniel know what my favorite flowers were? I didn't remember ever telling him.

When I got to the room, I fumbled with the key card, the flower box, the blueprints, and my briefcase. My umbrella dripped down my leg into one of my shoes. I grumbled and cursed, and finally shoved the stubborn card in the slot.

I pushed the door open and heard music. I hung my sopping coat on a rack by the door and propped my briefcase and drawings against the wall. Carrying the flowers with me, I walked through the entry foyer. Flickering light from the fireplace reflected on the marble floor. I wasn't sure which way to turn. The elegantly furnished suite smelled of scented candles—sandalwood, I thought.

"Danny?"

"Over here, Care," he called from somewhere on my right.

I entered the living room and stood there with my mouth hanging open. There must have been a hundred candles lighting the room. Danny was lying on his stomach on one of two massage tables, grinning at me.

Two men, dressed in white, like attendants in a mental hospital, stood next to the tables. On second thought, they looked more like male models of the Latino variety, young, tan, and muscular. I was totally confused.

"Meet Antonio and Raoul, babe. You are going to get the most fabulous massage of your life. Get out of those clothes and join me." He tilted his head to the side, pointing the way. "The bedroom is over there."

"Danny, have you lost it?" I laughed. "What are you doing?"

"Giving us a reward. One we've got coming. Now, get naked and get back in here. I left a big towel on the bed for you."

Raoul or Antonio, I didn't know which, smiled and took the flower box from me and said he would put them in water while I changed. I walked into the bedroom, thinking I would wake up any minute. If you added up all that had happened in the past few days, I was obviously in a dream. It bore no resemblance to my real life. None at all.

I changed into the towel, pulled my hair into an unruly bundle on top of my head, and returned to the living room. If this was a dream, I might as well enjoy it. I climbed onto the table, and smiling over at Danny, I reclined on my back and sighed.

"Go to it, Raoul. Start wherever you like."

"Antonio." He corrected me with a dazzling toothpaste ad smile. He arranged the sheets and towel and began working on my feet. I groaned and relaxed as Dan chuckled and reached across to squeeze my hand. I finally figured it out. I was dead and had made it to heaven.

After about an hour, my entire body felt as though it could have been poured into a bowl like a big puddle of vanilla pudding. I was dozing off when the doorbell rang. Two waiters brought in a cart with our supper. Antonio helped me into a terry robe. Danny was already in his. He walked over and put his arms around me and gave me a doozie of a kiss. Tongue and everything. You know the kind I mean.

Knees wobbling, I whispered, "Forget dinner. I want to—"

"Soon," he whispered back. "Eat first."

The waiters and masseurs had evaporated.

I never thought food was sexy, but that was the only way I could describe the dinner Daniel ordered for us. First, an ice bucket with a bottle of the best champagne I'd ever tasted. I couldn't think about how much it was costing him. I couldn't. Then a microscopic salad with an unbelievable balsamic vinaigrette dressing dripped over it and fresh baked bread sticks. The steak Diane entrée had some little asparagus thingies on the side. Everything melted in my mouth, and I swooned with pleasure after every bite. How gawdawful decadent, I giggled to myself. More than once.

Thinking we were finished, I saw Danny uncover a warming oven and pull out a small baking dish of double dark chocolate soufflé. He poured more champagne, and I sat there with a big stupid grin on my face. He enjoyed my reaction. All during dessert, he kept picking up my hands and kissing my fingertips. Heaven, no doubt about it.

Finally, he stood and extended his hand. He didn't say anything, didn't have to. His eyes told me everything I needed to know. He led me into the candle-lit bedroom. When that had happened, I didn't know. Somebody must have snuck in there while I was in massage nirvana. Dan pushed off my robe and dropped his on the floor. He picked me up and carried me to the bed. He'd never done that before. I felt like a fairy princess. I liked it a lot.

Well, all I'll tell you about what happened next is that he completely blew me away, completely.

~

I woke to the sound of the shower running the next morning. I couldn't be dead. Dead people didn't wake up. I knew last night happened because of all the burned down candles and the yellow roses on a table by the window.

I got up and staggered to the bathroom. It was steamy. I could see Danny through the mist-coated glass door. God, he was something. I slid open the door and watched him for a minute. His eyes were closed while he washed his hair.

He opened them and smiled at me. "Morning, babe."

I stepped inside, soaped up my hands, and turned him around so I could wash his back. I loved washing his broad, strong back. It gave me a chance to touch him without it turning into sex. Usually. I liked to torture myself. You know—touch, but don't take. It also gave me an opportunity to bite his scrumptious butt.

My arms around his waist, I pushed him closer to the showerhead to let it wash over both of us. He turned around, kissed me, then squirted shampoo on my head and washed my hair. He liked the torture, too.

"Babe, you are so beautiful." He held my face between his hands and rubbed his thumbs on my ears. "I want to say something, and I want you to promise me you won't jump and run. Okay?"

"Danny..." My antennae shot up.

"Caroline," he began, his face all serious and deep.

Oh Jeez, this is going to be bad. He only calls me Caroline when it's really serious.

He brushed my lips with a tender kiss. "I love you. I want you to marry me."

My stomach clenched, and I heard buzzing in my ears. All of a sudden, I was cold.

"Danny!" I cried and smacked him on the chest, pushing him backward. "Why did you have to go and say that? You're changing the rules. Why?" Tears threatened. I was scared out of my wits.

"It's okay. You don't have to answer right now. I had to throw it out there for you to consider."

I turned my back on him and put my forehead on the cold tile.

His hands gently washed my back. I jerked instinctively, but he didn't say anything more. He just kept gliding his hands over my back and shoulders. I sighed and let my head fall back onto his shoulder. He pressed himself against me, and leaning down, kissed me on the neck.

"I'm sorry, Danny. I didn't mean...I'm scared...that's all. You know that I..." Words clogged the back of my throat. I was terrified of losing him and afraid to say yes to marrying him.

Gently, he let me off the hook. "I'll order breakfast. It stopped raining. I have a big day planned for us. How does a ferry ride over to the Olympic Peninsula sound? They have great old buildings and shops over there. Right down your alley."

He turned off the shower, grabbed two towels, and handed one to me. I dried myself and stepped out of the enclosure. Danny shaved at one of the sinks. I took the hairdryer for the tedious process of drying the unruly mop on my head. We avoided eye contact.

He finished shaving, pulled on his boxers, gave me a little peck on the cheek, and went into the bedroom. I heard him ordering, in perfect Spanish, what sounded like enough food for an invading army.

"Caroline," I told myself, "it's not the end of the world. If you're ever going to get married it should be Danny. Right?" I figured if I acted like the proposal never happened, it might blow over.

Somehow, I know, don't ask me how I know, Matthew is involved in this.

We had a good day, laughed a lot and ran around like tourists. Daniel didn't mention you-know-what again, and I was beginning to think I'd imagined the whole thing.

We got back to the hotel late. The long ferry ride was as hypnotic as a baby cradle swaying in the breeze. We undressed and crawled between the sheets. He pulled me tight against him, and in a matter of seconds, he was asleep. His warm breath brushed the back of my neck, his breathing steady and slow. I rested my face on his biceps and his legs were tangled with mine. I love the feel and smell of his skin.

Taking a deep breath, I tried to relax, totally beat but unable to fall asleep. My stomach felt like a little hamster in there running on one of those round wire thingies. This new development was frightening. Things were going so smooth. Why did he have to mess everything up? He never said the *three little words* before. Not to mention the *M* word!

Being in love made life a living hell. I wanted to stay with Danny, I did, but I didn't want to be chained to him by a stack of legal papers and a stupid ritual acted out in front of a bunch of people, where you promise all sorts of things that you'll probably never follow through on.

I fell asleep and didn't remember anything else until I felt his erection against my back. I lifted my eyelid a crack and saw the dawning light outside. I rolled over and faced him.

"Mmm," I groaned, trying to wake him. Man, he was dead to the world. I squirmed against him and ran my hand down his chest. "Danny," I whispered. That did it.

∽

He didn't mention marriage again the rest of the week. Seattle is a neat town if you can stand the weather. We ate like pigs and went to the movies and shopped and even went to the top of the Space Needle. I never drank so much coffee in my life. If you don't watch where you're going, you'll trip over a coffee bar every time you turn around. Dan bought about six pounds of different kinds of beans and a little grinder. He claims to be an authority on coffee now. I put him in charge of breakfast from here on out.

I got a phone message from the Libertine. He wanted me to call as soon as I got back, but I ignored it. I figured it could wait until Monday morning.

We arrived home Saturday afternoon and spent the rest of the day doing laundry and grocery shopping and stuff. Like an old married couple. The hair on my neck stood up whenever that darn *M* word got close to my lips.

CHAPTER 5
Matthew

That went well.

CHAPTER 6

Daniel

Daniel put his new coffee grinder on the kitchen counter and was dying to try it out. He'd lined up all the varieties of beans in their shiny little bags, eager to help, then jump out and into his grinder. He and Caroline had been back from Seattle for a week, and they were still wired from all the coffee they'd sampled.

He'd finished his assigned KP duties after a serious dressing down from Sergeant Clayton about the condition of his barracks. He could finally see the bottom of his kitchen sink. Sarge was doing their laundry on his promise that the apartment would be fit for human habitation by the time she finished.

Daniel had been in this apartment for almost five years. He didn't seem to notice any mess until Caroline brought it to his attention, which she did on a regular basis. His logic of "Why should I make the bed if I'm going to get back into it in a few hours?" or "I do wash dishes once in a while, whenever there aren't any clean ones," didn't impress her. He felt he had more important things to do. Hey, he was a guy, right?

"Hey, babe, want some coffee?" he called to her over the rumble of the washer.

"Okay, Danny, but make it decaf this time. I have to get up early tomorrow to be in before the boss shows up. I want to see which of my design proposals he's been messing with."

He took an extra moment to admire her backside as she pulled some clothes from the dryer. "I bought some great Costa Rican Atitlan gourmet decaf. I'll grind some. Be ready by the time you have your unmentionables folded."

"It's your unmentionables I'm folding at the moment, smart guy."

"That's my girl. I knew I kept you around for something." He never claimed to be above enjoying some of the domestic perks.

"Very funny, see when I do your wash again." She sashayed into the kitchen carrying his laundry basket.

If he didn't love the frowsy way she looked in that tacky old robe of hers, he'd go out and get her a new one. "Hey, I fixed dinner, didn't I?" he asked in protest.

"For some reason, I never thought of raisin bran as dinner." She stuck her tongue out at him on her way to the bedroom to put his stuff away. "Don't make it so weak this time or you're fired as my personal barista."

"Bitch, bitch, bitch, I don't get no respect around here." He watched her walk away, wanting to pull the plug on the grinder and follow her to the bedroom. She wasn't wearing anything under her robe.

"Pay attention to what you're supposed to be doing, Kavanaugh. I expect that coffee to be ready when I get out of the shower." She made a face at him over her shoulder and walked through the door.

What a babe.

The next morning, he could tell she wasn't looking forward to going to her office. It was a shame she wasn't happy there. She loved her work and took a lot of pride in it. It's the one area of her life she should have had control of, but anytime you work for somebody else, shit happens.

He knew it well. All the bull he endured at the firm the first few years. Now that he finally made partner, he could look back and say it was all worth it, but there were times.

He didn't think she had much future with her company. She should be running the division, but her boss took credit for everything she did. Danny doesn't give advice to Caroline. One sure way for him to really stick his foot in it would be to start giving her job advice. Danny wants to live a little longer.

She told him in an offhand way, a couple years ago, that her boss was hitting on her. He was so angry he wanted to go to her office and strangle the jerk. She insisted he mind his own business. Said she never should have told him, and she could take care of herself.

Caroline could take care of herself, and that nagged him. He'd like her to let him take care of her once in a while, to trust him, and once, just once, to hear her say out loud, I love you, Danny.

She was funny as hell sometimes. For instance, she didn't like him to call her Care. Since she seemed determined not to confront him about it, they were at a stalemate. He got a devilish kick out of watching that little spark in her greenish-blue eyes when he called her Care. He could almost hear her teeth grind. One of these days, she'd probably get so riled she'll pop him. Serve him right, too.

~

When they got to his parents' house, his father and brothers were all gathered around the barbecue, shooting the bull. His mother, Mary, and the four sisters-in-law were fussing with the kids and organizing the meal.

The first thing Caroline did was stick her finger in the frosting of his dad's birthday cake. It won her a finger wagging from sister-in-law Claire, and the undying admiration of her son, twelve-year-old, Ryan. Caroline had scooped enough in that one swipe for both of them. Dan's nephew, Ryan–Flynn and Claire's son–was madly in love with Caroline. Danny admired the kid's good taste in women.

He went up behind Claire, put his arms around her, and nibbled at her neck. "How you doing, beautiful?" he whispered seductively, and ran his hands over her very pregnant belly. "When's Flynn Junior making his appearance?"

"How's yourself handsome?" She covered Dan's hands with hers and leaned back against him. "It's Claire Junior. I refuse to be the mother of four boys."

He laughed and gave her a squeeze as Ryan and Caroline made a beeline for the back yard. He watched them toss around a football for a minute. Two of the younger boys tried to join in, but Ryan chased them away. He wanted Caroline all to himself.

Dan gave his mother a kiss and hugged Audrey. Grace sat in a rocking chair, breast-feeding the latest Kavanaugh. Linda darted down the hallway after her giggling twins. Those two were up to something.

Time for Daniel to join the menfolk around the barbecue.

"Hey, Ryan," he yelled, "quit hitting on my woman." Ryan's face turned as red as his hair, but he was so love-struck he just kept tossing Caroline the ball. Dan's brothers chuckled and sent the boy a few catcalls.

Dan didn't have to wait long for the ribbing he'd get from his brothers over the recent advancement at his firm.

Stewart attacked first. "Well, well, well, I guess congratulations are in order, Danny. Looks like you pulled the wool over the eyes of poor old Bill and George."

"Yeah," chimed in Wayne. "How'd a so-so lawyer like you pull that one off?"

Daniel flashed him a glare. "Ha-ha."

"Leave Dan alone, guys," Grant said. "He took advantage of an opportunity to get ahead. That's all." His wicked grin gave Danny no comfort. "After all, he knew he'd never be able to make the cut at Kavanaugh."

"Very funny." Dan glanced toward his dad, but Dad never bailed him out when his big brothers ganged up, so he wasn't expecting any help from that quarter.

"Lay off, you bullies," Flynn the *big*, big brother, ordered. He assumed the divine right to boss his four younger siblings around. "Danny's our baby brother. We should be supportive." With that, he grabbed Dan in a head lock and pretended to be choking him as the others took turns raining down light smacks and jabs. Daniel knew he could knock any one of his big brothers on their butts, and they knew it too.

His dad finally intervened. "Okay, boys, one at a time. You know I disapprove when you gang up on one another." He pushed his way through the melee. "Hold him down," he added and playfully landed his own marshmallow shot to his youngest son's gut.

"Gee, thanks, Dad."

Dan twisted to free himself from Flynn's grip. He finally let go, but twisted a knuckle noogie to his scalp first.

Now you know why Daniel went to work for Bill Knight after graduation. His dad and Bill went to law school together. Dan liked working for Bill, so he stayed. That was six years ago.

"I'd think you guys should be past this by now," Dan complained.

Wayne piped up. "Dad, we had a meeting and decided you should disinherit Dan and send him a bill for his fancy law school education."

"You boys lay off now," Liam said. "We got our licks in, so let's move on. Dan has a right to make his own decisions. I placed no conditions on any of your 'fancy law school educations.'"

They were all joking, but it still rankled. Danny had been on their lawyerly shit-list ever since he turned down his dad's offer to work at the family firm. Maybe the brothers thought it was disrespectful. Dan mentally shrugged. He wasn't sure he cared why they kept up the teasing.

Dad was disappointed when he didn't join with the rest of his sons, but he understood that he was tired of taking the leftovers. He'd had enough of being baby brother. The pecking order from Flynn down was too long for a man in a hurry.

They get their digs in every now and again, then they'd drop it. This he knew—if he ever needed backup in a tough situation, his brothers would be there for him one-hundred-percent. No question.

"Now, let's pay attention to these steaks and ribs," Liam said. "We'll catch hell from your mother if we mess up."

Caroline joined them at the barbecue moments later. She gave Danny a sharp glare and between gritted teeth said, "Quit embarrassing Ryan."

Her arm went around Liam. She hugged him and wished him a happy birthday.

Liam grinned and hugged her back.

Danny gave her a little pat on the bottom and headed for safe territory, the kitchen crew. He'd play mama's boy for a while.

He entered the family-room through the patio door. The gals chattered away in the kitchen. About to go in, he paused when he heard Audrey say something about Caroline. He stopped and stood there like the eavesdropper he was.

"I guess I don't understand her, Mom. She's so different from the rest of us."

Linda agreed. "What exactly it is that Danny sees in her?"

"Come on, she's gorgeous," Claire answered, "and just as smart as he is. What's not to see?"

Grace chimed in, "Good heavens, they've been together three years now. Do you think they'll ever get married?"

Gracie was the quietest and shyest of his sisters-in-law. He remembered the first time Wayne brought her home. It took her some time to get used to all the boisterousness in that house.

"Mom," Audrey said, "why do you suppose Dan has stayed with her so long? I always figured him for a marrying man. Caroline doesn't seem the type of woman he'd choose."

"You know what I think?" Mom said. "I think Caroline is heaven sent. She's perfect for Danny. Your father-in-law agrees. She's just what our boy needs."

Good old Ma.

Linda sounded surprised. "No kidding? Why do you think so?"

"Well, it's a bit hard to explain," Mary answered, "but our Dan has always been a bit unlike his brothers. I remember when I brought him home from the hospital. He was so tiny, but somehow I knew, even then, he was different."

"I don't understand?" Claire said.

"You know I named all your husbands after my favorite hunky, old-time movie stars. I even had a name picked out for Dan, but when I brought him home, all I could think to name him was Daniel. I was throwing him right into that lion's den of big brothers."

His sisters-in-law all laughed at that. He'd heard the story before, but still liked to hear Ma telling it. She had a soft spot for her youngest.

"That's so funny, Mom," Claire said. "How is it you never told us that before?"

"Because I don't want any of my boys to think I'm playing favorites, besides Daniel would die if he knew I still think of him as my baby."

More laughter, Daniel's cue, time to make a little noise. He pretended he'd just walked into the house.

The women were happy to see him and promptly put him to work lugging the folding chairs from the guest room closet out to the patio.

When he finally sat down, Audrey handed him a baby and a bottle. That's the way Caroline found him. As soon as she plopped down next to Dan, one of the little nieces crawled onto her lap and offered to share her Tootsie Pop. She didn't blink, just opened her mouth and laughed when the kid missed the mark completely, almost putting out one of her eyes.

Liam hollered that the steaks and ribs were ready. The kitchen crew carried out the rest of the food. Caroline jumped out of her chair and herded the little ones to the patio. She was so good with kids, Danny thought it a shame she was set on never having her own.

Danny watched his dad at the head of the long table surveying his family—five sons, four daughters-in-law, ten grandchildren, his wife, Mary, and Caroline. Twenty-two and counting. Liam included Caroline, because he considered her a member of his family.

The table groaned under the weight of food. It was like those old paintings of a royal feast. It didn't seem possible they could consume all that food, but Danny knew there'd be little of it left by the time they pushed back from the table.

"Liam, why don't you say the blessing?" Mary said. "It's your birthday and a special one at that."

His dad nodded. "Okay, boys and girls. Let's all join hands and thank the Lord for this fine feast your grandma has put before us today."

He reached out for the nearest hands, and they all followed his lead.

Caroline had never quite gotten used to this family tradition. Danny winked at her, and she smiled back. She took Ryan's hand, and he flushed beet red.

"Our Father, we give thanks for this bountiful meal and for the company of all our children and grandchildren. We're grateful for our privileged lives and our good health. Amen."

"Amen!" they shouted as bedlam broke out. Plates were soon heaped under the weight of the feast. The ladies must have made ten pounds of red potato salad and within minutes, it was nearly gone. Platters of steak, ribs, and hotdogs made their way from one end of the table to the other.

Everybody talked at once, and Dan picked up snatches of a debate about the stock market, between Caroline and Wayne.

"Oh, come on, Wayne," she said, "it's not whether your portfolio manager can beat the S&P 500. That's not the only yardstick for judging her performance."

"Well, it's the yardstick I use."

"The S&P 500 only represents a segment of the market. It has strengths and limitations. The long-term goal is what you should be concerned with, not the performance day-to-day."

"My long-term goal is to be rich." He grinned. "I think she should be putting more into technology stocks.

"You are young enough to take some risk," she replied, "but with two kids and another on the way, maybe you'd be better off to buy shares in a tech-heavy mutual fund, instead of single stocks."

Wayne mumbled some sort of answer, which Dan couldn't hear over the chatter of the kids. Caroline held her own whenever the talk was about the economy or sports. They kept forgetting how smart she was. Grace nudged Wayne in a way that indicated she agreed with Caroline.

They merrily gorged themselves for the next forty minutes. It was comical the way they started out in high gear and things wound down. Not so many platters being passed around and the littlest of the kids beginning to stare into space or nod off in their chairs, while the older ones squirmed.

Mary stood. "I think we'll hold off serving cake and ice cream until the children have been cleaned up and had their naps." She signaled for the rest of them to carry things to the kitchen.

"I want to teach Caroline how to skate-board," Ryan announced.

"Go ahead then," Claire, said "but take Jimmy with you. I'll clean up Brian and help Linda with the twins."

"How about a cigar, boys?" Liam asked. "Bill gave me a box of Cubans for my birthday."

"You keep those smelly things as far away from this house as you can," Mary ordered. "Go for a walk around the block or something."

"Yes, ma'am." He snapped off a salute. "Who's going with me?"

The brothers fell in line, turning toward the garage, where he apparently had his stash.

"I'll pass," Daniel said. "I'm going to help Ma clean up."

"Mama's boy," Grant muttered sotto voce as he passed. Danny punched him in the shoulder. He howled as if mortally wounded.

"Will you boys ever outgrow that behavior?" their mother asked on her way through the door with a stack of plates. "You'll make me old before my time."

Dan took the rest of the plates and followed her into the kitchen. They were alone. He filled the sink with soapy water and washed the cooking pots. The dishwasher wasn't big enough to accommodate all of the mess.

"Ma," he said, after checking around to make sure they were alone. "I asked Caroline to marry me when we were in Seattle."

"You did? Honey, that's wonderful." She gave him a hug and a brilliant smile. "When's the wedding?"

He shrugged. "She didn't say yes."

Disbelief washed over her face. "She didn't?"

"No. I nearly blew it, but I was still so hyped about the partner thing. We were in the shower together, and she looked so luscious, all wet and sleepy. I got carried away and proposed. The minute the words were out of my mouth, I wanted to hang myself."

"I don't understand, son. She loves you, doesn't she?"

He nodded. "I know she does, but she's terrified to commit to marriage."

"You two are perfect together and look at her out there with Ryan and Jimmy." She nodded to the window. The boys laughed at Care trying to keep her balance on Ryan's skateboard. "She's so good with children. I don't understand why she's afraid of marriage."

"She got jilted when she was twenty-two. It was pretty messy." She took the pot Dan handed her and dried it, shaking her head in sympathy for Caroline.

"Yeah, she had stars in her eyes. She was totally in love with the guy. A day before the big, ostentatious Christmas wedding he ran off with one of her bridesmaids."

"Why, the cad!" Outrage suffused her lovely face.

"You got that right, and if that weren't bad enough, her parents blamed her for it. They were convinced it was all her fault."

"Oh, that's just awful." She shook her head with disgust.

"Care told me he'd been handpicked by them. They figured she must have done something to cause him to leave. Her way of rebelling, they told her. They went on and on about all the sacrifices they made for her all her life. That's how she showed her gratitude, by alienating such a decent and promising young man from such a good family. They doubted she'd ever make a suitable match."

Mary shook her head slowly. "That's so sad. Just when she needed their support the most, they failed her."

"It's a pattern they specialize in." Dan's anger at them burned inside.

"What do they think of you?"

His shoulders shook with a chuckle. "They don't like me much. My pedigree is lacking."

"Well, they're just plain wrong! It's their loss if they don't know a fine young man when they see one." She stood with her fists on her hips, ready to take up the fight for him.

"You're a little prejudiced, Ma," he said with a grin, leaned over, and kissed her cheek.

"Why is it we've never met Caroline's parents? Is she ashamed of us?"

"Just the opposite—she's ashamed of them. Anyway, they only blow through town now and then. Just long enough to get her completely screwed up. Then they blow out again, back to one of their villas on the Med or their apartment in Paris or New York."

Mary's lips pursed with distaste. "They don't sound like nice people."

"They're assholes."

"How could they have raised such a sweet girl, I wonder?"

Chuckling, he said, "She would cringe if she heard herself referred to as sweet. Care *is* sweet. Tender-hearted, too. Her late grandmother did most of the raising."

"I know you told me some time ago that Caroline wasn't interested in having children of her own. I thought that was why you two weren't planning marriage."

He sighed with frustration. "She says she's afraid she might do to a child what her parents did to her. I told her that was a crock."

"I should think it would be all the more reason she'd be a fine mother, but then I don't understand how any woman could not want children."

"You know what, Ma? I can easily live with the no-kids policy. You and Dad already have ten grandchildren and more on the way. I think we would have a good life together, with or without kids. We're already everyone's favorite aunt and uncle."

"I don't know what to say, honey. Do you think she'll come around?"

"I sure hope so. I can't imagine spending my life with any other woman. I'm crazy about her."

She patted his back and murmured reassurances.

Ma was one in a million.

CHAPTER 7

Matthew

After Liam's birthday cake that blazed like a forest fire, they had a hot game of Trivial Pursuit. It was Caroline, Ryan, Jimmy, and the rest of the kids old enough to talk, against Dan and his brothers. I won't bore you with details. The lawyers lost.

By the time Daniel drove them to Caroline's place, they were dirty, stuffed, and tired, and she hadn't given a thought about her job for a few hours. He loved it that she felt carefree around his family.

He'd cool it on the subject of marriage for a while, concentrate on trying to convince her they should live together. I was in his corner all the way. After all, my job was in jeopardy.

Daniel's mother, Mary, is a perceptive woman, indeed. Caroline *was* Heaven-sent. She *is* Daniel's destiny. The problem I face is how to convince her? She deeply fears being hurt or betrayed again.

Believe you me, I was surprised when they fell into bed the first day they met. I didn't expect my behind-the-scenes maneuvering, getting them both invited to Jack's–you remember the young golf pro?–and Karen's New Year's soiree would result in such spontaneous combustion. My task was going to be easy. Well, that's what I thought at the time.

I had subliminally suggested to Caroline that she take golf lessons, to further her career, you know. Daniel's old school mate was employed at the local public golf course as a teaching pro.

I digress, often.

Caroline signed up for a series of golf lessons with Jack, and they became good buddies. When Jack and Karen planned their party, they invited Caroline as well as Daniel.

As I had planned, Daniel and Caroline were immediately attracted to each other. The words from South Pacific seemed justly appropriate. You know the song, "Across a crowded room," etcetera. I was overly proud of myself. Come to think of it, I have a problem managing pride. I will work on that. I will.

In any case, they soon disappeared from the party and before I knew it, were in Daniel's apartment tearing at each other's clothing. Daniel had never met a woman he wanted to get his hands on more. Caroline was equally enamored. She wanted him the moment she saw him, even though when he glanced at her she gave him her best *Get lost, Buster* glare. The woman has perfected that expression. He countered with his world-class smile, and that broke the ice dam in her resistance.

Poor boy, he was a goner. Of course, that's the reaction I'd expected. At that juncture, I was convinced things would progress in an orderly fashion, allowing me more time for the other Kavanaughs. I hate to whine, but it is difficult managing such a large family.

I had not counted on her being so perplexing. I'd been brought up to speed on her past, the aborted wedding and indifferent parents. I was not unprepared for the fact that she would still be silently suffering the aftereffects. She was a young twenty-two then. One would think the old wounds should be mostly healed in those intervening years.

Obviously, I was wrong on that score.

I now needed to find a plausible way to see Caroline, and frequently. Chance meetings at the tavern and the airport would not do the trick. I had used those tactics, and while I was satisfied with the results, there was a limit to their effectiveness. She thought me a pest, and she's not completely convinced I was not trying to make a move on her. God forbid.

I tapped the number for her firm. These cellular phones are a marvelous innovation. I do love technology. "This is Matthew Angeli calling. I'd like to speak to Mr. Moody."

"I'll see if he is available, please hold."

After a few seconds, a disinterested male voice came on the line. "Moody."

Hmm, yes, I could see that he was.

"Mr. Moody, my name is Matthew Angeli. I've just now leased offices in the Wilshire Bank building, and I would like to hire the design services of your firm."

He brightened up considerably at the prospect of new business. "Very good, Mr. Angeli. Would you like to make an appointment to discuss your needs?"

"Yes, I would. I'm interested in working with a Ms. Clayton. She's been referred to me by an associate."

I threw that last bit in for good measure.

"We have several talented designers here. I'm sure any one of them would do an excellent job for you. Let's set up an appointment to discuss your project." I could hear him flipping pages. "Would this afternoon be convenient? I have two-fifteen open."

"Good. I'll see you then."

"Excellent."

Hanging up, I visualized him gleefully rubbing his hands together. The Wilshire Bank project had been one of Caroline's biggest jobs. Before-and-after photos had appeared in Architectural Digest, and she had received kudos from her peers. Moody was no doubt envisioning a similar project.

My Boss had approved a lease on a small office suite, for the specific purpose of placing me in close contact with Caroline over an extended period of time. Moody would be disappointed about the limited scope of the project. I'd make up for that by ordering the office fixtures and design to suit my expensive and eclectic tastes. I do love nice things.

CHAPTER 8

Caroline

"I can't be here at two-fifteen," I told Moody Boy. "I have a previous appointment clear across town." I gritted my teeth with frustration. He's the boss from hell.

"Cancel or reschedule it, Clayton. The man who's coming in has leased offices in the Wilshire Bank building. He specifically asked for you."

I slammed my hand on the desk and closed my eyes. "Why didn't you check my schedule? I coordinated this meeting with two different furniture designers. It was a bitch finding a time when they could both be at the factory."

"Look, Clayton, do you want to argue about it? I said cancel or reschedule your meeting. This could be an important job."

"And the new Seattle project isn't important? I'm working on a deadline here."

"If you hadn't spent so much time pussyfooting around in Seattle with your boyfriend, you wouldn't be so far behind. Now change your meeting. I expect you to be here to meet this Angeli person at two-fifteen."

He turned and stalked back to his little ivory tower. I burned with anger at the obnoxious toad, but a weird feeling came over me about the name Angeli.

Had I previously met the guy someplace? I didn't have time to agonize over it. I had to get on the phone and try to rearrange my meeting at the furniture woodworks. If it wasn't one darn thing, it was another. I hoped my entire day wouldn't go like this.

∼

At two o'clock I was in the employee's lounge rinsing out my coffee cup, no lunch again, and trying to find time to go to the girls' room. Even though Tiffany pitched in like a pro to help me, I'd been on a dead run all day. Glancing at my smudgy reflection in the paper towel dispenser, I accepted that this was as good as I was going to look for the new client.

The receptionist greeted someone as I passed the lobby on the way back to my workstation. I glanced up when I recognized the man's voice. I was shocked to see Matthew standing there, oozing charm for Sandra, the receptionist. She blushed and fumbled with the intercom.

What the hell is he doing here! I hoped he hadn't shown up on our doorstep looking for me. I ducked behind the door before he saw me.

Sandra said, "Mr. Moody, Mr. Angeli is here to see you. Please have a seat, Mr. Angeli. Mr. Moody will be out in a moment."

"Thank you, Ms. Russell," he answered with his sweet smile.

Turning to take a seat, he spotted me before I could duck behind the doorway again. He waved and flashed me a wink. I jumped like a spooked cat and hightailed it back to my desk.

Matthew was the Angeli who had the two-fifteen!

Mental warning bells clanged. There was something about the whole setup I didn't like.

"Where the hell have you been, Clayton?" Moody fumed when I got back to my station.

"Jeez, is it okay if I break for a pee once in a while?" I was in no mood to take crap from anyone, especially him.

He fumed like a flustered old lady. "Don't give me attitude. We have an important new client waiting. I want to see an accommodating smile on that face of yours."

Standing my ground with hands on my hips, I said, "That important new client is some kind of weirdo. I've met him before, and he's creepy. I will *not* work with him. Assign someone else to the project."

"I don't give a rat's patootie if he's a two-headed, fire-breathing dragon. He asked for you, dammit. Now let's go."

He headed toward reception. Trailing after him, I asked, "Why can't

Tiffany work on it? She's really coming along. I'd like to see her get her own project."

I really hate it when I whine.

"Oh, just shut up. How about I fire your ass out of here and give *all* your clients to Tiffany. Would that make you happy?"

I mumbled an inaudible response, one sure to get me canned, and decided it wasn't wise to push him any further. Anyway, by now we were entering the lobby, and Matthew was standing to greet us.

CHAPTER 9

Matthew

I, Matthew, angel extraordinaire, smiled and extended my hand to Moody. Caroline was not happy to see me. I had anticipated as much and prepared myself.

"Hello, Caroline." I shook her hand. "How nice to see you again."

Moody was surprised. "You know each other?"

She gave him a furious glare. "Yes, I told you we'd met before. We have mutual friends. At least, that's what Matthew tells me. How are you, Matt?"

"I'm well, thank you. As I informed Mr. Moody, I've leased space in the Wilshire Bank building and would like you to design my office and reception area."

"I don't believe I can manage that right now," Caroline answered icily. "I'm very busy." She looked across the room and motioned to a young lady who'd just stepped off the elevator.

"Tiffany," Caroline called, "would you join us?" The young woman approached, and Caroline introduced me. I shook her hand. "Matthew Angeli, this is Tiffany Gaines. She's been working with me on several of my projects. She's very talented, and I'm sure she'd be happy to work on your design."

Moody was so flustered, he said, "Now just a minute here, Clayton. If Mr. Angeli wants you to work on his design, I'm sure you can manage it."

"Can't possibly," she answered. "I wouldn't be able to give it the proper attention. I'm too backed up right now. I'm sure Mr. Angeli will understand." Her eyebrows went up in question.

Moody seemed about to suffer a stroke at the threat of losing a new customer. "Now hold it right there, Clayton. I decide which projects you will be assigned."

He was clearly embarrassed. Caroline had caught me by surprise, as well as Moody. I hadn't expected her to throw that little curve. I tried to think of a way around her when I got a divine inspiration.

I cut in before the fur could fly. "I think we can work something out. I'd be happy to work with Ms. Gaines if Caroline could find time to oversee the project."

Ms. Gaines seemed clearly delighted, and Moody regained some of his natural color. Caroline crossed her arms and set her feet apart with annoyance.

I told her, "It's not a large project, and since it's only a few blocks from here, I think we can fit it into all our schedules. I'm not going to be on the road for a while, so I'll be happy to arrange my time to suit yours."

Tiffany's face brightened with animation. "I'd love to work on your design, Mr. Angeli." She gestured with enthusiasm. "Perhaps Caroline and I could set an appointment to have a look at your suite later today?"

"I can't possibly do it today," Caroline stated flatly.

Moody's face went deep red again. He was speechless.

I quickly threw myself into the breach. "No problem. No problem at all." I looked directly at him. "Tomorrow or later in the week will be fine. I'm flexible." I directed my most charming smile to reassure the man.

"I must apologize for Clayton's abruptness." Moody glared daggers at Caroline. "She *is* quite busy now. If you like, Ms. Gaines could have a look this afternoon, and Clayton will consult with you in a day or so."

His expression clearly told Caroline that he'd reached the end of his patience.

"Yes," Tiffany said. "I'd love to do that."

"Fine, that's settled then," Moody declared. "Ms. Gaines will drop in this afternoon. She'll do preliminary measurements and sketches. Then later we'll discuss what you want in greater detail."

"Excellent. I expect to be back at my new office around four. Perhaps you could meet me there, Ms. Gaines?" The Ms. nominative sets my teeth on edge. I prefer Miss, but must recognize the changes that take place among humans and their social structures.

"Call me Tiffany, please. I'll be there." Her smile dazzled me. She stirred up an unexpected and nearly forgotten sensual response in my temporary human body. I was taken off guard by her personality and physical appeal.

"Ms. Gaines will do a fine job for you," Moody broke in, still giving Caroline the evil eye.

I got a grip on myself. "I have no doubt she will. I look forward to working with both of these ladies." I shot a look at Caroline to let her know she wasn't completely off the hook.

"If you'll excuse me," Caroline said. "I must get my things together and head out for my meeting." She extended her hand. "Nice seeing you, Matt," she added insincerely.

"Yes, it is nice to see you again," I replied to her back as she turned and left the reception area.

"I apologize once more." Moody said darkly. "She's been very temperamental lately, and she's overdue for disciplinary action."

Tiffany jumped to her defense. "Caroline's overwhelmed with work right now. I'm sure she didn't mean to be rude."

"I'll do the managing around here, if you don't mind, Gaines. Don't *you* start giving me attitude."

I sighed at the way nouns and verbs were used interchangeably in today's world.

Tiffany lowered her head. A dark blush rose from her neck. I understood why Caroline had such deep disrespect for their boss. To embarrass an employee in the presence of a customer is unforgivable. Moody was the one who needed discipline.

I *accidentally* dropped some paperwork I carried. Moody jumped to retrieve it for me. As he bent over, a large rip appeared in the seat of his pants. Tiffany's eyes grew large. She slapped a hand over her mouth to stifle a giggle. I winked at her, then thanked the chagrined Moody and made a hasty departure.

All I could think of after my visit with that pathetic man was where was his guardian angel when he so obviously needed one?

CHAPTER 10

Daniel

Daniel and Caroline sat at her kitchen table talking after an early dinner. She was unhappy about her job situation. Her boss was driving her up the wall, piling on more work than she could handle, disrespecting her schedule, and her insistence on good customer follow through.

Nothing new on that front.

He brought the conversation around to her dream to open her own firm, not for the first time.

"Danny, that isn't realistic. I only have twenty-four thousand dollars in my savings. I need at least a hundred thousand to get me through the first year, and that would be if I retained some of my best clients."

He reached across and brushed her knuckles with his fingertips. "You should seriously consider it."

Gloomy, she shook her head and sipped the last of the iced tea in her glass.

"What about your grandmother's inheritance, your trust fund?" He leaned forward on his elbows. It put him closer to her.

"I can't get access to the money until my thirty-fifth birthday. That's years away. My parents have total control until then. There's a good chunk of money in the fund, but in truth, I don't know how much. I'm sure it's increased in value since she set it up." She shook her head with a hopeless expression on her beautiful face.

Searching for a solution, Dan asked, "Don't they have the option of releasing all or part of it earlier?" He reached into her refrigerator and retrieved the pitcher of cold tea and a beer.

"Of course, but they would never do it. Forget that." Her voice was fat with frustration.

Dan grinned and waggled his eyebrows. "I know how you could save twenty-five thousand a year." He leaned back from the table, stretched out his legs, and then ran his bare foot up the inside of her thigh.

She flashed him her funny little you-can-be-so-clueless look and shook her head. "Yeah, what, give up eating altogether?"

"Move in with me. You pay too much rent on this place."

"Don't even go there," she warned, her lips pressed in a thin line.

"It makes perfect sense."

"Dan, do you like being with me?"

He crossed his eyes and let his tongue hang out. She already thought he was an idiot, so he dramatized it a bit. At least it got a smile out of her.

"Moving in together would be the end of us. After about a month of picking up after you, I'd probably kill myself, or better yet...you." She aimed her finger at his face, in imitation of a gun, and pulled the thumb hammer.

"Oh, come on," he protested. "I'm not that bad. Do I make a mess when I stay here?"

"No, because you know I'd never put up with it."

"In that case, the defense rests, your honor." He mimed the closing a brief.

"My grandmother told me something very wise. She said if something about a man *annoys* you when he's courting you, it will drive you absolutely *insane* once you're married."

"Who said anything about marriage?" He tried on what he thought was his most lascivious facial expression. Who was he kidding? Marriage was exactly what he wanted.

She gave him a baleful stare, pushed away from the table and carried her plate to the sink. "I think it's time for you to go home, Kavanaugh."

"Oh, really?" he whispered as he came up behind her and kissed her on the neck. "I wasn't planning on leaving till tomorrow morning."

"Then you'd better behave yourself."

"I wasn't planning on doing that either." He turned her around and kissed her firmly. "Why don't you slip out of something while I load the dishwasher?"

"Who could pass up such an offer?" She kissed him back, reached around his waist, and yanked up his T-shirt. The next thing he knew, they were both naked. She did insist, however, they finish the dishes before proceeding with his plan. The sight of Caroline loading the dishwasher in the buff made it worth waiting for.

∼

Early the next morning, they sat in the bagel shop at the corner by Dan's office. They rose early, which wasn't surprising, considering they'd gone to bed before eight o'clock. They'd already had two cups of coffee and it was still before seven a.m. Neither of them was ready to go in to work.

"Oh, here's something weird," she said. "Remember that guy I told you about? Matthew? He was in the studio yesterday. Seems he rented a suite of offices in the Wilshire Bank building and wants me to design it for him."

"No kidding? Did I tell you that Dad, Bill, and I had a game of golf with him?"

"What?" She jerked with shock. "No, you didn't."

"Let me think. It must have been the day you went to Seattle. Yeah, I left for the country club right after you called to tell me you were on your way home to pack."

"No." She was puzzled, shook her head. "It couldn't have been that day. He was on my flight, only he got off in Portland."

"Maybe it's not the same guy. He said he knew you though."

"This is odd. How could there be two guys named Matthew, whom we don't know, but who professes to know both of us? Something about him unnerves me. Anyway, I told him I was booked solid and sloughed him off on Tiffany."

It was unlikely there could be two Matthews or the same Matthew in two different places at the same time. Dan searched for his last name. "The guy we played golf with is named Angeli."

Her eyes flew open like she'd seen a ghost. He thought maybe she'd had too much caffeine, or not enough sleep, or both.

"What does he look like?" She backed up in her chair, like she didn't really want to know.

"He's about five-eleven. Slender build, curly dark hair, and light blue eyes. Maybe not light blue, but an odd color of blue. He's maybe forty, I'd guess."

She groaned and laid her head down on her arms, rolling it side to side. "Why me, God, why me?"

Daniel couldn't figure out why she was so upset. "What's the problem? Angeli seemed rather ordinary to me, congenial, a good golfer. Is he the same guy?"

Her eyes flew open, her cheeks flushed. "Yes, he's the same guy. So, you tell me, genius lawyer, how could he have been playing golf with you and also be on a flight with me?"

Dan drew himself up, waved a hand, "There has to be a logical explanation. We must have the dates wrong. Maybe it was the day before you went to Seattle. Anyway, what are you so disturbed about? I didn't like him much, but he seemed harmless."

"I don't want to talk about it. I gotta go to work." She stood and gathered her things, turned without saying anything else, and started for the door.

"You coming over tonight?" he called.

She paused with her hand on the door. "I don't know. I'll call you later."

"I'll fix dinner."

"What this time, Froot Loops?"

CHAPTER 11

Caroline

Needing some air to get my brain working, I walked all the way to my office, a good two miles from the bagel place. I couldn't sort out the Matthew puzzle. Either I was going completely nuts or there was a logical explanation. I wanted the latter.

First thing I did when I walked in the door of the office was drop my portfolio. Not intentionally. Papers and drawings went everywhere, flying and sliding on the marble floor, like a huge aerodynamic science project. I uttered some choice curses I'd overheard when walking past the construction site next door.

"Caroline, how nice to see you in such a congenial mood this morning," said Guess Who.

"A very good morning to you, Mr. Moody."

Just what I needed first thing. He probably didn't get any last night. From his pinched face, it appeared as if he'd been constipated for a week. I don't know how his wife stands him. She must have an iron stomach, and she's the one with the money. Go figure.

"See Tiffany as soon as you get organized," he ordered. "She went to see Angeli yesterday afternoon, and I want her to get started right away so I can give him a cost estimate."

Angeli. Angeli. Was I destined to have this guy pushed in my face every day for the rest of my life?

Midget Brain walked out of reception without offering to help me retrieve my stuff. Such a gentleman.

Tiffany spotted me and came bouncing over. She looked, as my grandmother would have said, bright-eyed and bushy-tailed.

"You look like the cat that got all the cream." I shook my head and suppressed a smile.

"I'm so excited." If she'd had a tail, it would have been wagging.

I had to smile in spite of myself. How could I stay in my rotten mood in the face of such innocent cheerfulness? No wonder the Moodster had such a hard time keeping his hands off her.

"Yeah, about what, wiggles?" I continued to shuffle papers, stood, and walked into the inner sanctum.

"Matthew Angeli," she said with a grin, her eyes sparkling.

I kid you not. Him again! I didn't say anything. I looked at her with a yeah, so what? expression.

"I like him. Really." Her face turned pink, and she shifted from foot to foot.

"What do you mean, you really like him?" As if I didn't know. "Tiffany. Stand still!"

"I don't know...he's so sweet and kind, and he's so good-looking. I'm going to love working for him." Her face was flushed some more, and her freckles lit up. "He's not married, and did you notice his eyes?" She put her hand over her heart and went all wobbly in the knees.

All I could think was; you poor kid. Having encountered him myself, I knew what she meant about sweet and kind. I also knew that for some reason he seemed able to see right through me with those aqua eyes, and what he didn't already know, I felt compelled to tell him in great detail.

"Look, Tiffany, it's none of my business, but something about him bothers me." She started to protest, but I put my hand out like a traffic cop. "Let me finish, okay?"

"Okay," she said reluctantly.

"I don't want to rain on your parade, and you're a big girl, but ask yourself this, if he's such a great catch, why is he still single at his age? Huh? Maybe he's gay, or a priest, or something. Think about it."

"Oh, for heaven's sake, Caroline, I'm not planning to marry the guy. I like him a lot, and I'd like to spend some time with him. I think it's going to be a lot of fun working on his office. Be nice, okay?"

"Okay. I'm sorry. I didn't get much sleep last night."

"What time did you go to bed?" She cocked her head.

"I don't know, around eight I guess." I pretended to concentrate on the drawings on my drafting board.

She waited silently for me to look up. "Oh, I see," she said with a knowing smile. "Did Daniel sleep over by any chance?"

"Yeah, forget it, all right? Let's get to work on this before Randy Man comes out here and starts bugging us. Let me see your prelims."

She went back to her table to get her notes as Sandra came with coffee. "Looks like you could use this."

"Thanks. I can."

Tiffany returned with her stuff. We spread it out and started analyzing how best to use the space.

"Is he into modern, traditional, art deco, what?"

I was in all-business mode as I looked at her paperwork. Our office was so busy it sounded like a giant beehive.

"Well, get this, Matthew told me he's a big fan of Charles Rennie Mackintosh, of all things. He said he's traveled a lot in Scotland, and he took a liking to the style. Even said he spent almost a week in the Glasgow School of Art, some years back, studying and admiring Mackintosh's work."

"Mackintosh, huh? That'll make the boss happy. Sounds expensive. There are only a few places where his reproductions can be had. You'd better start with Jenna Lewis. She'll either be at the warehouse in Santa Monica or her office in London."

"I thought Lewis specialized in antique woodwork and doors." Tiffany cocked her head with a puzzled puppy look, like the Victrola ads in the antique magazines Gramma used to collect. They'd been all around our house.

"Lewis specializes in old and recovered woods, but a couple of years ago, she came across a manor house in Ft. William that was about to be dismantled. It turned out to be a treasure trove of Mackintosh. She secured a ton of windows, light fixtures, carved furniture, and fixtures. She salvaged all of it. That's when she became widely known. Her business took off like a rocket."

"Matthew told me he'd like the decorator touches to be Mackintosh, the desks and furniture to be understated and functional."

"He has taste, I'll give him that," I allowed begrudgingly. It intrigued me that he liked Mackintosh, my favorite architect and artist next to Frank Lloyd Wright.

∽

All morning, we worked together on Angeli's design, then I had to get back to the new Seattle project.

When we broke for lunch, Tiffany and I walked to the Mexican lunch wagon and ordered our favorites. We carried it to a little greenbelt nearby and sat on the grass to eat. It was one of those rare, perfect fall days in L.A. Not too hot, not too cold, and not too windy.

"Where are you?" I heard Tiffany say.

"Sorry, I was thinking about the Schumann and Sinclair law offices project in Seattle. I got the contract through Danny's dad, Liam. He and Harry Sinclair were fraternity brothers. I want everything to be perfect. I won't let Liam down."

She tilted her head back to catch some sun. "You were off in neverland there for a few minutes," she said with a laugh.

"Huh." I drifted off into my own space once more.

She poked my arm. "There you go again. Am I that boring?"

"No, my brain is going in circles with a lot of stuff right now. I was thinking of something Danny and I talked about this morning." I chewed my taco slowly, unable to get my mind off the idea of going out on my own.

"Anything my innocent little ears could stand to hear?" She dumped packet after packet of jalapeno sauce on her taco.

I emitted something that was halfway between a snort and a chuckle. "You must think we spend all our time together in bed."

"I certainly hope so. I can't imagine wasting a hottie like Daniel sitting around watching TV or playing checkers."

I was astonished when I noticed her lick the extra pepper sauce off her fingers. "God, how can you swallow all that liquid fire and not even blink?"

"I love it. I eat it on everything." She grinned and dumped on some more.

My eyes watered just thinking about that fiery condiment.

"Anyway, a long time ago I told Danny that I...Oh, forget it, Tiffany, it's nothing more than a dream."

"Come on, Caroline, you can't leave me hanging now. Tell, tell."

I sighed and began, "A couple of years ago, I confessed to Danny that I'd like to open my own design firm one day, okay? He brought it up again after dinner last night. He thinks I could do it now if I'm serious about it. Not likely. End of story."

"Wow, Caroline, how exciting. Your own firm."

More jalapeno on the taco.

"Yeah, well." I shrugged and sighed.

"No, really, what would it take?"

"A lot more money than I have saved. I figure I need enough to cover all my costs for at least a year. I'm looking at a hundred K, at least."

She grimaced. "Ooh, that is a lot of money. If you ever do decide to do it, I'll come and work for you. I wouldn't feel the least regret leaving L.E.H." She took a big bite of that flaming hot taco without as much as a tear or sniff.

"How much money do *you* have, Tiffany?" *It didn't hurt to ask, does it?*

Eyes big, she sat straight. "Me? You have to be kidding. I've only been out of design school for three years. I'm still paying off student loans." She wiped her lips with her napkin and took a long sip of diet cola.

"The reason I asked if you have any money to invest is that I'd rather have you for a business partner than an employee. I think we're a good team."

"Gosh, Caroline, I wish I did."

Jeez, there was that pathetic face again, the worshipful one that she's so good at. She even had tears in her eyes. I swear. Maybe it was the pepper sauce.

"For Pete's sake, Tiffany, quit looking at me like that. I'm not the goddess of office design. A lot of the time I'm not even nice to be around."

"I'm sorry," she sniffed. "You took me by surprise. Do you really think you'd want me for a partner? I'd love that. Wouldn't it be wonderful to pick and choose, to work on the designs we wanted and not have someone like The Ogre breathing down our necks?"

"Yeah, well, it's only a dream. For now, anyway. I'd be the one breathing down your neck instead of him. You'd be switching one ogre for another. Let's get back to work." I stood and brushed off my skirt.

She jumped up and gave me a quick hug. It took both of us by surprise. There she was with her freckles all lit up again and me speechless.

CHAPTER 12

Matthew

I held the end of the tape measure for Tiffany and called out the numbers as she made quick sketches and jotted measurements. The empty suite appeared cavernous on this second visit, without furniture or fixtures. One entire wall of my *Angel Office* consisted of windows overlooking Wilshire Boulevard from the seventh floor. While enjoying her running commentary, I even began to fantasize that I actually would be working from here. Fantasizing is not in the Policies and Procedures Handbook for angels.

After Tiffany and I finished our preliminary discussion on the possibilities for the office design, I invited her to have a cup of coffee.

"I'd love to," she said. "There's a coffee bar about two blocks away, a hangout for the people who work around here. It's a funky little dive. Would you like to go there?" She tilted her head to one side in a most charming manner.

The other day, when Caroline introduced Tiffany to me in the foyer of L.E.H., I was struck by how engaging she was. Prolonging conversation with this appealing young woman would be very pleasant. I was struck by the fact that she was truly beautiful. How could I have missed that?

"Everything they make is good," she went on, "and the people who work there are always breaking out into song, telling jokes, or teasing the customers. I think you'll like it."

With that, she took her coat and turned to see if I was following, a small tilt of her head toward the door. She picked up the briefcase stuffed with notes and measurements. "We can talk a little more about the details. It's going to be fun creating the look you want to achieve here, the mood you'd like to create."

Creation is best left to the Supreme Director, not mere underlings such as myself.

She reached into her coat pocket. "I got some great photos on my phone." She held out the device she'd used to snap photos of the empty suite. "I'd like Caroline to see the pictures before I really get into your space."

"Excellent." I held the door for her.

She flashed me a brilliant smile.

I felt a little catch in my chest. My attraction to her took me by surprise. I had a brief urge to reach out and touch her but held myself in check. We strolled the short distance to the coffee bar. Her happy demeanor enchanted me.

The cozy bistro was noisy and crowded, but Tiffany wove her way expertly through the crush to a postage-stamp sized table in the far corner. I helped her out of her jacket, took mine off, and hung them on a rickety bamboo coat rack between our table and the doorway to the kitchen.

"Funky is putting it mildly," I observed, doing my best to keep up with modern vernacular. The walls were painted in vivid primary colors, with almost every inch covered in candid snapshots of what I took to be the help and patrons. Several photos had autographs and messages scrawled across them. Our table was cardinal red, Tiffany's chair jade green, and mine yellow. A primitive hand-painted bouquet of pink cabbage roses graced the tabletop.

"Yes, isn't it great?" She raised her hand and gestured for service.

A tall, slim, young waiter with a thick dark ponytail and a van Dyke beard took our order. He winked at Tiffany, and I felt a pang of jealousy. How inappropriate. Angels in my line of work don't usually experience such emotion. Emotion is strictly reserved for humans.

"Noel's a cutie," she whispered. "He always flirts, but he's way too young for me, can't be more than twenty."

"What would you be?" I queried, "A middle-aged woman of say, twenty-four?"

"Exactly," she laughed. "What a good guess."

"Let's see," I mused. "That would make me fourteen years your senior."

I'd drowned at the age of thirty-eight. Time had stopped for me then. I would forever remain thirty-eight.

"Fourteen years? Hmm." She rested her chin in her hands as she contemplated that. "My dad is sixteen years older than my mom."

"You don't say?" Not knowing where to go with that, I turned the conversation to our project again. "Have you been partnering with Caroline on a regular basis?"

"No, just a few weeks, actually. She's so smart and talented. I love working with her. Mr. Moody doesn't appreciate what a treasure he has. Almost all our most lucrative jobs in the past year have been hers."

"She came highly recommended to me. I was looking forward to working with her." The second the words were out of my mouth, I realized how they must have sounded to her.

"I'm sorry, Tiffany. I didn't mean to say I'm not happy to have you working on the design. I just hadn't expected..." I trailed off helplessly.

"That's okay, Mr. Angeli. Don't be concerned. She'll be supervising everything I do for you."

"I know, but I'm embarrassed, nevertheless. Forgive me."

"No problem. Look, here's our cappuccino." After the waiter left, she raised her cup and smiled. "Cheers."

"Yes, cheers indeed. This will be a happy project."

Tiffany Gaines had me completely disarmed.

"Guess what?" She set her mug on a purple napkin. "Caroline told me that she'd like to go into business for herself. She even said she'd like me for a business partner. Isn't that great?" She raised her voice because Noel broke into a rap version of "Happy Birthday" embarrassing a patron. The birthday girl's tablemates gamely joined in.

"Caroline would be lucky to have you."

"What?" She giggled and put her hand behind her ear to hear me above the racket.

I leaned across the tiny table. "I said she'd be lucky to have you."

"Mr. Angeli, what a sweet thing to say." She blushed, that charming blush she seemed unable to control.

"Call me Matthew, please. It's after business hours." I saluted her with my cup. "I think you and Caroline would make a fine team."

"Okay...uh...Matthew," she said hesitantly. "That's what Caroline said. It took me by surprise. Only a few weeks ago, I didn't think she even liked me."

"I'm sure you're wrong about that." I smiled foolishly at her over my cup. I was ridiculously happy.

The pervasive aroma of chocolate drifted to our noses as two steaming cups of mocha, heaped with mounds of whipped cream and chocolate shavings, was served to the couple at the table next to ours.

Tiffany sighed and sniffed the air like a bloodhound catching the scent. She grinned and crooked her finger at young Noel.

"Yeah, Tiff. What's up?"

"I think I need to have one of those, Noel."

"Make it two," I added and laughed for the sheer pleasure of her company.

As I studied her across the table, she looked down shyly. "I just realized," I said. "You remind me of someone."

"I do?"

"Yes, it's amazing. You're so like her." I warmed at the unexpected memory.

"Like who?"

"You'll think this silly, but you remind me of my stepmother. Goodness, it's been so long since I saw her last." I shook my head in amazement at the resemblance.

"That *is* funny. I thought you were going to say I reminded you of an old schoolmate or girlfriend, but your stepmother?" She was clearly intrigued.

"She was quite young when she and my father married. I was only fourteen at the time and fancied myself in love with her."

"How sweet. What was her name?"

"Ariel. A wonderful creature. She came to help us after my mother died in childbirth. She'd recently lost her own husband and baby to an epidemic. She took my infant sister and nursed her as if she were her own. Ariel was the only mother some of my younger siblings ever knew."

"Oh, Matthew, what a sad and beautiful story. Did you come from a large family?"

"Yes, I was the eldest, and I had eight brothers and sisters. Then Ariel and my father had three more children, an even dozen. A large, happy family." I smiled, remembering.

"Gosh, how did your father manage to support such a big family?" Her rusty brown eyes were filled with innocent curiosity.

"I expect we were poor, but I didn't realize it at the time. Papa had a modest wine business, and we all worked at it. I had to leave school when I was twelve to work the press."

"You had to leave school in the sixth grade?" She stared, astonished.

"Yes. After that, I was home schooled by Papa and later Ariel. I took my turn teaching the younger ones to read and do their sums. I wasn't able to finish my formal education until I served a tour of duty in the armed services. I was a few years older than you when I finally managed to return to school."

I was amazed at how much I told her about myself. Getting others to bare their souls was my area of expertise. Now here was the lovely Tiffany, smiling at me across the tiny table in the noisy café, and I couldn't stop talking. "Enough about me." I took a breath. "Tell me about yourself, Tiffany, your parents. Do you have brothers and sisters?"

"Oh, gee, it's pretty boring, but here goes. My father is a jeweler to the rich and famous, my mother a fulltime homemaker, but she's a former child actress. She has lots of show biz friends. I've got the world's best parents. I love them so much. Everything they do is for us. I have two younger brothers and a sister who still live at home with my parents. Avi is at UCLA, studying to be a doctor. Jake will graduate from high school this year and has no idea what he wants to do. They're both tall, blond, and devastatingly handsome, of course.

"Then there's my sister, Melody. She's only thirteen, and she's been on TV since she was about four. She's a former regular on the Mickey Mouse Club. Now she does mostly commercials so that she can attend school full time. I was a TV kid, too, for a few years, but decided I didn't want to be in movies or TV. I went to college instead and got a design degree."

Tiffany sat with her chin in her hand, smiling at me. The love for her family glowed in her face and eyes.

"My, that sounds like a lively household, not boring in any sense." I returned her smile.

"You're not from around here, are you? There's something about your speech that's different. I can't quite put my finger on it."

"No. I'm not from around here. In fact, I've only been in L.A. a short while. My childhood home is far away. I haven't been there in many years."

"Don't tell me where you're from. I want to think about it for a while. After we've spent some time together, I bet I can figure it out. I've always been pretty good with regional accents and speech patterns."

"All right, I'll let you ponder it."

"See? There you go again. Nobody says ponder anymore."

She smiled at the challenge. I wanted very much to kiss her. How shocking.

Later, I saw her safely to her automobile. After she waved goodbye from the side window, I took a long walk, trying hard to focus. Tiffany is enchanting. She is a woman I would be drawn to if my circumstances were different.

Such a sweet heart she has. That's where the expression came from, you know. A man could settle down with a young lady like Tiffany, have a passel of kiddies, and look forward to coming home every night. She was easy on the eyes, that curly, flaxen hair, her slender, long, and beautiful tapered hands. Like Ariel, she had a lovely, rounded figure and rosy complexion. You may think it odd, but there are times when it's a real drag to be an angel.

I admonished myself. "Stop it, Matthew. You cannot go down this path."

I sat on a bus bench and leaned forward on my elbows, feeling sorry for myself when I sensed something around a mild three-point-five earthquake. The sweet looking elderly lady sitting on the other end of the bench uttered a shocking expletive. I shared a startled look with her and raised my eyes Heavenward.

Okay, so I'm not perfect. You don't have to frighten half the population of Los Angeles to make a point.

I stood and strolled down Wilshire Boulevard for several blocks, attempting to sort out matters cluttering my mind. Traffic was heavy, and the sidewalk crowded with people going about their business, but I noticed little detail. I felt pervasive fatigue. It had been so long since I'd had such an extended period of actual physical contact with people, I had forgotten how stressful day-to-day mortal living could be. I was weary of being an angel and having fantasies about being a real flesh-and-blood man again. Heaven help me. This should have been a simple assignment. Instead, look what was happening to my judgment and ability.

I decided to take a few days off and go to the home office for some R and R. I prayed my superiors would have words of wisdom for me and would help me get back on task. I repeat myself, but how I ever got this job in the first place was still a mystery to me. Caroline was going to face serious challenges in the coming weeks. I would not desert her. I must find a way to fulfill my responsibility to both Caroline and Daniel and the Grand Plan.

CHAPTER 13

Caroline

Darn Danny, anyway. I had more or less made peace with myself over the business of starting my own firm when he got me thinking about it again. If that wasn't bad enough, Tiffany had a long face all morning because Matthew left her a message that he was called out of town. All starry-eyed when she came in this morning, she now looked as if her best friend died.

I helped her with the design when she asked me, but I didn't offer her any more advice where Matthew Angeli was concerned. If I had my way, I'd never lay eyes on him again.

Let her get her heart broken. What did I care?

Who was I kidding? Jeez, why did I have to like her? It was much easier when I just came into this place, did my work and went home. Now, I'm worried about putting my nose in her business. I should be glad she's working with Matthew Angeli. It got me off the hook. I could focus my concentration on the Schumann and Sinclair job.

I asked Moody if I could go to Seattle for a few days. I needed another face-to-face with them and some time to look at what's happened with the construction. Not that I needed to leave to avoid Angeli. If what he told Tiffany was true, he'd already left town.

I could use time by myself, to think through the feasibility of starting my own firm. If I talked about it with Daniel, I would lose my perspective.

Good grief, here comes God's Gift.

"All right, Clayton. You may leave in the morning. I told Russell to order your airline tickets. You shouldn't need more than two days up there. Be back here by the time Angeli returns. I want you to review Tiffany's prelim before we present it to him."

Everyone in the drafting area was all ears, all six of them. They always tuned in to the latest encounter between Moody and me. Coffee cups were raised to suddenly stilled lips. It was comical how it became quiet whenever they suspected Moody and I might have a showdown.

The three junior designers were busy staring at their drawings, their ears practically wriggling, straining to hear what we would say. The model makers, Bill Murphy and Janet Hampton, who'd been arguing non-stop over a project they were working on, suddenly quieted. Tiffany was the only one who had the decency to feign disinterest. She went to the blueprint copier and turned on the noisy thing. Those closest to the huge machine glared at her.

Usually there was a constant stream of conversation and the muffled sounds of the TV tuned to HGTV, which made the big room sound like a doctor's waiting room. I chuckled in spite of myself.

"Great," I said with uncharacteristic niceness and asked sweetly, "Is Sandra getting my hotel booked, or should I do it myself?"

Oh, how disappointed Bill and Janet appeared to be. No battle this time.

"I don't think I need to be there more than one night, but I may want to use the opportunity to take another look at how the Harrison Publishing project is going."

"Whatever. Book it yourself. I told her to leave your flight return open. Just be sure you get your tush back here as soon as you're done. This isn't another excuse for you and Litigator Boy to have a vacation at company expense."

"He doesn't litigate."

"What?" He whipped around looking as if he'd eaten a green persimmon.

"Daniel Kavanaugh is not a litigator. He's a contracts attorney."

"Kiss my ass, Clayton." He made his parting shot to the amusement of the room, so their eavesdropping wasn't wasted after all.

"You wish," I murmured.

Okay, I sacrificed my pride for a few laughs. So what? I was getting away for a couple of days. Now maybe I could do some clear thinking. Clear my head. Something.

∼

I called Danny's office and Billie put me through to his extension. "Don't come over tonight. I have to sort out my papers and pack. My flight is at six-forty-five in the morning."

I held the phone precariously on my shoulder while trying to get my travel bag from the top shelf of the hall closet. The phone squirted out from under my chin and banged against the wall before hitting the floor with a loud crack.

"Crap!" I dropped the bag, and it landed on my foot. "Crap, crap!"

I picked up the phone, still hopping on one foot, and asked Danny if he was still there.

"Yes, I'm here, but I think you gave me a brain hemorrhage. What the hell happened?"

"Sorry, I was trying to get my bag down from the closet and dropped the phone. I'm surprised it didn't break when it hit the wall."

"I'm surprised my eardrum didn't break. Do you want me to drive you to the airport? That's assuming I'll get my normal hearing and vision back by morning."

I could picture him sitting at his computer banging out a contract or legal correspondence or something. When I'm at his place, I sometimes stand in the doorway to his den and observe him working when he doesn't know I'm watching. He always sits real straight, and I can see the muscles in his back and shoulders moving under his t-shirt as he types away. He must type a million words a minute. At times, I think if I set off a bomb, he wouldn't even notice. That's how good his concentration is.

One time I took off all my clothes and stood next to his chair for about five minutes waiting for him to notice. Finally, he looked up. He let out a whoop and made a grab for me. I shrieked and jumped back, tripping over a big stack of books. He tried to stop me from falling but stepped on one of the books himself. We both sat down hard on the floor and burst out laughing.

"No, you don't need to get up that early. Anyway, hopefully I'll only be gone for one night, and I'm not sure what flight I'll be coming back on. I'll leave my car at the airport."

"Call me when you get there, babe."

"I'm staying at the Water's Edge again, but no showing up there this time. I've already been put on notice by Mr. High and Mighty." I limped back to my bedroom with my flight bag in one hand and the phone in the other.

Dan snorted. "He's a world-class schlemiel."

"Yeah, well." I tossed the bag on my bed and flopped down beside it. "What else is new?" I was attempting to shimmy out of my thigh-high hose, using my hips and one hand. "Criminy these things are impossible!"

"What's happening?"

Finally, they were off. I sighed with relief. "Huh?"

"You were grumbling. What are you doing?"

"I was trying to get my stockings off. You know, those things invented by the Marquis de Sade."

"If I were there, I could help you off with your clothes. Just say the word." The sexy grin in his voice came right through the phone.

"Very funny. Actually, I don't want you to come over right now. My other lover will be here any minute, and it would be awkward."

"Okay, I don't want to put a crimp in your extracurricular love life, but why not humor me and tell me what else you're taking off?"

"Bye, Danny, I'll call you later."

"Spoil sport."

～

The next morning I was up before the crack of dawn, having slept like a rock. Guess my conscience was clear. The traffic wasn't too lousy at that time of the morning, so I made good time to LAX. It was too early to check in, the boarding gate still deserted. I decided to go over to the fast-food place and have something for breakfast. My stomach was finally in a place that didn't entirely reject the idea of welcoming food.

It was a good thing I ate. Murphy's Law reigns supreme. The flight crew was late arriving, the gal operating the Jetway couldn't get it lined up to the door of the aircraft, and when we finally boarded, the door wouldn't close. We cooled our heels for forty minutes, waiting for a mechanic to fix it. The flight finally took off after eight. I would have been starving by the time we arrived in Seattle. There was no way I could eat the meal they serve on those early morning business class flights. It was a ghastly, greasy, cold cheese omelet or cold rubbery waffles. I'm sure the inmates at San Quentin get better food than what they serve on the airlines these days.

∼

When my flight arrived, the Seattle airport was a mess with disgruntled picketers and noises everywhere. I learned the World Trade Organization Conference was taking place in town. Near the downtown convention center, police had cordoned off the entire area while they and the K-9's searched the interior of the building. Wouldn't you know that the office building I was headed for was a half block away from all the commotion? The taxi driver couldn't go more than a few yards at a time without stopping. A large group of chanting demonstrators marched up Sixth Avenue waving placards, following behind a flatbed truck.

"This is nuts," I said. "I'll walk from here."

I paid him off and left the cab. I had my carry-on bag, purse, briefcase, coat, and umbrella. It was a pain trying to maneuver through the milling crowd on the sidewalk, something like running the gauntlet at an initiation ritual. Some of the crowd looked like college students and some like dock workers. Across the street, a large group of priests and nuns stood quietly, eyes closed as if in silent prayer.

At the building entrance, a burly security guard stood behind the locked glass door, watching the street scene. I kicked the door with my foot to get his attention.

When he looked my way, I shouted through the glass, "I have an appointment with Harry Sinclair."

He nodded and unlocked the door. I stepped inside as the crowd surged, and a large stevedore type began yelling obscenities at a little female police officer. I was glad to be inside.

"How long has this been going on?" I gasped, breathless.

"Couple of days, they get meaner every hour." He locked the door behind me. "The police aren't doing enough to keep them under control."

"I picked a great time to come here. I wish I'd known this was happening." I shifted my overnight bag to my shoulder and my umbrella from under my arm to my hand.

"It's been all over the TV and internet, lady." He looked at me as if I'd stepped off an alien spaceship.

"Where's the restroom?" I asked, instead of giving him the snarky answer right on the tip of my tongue.

He cocked his head to the side, indicating the large sign which read: *Restrooms and Telephones.* I was sure he thought I was a moron.

After making a futile attempt to push my hair down to manageable size–the climate in Seattle gives me Diana Ross hair–and refreshing my lipstick, I aimed for the bank of elevators. The suite I headed for was on the twentieth floor. I had to go to nineteen, then use a courtesy phone to have their receptionist send down the private elevator to their level. The previous tenants of the suite must have been an international money laundering ring or the CIA.

When I stepped off the elevator, I smelled paint and heard the sounds of construction going on in the back. It looked as if things were moving along.

Harry's secretary took my suitcase, umbrella, and coat and showed me in. Two men stood at the window of Harry's office, watching the commotion below. Imagine my surprise when they turned and one of them was Danny's father, Liam.

"Dad! What are you doing here?" I surprised myself. I wasn't sure I had ever called him Dad before.

"Hello, my dear girl." He came over and embraced me. "Harry and I have an appointment with a mutual customer this afternoon. I didn't know you were coming until I arrived an hour ago. We could have flown together."

"I never dreamed you'd be here, or I would have called you. I only decided yesterday to check on the progress of the new offices." I put my briefcase on the floor and extended my hand to Harry, "Nice to see you again, Mr. Sinclair."

Harry Sinclair was your stereotypical Silver Fox, about sixty and as slim as a distance runner with a full head of thick white hair. His suit must have cost well over a couple thousand bucks. He could give a movie star a run for the money. Heck, I could go for him myself.

"Call me Harry, please." He indicated the sofa and sat across from us in an armchair. "Lee assures me you're practically a member of his family."

I cast a sidewise look at Liam after Harry's remark. He kept a sober face but winked at me. I suddenly had the strange feeling Daniel must have told him he'd proposed to me. No. I was imagining things.

"How is the reconstruction progressing, Harry?" I asked Sinclair, putting my professional face back on.

"Until the last couple of days, we were moving right along. Now the contractor has a problem trying to get his vehicles around to the service entrance. Looks like things will slow down until this brouhaha is over."

"Is Al here? I have some samples of the crown moldings and a piece of the wall covering we selected for the conference room."

"Yes, he's here. The architect, too. Should I call them in?" He made as if to rise.

I stood. "No, I'll find them. I don't wish to interrupt you and Liam."

"We're about ready to leave for our meeting. You may use my office if you like," he offered graciously.

"We should be on our way, Harry." Liam said. "With all that confusion going on down there, we need to plan on taking more time to get to our meeting."

Harry agreed. "Okay, Liam, let's go."

Liam smiled the smile that all the Kavanaugh men, including my little buddy Ryan, had perfected. You gotta love 'em.

"Caroline, perhaps you and I can have dinner later? My flight isn't scheduled until almost ten tonight."

"That would be great. I'm here all by my lonesome, and I hate eating solo in restaurants." I took off my jacket and placed it on the back of the sofa.

"What time are you leaving tonight?" He pulled his overcoat on, and picked up his briefcase.

"I'm not. I'm making a call at another job site in the morning. That one's about ready to wrap up. I'm here until tomorrow evening, at least."

"All right then, my dear, I'll look for you when we return." He put his arm around my shoulders and gave me a brief hug.

∾

The contractor on this job wasn't the same as the one working on my other Seattle project, but they used the same architect, Peter Langley. I found them in the new suite area, in the middle of a heated argument over some detail on the custom cabinetry the architect and I had ordered.

Peter, in his mid-forties, still had that fresh college-boy, preppy look about him. Al Guererro, the contractor, always reminded me of a pugnacious Chihuahua. Undersized, he made up for it by being tough and stubborn.

Peter stood his ground. "Look, Al, I don't give a damn whether you think it's practical or not. It's what Clayton and I ordered, and it's what the customer wants. Just install the goddamned thing."

Al's big, brown, Chihuahua eyes bulged. "What I'm trying to tell you, you stubborn prick, is that it won't work the way you want it to. I don't want to have to come back here and dismantle the whole damn unit once they realize the problems with it."

I announced my presence. "Sorry to interrupt your little love-fest, guys. What *is* the problem?"

Al looked up and gave me a large lustful grin. I had to admire his chutzpah. I stood at least six inches taller.

"Your design stinks, beautiful. Other than that, Pete and I are best pals." He wiped his forehead with his shirtsleeve.

"Is that all?" I raised my eyebrows at Peter Langley. "And here I thought I was pretty good."

"You are good, Caroline. This bonehead thinks he's better," Langley said.

I lowered my eyes. "Other than 'stinks' could you be more specific, Al?"

"Yeah, come over here and I'll show you." He walked through the archway to the back of the next room, stood by the window, and pointed at the corner.

"See this?" He touched the bottom of the window. "You wanted this fancy sill, but the cabinet you designed has a door that opens slam-bam into it. The first ditzy secretary who opens that door is going to put a big ding in the expensive mahogany, and guess who's going to be blamed?"

What a classy guy. I just love a confrontation with a real macho man.

"Well, Al." I took on the tone of an overworked schoolteacher explaining two and two to a dopey kid. "If you could read a blueprint, you'd see that the door is designed to be hinged on either side. So why, when you install the unit, don't you put the hinges here?" I placed my finger on the blueprint.

None of this was lost on Langley. He turned slightly away and put his hand to his mouth to hide his grin.

Al, speechless for the moment, stalked to the blueprint table and leaned over, studying it closely. "Aw, hell."

"Okay, then. Can we move on now? Show me the prep work that's been in the conference room. I brought a sample of the crown molding and the wallpaper."

The next two hours went by without further tantrums on Al's part. He was an excellent contractor, and I've worked with him on two other projects. One here in town and another at the administrative offices of a hotel near SeaTac. He's dependable, honest, and a perfectionist, but never a dull moment.

By the time Liam and Harry returned, Al had left for the day. Peter and I were discussing the finishing work.

"How are we progressing?" Harry asked, "Everything on schedule for our big open house next month?"

"Should come in right on time," Peter answered. "We ironed out a few minor problems today. Al has everything under control, as usual."

"Yes," Harry said, "he did a great job on the renovations of our Whidbey Island house. Drove Muriel crazy though." He laughed. "I remember our first encounter with Al."

"The only reason I can stomach working with him is I know he'll do a quality job." Peter nodded. "And he rarely has cost overruns."

"It's going to be beautiful, Harry," I said. "You'll love it." I retrieved my jacket from the back of the sofa and slipped into it.

"How about that dinner, sweetheart?" Liam put his briefcase in order. "I'd enjoy a nice leisurely evening with you, rather than sitting, waiting hours for my flight."

"I'm ready." I gathered up my rain coat and umbrella. "Harry, I'm pleased with the job. Call me if you have any concerns. You've got my cell phone number. I'll do a final walk-through when everything is finished."

"Glad you came today. I'm expecting you and Lee to be here for our open house. Bring Daniel and Mary."

"Wouldn't miss it," I promised.

He did a quick tilt of his head toward the window. "You two be careful out there."

Liam took my overnight bag, and we made our way to the main lobby. The security guard stood at the door, intent on the goings on outside.

I peered around him. "What's happening?"

"Looks pretty calm right now," he said, without looking away from the sidewalk scene. "Most of them have put in a long day, and they're about ready to throw in the towel."

He unlocked the door for us. "You watch yourselves."

We stepped into the throng. People on the sidewalk at that hour seemed to be looky-loos or office workers heading home.

Liam tilted his head to the right. "There's a nice restaurant right down the block. Let's see if they're open."

We elbowed through the multitude and moved away from the noise. The block ahead was much less crowded, but I heard a ruckus across the street. A mob milled around a TV crew and their van. Someone shouted as the shoving pack suddenly surged across the street toward us.

"Dad." I tugged his sleeve, and he turned toward the commotion. "What the...?"

A beer bottle flew through the air, headed right for us.

I saw that it was going to hit Liam. "Dad, look out!" I yelled and gave him a shove. Out of nowhere, Matthew Angeli jumped right in front of Liam and the bottle caught him squarely in the face.

He fell to the ground, blood gushing from his forehead.

"Matthew!" I shrieked and rushed to his side. He didn't move. "Somebody call a doctor!" I knelt beside him and cradled his head in my lap. "Oh, God," I moaned with fear. I thought he was dead.

"Is that Matthew Angeli?" Liam asked as he knelt beside me. "Where in daylights did he come from?"

"Yes, it's him. I don't know where he came from. He's hurt."

Glaring lights were everywhere. Suddenly a TV reporter and cameraman shoved their way through the gathering crowd. The reporter stuck a microphone in my face.

"Do you know this man?" the obnoxious brunette demanded.

"Get away!" I yelled at her, pushed her with my hand. "He can't breathe. Did anyone call an ambulance?" I held Matthew's head and rocked back and forth. "Please, Matt, don't be dead."

Liam put pressure on Matt's head wound with his neck scarf, while he dialed nine-one-one on his cellphone with his thumb. I rubbed Matthew's cheek over and over.

"Please, God," I murmured, "don't let him be dead. Please."

Liam held the scarf to Matthew's wound. He extended his elbow to shove back against the crowd. My baggage got a good trampling in the melee.

"Matthew. Matthew, wake up. Wake up dammit!" His eyes opened, and he moaned. "Thank you, God," I said.

The TV reporter and the cameraman moved in closer.

"Get away, you ghouls! Can't you see he's hurt? Where's the dammed ambulance?" I batted at the microphone again.

"I hear a siren now," Liam said.

"Caroline?" Matthew groaned weakly. "Caroline, is Liam all right?"

"Shush now. Dad's okay." I leaned over with relief washing over me and put my cheek against his head.

"Move aside. Move aside," a police officer ordered, making an opening in the crowd for the paramedics and their stretcher.

A skinny guy in uniform, who looked too young to be of any help, knelt beside me. He peered into Matthew's eyes with a slim flashlight and lifted Liam's scarf to see the wound. Matthew groaned.

"Be careful," I begged. "He's hurt."

"Yes, ma'am, I know. That's why we're here. It doesn't look life threatening. Let's get him into the ambulance."

The two paramedics lifted Matthew gently onto the stretcher. The police held people back, then noise erupted down the street and attention was diverted from us. We were in the middle of a riot.

I gripped Matthew's hand like it was the only piece of driftwood in a cold, lonely sea. I knew if I let go, he'd die on me. I trembled from head to toe. There was no way they were going to pry me loose.

"Where are you taking him?" I demanded.

"Harborview Medical Center."

"I'm coming with you." I had completely forgotten about Liam, my luggage, and my briefcase. All I could think of was Matthew and how seriously he might be hurt.

"Caroline?" Liam touched my arm. "You go ahead in the ambulance; I'll retrieve your things, get a cab, and meet you there. Take a breath. He's going to be okay." He seemed perplexed at my hysterical concern for Matt. I was puzzled about it myself.

I jogged alongside the stretcher and climbed into the ambulance. The detestable news crew had to be pushed out of the way so the paramedics could close the doors.

"Caroline?"

Heart pounding, I looked down at Matthew. "Yes?"

"You're hurting my hand."

CHAPTER 14

Matthew

My head pain is like hell, figuratively speaking, of course. I do not like pain, never did, never will. My bright idea to work in the physical certainly has not yielded the quick result I counted on. If things keep going the way they are, I will get myself killed again. It was no fun the first time, and I don't care to repeat it.

I've never been in a hospital before, not as a patient in any case. The sights, sounds, and smells fascinate me. It is quiet, yet at the same time, the clamor of healing, pain, and complaint are clear. I am conscious of my own groaning and behaving like a baby. Down the hallway, a human baby cries. I hear the muffled sounds of his mother attempting to soothe away the pain and fear. I hope the child isn't seriously hurt or ill. *God help him.*

The doctors and nurses have quit torturing me for the moment. The local anesthetic did not start working until nearly all the stitches were in. I have the strange sensation my head is ballooning, larger then smaller with each beat of my pulse. That beer bottle hit me hard enough to dislodge my halo–if I had one.

The baby wails again. *Whatever are they doing to him?*

I had intended to deflect the missile thrown at Liam with my hand. Clearly, I am not as nimble of foot as I should be in this body. Getting knocked squarely on the forehead was not part of the plan and the blood! In my eyes, my mouth, all down the front of my shirt. Why, it was downright frightening.

The harried young Asian doctor leaned over me, shining a bright light into my eyes. "You have unusual eyes, Mr. Angeli." He leans this way and that until he is apparently satisfied with what he sees. "Well then, how are we doing?"

It amuses me how medical personnel tend to speak in the *royal* sense.

"*We're* doing as well as can be expected under the circumstances," I say. "Any permanent damage to the noggin?"

"Probably not." His smile is gentle and compassionate. "We won't know for sure until hours from now. I should admit you for the night. I'd like to make sure you're not working on a concussion." He picks up my chart and scribbles some notes.

I'm unable to keep the alarm out of my voice. "I can't possibly stay. I have an early morning flight back to Los Angeles. I'm behind schedule as is." Behind schedule is putting it mildly.

"I'll release you if you insist. However, I'd advise you to stay put here for at least another hour. We'll monitor your vitals, keep an eye on you for a while longer. Now, if you'll excuse me, I have a few more casualties to look after from the melee downtown." He patted my arm and exited the curtained-off area next to my bed.

"Matthew?" Caroline's voice comes from the other side of the curtain. "May we come in?"

I uttered a groan for emphasis. "Come ahead but speak softly if you don't mind. I have a monstrous headache."

Caroline and Liam pull the curtain back and approach my bed. They smile tentatively.

"I was so worried about you, Matt," Caroline said. "I thought for sure you were dead. What in the heck were you doing there in the middle of all that?"

Her tone was accusatory. That's probably why she addressed me as Matt. She knows I don't like it.

"Yes, you gave both of us a scare," Liam added. "If you hadn't been right there in front of me, I'd be the one nursing a headache."

To answer Caroline, I said, "I'm here on company business. I was about to say hello, when the next thing I know I'm on the ground with my head in your lap." I turn to look at her. "I think you were yelling at me." I chuckled, then winced. "Ouch."

"I *was* yelling at you. You scared me half to death. The way your head bounced on the pavement, blood flying everywhere. I was trying to wake you."

"You have a beaut of a knot on your head, my friend." Liam leaned over to study the doctor's handiwork. "Nasty scar, maybe. Shouldn't affect the golf game, though." He gave me a sympathetic smile and a pat on the shoulder.

"Caroline, do you have a mirror in your purse?" I asked. "I want to see what you're both gaping at."

She fumbled through her bag and came up with a hand mirror. "You sure you want to see that?" She held the mirror out of arm's reach. "It's pretty ugly."

"I'll have to, sooner or later."

"Okay, here goes." She held the mirror in front of my face.

"Heaven forbid! I look like I've been in a knock down at an Irish pub and not a drop of good Irish Whisky to show for it."

Liam chuckled. "You made the seven o'clock news. Caroline, too."

I looked at Caroline and noticed for the first time that she had blood all over the front of her suit and blouse. The suit was the same color as her eyes, the silk blouse a shade lighter. She is a stunner, even splattered with my blood. Her angular face is framed in a mass of auburn hair. It was in disarray, and instead of detracting, it actually added to her appeal. My sympathy went out to Daniel. Heaven help him.

"Caroline, I'm sorry about that mess on your beautiful suit. It looks ruined."

She looked down, shook her head, and shrugged. "Don't worry about it."

Young doctor Han pulled aside the curtain and came to my bedside, accompanied by an orderly pushing a gurney. Holding the chart in his right hand, he took my wrist to check my pulse with his left.

"Whatever are they doing to that poor baby? It sounds as if he's being tortured."

I don't like being treated like an infant, but then again, I was acting like one.

He paused while he counted, then smiled. "He's a she, and she ate her mother's birth control pills. We did a gastric lavage. She's more insulted than hurt. It took three of us to hold her down." He shook his head at the memory.

"Gastric lavage? I don't know what that is, but I do know I don't want you to do it to me." I shuddered.

"Pumped her stomach," he replied.

"Oh." The visual was disgusting.

"I'm afraid we'll have to move you to a room, Mr. Angeli. Seems we're about to receive more guests from Seattle's little party."

"That's not necessary. I'm fine. If you'll sign me out, I'll be on my way." I attempted to sit up and a wave of pain rushed upward in my skull, sending me quickly back to my pillow. Nausea washed over me. I groaned and wanted to cry. What I craved was Ariel's sweet and tender touch.

Caroline pushed back on my shoulders. "You're not going anywhere, Matt. Just do as the doctor says."

Her touch is neither sweet nor tender, but I'm in no condition to argue.

She hailed the doctor. "How long does he have to stay here?"

"I could release him if he has someone to check on him every hour or so. We need to make sure he doesn't have a concussion or anything more serious going on in here." He gently tapped my head.

"Okay, then. He's coming with me," Caroline stated, in a that's settled tone of voice.

Liam gave her a startled look, which I'm sure mirrored my own.

She gave a dismissive wave. "I have a large room at the Water's Edge. He'll stay with me tonight. I'll watch him. If he shows any symptoms of concussion, I'll bring him right back here."

I was about to refuse her offer when I realized it was the perfect opportunity for me to spend time with her. She made it clear the day I went to her firm that she had no intention of being in my company if she could avoid it. Her sudden solicitousness was surprising, and it gave me the opportunity to make progress.

Still, it seemed appropriate at this juncture to make a mild protest. "That's kind of you, Caroline, but, I couldn't..."

"Don't be silly, Matthew. You helped me out once. I'm only returning the favor. I insist unless you have someone else to stay with?"

"No, but it might seem inappropriate for us to..."

She laughs. "The hotel will bring in a rollaway bed for you. Trust me, I feel perfectly safe, or are you the one who's worried?"

Not sure how to answer that, I remained silent. *Man proposes—God disposes.*

Liam observed the foregoing exchange with a mixture of puzzlement and enjoyment. I am reminded again how much Daniel resembles him. All five of his sons do, but more markedly, Daniel. I got a flash of insight about what Caroline's and Daniel's children might look like. If I ever got them to the altar, that is.

"I'd be happy to stay the night and help look after Matthew," Liam volunteered. "If he hadn't been there, I'd be the one needing your nursing. I'm in his debt."

"Not necessary, Dad." Matthew noticed Caroline had unconsciously called him Dad again.

I am pleased that my influence has softened her. I wondered if she was aware of that little adjustment in her psyche. I think I am responsible and have made progress, after all. A cheering thought.

"I'm staying over anyway," she continued. "You have a flight to catch in a couple of hours. Go on home, Dad. Matt and I will be fine."

"If that's been settled," the physician interjected, "I'll sign the release."

"Yes, it's settled," she said. "Come on, Matthew, I'll help you get your shoes back on."

"I'll stay till we get him into a cab," Liam added. "Then I'll be on my way."

Liam and I both recognize it is a waste of energy to argue with her now that her mind was made up.

∽

We settled into the taxi. I leaned my head on the seat back while Caroline instructed the driver where to go. I couldn't help groaning.

She chided me, "Quit being such a baby, Matthew. It's a lump on the head and a few stitches, not an organ transplant."

"Yes. *My* head, thank you." I glared at her.

"Behave and I'll tell you what caused the ruckus that landed you in the emergency room."

"I'm doing my best. I don't handle pain well."

"Men are such infants when it comes to being hurt or sick." She pursed her lips, shaking her head with disgust.

I began to wish I had stayed at the hospital. I mutter sullenly, "Tell me what happened."

"According to that detestable female television reporter—just before we stepped outside the building, an elderly man and a middle-aged woman had just read a Citizen's Arrest Warrant. They were planning to serve it on a World Trade Organization minister. Their mistake was trying to cross the police line. They got handcuffed and arrested. The crowd grew angry and began shouting at the police. That's when the riot broke out."

"Hmm, bad timing on your part, I'd say."

"Look who's talking," she replied with a chuckle.

"Indeed."

We arrived at the hotel and the doorman gasped when Caroline helped me out of the cab.

"I saw you on the evening news," he exclaimed. "I thought you were a goner." He immediately helped steady me. He helped me to stand, supported me to the entrance doors.

"Close enough," I groaned.

"This thing has turned into a big mess," he said, "and it doesn't officially start until tomorrow.".

"If you'll help him into the elevator and up to room four-thirty-one, I'll pay the cab driver." Caroline handed her keycard to the doorman.

"More than happy to, ma'am."

The kind doorman saw me all the way into her room and made sure I was settled comfortably on the sofa. It was a lovely room. Large windows overlooked the harbor.

"Thank you, young man. I'm not sure I could have made it on my own. I'm woozier than I thought." I sighed and sank into the sofa cushions.

"I feel embarrassed for my hometown, sir. May I call room service? Have them send up a pot of tea or a light snack? My guess is you and your wife haven't had dinner yet." He adjusted the thermostat and turned on the lamps, then hung my jacket in the closet.

"She's not..."

Caroline walked through the door. I realized that it didn't matter whether he thought she was my wife or not. I groaned a little and rested my head on the cushion. "What I *could* use is a drop of the Irish," I moaned.

"No alcohol," Caroline stated. "The instructions say you can't have alcohol or caffeine for at least twenty-four-hours."

She handed the doorman a tip, thanked him, and closed the door behind him.

"Thank you, Mother Superior," I grumbled. "Am I allowed to eat?" I was suddenly famished. After a few centuries, one becomes unaccustomed to such things as hunger, desire, and pain.

"Oh? Is someone feeling a little sorry for himself, Matty Watty?"

Her imitation of baby talk was most annoying. "I have a headache!" Yes, I felt sorry for myself. I sat there and pouted like a small boy wanting his mother's sympathy.

"I'm not surprised, hero." She took the room-service menu and opened it to Late Night Dining. "Here, do you see anything you'd like?"

"Just pick something. I don't care, anything."

"All right—let's see—how about a nice omelet?"

My stomach heaved at the thought. "Not an omelet. I dislike eggs intensely."

"Me, too, okay? What else do they have?" She sat next to me and studied the menu. She placed her hand on mine and gave it a little squeeze, which was instantly comforting. We settled on grilled cheese sandwiches, fries, and root beer.

After calling in the order, Caroline brought a pillow and made me comfortable on the sofa. "I'm turning on the TV. No sleeping now," she instructed me.

She excused herself and went to take a shower while we waited. She came out of the bathroom wearing baggy men's pajamas, rolled up at the sleeves. A pair of Daniel's, I suspected. Her intention was to be unattractive, I am sure; but it had the opposite effect. There is little she can do to look unattractive. I marveled at how oblivious she was of her appearance. Idly, I wondered how Tiffany Gaines might look in my pajamas. *Forgive me. It must be the bump on the head.*

"Why don't you get out of those bloody clothes?" she asked. "There's a terry robe in the bathroom you can wear. After dinner, I'll fill the tub, and you can take a nice warm bath. That might make you feel better."

"I didn't come prepared to spend the night. I'm afraid I'll have to put these things on again in the morning. It would be nice, though, to get out of them now. I wish I had a toothbrush."

She took a few things out of her valise and hung them in the closet while she talked. "I'm sure they can send one up. I'll call while you change. Go on, fill the sink with cold water and put your shirt in it. I'll rinse it out later. If it's not dry by morning, I'll pick up a T-shirt for you from the lobby shop."

I did feel better getting out of those clothes. That is another thing I am unused to dealing with. Earthly life is endlessly bothersome. One has so many things to think of. I am amazed that anyone escapes unscathed. When this project is concluded, I have no intention of making any more appearances in the flesh, not for a very long time, at least.

I watched the TV with fascination as we ate our supper. News coverage was almost exclusively of the World Trade Organization protests. The WTO conference had brought everyone out of the woodwork. Every group that had an ax to grind was on the street with bullhorns, protest signs, and memorized chants.

The stunt that proved to be the most noteworthy was when a group of environmentalists, with the Rainforest Action Network, entered a construction site on Aloha Street after dark. Using safety harnesses and mountain-climbing gear, they attached themselves to a giant crane next to the cancer research center and unfurled a huge anti-WTO banner. I strained to make out what it said, with no luck. Once the police convinced them to come down, they were promptly arrested for criminal trespassing and reckless endangerment.

A group of witches up from the Bay Area, who call themselves Reclaiming—claim they are working their magic with the elements to ensure beautiful weather throughout the event. They constitute a bizarre assortment of women of all ages. Witches make my skin crawl. I usually steer clear of them.

I am about to head for that hot bath when Caroline excitedly summons me back to the television set. There we are for the entire world to see, me, knocked out cold with my head cradled in Caroline's arms, she, calling for an ambulance and batting away the microphone that has been thrust into her face.

"I was ready to belt that woman," Caroline declared. "I was trying to see if you were still alive, and all she wanted to do was ask inane questions. Jeez, what a lousy job that must be."

"Indeed," I agreed, "What a lousy job."

∼

It was nearly worth the blow to my head. I make some progress with Miss Caroline at last. While she tends my injured noggin, I have a perfect excuse to engage her in conversation. She told me about her dream to own and operate her own business. That could very well be the key to working out her commitment problems with Daniel. If she was independent and satisfied in her work, her personal life may fall like a happy domino effect.

It will be such a relief to get the entire predicament back on Heaven's schedule. Humans have free will as part of the Great Plan. This causes no end of problems for those of us who are responsible to see that they don't get too far astray of the time schedule.

During the course of my work, I have developed an appreciation for the problems I must have caused for *my* guardian. She is now my supervisor, and I am sure she enjoys observing my trials and tribulations. Daniel would call it payback.

Off and on during the night in Caroline's room, we chatted about this and that. As she was vigilant about allowing me to sleep no more than an hour at a stretch, we talked to stay awake. When she was tired, she let down her guard and confessed that she is in love with Daniel. Of course, I already knew that.

The conundrum is her unfounded fear that if they were engaged to marry, he might end up betraying her the same way her former fiancé jilted her the day before their planned wedding. She still burns with that humiliation. Worse, she worries that if she and Daniel marry, their marriage will become no more than a passionless business relationship, as is the case of her parents.

Since given this particular assignment, I have become aware that all Caroline knows of real love is what she received unconditionally from her sainted grandmother. I thank Heaven frequently for that remarkable woman. I doubt it would be possible to bring this marriage about were it not for her.

I tried to reassure Caroline of the true depth of Daniel's feelings and his commitment to her without raising her suspicions. She masks her fears with an air of competence and bravado. So much cynicism resides in her brief thirty years.

Daniel understands her and has the wherewithal to cope with her insecurities. In truth, Daniel needs the marriage as much as Caroline. She challenges him constantly, and as a result, he gains growth and confidence. He will need those characteristics in his later years, as Daniel is fated to become the steadiest star in the Kavanaugh universe. He will be the most important mentor to his many nieces and nephews.

Their marriage was made in Heaven. I repeat myself. Sorry.

I am beginning to see how the lovely Tiffany fits into the puzzle. She empathizes with Caroline. She will become a true friend and confidant, the female element in Caroline's experience that has been missing since the death of her grandmother.

You'd think with all that destiny at work, my job would be less difficult. No doubt *I'm* still being tested.

CHAPTER 15

Daniel

Dan came home early to work on the Flanders' contract without distractions. With Caroline in Seattle, he had no excuse not to sit down at his computer and work.

He looked forward to going to her place tomorrow night, as usual. They'd spend the weekend together, relaxing, just enjoying each other's company.

Dan lost track of the time. It was late, dark outside. He stopped to make himself a peanut butter sandwich and flipped on the TV as he walked through what passed for a living room on his way to what passed for a kitchen in his small one bedroom and a study apartment.

He stopped, surprised, shocked. There was Care on the evening news with Angeli's head in her lap. At least he thought it was Matthew Angeli. Pandemonium surrounded them. That was the last thing he expected to see.

"What the hell?" He spoke to the TV screen, then began flipping channels, hoping for a clearer view of the guy with blood dripping down his face. The phone rang.

"Yeah!"

"Dan? It's Dad here."

"Yes, hi, Dad. I just caught a glimpse of the evening news, and the damnedest thing——"

"That's what I called you about. I just returned from Seattle, and I was telling your mother about what happened."

"You were there?" Dan interrupted him and continued to channel surf. All the news coverage was about the rioting in Seattle, but none of the other channels showed the scene with Care and the injured guy.

"Yes, Caroline and I had just stepped outside Harry Sinclair's building when all hell broke loose."

"Was that Matthew Angeli?" He gave up on the TV and dropped the remote onto a stack of newspapers on the coffee table. He'd have to clear out all that mess before Care got a look at his place.

"Yes, I could hardly believe it myself. Angeli came out of nowhere and ended up getting hit on the head with a beer bottle that was flying right for me. Caroline saw it and tried to push me out of the way."

"What the hell was Angeli doing there?" His brief look at the anxious expression on Caroline's face and the proprietary way she'd held Matthew wasn't sitting well. A niggling jealous anger burned in his chest.

"I asked him the same thing after they finished patching him up at the hospital. Said he was on company business, and it was coincidental that he happened to be in the neighborhood. He ended up with a big lump on his head and a nasty cut. Had about thirty sutures, I think."

Dan paced. "Where's Care now? Was she hurt? Did she come back with you?"

"No, she's back at her hotel by now, took Angeli with her."

That stopped him. "She what!"

"They wanted to keep him at the hospital overnight for observation, but he refused to stay, so Caroline offered to take him back to her hotel and monitor him. The doctor needed to be sure he didn't have a concussion."

"She doesn't even like him!" At least that's what she'd been saying.

"I don't know about that. She said she was returning a favor. Told me she'd be back home tomorrow afternoon. You can ask her about it then."

"I'll ask her about it all right!" He raked fingers through his hair and nursed the unwelcome suspicion she might be playing around on him.

"Dan, what are you so upset about? She wasn't hurt. The whole thing is perfectly innocent. She didn't know Angeli was in town. She was as shocked to see him as I. Caroline's a take charge person. You know her."

"Yeah, maybe, I don't know. I'm probably making a federal case out of it. I'll talk to her about it tomorrow. I gotta go, Dad." He wanted to call her right then, at the hotel, and have it out with her. No, that was childish. He'd talk to her tomorrow.

Pushing the disconnect button, he immediately looked for the Water's Edge number, only to put the phone on the coffee table and pace the room. Caroline always had her cell phone turned off when she finished work, so it was useless to call her number. Was he being stupid? What was he worried about anyway? She was his woman, and she loved him. Did he have any reason to suspect anything? No, he didn't.

He grabbed the phone and tapped the number. "Caroline Clayton's room," he barked the second they answered.

They put him on hold. After about five seconds, a voice came on the line. "I'm sorry, sir. Ms. Clayton has requested that no calls be put through to her room tonight."

Daniel stared at the phone in his hand, paralyzed for a moment. No calls?

"Sir, are you there?"

"Yeah, I'm here. Are you sure about that?"

"Yes, it's posted right here. I'm sorry."

"Uh, okay then." He disconnected and thought for a moment. What he wanted to do was go to the airport, fly to Seattle, go to the hotel, and finish the job on Angeli that the guy with the beer bottle had started. Instead, he poured a glass of water and went back to his computer, stared at the contract for several minutes, gave up, and went to bed.

∽

When he got up the next morning, he figured it was useless to call her. She was probably on her way to her appointment and would soon be on her way home. He didn't know what the hell he would say to her anyhow.

Hi, honey, just curious—why were you pressing Angeli's face into your tits, and looking like you'd lost your best pal? And, oh, by the way, what the hell was he doing with you in your room all night?

In a surly mood when he walked into his office lobby, he scowled when Billie signaled from the reception desk. She had a wide-eyed look of concern on her face.

"Danny, I saw Caroline on the TV last night. What happened? What was she doing there in all that mess? She wasn't hurt, was she?"

"Later, Billie, I'm behind on the Flanders' contract. Any messages?"

He'd cut her off, and she reacted like he'd slapped her. Old enough to be Daniel's mother, Billie looked like your sweet, old maiden aunt, but she was a former Marine pilot, married to a retired smoke jumper. They ran marathons, jumped out of airplanes, and practiced Tae Kwan Do for fun.

Dan knew he shouldn't have been so short with her, but he didn't want to talk about it. He didn't know anything more than Liam told him. He went straight to his private office and closed the door to work on the contract until the partner's meeting at ten.

~

He'd barely sat down at the conference table when Bill Knight asked him, "What was Caroline doing in all that commotion in Seattle? Norma and I saw her on the evening news last night."

"She and Dad were caught in the middle of the WTO fracas outside Harry Sinclair's building."

Dan didn't want to talk about it, but Bill wouldn't let up. "Was that Matthew Angeli she was, ah, helping? I wasn't aware they were such good friends." He peered over his glasses for a moment, then went back to the agenda documentation.

Dan waved him off. "It was a coincidence. Caroline and Dad were surprised to see him. He took a doozie of a blow to the head. I guess she was trying to help." He put his portfolio on the table, opened it, and studied the contents, signaling the conversation was over.

"No doubt," Bill said as he looked around the table. "I see we're all assembled. Shall we begin?"

Somehow, Dan managed to make it through the meeting and the rest of the morning. About the time he was ready to take a lunch break, Billie tapped on his door.

"Mr. Kavanaugh? I have a phone message for you. I wanted to catch you before I went to lunch." She tiptoed over to the desk and placed a pink note on his calendar, then turned quickly to go. She'd only called him Mr. Kavanaugh a couple of times in the past few years. As he recalled, it was because he'd behaved like an asshole then, too.

"Thanks, Billie." He reached for the note. "Sorry I was such a jerk this morning. I had a lot on my mind." Feeble, but an apology of sorts.

"No problem, Danny, sometimes I'm too nosey." She smiled as she turned to go.

"No, there's a difference between nosey and concerned. Tell me you still love me, Billie Girl."

"Love you, Danny Boy," she called back and chuckled.

The note was from Caroline. She was running late but expected to be home by seven-thirty. She wanted him to call her if he'd changed plans about dinner, otherwise she'd see him at her place. Cool as that. Who did she think she was kidding? She never calls when she's going to be late. That's something he'd been trying to get her to do for years. Something was up, and Dan was sure Angeli had a part in it.

∼

It was just after seven-fifteen when he got to her place. He let himself in and walked through the entire apartment. He didn't know what he was looking for or what he expected to find. All he knew was that she had some explaining to do.

Dan threw his briefcase on a chair and tossed his jacket over the back of the couch. He sat for a minute, then kicked his shoes off, left them right where they landed, and went to look in the refrigerator. She didn't have a decent thing in there to drink. He settled for a Diet Coke. Like she needs diet stuff—women—go figure. Would it be too much to ask her to keep a couple of beers cold for him?

About a quarter to eight, he'd finished the Coke and was getting more agitated by the minute. Finally, he said, "Screw it," picked up his coat and jammed his feet into his shoes. He had better things to do than wait around all evening for Her Royal Highness to show up. He reached for the knob as she opened the door and rushed in.

"Hi, Danny, you just get here? Sorry I'm late, somebody took my parking space, and I had to drive around for ten minutes to find another one. Wow, I'm bushed." She grinned and put her arms around his neck and laid a big smooch on his mouth. "I missed you."

Pissed, he didn't want to cave, but hell, it was a great kiss. He couldn't help himself. He put his arms around her waist and gave as good as he got.

She leaned back and gave him a wide, sexy smile, pressed her hips against him, and played the back of his neck like a harp. "I'm starved. How about you?" she purred against his mouth.

Of course, she got the reaction she was expecting. So much for his resolve. "I was gonna suggest we wander over to Riccio's, but for some reason I'm not hungry now."

"Hmm, maybe we should stay here, call, and have them deliver something." She tortured him with her hips. "I can tell you missed me," she crooned smugly.

Danny grabbed a fistful of her hair and crushed his mouth to hers. His hand slid to her bottom, and he slammed her hips against him hard, leaving no doubt about his intentions. When he kissed her enough to satisfy himself, he released her.

She leaned back big-eyed, her lips red and swollen. "Wow, Danny, what is that all about?"

"I'm pissed. That's what it's all about." He let her go and paced in a tight circle while dragging his hands through his hair. "Dammit, Caroline. Dammit!"

"Dammit what? Why are you so upset?" She lowered her chin, clearly puzzled at his outburst.

"How come you never have a damn thing in your refrigerator that I like to drink? Huh? Do you ever think of putting something in there for me!" He pounded a fist against his chest.

"That's it? All this because I don't put beer in my fridge? I don't believe you. What's really going on?" She crossed her arms and waited for his answer.

"That's exactly what I'd like to know. What's really going on? I saw you on TV, all hysterical, pressing Matthew Angeli's face into your chest. What's going on between you two? Huh? Are you playing me for a fool? How about telling me the truth!" Hands on his hips, he leaned forward with his face menacingly close to hers, daring her to come clean.

She straightened up and slammed her hands into his shoulders. "You want the truth? Before you answer me, think very carefully, Daniel Kavanaugh."

He clenched a handful of his hair. "Yes, goddammit! Tell me. Then I'll get the hell out of this apartment and your life. I've had it with you."

He knew he was treading on dangerous ground. He wished he

hadn't said that, but it was out there now. Whatever she had to say for herself, he'd deal with it.

"Okay." She nodded. "Maybe you'd like to sit. It's a long story." Her stony expression was as serious as a heart attack.

He swallowed the lump in this throat. His heart might crack from the hard pounding. He plopped on the sofa and attempted nonchalance by crossing his legs and throwing one arm casually over the back. "Go."

"I've been having a secret, steamy affair with Matthew for weeks. All those times I told you I hated him were lies. All those times I told you I kept bumping into him were actually planned meetings. I've had the breathless hots for him ever since I spent that first afternoon having drinks with him in the lobby bar of my office building. I swoon every time I look into those amazing eyes of his."

She paused and gestured with her finger like a schoolteacher giving a scolding to a troublesome kid. "I'm crazy for him. I can't get him out of my mind. It was no coincidence he was in Seattle. We'd planned a romantic weekend together. It wasn't on our schedule for him to get injured, but it gave me a plausible excuse to take him back to my hotel without raising Dad's suspicions.

"The doctors patched him up and gave me instructions to wake him every hour to make sure he didn't have a concussion. When we got to my room and out of our bloody clothes, we ordered room service dinner, a very romantic gourmet dinner. Wine and candles and everything. Then we went to bed.

"I woke him up every hour, and we had incredibly hot and frantic monkey sex for about fifteen minutes before we fell into exhausted sleep again. This went on all night."

The more dramatic and theatrical Caroline's story became, Daniel's jaw muscles worked against his will. He had to hand it to her. He opened his mouth to interrupt her.

Her fierce glare stopped him.

"Finally, morning came all too soon, and we had one last hot session of sex in the shower. I couldn't get enough of him. He's amazing. I had to get to the meeting with my customer, and Matty had to catch his flight back to L.A. so as not to raise Tiffany's suspicion about his prolonged absence. Like me, she's kind of sweet on him.

"I have to say I was barely able to walk straight after all that hot sex and had to work at keeping that satisfied smile off my face, because I've also been having an affair with the architect on the Seattle job, Peter Langley, for years now. I'm also very attracted to the construction boss, Al Guerrero. Al is rough around the edges, but you can't imagine how sexy he is with the big, heavy tool belt hanging around his muscular hips. Too yummy."

Danny pressed his lips together to suppress the smile screaming to be free. It took all his willpower. Care was magnificent. She not only gestured with her hands and arms; her facial expressions were priceless. "Can I say something?"

She glared at him. "No! I'm not finished. I also had a short fling with Moody, but he couldn't even stack up to *you*."

He looked away from her, uncrossed his legs, removed his shoes, and tossed them over his shoulder one after the other, where they bounced and bumped into her precious stereo console. He took the tie out of his pocket and dropped it on the coffee table, then placed his feet squarely in the middle of the glass top and flexed his toes. It drove her crazy when he put his feet on her precious coffee table.

Making an expansive gesture with his arm, he bowed his head and said, "Continue, please. I can't wait to hear the end of this confession if there is one."

Care's composure slipped for a second, then she gathered herself. "I'm quite certain I'm a woman who cannot control her sexual needs with only one man. It's obvious from what I told you that you're merely a cog in a big wheel of men in my life. I can no longer keep my secret. There, I said it. I'm done." She sighed and dropped her arms to her sides.

The corner of his mouth twitched. He raised his hands in surrender. "Okay, okay, I get it."

"That's the problem. You don't get it, and don't you dare smile. I'm serious."

"I can see that." He patted the spot next to him. "Why don't you have a seat, and we'll discuss where we're going to go from here?" He raised his eyebrows and watched her struggle to find a way to refuse.

She grabbed a heavy design catalog. "Get your big smelly feet off my table." She leaned forward and whacked his feet with the catalog.

"Ow!" He grabbed his foot and massaged his toes. "That hurt, babe."

Saying nothing, she plopped down next to him and crossed her arms, an uncharacteristic pout on her lips.

He touched her leg. "You need to apologize to me for hitting me and for all those affairs you've been hiding. I'm shocked beyond belief to learn all you've been doing behind my back, but I'm willing to work with you to see if we can come to an agreeable arrangement. Otherwise, I see no alternative but to start a breach of affections lawsuit against you for ruining my life. I'll never be able to trust another woman. I'll die a sick, brokenhearted, lonely old man, all by myself in that hovel of an apartment. I'll probably be dead for days before anyone discovers my body."

"Oh, good grief. Either grow up or go home, Danny." She shook her head and shoved his shoulder.

He got up and went behind the sofa.

"What are you doing back there?"

"Looking for my shoes." He found his loafers and slipped them on and rounded the end of the couch. "Come on."

He grabbed her hand. "I think we both need to grow up." He pulled her to her feet. "Let's walk to Riccio's. I'm starving."

Caroline smoothed her hair, then her skirt. "Me, too. Those garlic knots are calling my name." She grinned and grabbed her purse. "You coming?"

He caught up to her. "Um, after dinner, can we try some monkey sex?"

"Oh, shut up. I don't ever want to hear the words monkey sex again."

CHAPTER 16

Matthew

My appointment to meet Tiffany at my *Angel Office* was in the late afternoon, three days after my interesting Seattle adventure. She was solicitous of my health when we arranged the meeting. I assured her I would be fine and seeing her would speed my healing process. She, along with the others at Leebow Elvey Honnet, had witnessed the drama played out on the streets of Seattle on the evening news. The relief in her voice, as to my condition, was sweet and spontaneous. Such an enchanting young woman.

Upon entering the vacant suite, I was surprised to see that the painters had already begun working. Drop cloths and paint cans were neatly placed against the far wall, and the base coat had been completed. It's a shame that I would never use the office. Some lucky lawyer or accountant would probably lease the space once my work on *terra firma* was concluded.

Tiffany entered the office shortly after I arrived. She brought to mind the fresh field of flowers on the meadow behind my childhood home near Aix en Provence, in the mid-seventeen-hundreds. She stared wide-eyed for a brief moment, so open and without guile, the perfect foil for Caroline. Were I truly a man, I'd make her mine with nary a qualm.

Immediately, she walked to my side. "Matthew, you poor thing." She gently touched my bandaged forehead.

Her hand rested on my cheek. Adrenaline shot through my veins.

All those human responses I have tried to bury shouted to the heavens for release. I reached to remove her hand from my face, but when I felt the pulse pounding in her delicate, feminine wrist, I lost all reason. Before either of us knew what happened, I had my arms about her and kissed her with reawakened passion.

Her response was immediate and eager. Her hands framed my face, her sweet kiss carried a promise. Ardor overtook me. I crushed her to my chest, kissing her again and again.

I didn't want to release her. I could have held her like that forever, my heart soaring and my head swimming. Her arms went about my waist, and her fingers dug into my back. Caught up in the moment, we lost all sense of time and place. Finally, I relaxed my embrace, placed my trembling hands on her shoulders in an attempt to get a grip on my raging human maleness.

"Tiffany, Tiffany, my dear girl. You paralyze me, body and soul. I don't know what came over me." I gripped her shoulders and gently pushed her away from me.

Breathless, she laid her lovely head on my chest and sighed. "Matthew, that was wonderful."

"Please accept my apology."

There was hurt and disappointment in her fawn-brown eyes as she looked up. Her lips trembled slightly as she said, "You didn't want to kiss me?"

"Well, I...certainly. I..."

"I wanted to kiss you." A single tear brimmed unsteadily on her lower lid. Her sweet lips quivered.

How could I have hurt her so? "Yes, of course, I wanted to kiss you. What man would not?"

"I didn't want to kiss *what man*."

The tear slid down her cheek, and I brushed it away with my thumb and embraced her again. "My sweet, lovely Tiffany," I whispered into her hair. "I don't want to hurt you. I couldn't bear to hurt you. What have I done?"

Her soft, warm body fit perfectly against my own. She said nothing, merely rested her cheek once again against my chest. The pounding of my heart must have been thunderous in her ear. I looked Heavenward and shook my bewildered head. *Help me!*

"Matthew," she whispered, "I want to be with you."

"You don't know what you're saying. You barely know me." My physical response grew embarrassingly troublesome. What was I to do?

She peered innocently into my eyes. "Are you married?"

"No, I've never married." I saw deep into her beautiful soul. How rare, I thought, to be so open and unspoiled. Most young women in this *Sex and the City* age are worldly and cynical by the time they've reached her years.

She cocked her head to one side. "Are you gay?"

"Certainly not!" I jerked back, shocked at my unwarranted reaction. That she would think to question my masculinity was now a serious threat to my judgment.

"Then I know everything I need to know. I can see in your eyes how you feel about me. I feel the same."

Helpless, I held her in my arms. The desire to possess her nearly consumed me. I knew I had never wanted a woman so much when I was a mortal man as I wanted her. I tipped her face up and brushed my mouth lightly over hers. Her lips curved into a smile against mine.

Taking her by the arms, I gently moved her away from me again. "Perhaps we should discuss the progress of the office." I coughed to clear the roughness from my throat.

"If you like," she said with a smile, a smile with a touch of Beelzebub in it. She reached into her portfolio and brought out some drawings and catalogue pages. "Here's the furniture I've ordered. Everything is in stock except the repro MacIntosh lamp. It will be delivered in less than two weeks. See how beautifully it all goes together?"

"That's wonderful," I said with relief, jamming my hands in my pockets to prevent me from touching her again. I walked across the room to put some distance between us. As she spoke, I tried to concentrate on her design. It was clever, unique. If it were ordained for me to remain on this mortal coil, I'm sure I would have enjoyed using the space as my base of operations.

Thankfully, we continued to talk for some time about the plans for finishing the suite. Enjoying the opportunity to complete her own project from start to finish, she chattered on, sweeping her arm here and there, describing how the completed suite would look. She made a point of emphasizing that Caroline had overseen and approved every aspect of the job. Tiffany was a bit unsure of her work, probably because I had initially made such an issue of insisting that Caroline do the design.

"I bet you'll be able to move in here right after Thanksgiving."

"I'm pleased," I said, nodding with approval. "It's going to be wonderful. You're talented, Tiffany. You practically read my mind when we first started planning this. It's going to look exactly as I hoped it would, but better."

I smiled with natural sincerity, never mind the original intent for the project was to put me in close proximity to Caroline.

Obviously pleased by my compliment, her smile lit up the lowering afternoon gloom in the empty room.

"Matthew, would you take me to dinner when we finish here?" She turned and looked me squarely in the eye.

"Why, I hadn't——"

"You are having dinner, aren't you?"

"Well, yes, I suppose."

"Why not eat together? I'd like to hear more about Matthew and Caroline's Excellent Seattle Adventure. Okay?"

Seeing no graceful way out, I agreed. What harm could come of us sharing a meal in a public place? "All right, let's have dinner." I extended my arm toward the door.

"I have my car here, so if it doesn't bother you, I'll drive." She tilted her head to one side, her face a question mark.

"Since I don't own a car, I was about to suggest a taxi. Your car it is." I could not stop myself from smiling. She was so pleased that I agreed. I, too, was pleased.

∽

The restaurant Tiffany chose was a quaint bistro in the Melrose neighborhood. If one were unfamiliar with the area, it would have been possible to drive past it and never know it was there. She told me it was one of her favorite places, and that she would sometimes dine there alone because it was close to her residence.

An eclectic mix of Greek, French, and Italian filled the pages of the menu. We shared a bottle of Argentinean Malbec while we perused our choices. As I mentioned earlier, my father had a wine press, and I'd enjoyed the gift of the grape since childhood. The selection she chose was particularly good.

I studied Tiffany across the table. The wine brought a pink flush to her cheeks, and her eyes glistened as they reflected the light of the candle. I reached to touch her hand.

"Matthew." She tightened her fingers around my own.

Heavens above, what was I doing?

I cleared my throat. "Tiffany, I want you to believe that I'm very fond of you, but it is not possible for us to have a romantic relationship."

Her fingers tightened some more, and her expression grew sober. "Why?"

I racked my brain for something I could say that would make sense to her.

Stating the obvious, I said, "For one thing, I'm much too old for you." My pitiful attempt at making sense prompted her to smile again.

"You're not that much older, Matthew." She shook her head.

I nodded mournfully. "Yes, my dear, I am."

"How much? Just fourteen years, right?"

My goodness, the woman was relentless. "I'm thirty-eight, but trust me, I feel much, much older."

"That's not such a big difference. I'm almost twenty-five." She brought the wine to her lips and challenged me over the ruby red liquid in her glass.

I was speechless for the moment, unable to formulate any rational rejoinder.

"I'm not a virgin," she announced as the waiter approached our table with the appetizer. He turned quickly on his heel and went back through the swinging kitchen door. He returned and coughed discreetly to make us aware of his presence.

"Well, I'm not," she said, letting go of my hand as she turned to acknowledge him. He set the plates in front of us, mumbled something, and made a hasty retreat.

I chuckled at her ingenuousness. "My dear, I don't know how to respond to that."

"I wanted you to know, that's all." She picked up her cocktail fork, speared a rather large shrimp, put the entire thing in her mouth, smiled, and slowly chewed.

The sensuousness of her action astounded me. My physical response was instantaneous. Extremely grateful we were sitting, my immediate thought was, *Get thee behind me, Satan*. I downed my entire glass of wine and prayed for guidance.

Somehow, we made it through dinner with no further references to her chastity or my advanced age. When we stepped outside, the cool air of the evening was welcome and refreshing. Perhaps I would get my mind functioning again.

"Oh, no!" Tiffany pointed to her car. She'd left her lights on, and they had deteriorated into a dull glow. "I hope I can get it started."

I sighed softly and murmured a plea that her engine would engage. It was a very small favor, and I hoped those above were listening. No such luck. Knowing nothing about the workings of automobiles, I was helpless. She slid into the car and attempted to start it. Nothing.

"Matthew, I'm sorry. My battery is dead. How am I going to get you home?" Her distress sounded somehow faint.

"Don't be concerned about that. I'll call a taxi, see you home, and then go on."

She appeared briefly disappointed and then brightened. "I know," she said. "I only live about six blocks from here. Why don't you walk me home and call a cab from there?"

Alarm bells went off in my head. I knew as well as I had ever known anything that walking her home was simply, completely, out of the question. Absolutely.

"All right," I said, wondering who had taken over my mouth, body, and brain. "The walk will be refreshing."

"Good." She secured her car, buttoned her jacket, and put the strap of her handbag over her shoulder. "This way," she said, pointing up the street. She took my hand and gave me a little tug.

I'd only been in this body a few weeks and had wasted no time acquiring the weaknesses of mortal man. I trotted along beside her like an obedient pooch.

The side street took us through a quiet old neighborhood. The houses were built prior to the time when families had more than one vehicle, so there were many cars parked up and down both sides of the street. Old-fashioned streetlamps emitted a soft glow which barely reached the sidewalk. The strong scent of night-blooming jasmine hung in the evening air.

We walked four or five blocks before I realized we'd not spoken a word. Her hand in mine was warm and soft. It seemed so natural for it to be there. I squeezed gently, and her response was to look at me and smile. My heart tripped wildly, and I forgot to breathe for several steps.

Tiffany pulled me between the posts of a garden gate. "Here we are." She pointed to the left. "My apartment is there."

The complex was one of those very Los Angeles style structures which sprouted up in great numbers before World War II. Horseshoe shaped with small, detached units surrounding a shared courtyard. Daniel's parents, Liam and Mary Kavanaugh, had lived in a similar place when first wed.

Tiffany took out her keys and unlocked the door. She briefly touched the mezuzah on the doorframe and touched her fingers to her lips. I stood awkwardly for a moment, feeling like nothing so much as a green, young swain. Tongue-tied, I made as if to shake her hand and bid her goodnight.

"You're going to come in and stay until I check all the doors and windows, aren't you? At least wait till I've turned on the lights." She was the picture of innocence. "Then you can call for your taxi."

"Well, certainly." I felt helpless to refuse such a reasonable request. She was a young woman alone, after all. I would be irresponsible to leave her alone on her doorstep at this late hour. Wouldn't I?

"Good. Come in then." She snapped on the living room lamp, reaching behind me to close the door.

I heard the familiar voice of Miriam, Tiffany's G.A. "Tread very carefully here, Matthew. Remember who you are."

"Tiffany, I think I should call..." was all I managed before I found myself in Tiffany's embrace. She smiled into my face and closed her eyes, anticipating my kiss. What was I to do? I kissed her.

"Matthew, I want to be with you," she declared for the second time that day. "Really *be* with you." She pushed my coat off my shoulders.

Beset with passion, I swept her into my arms. I had no resistance, no second thought about what I was about to do.

"I want to be with you, too, my dear girl. More than you could ever know." I kissed her hungrily, desire flaming hot in my belly. I had to have her. I was bewitched.

There will be hell to pay for this night.

CHAPTER 17

Caroline

I didn't notice Tiffany standing beside my desk until she made a loud slurping sound with her cup of coffee. She bounced on her toes and grinned. I couldn't help myself. I laughed at her.

"What?" I asked. "Go away. I'm busy. I'm behind schedule on this." I ignored her. She didn't move. I did an exaggerated sigh and leaned back in my chair. She was positively glowing. "Okay, what?" I tossed my pencil in surrender.

"I seduced Matthew last night." Her smile was so big her face was in danger of breaking in two.

I sat straight. "You what!"

"You heard me." She did a pirouette. "It was great." The exaggerated knee wobble again.

I placed my hands over my ears. "Why are you telling me this?"

"Because I want to, and why should you be the only one who has a fabulous love life?"

She put her coffee cup on the corner of my desk, pulled my hands down, and leaned on her elbows, facing me.

"Oh, Caroline, he was so sweet. Pretended he hadn't had a woman in centuries and was afraid he wouldn't know what to do." She did the Groucho thing with her eyebrows.

In spite of myself, I wanted details. "And?"

"He remembered." There went those neon freckles of hers and those sparkly cinnamon eyes. "Twice."

I shook my head sure she was joking. "You're kidding me."

"Not kidding, twice. He stayed all night, and I fixed him breakfast this morning. He ate eight pancakes, and said he was as hungry as a man at haying time." She giggled. "He talks so funny sometimes."

I couldn't stop the smile growing on my face. "I'm amazed. He looks so harmless, all dreamy eyed and proper, kind of Saran wrapped."

Her hand went to her throat, and her eyes rolled upward. "Caroline, he has curly black hair on his chest."

"Wait! Stop! This is more information than I need." I pushed back from the desk a bit and shook my head.

"Come on, I have to tell somebody."

"Oh, for cripe's sake, Tiffany. What am I? Your shrink?"

"No, but I think you're almost my best girlfriend."

That last statement was so heartfelt, I didn't know what to say. Our heads practically touched across my desk. She quickly moved forward and bumped her forehead against mine.

"Ow! What the heck are you doing, Tiffany? Do you want everyone in here to think we're in love?" I glanced around to see if anyone had noticed what she'd done.

"I don't care what they think." Her grin was irresistible. "Wanna be my best girlfriend?"

"Do I have a choice?" The kid is a virtual steamroller.

"Nope."

I knew when to give up. "Okay then, girlfriend, carry on with your lurid story." I laced my fingers together and rested my chin on my hands.

"You know that curly, black, chest hair? I think I chewed some of it off." She straightened and put both hands over her mouth to stifle her laughter.

"You hussy! Have you no shame?"

"No way. I'm on cloud nine. He's an angel, and I'm in love." She crossed her hands over her heart and sighed like a teenager.

I thought those freckles would pop right off her nose.

"Good grief, Tiffany, after one night with the man? Get a grip, girl."

"I plan to. He's coming over to my place again tomorrow night. God! I can't wait." She made a growling sound, and I felt some concern for Matthew. I hoped he was up to her expectations.

"Look out. Here comes trouble." I pointed to a spec. "I think you might want to do a little glass brick treatment right here in the foyer area." It was my drawing, which was not Angeli's new office.

"That might be interesting." She grinned, "Yes, I like it."

"I'm not paying you two to stand around and gossip about the latest fashions and hairstyles all day," the Creep said, looming over my drawing board.

"Good morning, Mr. Moody. Actually, Caroline and I were discussing the Angeli project."

Tiffany turned slightly and winked at me. The color rose from her neck to her scalp like the indicator on a meat thermometer. She topped the medium-rare mark.

I jumped in. "Yes, it'll be stunning. Tiffany brings new meaning to total involvement in the customer's project."

I don't know how, but I was able to say that with a straight face.

Moody made some sort of grumbling, snorting sound and huffed away. Tiffany and I were in serious danger of giving ourselves away by bursting into laughter. It felt like being back in junior high.

"Get away from my desk," I said under my breath. "We'll discuss this further at lunch."

"You bet we will," she promised and, over her shoulder, added, "Three hours and counting."

~

I spent a lot of time that morning thinking about what Tiffany meant when she asked me if I wanted to be her best girlfriend. I don't think I've ever been anyone's *best* girlfriend. Oh, I had girlfriends from time to time, but mostly that was when I was in school. Come to think of it, none of them were *my* best friend, probably because I was never *their* best friend. The one girl I was closest to eloped with my fiancé on our wedding day. Some friend.

I guess, now that I thought about the whole friend thing, Daniel was my best friend. At least he was the one I talked to the most, even though I rarely shared my innermost secrets. I don't know if you can do that with a guy. Frankly, I don't know if I'm willing to do that with anyone.

Crazy as it seemed, I had shared more of my secrets with Matthew. He had a way of looking at me and before I knew it, I was blabbing away about thoughts that I'd never verbalized. There went my, *can't tell it to a guy* theory.

I guess I don't like people knowing too much about me. What I'm thinking and how I feel is mine, and it's nobody's business.

The thing is I really liked Tiffany. Odd, once I acknowledged it, considering that when she first came to work here, I thought she was just another brainless blonde. Boy, was I wrong. Even when I'd been my most *Caroline,* she was decent about it.

I didn't know why she would want me to be her friend. I did ask her if she'd like to be in business with me, but that has nothing to do with being friends. I had a feeling she'd be my friend anyway. Maybe she saw something in me, something I wasn't aware of. Wouldn't that be nice?

∽

On the dot of noon, Tiffany was standing at my drawing board with her purse slung over her shoulder. Ready to leave the office, she hissed between clenched teeth, "Come on, come on, come on. Let's go."

"Keep your pants on, bright eyes. I'm almost done with this." I studied the spec sheet I'd been working on.

"Finish it when we get back. We only have an hour," she pleaded.

"Good grief, how much do you have to tell me?"

"At least an hour's worth."

"I don't know if I'm up for this girlfriend stuff."

"Sure, you are. Admit it; you're dying to know the details."

"Not as much as you're dying to tell them to me." I glanced at her as I reached for my purse. She still glowed and must have burned up thousands of calories this morning, maintaining that irrepressible mood. I had to laugh. "Okay, let's go before you ignite."

"Good. We only have to get a couple of soft drinks. I brought two sandwiches. We can eat in the park."

"My word, you had this all planned out."

She made a beeline for the elevators, and I practically had to break into a run to keep up with her.

Ten minutes later, we were staking out one of the best benches in the shade of a big coral tree. Tiffany put a couple of napkins between us and laid out the sandwiches she'd brought. I popped open the Pepsi cans, leaned back and waited for her to begin.

Instead of launching into the Matthew Seduction Saga, she took a sip of her Pepsi and said, "How was your weekend?"

"I was sexually assaulted Friday night."

She shrieked and slopped soda on her leg. "Oh, my God! Caroline, oh God. How awful. How terrible. Are you okay? Why didn't you say something before?" She put down her drink and leaned toward me, a concerned hand on my shoulder.

"It's okay, I assaulted him back."

She took her solicitous hand from my shoulder and smacked me on the arm.

"Darn you, Caroline. You scared me to death. Jeepers!"

"What's with the jeepers?" I laughed at her and mopped up soda with a paper napkin. "You sound like a Mouseketeer."

"I *was* a Mouseketeer." She twisted a fingertip against her cheek and cocked her head to one side, adopting the look of an icky-sweet nine-year-old.

"Get out." I put my soda can down and stared at her.

"No, cross my heart. I was a Mouseketeer from the time I was seven until I was eleven. Maybe you saw me? I was really cute." She sang, "M-I-C-K-E-Y M-O-U-S-E."

"Oh, good Lord, you're serious, aren't you?"

"Yep, my little sister, too." She sat back and grinned at me.

"You have a sister?"

"And two brothers." She nodded, and her blonde curls bounced around her face. "There's lots about me you don't know, girlfriend."

I chuckled and took a bite of the tuna sandwich. "Mmm, this is good, Minnie. You can cook too. What am I going to learn next?"

"It shall all be revealed to you in good time." She winked and took a bite of her sandwich.

"Now, I definitely know I'm not up for this best girlfriend stuff." I shook my head sorrowfully.

"You are. You need me," she mumbled around her sandwich, both cheeks puffed out like a squirrel.

"Yeah, what for?" I brushed crumbs from my lap and took a swallow of my Pepsi.

"Well, for one thing, who else did you tell about your, um...assault?"

"Nobody."

"You see? You're already confiding in me." She adopted a serious expression. "This is the deal: I tell you everything, and you tell me everything."

"Oh, sure. I don't know if I should believe half of what you say." I swallowed a mouthful of her great tuna salad sandwich.

"Here's the thing. Complete honesty is essential. We can never lie to each other. We have to be one-hundred-percent truthful, even when it hurts. It's very therapeutic."

"Why me? Don't you have somebody else who's willing to bare their soul for your titillation?"

"Well, of course I did. Both my old girlfriends got married and moved away. We still talk on the phone, but it's not the same. They have problems now that I'm not much help with. You know, babies and husbands and mortgages. I figure you and I have more in common."

"Oh, really? Would you like to expand on that?" I wiped my mouth and took the last swallow of Pepsi.

"Sure. Let's see, we both work for the same lousy creep of a boss. We're both good at what we do. You're better, of course, but I'll catch up. We're both single, never been married. We're both educated, attractive, and in love with gorgeous men. How's that?"

"Wow. You've got me convinced," I answered, sarcasm in my tone.

"One more rule," she said, pointing her finger at my nose. "We have to be nice to each other."

"I'm seldom nice to anybody," I snorted.

"That's because you don't have a best girlfriend. Here I am. The answer to your prayers."

She put both her hands over her heart and gave me a big grin and an exaggerated sigh.

"You're too much, Tiffany. How do I get rid of you?"

"Sorry, you're stuck with me." She giggled and polished off her sandwich.

I shook my head and stared at her. I had a feeling I *was* stuck with her, but the idea was more amusing than disturbing. I'd never known anyone like her. We were total opposites. Maybe that was good. I was tall. She was short. I was dark. She was fair. I was a pessimist. She an optimist. I was crabby. She was cheerful. We were meant for each other.

"Okay," I said. "I'm willing to give it a try. I can always shoot you and hide the body if you really get on my nerves."

"Goody!" she squealed and smacked me on the knee. "Now tell me all about the assault." She rubbed her palms together like a medieval money lender.

"Nuh-uh, we came out here to talk about *your* love life, remember? I'll have to work my way up to mine, little by little."

"Okay." She shrugged with resignation. "Well, here goes. When Matthew called me to set an appointment to do a walk-through of his new office, I had a hunch he just wanted to see me again. Not that we didn't need to have an update on the progress and all, but you know what I mean. You can tell when a guy is interested."

"Then...?" I prompted her to continue.

"So, I made up my mind right then that we were going to move our relationship to the next level. I really, really like him, and I think we'd be perfect together. If I waited for him to make a move, I'd be old and gray when he got around to it."

"And...?"

"I made him kiss me at the new office. It was a great kiss, more than one actually, real knee knockers." She rolled her eyes. "I told him I wanted him. He was so shaken I was pretty sure I had him." She smiled and nodded.

"I had no idea you were such a schemer." I was truly getting into it. "I'll have to watch out for you. What happened next?"

"I convinced him we should have dinner together, and when we got to the restaurant by my house, I left the car lights on so my battery would go dead, and he'd have to walk me home."

"Clever."

"It worked."

"Okay, so far we have him kissing you at the office and walking you home. How do we get from there to you chewing the hair off his chest?" I raised my hands and shrugged.

"The rest was easy. I asked him to come in so he could call a cab and I could be sure the house was secure. He's such a gentleman, I knew he'd want to make sure I was safe. I closed the door behind him, threw myself into his arms, and told him again that I wanted him and started pulling at his clothes."

"The sure-fire direct approach," I mused.

"Yep, and the rest, as they say, is history. He's crazy about me." She stood up and brushed the crumbs off her skirt. "I need some chocolate ice cream. Let's go across the street and get some. You can fill me in on your reciprocal sexual assault while we're walking back."

"I'm not ready to start disclosing details, but I did find out Saturday morning why Danny was so, shall we say, forceful." I picked up the empty cans and dropped them into the recycle bin at the edge of the park.

"You're going to laugh when I tell you." I continued while we jaywalked and dodged cars on the way to Ben and Jerry's. "He was jealous of Matthew and my doorman."

"No!" She stopped right in the middle of Wilshire Boulevard. I had to yank her out of the path of an Audi with a lead-footed driver.

"Yes." I laughed at the preposterousness of it. "Somehow, he had it in his mind I was interested in Matthew, fooling around with him. Can you believe it?"

"I don't find that so hard to believe. I'm interested in Matthew. He's handsome and sweet."

She was actually offended because I wasn't after her boyfriend. "Come on, Tiffany. I didn't mean it like that. We're supposed to be honest, right? Isn't that part of the best girlfriend deal? Why would I even be looking at other guys when I have Danny?"

"Okay. Sorry. You're right." She shrugged. "So, give me some details. I might learn something I can use."

Already her face was brightening. Her bad mood had lasted all of ten seconds.

I opened the door of the shop and held it for her. "Let's get the ice cream, okay?" We bought our cones, hitched our bags onto our shoulders, and started a slow stroll back to the office.

"I don't want to talk about my love life," I said between catching drips from the edge of my cone. "I have something else to talk with you about."

"Okay, I can get the shocking details later. Shoot."

She did some fancy tongue work on her ice cream cone. I wiped unbidden images from my thoughts.

"I've made up my mind. I'm going to do it," I stated.

"Do what?"

There went that tongue again.

"I'm heading to the bank in the morning to see if I can get a business loan. I'm going out on my own. Daniel's been encouraging me for months to try for it, and in Seattle, Matthew urged me to do it."

It was the first time I had spoken the words aloud and my stomach did flips.

"Caroline, that's super. That's great! I know you'll be successful. I hope you meant it when you said you'd like me to come with you, because I want to. I think we'd make a good team."

"Me, too, and yes, I meant it. But it's all going to depend on if I can raise the money. We would need enough to get set up and expect no income for at least six months. I figure after that time we'd either be making money or deciding to scrap the whole venture."

"It'll work. I know it'll work. I could run the office part and do customer service and stuff while you went out and pulled in clients and sold them on your designs. I majored in design, but I minored in business and finance."

I stopped dead in my tracks. "You know about finances, how to structure a business?"

"Sure. Let's get together tonight and work out a business plan. That will impress the bankers. They'll want to know you have some idea what you're doing."

"Tiffany, you are an endless source of amazement."

There was much more to her than I had imagined. Real substance lurked beneath her cute and sunny exterior.

"I'll be your back-up," she said, "and I'd be willing to work twelve hours a day until, you know, until we could afford to hire some help. This is so exciting."

She stopped walking and reached out to hug me. People walking by smiled when they passed us, because I suppose they could tell she was happy and jazzed about something. I wasn't even embarrassed.

CHAPTER 18

Daniel

The phone rang, jangling Dan out of his concentration on the Lakers game. He hit the mute button on the remote.

"Yeah!"

"Jeez, Danny, is that any way to answer the phone?" He could tell by Caroline's voice that she was miffed. "I called to tell you not to come over until about eight-thirty."

"Why?" He was momentarily distracted when the Celtics blocked a shot.

"Tiffany and I put our heads together, working out numbers and a business plan to take to the loan officer at Wilshire Bank tomorrow."

Suddenly alert, he said, "Hey, babe, that's great. You're going to do it. Good for you. I'm so proud of you. Good luck on your project. I'll fix dinner at my place."

She scoffed, telling him his table was no bigger than a microchip and couldn't seat three. Not to mention that he probably hadn't picked up the place in days.

Danny looked around and could see her point. He preferred to think of it as lived-in, cozy. "Okay, babe. I'll think of someplace the three of us can go for a late supper."

"Good. I don't want Tiffany disillusioned by finding out you're such a slob. She thinks you're some kind of Superhero. She probably still believes in the tooth fairy."

"I'll guard our secret."

"Bye, Danny. Bring your jammies."

"Don't have to. I left them on the floor of your closet. Remember?"

"You're hopeless," she groaned. "Bye."

∼

He heard them chattering away when he opened her door, dropped his keys on the hall table, and followed their voices to the den. He entered the room just when Tiffany flew out and ran smack into him.

He grabbed her just in time to keep her from falling. "Whoa there, brown eyes. Where's the fire?"

She was breathless. "Sorry, Danny." Her cheeks turned adorably pink. "I have to do something with my face before Matthew gets here."

"Matthew?" He glanced at Care and raised his eyebrows, wondering why in hell they were expecting Angeli. She nailed him with a warning glare.

"He's joining us for dinner." Care answered his unspoken question and hardened her stare. "Tiffany called him a few minutes ago." She strolled over to him. "Hi."

"Hi." He embraced Caroline and ran his hands up and down her back. "How was your day?"

"The usual." She kissed him softly, and they were just getting into the mood when her doorbell rang.

"That's probably Mr. Wonderful now," Dan whispered against her neck.

Angeli was not his favorite person. He still couldn't get past the fact that he'd been in Caroline's hotel room all night.

Caroline gave him a little shove and a warning look. "Be nice, Danny."

Tiffany bolted from the bathroom. "I'll get it."

She opened the door and launched herself into Matthew's arms, emitting a squeal of delight.

Daniel and Caroline both laughed. Matthew looked stunned, then leaned in for Tiffany's welcoming kiss.

"How come *you* never do that when I come through the door?" Danny whispered to Caroline.

"You'd probably die from shock."

"You got that right."

Dan decided to be civil and crossed the hallway. "How's it going, Angeli?" He extended his hand, then withdrew it. "Never mind, I can see how it's going."

Matthew cleared his throat, transparently uneasy with Tiffany's unabashed enthusiasm. "Nice to see you again, Daniel." He gave her an affectionate squeeze before reaching for Dan's hand.

"Same here." They shook hands. "How's the golf game?"

"Haven't played since that day I went out with you and your dad."

Dan worked at sounding cordial. "We'll have to remedy that."

"Hey, it's getting late, guys," Caroline interjected. "We should get to the restaurant. Where are we going, Danny?"

∽

They walked the few blocks to Riccio's. The upscale neighborhood was mostly apartment buildings with Crape Myrtle trees with bright pink blossoms lined the sidewalk next to the curbing. They passed lots of people strolling and walking their dogs.

Daniel and Caroline took the lead, with Tiffany and Matthew following. Dan glanced back at the stragglers. They walked hand-in-hand several paces behind, smiling and whispering. Tiffany leaned into Matthew and put her hand on his chest. He lifted it to his mouth and kissed her fingers.

"They've got it bad," Dan whispered.

Caroline chuckled and squeezed his hand. "Poor Matt doesn't know what hit him. Pity any man Tiffany decides she wants. He doesn't stand a chance."

"I can think of worse fates. Tiffany's hot."

She looked at him with an uncharacteristic pout. "I thought you liked my type."

They stopped outside the door of Riccio's waiting for them to catch up. "There are lots of hot babes in the world, but you're the only one for me."

"That's more like it."

∽

The instant they stepped inside the aromas from the kitchen made Dan's mouth water and his gut rumbled at the combination of fresh bread, garlic, and marinara sauce. He sucked air through his nose and sighed contentedly. Caroline grinned and poked him in the ribs.

The tables wore red, green, and white cloths and a bowl of seasoned olive oil was placed in the center of each one. Riccio's most popular specialty was fresh Italian bread, which Riccio personally baked every morning. Dip a hunk of that bread in the olive oil and you were in taste bud heaven, Dan had often exclaimed.

Cleverly decorated by Riccio and his wife, they'd used muted yellows and white lattice intertwined with silk ivy. A garden right out of Tuscany. The midnight blue ceiling twinkled with hundreds of little white stars overhead.

Their daughter, Gina, greeted them with a handful of menus. "Hi, nice to see you. I hope you're hungry. Mom and Pop cooked up a batch of sauce big enough to ship to an aircraft carrier." She directed them to a table against one wall. "The special tonight is manicotti with a small filet of fresh halibut and a side of asparagus."

Tiffany heaved a sigh. "Oh, yummy,"

"Yes, sounds wonderful," Matthew added. He kissed the top of Tiffany's head when she sat in the chair he held for her.

Dan was disgusted by his syrupy, sweet tone of voice. The way Matthew looked at him with his unnerving blue-green eyes made Danny wonder for a second if he'd put his foot in it and said out loud what he was thinking.

"How about a bottle of the house Chianti?" Gina asked.

"Sounds great," Dan answered, grateful for the interruption. "Bring a boatload of your dad's bread with it."

"Looks like we're all having the special?" Caroline asked, glancing around for their assent.

"I'd like the fettuccine Alfredo, please." Angeli smiled at Tiffany and said, "You look beautiful tonight, sweetheart." He glanced across the table. "Doesn't she look beautiful?"

"Yes," Daniel answered honestly, "she does."

Danny reached under the table and put his hand on Caroline's thigh. Touching her never failed to give him a rush. It scared him how much he loved her. She turned and gazed with one of her rare, caught off guard, intimate looks. She covered his hand with hers and squeezed gently. Dan was astonished to see a flush on her cheek. *Amazing! The Control Queen let her vulnerability show for a split second.* He liked that.

Buddy, Gina's brother, came with the wine. "How're you folks doing tonight?" He expertly pulled the cork and placed it next to Daniel's glass.

"We're great, Buddy." He sniffed the cork and nodded approval. "We brought you some new converts, our friends, Tiffany Gaines and Matthew Angeli."

Buddy nodded politely and filled their glasses. "Hope you folks enjoy dinner. Come back to see us often."

Matthew raised his glass. "Here's to good wine, good food, and good company."

"And good luck at the bank tomorrow," Tiffany added.

"Oh, yes," Caroline said. "Luck at the bank."

Danny squeezed her leg, and she flashed a nervous smile.

"You're going to do great, babe."

"Yes," Matthew affirmed. "I'm sure they'll be amenable to the business loan. Your credentials are excellent, and they have personal knowledge of your talent."

Tiffany beamed at Matthew. "I just love it when he uses big words."

Dan swallowed half a glass of wine, stared at Matthew and wondered why he wanted to slug him every time he opened his mouth. Why didn't he mind his own damn business?

Matthew studied him. Dan felt as if Angeli could read his mind. Raising his glass, Dan saluted him and took another swallow. Matthew acknowledged him with a slight nod.

CHAPTER 19

Matthew

I knew precisely what Daniel was thinking. I was not surprised that he was jealous, but the fact he was jealous of *me* is ludicrous. I am on his side, for Heaven's sake.

I spent the entire day meditating on the best way to get this train back on track. My Boss is disappointed in the way I've handled things so far. I sense it will be my last bodily manifestation for eons. It is for the best. In truth, I'm far too susceptible to the weakness of the flesh.

Look at me, sitting here enjoying the lovely wine and wonderful meal with this enchanting young woman at my side. I might add, whom I love deeply and who's destined to be terribly hurt by me. I have no right to encourage the relationship. It has no future. I must get back to the reason for my being here. Immediately.

"Daniel," I began. "Any chance we can get in a game of golf in the next few days?"

His thoughts told me he'd rather kick my, uh, behind, than play a round of golf with me, but I soldiered on. "I'd enjoy going out again."

"I wish I knew how to golf," Tiffany said. "Caroline, you should teach me."

"I think any plans of giving you golf lessons will have to go on the back burner. If this bank loan goes through, we'll be up to our necks in work for the next several months."

Daniel sipped his wine quietly. He searched his mind for a good reason to refuse my request. I got out of his head and let him think for himself. He's shown far more intelligence than I in the past several days.

"Sure," he said, setting his glass down. He tore off a large piece of bread and methodically dipped it up and down in the olive oil, all the while studying me as if we were two male wolves, circling each other in a dance of dominance. "I'm going out at six tomorrow morning with Jack. Join us if that's not too early for you."

Caroline leaned back in her chair, a horrified look on her face. "Six! Danny, are you telling me you're going to get up tomorrow morning at five a.m. to play golf? I can't get up that early. I need my sleep."

Tiffany glanced at me with disappointment. "Matthew, that's really early."

I cast a regretful look in her direction. I had been looking forward to a long, sweet night with her. The thought of getting up that early gave me a headache. I'm becoming a veritable sloth.

"Six would be fine," I answered. "That's the best part of the day."

Daniel gave a perfunctory response. "Fine. Great."

Both women stared at us as if we'd taken leave of our senses, and I daresay we had. It will serve me right, having to rise from Tiffany's warm bed at such an ungodly hour. At least, that early, Daniel might not be in the mood to take a poke at me.

∼

Her soft, rhythmic breathing brushed my shoulder. The first steel gray light of day slid between the shutters covering her bedroom window. I was lying on my back with Tiffany snuggled against my side. Her head rested in the curve of my arm and shoulder, our legs tangled together like the plate of fettuccine I'd devoured a few hours earlier.

I moved her gently until she was lying face down on top of me. Stroking her back and hips, I was amazed, yet again, at the velvety smoothness of her skin and the softness of her flesh. She is heavenly perfection.

She stirred and raised her head, peering owlishly into my eyes, and then she smiled. "Hi," she whispered.

"Hi." I pulled her upwards until our lips met in a long, sweet kiss.

"I love you so much, Matthew." She brushed her lips against my ear.

"And I you, my angel."

She pushed herself upright and rose above me like the mythical Aphrodite, her hair a shining halo silhouetted in the faint glow from the window. Sitting astride me, she stroked my arms, shoulders, and chest. Moving downward, she took me in her hands. Bending her head, she held and kissed me, and a wave of ecstasy engulfed my entire being. I shuddered with pleasure.

Laughing, she moved higher and brushed her breasts against my face.

I clasped her hips and guided her home. Our dance as old as time and as close to Heaven as one could be without dying. God's special gift to humanity.

A wave of lucidity engulfed me, and I knew the love I felt for her was meant to be. It was right. It was pure. Somehow, Tiffany is part of The Plan.

Her face glowed in the early morning light. With our hands linked, she threw back her head as waves of sweet passion engulfed us. How beautiful she is. How beautiful we are together.

When spent, she slumped forward against my chest. I embraced her fiercely and rolled over, pinning her beneath me. "How could you use me so shamelessly?" I jested.

"You're a pushover." She reached up and brushed the hair from my forehead, gently touching my healing wound.

I pushed back on my elbows. "Am I crushing you?"

"Yes, but I love it. Don't move until I turn blue." She hugged me fiercely.

"There's nothing I'd enjoy more," I said, shifting to my side, "but the golf course beckons, my love."

"It's so early."

"You go back to sleep, sweetheart. You don't have to rise for another hour."

"Okay," she sighed, already slipping under the spell of Morpheus.

I slid off the bed and knelt beside her, gently drawing the sheet over her shoulders. I lowered my head and rested it on my clasped hands.

She stared at me with drowsy eyes. "What are you doing, Matthew?"

"Praying."

"For a good golf game?"

I chuckled quietly. "Nothing so trivial, my darling, I'm thanking God for you."

"Oh, Matthew," she said, rising on her elbow. Tears sparkled in her eyes.

Mine grew moist in response. I embraced her and pushed her back against the pillow.

"You sleep now, love. I'll see you in a few hours. I've work to do."

"I'll never be able to sleep now," she protested, even as her eyelids grew heavy.

"Yes, you will." I stroked her cheek, then headed for the shower. My heart thudded with joy as I dressed for the golf game with Daniel and Jack. I had a feeling this would be a productive day.

As I lifted my new custom set of PXG clubs out of the trunk of the taxi, I spotted Daniel parking his car at the other end of the country club lot. The golf clubs are an unjustifiable extravagance, but I'm behaving more like a modern mortal every day. Once I saw them in the pro shop, I had to have them. They were specially priced for Christmas, after all.

Daniel spotted me through the early morning sunlight when he stepped out and opened his trunk. He raised his hand in greeting. I paid the cab driver and headed in Daniel's direction, the soft cleats on my new hundred-ninety-dollar Foot Joys clicking quietly on the macadam. The sky was overcast and the air unseasonably sultry. As soon as I reached Daniel's car, I put down my golf bag and removed my sweater.

"Yeah," Daniel observed, "looks like you won't need that thing today. Hotter'n hell already."

An uninformed observation on his part, but I nodded and agreed with him, nevertheless. "Yes, looks like we're in for a swelter."

He cocked his head in the direction of the departing taxi. "You came in a cab. Car trouble?"

"I don't own a car." Then confessed, "I never learned to drive."

"Are you shitin' me?" he asked with an unconvinced smile.

I shrugged. "No, strange as it may seem, until recently, I've been someplace where an automobile is unnecessary."

He shook his head in wonder and picked up his golf bag. I followed him in the direction of the pro shop.

As we approached the door, the lights went on inside. Jack stood behind the counter, unlocking the cash register. He placed the Starter's electronic time-log on the glass countertop and scanned the page. He looked up and smiled a greeting when Daniel opened the door.

"Hey, right on time. How's it going, Dan? Nice to see you again, Mr. Angeli." Jack extended his hand to me across the counter.

"Matthew, please." I shook his hand. "I'm looking forward to our round with my new clubs."

"Anything cold in that cooler?" Daniel asked. He walked across the room to the large glass doors of the refrigerator. "I'm parched already."

"We're expecting the delivery truck this morning with soft drinks, water, and juice," Jack said. "It was hot yesterday afternoon, and we got cleaned out. Nothing but beer left in there. Little early for that though."

Daniel pulled two six-packs of Budweiser out of the cooler and snapped one can out of the plastic collar. "These go on my tab. I'll put them in the cooler on the cart." He placed the beer on the counter, popped open the can in his hand, and took a long swallow. Looking at me, he pointed to the other cans with a question on his brow.

"Don't think I'd better," I said. "I haven't had breakfast."

"Me, neither." He took another swallow. "Didn't have time. Somebody told me once that beer had nutritional properties." He pulled off another can and handed it to me.

"Guess one won't hurt," I said. "In fact, it's looking pretty good right now with this early morning heat." The cold beads of sweat on the aluminum were refreshing in my hand. The beer went down smoothly. "Good," I added, enjoying the cool bite.

"I'd better have one of those," Jack said, taking a can for himself. "Can't be the only sober one in the threesome. We're playing for money, and I wouldn't want to take advantage of you gentlemen. Karen made me a big breakfast this morning." His grin told us he considered himself a lucky man.

Daniel tossed his empty beer can in the wastebasket on Jack's side of the counter and opened another. I raised my eyebrows and glanced at Jack. He merely shrugged and went back to the log.

Daniel took another long swallow. "Nice looking set of clubs there, Matt."

"Yes, bought them from Jack here." I smoothed my fingers lovingly across the polished surface of the driver. "I couldn't resist the possibility of knocking a couple of strokes off my game."

Jack tossed a set of keys to Daniel. "Why don't you go unlock the cart shed, buddy. I'll finish here. We can get off the tee, soon as Pete shows. Take Matthew with you and drive a couple of carts to the first tee. It's going to be too hot to walk today. I'll meet you there."

"I've never driven one of those things," I said, unable to keep the trepidation out of my voice.

"Nothing to it," Daniel promised. "Come on, I'll give you a quick lesson." He hoisted his clubs over his shoulder, grabbed the beer, and threaded his way through the racks of pants and shirts. I followed closely, feeling foolish in that I hadn't taken the time to consider learning how to drive. I am an anomaly in The City of Our Lady of the Angels.

Daniel led me to the cart shed, flipping on an overhead light next to the gateway. He quickly found the correct key, pulled the gate toward us, and slid it back against the outside wall. Stepping into the first golf cart, he started the motor and backed it out. Helpless, I watched, wondering if there was "nothing to it."

When the cart was clear of the building, Daniel turned off the key and stepped out. He motioned me over.

"The key stays in the ignition," he said. "When that lever is in the down position, the cart goes forward and when it's up, it goes backward. There are two foot pedals. This one's the brake. That one engages the engine." He looked at me. "Got it?"

I nodded. What could be easier? Taking a seat behind the wheel, I lowered the lever and stepped on the right pedal. The cart leapt forward and sent a shower of gravel flying out from under the back tires. Rocks clattered loudly against the side of the shack.

"Holy crap!" Daniel shouted, covered his face with his forearms, and jumped clear.

I slammed my foot on the brake pedal and nearly flew over the steering wheel when the cart skidded to a sudden stop.

"Easy does it, Matt." Daniel stood with his hands on his hips and laughed. Soon he was doubled over.

I felt entirely foolish but saw the humor in the situation and laughed also. I took a deep breath and leaned back in the seat. "This thing is touchier than a temperamental cart horse," I declared, once I'd recovered my breath.

"Stay right there, Matt. Don't touch anything. I'll get the other cart." Daniel wagged his head in amusement and re-entered the building. In a couple of seconds, I heard the other engine fire up, and he appeared in the doorway. He was still grinning as he maneuvered the little cart next to mine.

"Set the brake by pushing down on the pedal until you hear a click," he said. "We'll strap our clubs in place, and I'll give you a short driving lesson on the way to the first tee, but don't get your nose out of joint if I give you a wide berth."

"I nearly got my nose out of joint permanently. Thank goodness you weren't standing directly behind me." I was grateful someone had looked out for Daniel while my attention was on the golf cart.

"I'm going to drive alongside you, and you do what I do, okay?" He sat, clipped the score card onto the steering wheel and tossed the balls and tees in the carry tray. Flipping the switch to the forward position, he slowly pressed on the power pedal, and the cart inched forward.

"Got the idea?" He raised his eyebrows and tapped his temple.

"I had the idea before, but the result was jarring. I'll give it another go." Pressing carefully on the pedal, I was exhilarated when the cart moved ahead without a jolt. Smiling at my success, I pulled even with Daniel. "I think I've got it."

"Don't get overconfident," he warned. "These little buggers can be tricky. Remember, easy does it."

We arrived at the first tee without incident. Thank you, Heaven.

Jack approached on foot, his heavy bag slung over his shoulder. He began to put his clubs on the back of my cart.

"I'll drive this cart and Jack will drive the other one."

I agreed immediately.

"Matt doesn't drive," Daniel stated.

Jack stared at me. "No kidding?" He wasn't sure he believed Daniel.

"Yes, I'm afraid it's true. I've never had need of an automobile, and so I never learned to drive."

"I thought every boy was champing at the bit from the age of fourteen, bugging their dads to teach them to drive," Jack said.

"It's a long story. My father didn't drive either, so it was never an issue."

Jack wore a dubious expression. "It's near impossible to live here without a car."

"Yes, I've been spending a lot of money on taxis and Ubers. Shall we start?"

"You toss it, Matt," Jack said and pulled a coin from his pocket. "Head's you start, tails, Dan starts. I expect to beat the pants off both of you, so I'll have the honors for the rest of the round." He flashed a wide smile.

"I can beat you on any given day, pal, any given day," Daniel declared with a grin. "I'm going to make you eat those words." He polished off the rest of the second beer and tossed the empty can into the recycle container.

The sun was up and hot. The moisture on the grass evaporated rapidly, the air steamy. I quickly downed the last of my beer and flipped the coin high in the air. As I watched it twirl upward, I felt the dizzying influence of the alcohol.

For a split second, the coin appeared to hang suspended. I was being cautioned. I glanced at my companions to see if they noticed it. They had not, so when it fell, I bent down and studied it with a silent promise to be on my best behavior.

"Looks like you're up first, Daniel."

"Watch me, boys, and see how it's done."

Jack smirked. "Give it your best shot, Danny boy."

Daniel lined up his shot with precision. He went into a classic backswing and completed what looked like the perfect drive. He caught the ball with the toe of his driver and sliced it neatly into the middle of the pond halfway down the fairway.

"Aw, hell!"

"Want to take your Mulligan now or save it for later?" Jack asked. He laughed, fully enjoying Daniel's frustration. These young friends are frequent competitors.

Daniel glared at Jack, then glanced at me. I kept my face perfectly straight with perhaps a hint of sympathy. He gestured for me to step to the tee. "Take your shot, Matt." He strode back to the cart, opened the cooler and pulled out a third Bud.

"Better go easy on that stuff, Dan," Jack warned, still laughing. "By the time we get to the second tee you won't even be able to see the ball."

Daniel muttered a few choice profanities and slouched in the cart under the shade of the canopy. He took long swallows of the icy cold beer, then emitted a manly burp.

My drive was my best ever, and then Jack out drove me by thirty yards. I sat back in the cart next to Daniel. He mumbled a compliment on my drive. We were off to a perplexing beginning.

At the second tee, Jack, as he'd predicted, had the honors. I followed him and hit a strong, straight drive down the middle of the fairway, leaving me in perfect position for my chip shot to the green. It was a beautiful little three par hole, surrounded at the back by oleanders in riotous bloom with deep sand traps on either side.

Daniel, having taken a bogey on the first hole, teed off last. He hit a beautiful drive, the ball flew high and true. We watched with awe as it sailed straight for the flag.

"Go, baby, go, baby, go, go, go," Daniel pleaded.

"Well, I'll be a sumbitch," Jack exclaimed. "You're on target for a hole-in-one, pal."

Speechless, I watched the ball as it dropped on the grass about four feet in front of the pin. It rolled straight and fast toward the cup. We jumped and cheered excitedly. There was no way it could miss.

Suddenly we heard a loud, metallic *thoing*. The golf ball hit the metal flag stick hard and ricocheted right into the large sand trap on the left side of the green. We stared, horrified, as it rolled right up underneath the shaggy rye grass on the overhanging lip of the trap.

Jack and I both groaned and cast Daniel sympathetic looks. He stared down the fairway in utter disbelief. "I don't believe it. I just don't believe it." Hands on his hips, he shook his head slowly from side to side.

"You were robbed, man," Jack said. "Robbed. I thought for sure you had that one. It was frickin' beautiful."

Mystified as to why Daniel's luck was running so poorly, I had put in a tremendous amount of energy, praying to prevent a repeat of the last hole. The reason I chose the opportunity to have a game of golf with him was to do some fence mending, gain his confidence. I tried to slow his ball as it ran toward the cup, but somehow had only succeeded in creating another minor disaster. Not what I had in mind at all.

Daniel walked past me, shaking his head dejectedly. He slipped his three wood back in the golf bag, sat down in the cart, and reached for another can of beer.

"I don't know what to say, Daniel. I suppose even Dustin Johnson has days like this."

Baleful, he grumbled, "Not likely."

Distressed, I was having misgivings about my backup team upstairs. We were working at cross purposes. To what end, I could not imagine.

When we drove to the fourth tee, Daniel was polishing off the last of the first six-pack and was in a dark mood, indeed. I behaved scrupulously, and Jack wisely discontinued his jesting.

When I stood to take my tee shot, I decided to alter my strategy. Instead of trying to influence Daniel's game, I would take steps to make my own game more common. *I must not continue to play so well.* So, I closed my eyes on the back swing. The sound of the club face striking the ball told me my tactic failed.

"Way to go, Matthew!" exclaimed Jack. "You and those new clubs are a match made in Heaven. You haven't had a bad shot all morning." He clapped me on the shoulder.

Match made in Heaven. *Pah!* Something is clearly going on here, something over which I have no control.

"Where did it go?" I asked, unable to see my ball.

"I spot it at least two-hundred-fifty yards on the other side of that rise in the middle of the fairway," Daniel said, pointing into the distance.

"I believe that's the longest ball I've ever hit. I can't imagine how it happened."

Daniel teed up his ball. "You sure as hell don't have to apologize for it. You're having a good day, and I'm having a bad one. It happens."

I gazed toward the heavens. *Would it be too much to ask that the man be allowed at least one good shot? Am I to be made privy to what is going on here?*

Apparently not.

Daniel went into his backswing. I glanced at my watch, which caught the sun and sent a bright flash right into his eyes. He grounded his club behind the ball, leaving a dark scuff in the grass, and sending the shot a mere hundred feet or so. He strode swiftly to the cart, slammed his driver into his golf bag and sat in the passenger seat, thoroughly disgusted.

"You drive," he growled.

"Me?"

"You see anybody else around? I'm too drunk to drive. I shouldn't have had that last beer. I don't feel so good."

I sat behind the wheel and released the brake. I thought it was a good time to change the subject from golf to Caroline. Perhaps that would lighten his mood.

"Caroline is going to the bank this morning to see about her loan, isn't she?" I said in a chirpy, upbeat tone.

Daniel turned and glowered at me. "Just why in hell are you so goddammed interested in my girlfriend, huh?"

"Well, I merely..."

"You're not fooling me, pal," he sneered and made wiggly fingers. "All the time oozing around, acting the picture of innocence. You're no goddamn angel."

I turned and stared at him with shock. "Daniel, I assure you..."

"Look out!" he shouted. "You're going in the water!"

I slammed on the brake, gripping the wheel for dear life. We skidded a good six feet on the damp grass. Daniel almost flew over the dashboard when we came to an abrupt stop a foot or so from the pond. Our golf clubs flew like arrows shot from their bags.

"Jesus!" Daniel yelled, when he recovered his breath. "If you had half a brain, you'd be dangerous!"

"There's no need to be rude!" I shouted back, trembling from our near fiasco. I switched the gear to reverse and applied gentle pressure to the accelerator. The cart leapt backward, and I drove over our golf clubs, bouncing the cart like a carnival ride and nearly tipping us over.

"Dammit!" I muttered, both in anger and humiliation.

When I stopped the cart, Daniel stepped off and staggered forward to survey the damage to our clubs. I followed him and was dismayed to see that I'd killed my new three wood. The shaft was bent in a perfect V, the grip shredded. I assumed this exercise had some point. So far, it had escaped me.

Jack drove up. He sat in his cart and appraised the sorry scene for a moment, then stepped out and approached us.

"Looks like you boys aren't having an ideal round." He stood, arms akimbo, shaking his head sorrowfully.

"Well, duh," Daniel slurred. He picked up his clubs and slammed them back into his bag, angrily yanking the locking strap tighter.

"We may have to order you another three wood, Matthew," Jack said. "I don't think that one is fixable." He bent to help me retrieve the contents of my bag.

"I think perhaps we should call it a day," I said. "Daniel isn't feeling well, and now I'm in no mood to continue."

"I feel fine, old buddy, old pal. I'm just drunk." Daniel leaned forward with elbows on his knees, looking greener by the moment.

Jack shook his head and chuckled. "Let's head back to the clubhouse. It's too darn hot to play today, anyway. Follow me. We'll cut across the fairway after the fifth hole."

"Good idea," I slipped behind the wheel. "Hang on," I warned Daniel, as I released the brake and started forward.

"No shit," he mumbled.

We continued without incident until we started across the fairway between five and eight. A big sprinkler sprang into action right in front of us. I swerved sharply to avoid running over it. We skidded sideways and Daniel went flying out of the cart onto the grass, landing in a heap. I leapt out and ran to see if he was injured. The cart continued rolling forward.

Daniel groaned as I bent down to have a look at him. At the same instant, he sat up, striking me squarely in the nose with his head. The blood spurted as I dropped to my knees, hitting him sharply in the eye with my elbow when I reached for my face to stanch the bleeding. He fell backward, clutching his eyebrow. Out of the corner of my eye, I saw the cart bounce to a stop. The sprinkler continued to spray, soaking us through.

Jack hollered to a greens-keeper to turn off the water. He drove over to where we lay sprawled on the sopping wet grass, stepped out of his cart, and stood over us. He sighed and shook his head in disbelief and, no doubt, more than a little disgust.

We were soon ensconced in the clubhouse kitchen, I holding a bag of ice to my nose and Daniel holding one over his eye. We stared menacingly at each other.

Jack entered the kitchen and approached us. "Your ride is here. I called Caroline and told her you were on your way to her place. I still think you should go to the clinic and get checked out, Dan. That's a nasty bruise coming up around your eye, and Matthew's nose is probably broken."

"No, jus' get me to Care's place," Daniel moaned. "I feel like I'm going to puke."

"Not in here, you're not," Jack warned. "Come on, both of you. I'll help you out to the parking lot. We'll take the service door. I don't want any members to see you."

Daniel groaned, and I snuffled. We made our way to the waiting car, holding each other up like two soldiers returning from a battlefield skirmish.

CHAPTER 20

Caroline

I was a wreck. After sitting for an hour at the bank during the loan interview, I felt like an international spy getting an intense questioning. The only thing missing were thumb screws and interrogation lights.

I had the business plan all ready and organized. After Tiffany running me through the numbers several times, I expected to be comfortable with my presentation. How wrong could I be? I was so darn nervous parts of the interview were a total blank by the time I left the banker's office.

My cell phone rang as I opened my apartment door. Jack called to tell me that he was sending Danny and Matthew to my apartment in an Uber.

I dropped my briefcase on the hall floor with a *thud*. "You're what?"

"It's a long story, but here's the skinny: Dan's drunk, and Matthew doesn't drive. I've put them in a car and sent them to you."

I grabbed a handful of my hair. "This is a joke, right?"

"No, I'm not kidding."

"Come on, Jack. What's going on? I'm supposed to be at work. I've had one hellish morning, and I'm not in the mood. Okay?"

"Sorry, kiddo. It's no joke. They're on the way. Somebody's got to be their nursemaid. I gotta go. A line is forming here, and I'm short-handed. Have Dan call me later when he sobers up."

Before I could form words around a reply, I heard a loud click, and the phone went dead.

Oh great! Nursemaid for a drunk, just what I need!

~

To say I wasn't prepared for how they would look when I opened my door would be putting it mildly. Blood spatters decorated the front of Matthew's shirt. He held a dishcloth to his nose with one hand and supported Danny with the other. Dan sported a big shiner and a lump the size of an egg above his eyebrow.

"Oh, my, God! What happened? Were you in an accident?" Real alarm turned me cold.

"I'll explain later," Matthew said. "Help me get Daniel to a bed. He's wobbly on his feet."

Danny gave me a pathetic look and whimpered, "Hi, babe. I don't feel so good." He reached for me, and, with Matthew on one side and me on the other, we dragged him to the bedroom. He whimpered and started to lie down.

"Wait! Not on my bedspread." I yanked it back just as he flopped back, groaning against the pillows. "Daniel Kavanaugh, you are drunk!"

"It was an accident."

"An accident? You're drunk by accident?"

I looked at Matthew. "And what happened to you?"

He lifted the towel to show me his swollen nose and pointed at Danny. "He did it."

I stared at him. "Danny hit you?"

"It was an accident."

Danny pointed at his black eye. "Anyway, Matthew did this."

"You hit him in the nose by accident?" I raised my arms in frustration. "Will one of you please tell me what's going on here?" I was fast running out of sympathy and patience for both of them.

Danny rolled onto his side. "I gotta get up. I'm gonna puke."

He turned a nice shade of gray-green and clutched his mid-section.

Matthew grabbed a wastebasket and thrust it under Danny's chin in the nick of time. We were overwhelmed by the rank stench of sour beer as Danny lost the contents of his stomach. I heard a suspicious retching and looked to see Matthew grimacing and choking, the wastebasket wobbling in his hands.

I made a grab for it and yelled, "In the bathroom, Matt. Over there!"

Danny fell back on the pillows and moaned. Matthew threw up in the toilet.

Snatching a clean wastebasket, I set it on the floor next to the bed. I gave Danny a threatening stare and pointed at the soiled container. "I'm going to take this revolting thing to the bathroom and check on Matt. Don't you dare throw up on the bed or the floor!"

He nodded obediently and closed his eyes.

Matthew knelt pitifully in front of the toilet with his forehead resting on the rim.

"Don't put your head on the toilet bowl. That's disgusting."

Really, am I taking care of him again?

"It feels so good. Nice and cool. I have a headache."

"I'm not surprised. I think your nose is broken." I dunked a washcloth in cold water, wrung it out, and put it on the back of his neck. "Come on," I tugged until he was on his feet. "Lie down on the bed next to Danny. I'll get an ice pack for you. You're not going to throw up again, are you?"

"No." He put his arm around my shoulders, and I helped him back to the bedroom. I led him around to the opposite side and sat him down. He gingerly lowered himself to the pillow, and I placed the cold cloth over his forehead.

Danny opened his eyes and grimaced. "What's he doing here?"

"Shut up, Danny. You're in enough trouble already." I pulled off Matt's golf shoes and dropped them on the floor, then went to the other side and removed Danny's. "I'm going to get the ice bag for Matthew, then I'll figure out something for that shiner of yours."

"You need to put a piece of raw steak on it," he mumbled.

"Don't be silly. That's an old wives' tale. Lie still, I'll think of something."

He was pathetic. I could feel sympathy creeping back in, in spite of myself.

"You could kiss it and make it all better."

"I'm not your mother, Kavanaugh. I'm more inclined to give you another black eye than kiss you."

He was so pitiful I did lean down and kiss him.

Matthew sighed and pressed his hand against his forehead.

"Forget it, Matt," I muttered, "I'm all kissed out."

I left them to their misery and went into the kitchen to fill the ice bag.

Just when I opened the freezer, the phone rang.

"Hello!"

"Caroline?" I recognized Tiffany's voice. "How did it go?"

"Come over here and get your boyfriend!"

I put a bowl under the ice dispenser and ice clattered into it.

"Excuse me?"

"I said, come over here and get your boyfriend. He's bleeding all over my eight-hundred-thread-count sheets."

I pulled open one drawer after the other, looking for the ice bag. I knew it was in there somewhere.

"Caroline, what are you talking about? Matthew and Daniel are out golfing this morning."

"Were—not are. They had a slug fest, and Jack sent them to my apartment in a hired car. Ah, there you are." I pulled the ice bag out from the back of my towel drawer. "I knew you were hiding in here somewhere."

"Are you drunk?"

I detected suspicion in her voice. "No, but that's not a bad idea. Come on over, and we'll both *get* drunk."

I dropped ice cubes into the bag and pushed on it to squeeze the air out. I screwed the cap on tight and opened the refrigerator to take out a bottle of seltzer for Danny.

"I don't know what's going on, but I'll be there in twenty minutes."

She hung up.

"Goody, we'll have a party," I muttered to myself and went back into my bedroom to tend the wounded.

∽

Tiffany stood beside me, gawking at Danny and Matthew. Dan slept and snored loudly. Matthew may have been asleep. I couldn't tell. His face was mostly covered by the ice bag.

She tiptoed to Matt's side of the bed.

"Honey?" she whispered. She put her hand tentatively on his chest. "It's me. Are you all right?"

Matt moaned and lifted the ice bag to peek at her. "No." He put it back and sighed.

"What happened?"

"Don't bother," I said. "We aren't going to get a straight answer from either of them for a while." I took her arm and pulled her toward the door. "Let's have a glass of wine while they sleep it off. They're snockered."

Tiffany followed me to the kitchen. I reached in the cupboard for a bottle of Syrah and took a hunk of cheese from the refrigerator. "There are some little cracker thingies in the pantry." I pointed across the island. "Put some on that plate. What did the Prince of Darkness say when you left the office early?" I pulled the cork from the bottle and took a deep sniff. The wine smelled heavenly.

"I told him I had severe cramps and was coming down with PMS," she said with a giggle. "He actually blushed and said something like, 'Well, uh, uh, go on home then.'"

She mimicked Moody's voice pattern perfectly.

Tiffany dumped crackers on the plate. I handed her the cheese board and a knife. I reached for two of my best crystal wine glasses, and we sat across the table from each other.

She sliced some cheese. "I was dying to hear how your interview went at the bank. Then when you told me to come and pick up Matthew, I forgot all about it. How did it go?"

"To tell you the truth, it's mostly a blur. I think it went well. The loan officer seemed impressed with your business plan. I blanked out on the numbers though and had to keep referring to my notes."

"I'm sure he didn't expect you to have all that stuff memorized. I bet you did great." She raised her glass and gave me a wink. "Here's to us and our future business."

I took a big sip of the wine and leaned back in my chair. "I hope you're right. This is something I've wanted to do for so long."

Tiffany placed cheese slices on top of the crackers, arranging them on the plate. Almost every other one went into her mouth.

"I thought you were dieting."

"I am, but this is a special occasion. You applied for the loan, and our boyfriends got drunk together and beat each other up. What better reasons do I need?" She grinned at the absurdity of it, and I had to laugh.

"Yes, what better reason could there be to get drunk and fat?" Both our glasses were half empty, so I topped them off. "Bottoms up, girlfriend."

CHAPTER 21

Daniel

Dan had one hell of a headache, and his mouth tasted like he'd been chewing on a dirty gym sock. It was dark, and he didn't know where he was. He slid a hand to the side and found the edge of the mattress. He moved his other hand sideways and found something soft and warm.

Caroline murmured, rolled over, and threw her leg across his hips. He was in her bed. Everything started to come back. The bad news—he remembered what happened at the golf course. The good news—it wasn't Matthew snuggling up to him.

His eye throbbed, and he gingerly reached to explore the damage. "Ouch! Goddammit!" It was worse than he thought. It felt as if he was growing a second head. Perhaps the new one would work better than the one he'd taken to the golf course that morning. At least, he was pretty sure it was that morning.

"Danny?" Caroline whispered thickly. "You okay?" She rubbed his arm and moved her head onto his chest.

"I'm okay, but I have to get up and take a leak. I don't want to turn on the light. Are we at your place or mine?"

She sighed and turned away. "Mine."

"Are we alone in here? What happened to Matthew?"

"Tiffany took him home. Quit talking and go pee. I'm sleeping."

When he sat on the edge of the bed, head swimming, he realized he was still dressed and pulled his polo shirt off. The collar rubbed against his sore eyebrow. It felt like sixty grit sandpaper applied with maximum force.

"Shit!"

"Be quiet."

"Have a little sympathy, will ya? I'm in pain here." He gave her a little smack on the bottom.

"What is this? Danny can't sleep—nobody sleeps?" She knocked over something on the nightstand. A click and the room suddenly filled with light.

"Oh, dammit," he groaned, covering his eyes. "Oh, oh that hurts."

"Good grief, you and Matthew are two of the biggest babies I've ever known."

She rolled out of bed and shuffled sleepily to his side. Bending down, she squinted at his face and grimaced. "Believe it or not, it looks better than it did a few hours ago." She tugged him to his feet.

"It doesn't feel any better." He undid his belt and dropped his pants on the floor.

"How would you know? You were under anesthesia." She reached down and picked up the pants as he stumbled into the bathroom.

"Anesthesia?"

"You were stinko, blotto, snockered, drunk, lover boy."

Hangers scraped on the closet bar. She was hanging his pants and shirt. She couldn't stand it when he left clothes lying around, even in the middle of the night. "Danny, you are a world class slob," she grumbled.

"Yeah, sorry."

"It wouldn't hurt if you brushed your teeth while you were in there. You're very aromatic."

The closet door closed with a whish followed by a muted *thud*.

"Okay, babe." He rummaged through her medicine cabinet for his toothbrush.

When he crept back to the bedroom, he eased himself down on the sheets with a loud groan. "Come snuggle with me, babe. I need some T.L.C."

She snapped off the lamp and crawled back into bed.

"What you need is a spanking."

She did scooch back in his direction. Dan pulled her close and nuzzled the back of her neck. "Can I have a rain-check?"

She was warm and soft and naked, and she smelled like spice cake. All of a sudden, he wasn't sleepy anymore. He forgot about his throbbing headache, his equipment on full alert.

"Very funny. Go back to sleep."

"I'm not sleepy anymore." He ran a hand up and down her leg and across her belly, her skin like warm cream under his fingers. There's no way he would ever get enough of her.

"Well, *I'm* sleepy," she said. "You slept like a corpse all afternoon." She shifted slightly, bumping her bottom against his pelvis. "Danny, you pick the most inconvenient times to get horny."

"What do you mean? This is a very convenient time." He kissed her shoulder and fondled her breast. He thought she had the most perfect, beautiful breasts possible. He tugged her over onto her back and moved to taste them. She sighed with reluctant pleasure.

He chuckled against her rigid nipple. A thousand times every day he thought about different ways to turn her on, about how she'd respond to his touch, and ran his tongue between her breasts all the way to her miraculous love nest.

"God, Danny," she whimpered. "Have you no heart?"

Even as she protested, her hips rose to meet him. He knelt between her legs and ran his hands over her body, studied her in the moonlight slanting through the bedroom window. In no hurry, he lifted her legs onto his shoulders, pressed forward, and teased her by rubbing himself against her inner thighs.

Before long, she gasped excitedly, grasped the back of his neck, and pulled his face to hers, her kiss hot and fierce. The instant he pushed forward a thrill shot through him that shook him to his bones.

He rolled over, carrying her with him. They were still together physically and emotionally. He felt moisture on his neck and put his hand under her chin to raise her head. Tears glistened on her cheeks. He went still. "Babe, did I hurt you?"

"I'm fine, Danny. I'm wonderful. I love you."

He hugged her tight, sure his heart would burst.

CHAPTER 22

Caroline

Tiffany made her way to my desk the minute I walked into work. The Big Drip glowered from his office window, probably thinking we might be discussing him. I think he had a hunch something was up, and it no doubt drove him batty.

Tiffany dropped a pile of specs on my desk. "How's Daniel this morning?" She pointed to something on the top page, pretended she was asking me about a project.

I grinned. "He's wonderful."

"I see." Her face was aglow, and her smile cranked up the wattage even further.

My eyebrows rose. "You, too, huh?"

"Yes," she sighed. "His nose looks pretty bad, all puffy and purply this morning. Didn't affect anything else though."

"I'd like to be a mouse in Danny's pocket when he arrives at work and tries to explain how he got his black eye. He'll probably tell the truth. He's not good at fibbing."

"Yet, he passed the bar exam," Tiffany teased. "How odd."

"Ha-ha." I shuffled through the papers she dropped in front of me. "Am I supposed to be doing something with this?"

"Believe it or not, yes. Peter Langley sent these from Seattle. He and Al Guererro are working on another job up there. They aren't happy with the designer their client hired. He would like you to comment on the flow pattern of the work stations. He's trying to get them to hire you."

"That's nice." I warmed with a satisfied smile. "What sort of company is it?"

"Software development."

I flipped through the drawings, then carried them to the nearest drafting table. We spread them out, put our heads together, and studied them for several minutes.

"I can barely concentrate on this. I'm on pins and needles about the loan," I told her. "Wouldn't it be nice if we could stall Langley until we set up our own place? No, he's a customer of this firm. It wouldn't be ethical."

Tiffany weighted down a corner of the drawing with a lead plug. "Do you think the bank will call you today?"

"I hope so. Heads up," I warned. "Here comes our dream date."

"Good morning, ladies. I see we're actually working for a change." He stood with his legs apart, arms crossed over his chest.

"Good morning, Mr. Moody," Tiffany and I answered in unison.

"How charming. Now Clayton, before you spend too much time on this, I'd like you to get on over to Magnificent Marble. Look over the stuff they cut for the Jones project. I don't want any more of that cracked crap shipped to them."

With him in his Monday morning whip-cracking mood, I thought I'd have some fun.

"You're absolutely right, Mr. Moody. I'll get right on it. That is an excellent idea. I'm amazed how you always anticipate potential problems. That's why you're the boss. I won't waste any more time on this. Tiffany can work on it." I went to my desk, picked up my purse, and headed out.

His mouth still hung open when I turned into the lobby and glanced back. Tiffany struggled keeping a straight face. Other staffers had their heads down, smiling at their drawings or computer screens.

∽

When I returned from the marble yard, there was a note on my desk with the name of the loan officer at Wilshire Bank. My heart was in my throat when I picked up the phone. I checked around to see if Simple Simon was anywhere in sight. Tiffany wasn't around, so I figured she'd gone to lunch.

I had to punch the number three times before I got it right. When they answered, I asked for Mr. Reynolds, pulse pounding in my ears. *Please, please, please. Let this be good news.* I fidgeted, rapped my nails on the desktop, and stared into space for what seemed an eternity. I thought I'd been disconnected when a plastic voice answered and told me Reynolds was out of the office. "Would you like his voice mail?"

No, I wouldn't like his voice mail. I wanted an answer to my loan application. What choice did I have? I left my message. It would be a long afternoon. I drummed my fingers on the desk some more, then reached for the phone again to call Danny's office. When Billie answered, I asked if Danny was in. I hoped he could get away for a quick lunch. Otherwise, it was Coke or coffee for me again.

"Sorry, hon. He left with a client. Said he'd be back in about two hours. That's a lovely black eye you gave him." I heard her snickering.

"Did he say I did that?"

"No, I'm teasing. He said he had an accident on the golf course, ran into somebody's elbow. Sounds pretty thin to me."

"Believe it or not, Billie, it's the truth. Did he happen to mention the other poor guy? He got his nose broken. They ran one of the carts right over a sprinkler in the fairway. Jack probably won't let either of them back on the course any time soon."

"Here I thought golf was safer than skydiving."

We both laughed about Danny and Matthew's exploits then exchanged small talk for a couple of minutes before disconnecting.

My stomach grumbled as I went downstairs to the lobby bar and had Jimmy whip up two large cherry Cokes for me. I juggled them back onto the elevator and up to the office. I'd eat something later. If I kept busy working, the time would go faster, get my mind off the guy from the bank.

The call came at quarter to five. Wilshire Bank turned me down. If I got a qualified co-signer, they'd be happy to do the funding. Since I had no real assets, except my savings and car, they were very sorry, they'd have to say no.

Tiffany watched me from across the room. I pressed my lips

together and shook my head. She gave me an incredulous look and started in my direction. I raised my hand to stop her, reached for my purse, and left the office.

CHAPTER 23

Daniel

The minute he walked into Caroline's apartment, Daniel sensed gloom. He put down his briefcase and hung his jacket on the coat tree in the hall. A light shone from the den. He headed in that direction.

Caroline was bent over a stack of papers on her desk. She wore her clunky red reading glasses and moved a pencil furiously across one of the pages. Immersed in the papers, Dan didn't think she heard him come in.

"Hey, babe, everything okay?"

She didn't look up from the paperwork. He could see by the set of her back she was stressed. He put his hands on her shoulders and massaged her neck. She sighed, removed the glasses, and leaned back into him. He kissed her on the forehead.

"Wilshire bank turned me down," she said with a sigh. "I'm getting organized here so I can shop some other banks." She flipped her pencil onto the desk and rose from the chair.

He embraced her. "I'm sorry, babe. Did they say why?"

She rested her forehead on his chin. "No credit history, no real estate, too little money in the bank, blah, blah, blah. Said they wouldn't loan without a co-signer." She tilted her face and managed a weak smile. "They're not the only bank in town, are they?"

"Damn right." He pointed at himself and pantomimed co-signing with his finger. "My offer still stands, you know."

"I know. Thanks, but no thanks." She smacked her hands on his chest and said, "However, there is something you can do for me." She tenderly explored the lump above his eye.

Dan jerked at her touch. "Ow! And that would be?"

"Take me out to dinner and buy me about a gallon of scotch and soda. I'm totally frazzled, and half starved. I didn't have lunch today."

"I was hoping you'd say something else, but dinner it is."

"One thing though, okay?"

"Anything, you name it."

"I don't want to talk about the loan." She sparkled with a feisty smile. "Let's spend all evening talking dirty sex and speculating about what Matthew and Tiffany do when they're alone."

His heart warmed. She was handling it well. "You know me. I'd rather do it than talk about it, but maybe after I've plied you with liquor and food, you'll change your mind."

"One never knows."

CHAPTER 24

Caroline

My beloved parents were about to blow through town. Their travel agent called to give me their arrival flight information. They expected me to pick them up. They always expect me to pick them up. Just drop everything I'm doing and drive through that hellish traffic on the 405 to meet their flight, as if anything I'm involved in at the time is completely unimportant.

I don't know why that surprised me because all my life, anything I'd done seemed unimportant to them. Heaven help them if they had to interrupt their busy social schedule to attend a school function or maybe invite me to spend the upcoming holidays with them, wherever they happened to be in the world at the time.

I suppose someday I'll get over being hurt by them and behave like another one of their retainers. I'm sure that's how they think of me anyway. I'm always an afterthought, until I can be of some service, such as picking them up at the airport. They pretend it's because they want to see me, and I suppose on some level they believe that.

Dad still has Grandma's house in Hancock Park, but they stay at the Hotel Bel Air. They could have asked the concierge to send a car, but that would not ease their conscience about seeing their precious daughter while they're in town. I'd no doubt have to suffer through dinner, listening to all the drivel about their ski trip to the Alps and the progress on their villa in Porto Venere. I've been there twice. How I hate the place. Why that darling, ancient town allowed them to build a monstrosity on that hillside is a mystery to me. No doubt the exchange of money was involved.

Well, okay. Now that they are coming into L.A., I'll bite the bullet and ask them to do the paperwork to release the trust fund my grandmother set up for me. They would turn me down flat if I asked over the phone but face to face, I think I might have a pretty good shot at getting them to do it. I need my money, or I won't be able to break out on my own.

Every bank has turned me down. Wilshire Bank was thrilled with the new executive offices I designed for them last year and which were subsequently featured in Architectural Digest did as well. I was sure they would consider me a good risk. I'm still designing things for their offices. I found out that you can't borrow money unless you don't really need any.

I sure as heck hate to think of working for Lewd Lips for three or four more years. I'll be completely nuts by then. Dear old Mommy and Daddy just have to agree to let me have my dough. It is mine, after all.

I knew I'd better not be late picking them up. Flying first class, they'd be among the first to deplane. They would expect to see me standing right there at baggage claim with a look of adoring anticipation on my face. So, I got in the car and headed for the freeway.

I should have allowed more time. Freeway, what a joke. I have no idea where all those cars are going twenty-four hours a day. It doesn't seem to matter whether it's the middle of the day or the middle of the night. If I was late, I'd either never hear the end of it or get the silent treatment.

With about three minutes to spare, I parked the car and ran for baggage claim. I sucked in several deep breaths and prepared myself.

They entered from the far end of the hall. I had to admit, they are an elegant couple. My mother doesn't look much older than me, and my dad is gorgeous, in spite of his prematurely white hair, or maybe because of it. They spotted me, and those dazzling phony smiles appeared on their faces, all gleaming white teeth against perfectly tanned skin. They looked as if they had nothing but money and have never done a day's work in their spoiled lives. Yes, they have money and haven't worked, so why not look the part?

"Caroline, darling, you look wonderful!"

That's Mother. I'm not allowed to call her *that*, though.

"Hello, Beth, you look fabulous as usual." Her name is Elizabeth. I wondered how much she'd spent at the spa the past year. *Looks like she's had a little work done on her neck.* Last I heard, she was getting those placenta shots or something at that clinic in Romania. The one where gullible, rich people are parted from their money.

"Hi, Dad." I stood on tiptoe and brushed an air kiss past his cheek. The last time I actually kissed him, more than five years ago, he stiffened uncomfortably. I never tried again.

"Good to see you, my dear." He gave my shoulders a perfunctory squeeze, then put his arm around Mommy Dearest.

"How was the flight from Paris?" Like I cared.

"Long," complained Beth. "Service in first class is not what it used to be. The fares get higher, and the service deteriorates. They didn't even have freshly prepared appetizers this time. Would you believe they served us little crackers in plastic wrap with very inferior caviar?"

"Gee, that's rough." I hadn't flown first class since they took me to Italy with them, right after my botched, almost-wedding. "I hope you don't mind if I take you right to your hotel. I have to get back to work. The boss wasn't too happy with me when I left in the middle of the day. I'll meet you for dinner about sevenish. Will that be okay?"

"I'll never understand why you continue to work for that boorish man, darling," Beth said. "You should get married and get on with your life. Are you still seeing that Daniel Kavanaugh? I hope not. An entire family of Presbyterian lawyers. It simply unnerves me."

"Please, Beth, don't start, okay? You can fuss about it over dinner, and they're not Presbyterian lawyers. They're lawyers who happen to be Presbyterians. Let's get your bags, and I'll bring the car around."

Don't lose your cool, Caroline. You want them in a good mood, remember?

We drove in disapproving silence to the hotel. Dad, as usual, said little, and Mommy said volumes with her attitude and body language. She must hate me for being such an inconvenience in her life.

Excuse me for living.

The general manager greeted them at the graceful entrance of the Bel Air Hotel and fawned over them while I popped my trunk and began pulling out the bags. A red-faced bellman rushed over and apologized for not being Johnny-on-the-spot. Mamacita glared, spun around and huffed into the lobby.

I must have done *something* to disappoint her. What, I don't know. Probably touching the luggage that the lowly bellman should have handled. Father gave me an apologetic nod and said they expected to see me in their suite by seven. I quashed the urge to bow and say, "As you wish, Sire."

When I arrived at work, Tiffany warned me that The Fiend was in a rare mood. I snorted and asked her how she could tell. She rolled her eyes, indicating with a little walking movement of her fingers that he was fast approaching.

"Did we have a nice Friday afternoon off, Clayton?" Sarcasm dripped from his fat lips.

"Yes, wonderful," I chirped. "How was yours?"

"You're living dangerously," he warned. He's always warning me about something. "Paulsen called while you were out. He wants the drawings on those wall units today. The owner of the company is flying in first thing in the morning. She wants to see how her new suite is progressing. Get your ass over there and go over the plans with him. Make him look good with the old bat. He sends us a lot of referrals."

I waited patiently for him to stop blabbing. "You mean he sends *me* lots of referrals."

"Yeah, whatever. Just move it. I promised him you'd be there by four. You're late."

He swaggered away, and Tiffany looked at me under the bottom of her eyebrows and shook her head ever so slightly. I wrinkled my nose at his back, and she giggled.

"Tif?" He growled. "You not busy enough?" He entered his lair and slammed the door.

"God, he's really having a good day, isn't he?"

"All day," she groaned.

"Have you been working on the Sentinel job at all?" I ask, as I put materials in my portfolio and briefcase.

"I went through and scoped out all the area for the marble, but I couldn't finish it. I'll try to wrap it up Monday morning. I think you should consider taking the marble all the way to the glass doors. It would raise the cost but would look great. Maybe you can get them to go for it."

"Re-sketch it and we'll present it to them both ways," I said. The kid was showing me some good stuff. "I gotta scram to see Paulsen. I won't be back this afternoon. By the time I'm finished with him, I'll barely have time to run home and change. I'm having dinner with my parents this evening, and I cannot be late."

I grabbed the drawings folder and headed for the door.

"Thanks for leaving me alone to cope with Captain Charm again. Others around here are no help."

"You can handle it," I assured her, over my shoulder.

∽

After the meeting with Paulsen, I rushed back to my apartment to change. I had to wear something that would meet with Beth's approval. It might make my request go down a little easier. I turned the lock on my door and flew into my apartment.

"Hey, babe, you're running late, aren't you?" Danny's voice startled me. He sat on the sofa and closed his laptop. "I was about to call your folks and tell them we might be a little bit late."

I slapped my hand on my chest. "Danny, you scared the bejabbers out of me." I gasped. "We?"

"Your dad called and invited me to join them. That's okay, isn't it?" Daniel was scrumptious in his black pinstripe with a white silk shirt and the new tie I bought him.

I looked him up and down, shook my head, and my grin was wide. I was so glad to see him.

"What?"

"Daniel Kavanaugh, you're the sexiest man on the planet."

"Yeah?" He cocked his head and gave me the Kavanaugh smile.

"Yeah, you are." I gave him a peck on the cheek. "I was planning to discuss some business with them. I'm going to ask them to release my trust fund, so I'll have the money to get my business started."

"I'll opt out then, if you prefer." He raised his hands and backed up a step.

"No, it's okay. You come. You're my moral support." I went into the bedroom and undressed. I jumped in the shower, slipped, and nearly fell on my butt. Hurriedly, I pulled my hair up out of the way. I didn't have time to wash it. It takes forever to dry, and I was really running late.

I put my face on and stood in front of the mirror, tugging my hair this way and that, trying to do something with it. "God, this is making me nuts!"

"What is?" Danny walked into the bedroom and leaned against the door frame. He smiled at me standing there in my underwear.

"This hair, I can't do anything with it!" I pinned it up on one side and tried to clamp it down with a comb. "What do you think?" I turned and faced him.

He looked at me with a crooked, sexy little smile and winked. "Just let it hang there, babe. You know the wilder it looks, the more I love it."

"You're a real big help, Kavanaugh." I threw down the brush and pulled on the little midnight blue dress. "Here, zip me."

Daniel dutifully pulled up the zipper and nuzzled the back of my neck. "Mmm, you smell great." He slid his hands down my bare arms and pressed himself against me.

I smacked him playfully and wriggled out of his embrace. "Don't even think about it. We're already late." I put on my grandmother's diamond earrings and bracelet.

He jingled his car keys. "Okay, if that's the way it's going to be. Let's go face Lizzie and Lyle. Give me a wink or a nod anytime you want me to jump in and add my two cents worth. I'm on your side." He gave me a little pat on the bottom.

"They'd have a cow if you ever called them that."

"Trust me, babe. I won't slip up. I'm a sneaky-slimy, bottom-feeding lawyer. Remember?"

"Oh, yeah, I forgot you know how to handle yourself when the piranha circle."

∽

We were halfway to the car when I ran back to my apartment to retrieve the business plan Tiffany and I prepared for the bank. I was a nervous wreck, and I hadn't even broached the subject with them yet.

The first thing Mother said when we arrived at their suite was, "Really, Caroline. Can't you do something with that hair? I'm going to call and make an appointment for you with Alfredo. He can do wonders with unruly hair."

"No thanks, Beth." I reached over and took Dan's arm. "Danny likes it this way. He says it's sexy."

"How nice." Lemon juice was sweet as sugar compared to Mommy's tone.

Danny smiled charmingly at the sour look of disapproval she flashed him.

"Nice dress, dear," she added grudgingly, having dismissed Daniel's taste in hair styles.

"Thanks. You sent it on my last birthday. I thought you'd like to see it on me."

I hoped my smile passed as a sincere.

All the while Beth and I were sparring, Danny and Dad uncomfortably observed us.

"Yes, I remember now," Pops spoke up. "We purchased that dress at the De Salle designer studio in Milan when Elizabeth selected her new wardrobe last spring. The color is charming with your eyes."

He was obviously relieved that he could add something to the conversation. How he knew it would look "charming with my eyes" was a mystery, because the last time I was with them I wore contacts that colored them brown. I was not sure he even knew what my natural eye color was.

Daniel cleared his throat and said that perhaps we should be heading out to the restaurant.

Mother agreed, adding that Wolfie hated it when they arrived late. He was personally preparing a special dish for us. It was most important that we be civilized and get there on time to chat with him before dinner. He is, after all, a busy and important restaurateur, and we should respect that.

Mother always lectured. She was convinced I had only a partial brain in my head, and she's never accepted that Daniel is next to being a genius. I guess she thought that just because one could think, one wasn't necessarily imbued with all the proper social graces. After all, it is so very important what others think about one, isn't it? One must always be aware of the impression one is making.

Except perhaps one's own child. When would I ever get past caring what they thought of me?

In spite of Beth's insufferable pretentiousness, dinner was pleasant. Wolfie was, as always, an amusing and gentle host. He even asked why Danny and I hadn't been in to see him in over a year. I was surprised he remembered us.

Danny said, "We haven't dined out much lately. We're both so busy we usually end up with some simple dinner prepared at home."

"How domestic," Mommy commented.

Wolfie graciously confessed that he usually preferred simple home-cooked meals himself.

The dinner *was* special. He started us off with fresh oysters in some kind of green chili sauce and black pepper mignonette. The entrée of roasted cumin lamb on lentil salad, with fresh coriander and yogurt mango chutney, was simply marvelous. For a while, I forgot my apprehension over the money request.

I nodded and smiled with polite attentiveness while my parents rambled on and on about their boring, pointless lives. The time passed bearably.

Not being a fan of oysters, Danny ordered the spicy corn chowder as his appetizer. I could tell Mother felt offended when he didn't go along with the rest of us. He said he liked Wolfie's corn chowder and saw no reason to try something different. He's a proponent of the 'if it ain't broke, don't fix it' school of food.

Dan attacked the lamb entrée with gusto and ordered some decadent cheesecake invention for dessert. I wished I had his wonderful guilt free appetite.

He acted as if he were interested in what my parents had to say. I have to hand it to him. He's the grease between the gears of them and me.

Finally, it was time to face the music. I excused myself to visit the ladies' room and take a moment to go over my little speech. I was pretty sure I'd covered all the objections they could possibly come up with. Hopefully, I would leave tonight with their agreement to release my trust fund.

When I returned to the table, Dad and Dan were discussing golf. It was something they were both good at and enjoyed. Beth was nowhere to be seen, and then I spotted her across the room schmoozing with a soap opera queen and her oh-so-young escort. I'm always amazed at how many people are Beth's "best friends."

"Well, Caroline dear," she purred as she returned to our table, "how are you managing at your little job?"

I gritted my teeth. "As a matter of fact, Beth, I'm seriously thinking of starting my own business. I have it all planned out." I reached into my purse to remove the business plan and slid it under my plate. My heart banged against my ribs and a fine trickle of sweat slid between my shoulder blades.

"Really," she replied woodenly. She gazed about the room to make sure she hadn't missed anyone important.

I glanced at Danny, and he gave me a wink of encouragement.

"Yes." I swallowed, then pasted a smile on my face. "It's time to strike out on my own, Beth, Dad. I have a good reputation and a number of loyal customers. One of my colleagues at work is ready to go with me. She's a talented designer and has a degree in business."

"How interesting," she said with absolute disinterest. "Daniel dear, have you decided to join your father's law firm, or are you still acting the young rebel?"

I glanced at Danny, wondering how he was going to handle that little put-down.

"As a matter of fact," he answered, stifling a smile, "I've recently made partner. Looks like I'll be staying put for the foreseeable future with Knight Kristensen *Kavanaugh*."

"Congratulations, old man," Father said. "I should think you and Caroline will be thinking about settling down now."

"Actually," I interrupted, "I want to talk to you both about my inheritance, my trust fund. I know I'm not due to receive the principal for three more years, but right now I need about a hundred thousand dollars to finance my new business."

There. I said it.

Beth's face froze, and she stiffened. "That's completely out of the question," she stated with a wave of dismissal.

"Definitely out of the question," echoed Father, nodding at Mommy for her approval.

"But why? It's my money." In spite of myself, I sounded a tad shrill.

"Well, for one thing, you have no experience in running a business," Beth said. "It would be very risky and most unwise. It's our responsibility to protect and preserve the money your grandmother set aside for you. We could not consider letting you squander it on a whim."

"A whim! Is that what you think?" I had to rein in my feelings because I'd nearly shouted. I took a sip of wine and a couple of slow breaths.

Mother patted my hand and said, "Perhaps I chose the wrong word, dear."

"I've thought this through carefully," I said with all the calm I could muster. "I know I can make a success of it. I've drawn up a complete business plan." I pulled the paperwork from under my plate and held in a trembling hand. "I would not be squandering the money. There is risk in starting any new business. I know that, but I'm *good* at what I do. If Gramma were alive, she'd gladly let me have the starter funds. It's not as if I'm planning to go out and buy lotto tickets. I plan to build something solid for my future. I thought you'd be pleased."

She didn't look pleased. "Caroline, dear, don't create a scene," she whispered. "What will people think?"

"I don't give a damn what people think, Mother. For once, why don't you have a little faith in me? Why is it you never recognize anything I do has value? I know I can be successful." I thrust the business plan in their direction. "I wouldn't even consider doing it if I thought I wasn't capable. I can make it work."

I glanced at Danny, and he gave me another nod of encouragement and rubbed his knee against mine.

Daddy pleaded, "Caroline, be calm, darling. It isn't that we doubt your ability. We think you need a little more maturity and experience before foolishly risking your inheritance."

I almost yelled. "Foolishly? Didn't you hear anything I said—either of you? Can't you just once have some faith in my judgment? It's *my* money. She left it for *me*. Why do you even care what I do with it?"

"In another three years, you may do with it as you like," Mother stated. "For now, we have no choice but to say no." She wore her authoritative, judgmental face. The one that used to make me stare at the toes of my Mary Janes and wonder why I had said or done such an unacceptable thing.

Danny shifted in his chair. I thought he was about to jump to my defense, so I bumped his knee to stop him.

"Yes, you do have a choice. I guess you've made it." I threw my napkin on the table and stood so abruptly I knocked over the chair. Every head in the room turned in our direction, mortifying Beth and Lyle. Grabbing my purse and paperwork, I headed for the door.

"Caroline, babe, wait," Daniel said as he caught up with me. "We came in my car. I can't leave them stranded here."

"Sorry, Danny, I have to leave now. I have to go. I don't care what they do."

By now, I was out the door and had signaled for the doorman to get me a taxi. One pulled up, and I jumped in, leaving Daniel standing perplexed at the curb.

CHAPTER 25

Daniel

After Caroline's cab left, Daniel stood outside the restaurant for a moment, then walked back inside. Liz and Lyle had their heads together, smiling phony smiles, nodding reassuringly to people around the room, pretending nothing had happened. He figured they were trying to diffuse any idea that there had been a disagreement between them and their darling daughter.

"She took a cab," he stated.

He sat and leaned back in his chair, wondering what he was still doing there.

"She'll see the wisdom of our judgment," Lizzie said. "This little whim will pass." She smiled and tickled her fingertips at someone who'd just entered the dining room.

"Yes, of course it will."

Lyle, the echo. Every time he utters a word, he looked to Lizzie for approval.

"Perhaps I should get you back to your hotel," Dan suggested.

He didn't want to spend one minute with these shallow nitwits than wasn't necessary, and he was determined not to say or do anything that would add to Care's grief. The sooner he was shed of her parents the better.

"That's very kind, old man," Lyle said. "But we promised our friends across the room that we'd stay and have a nightcap with them."

"Yes," agreed Liz. "We haven't seen them since they were our guests last spring at the villa on Elba. Perhaps you'd like to meet them?" She gave Dan a look that told him there was no way in hell she wanted to introduce him to her *dear* friends.

"Thanks, but I'll pass. I'd like to make sure Caroline is home safely, and I still have some work to do tonight." Anger at their cold indifference burned behind his eyes.

"I wish Caroline weren't so emotional. She's always had that little character flaw," Beth said. "I believe she takes after Lyle's mother."

"Would that be the grandmother who left her the inheritance?" he inquired blandly, while his blood simmered.

"Yes," Lyle said. "She was a dear, of course. A remarkable woman actually but had a propensity to get worked up about the most trivial things."

He looked at his wife for her approval once again.

Daniel couldn't let that pass. "The same grandmother who raised your daughter while you two were out jet-setting around the world?"

"Well, yes...but I don't see that is any of..."

"The only adult in her world who gave her unconditional love? Until I came along, that is."

Liz's face became alarmingly blotchy. An unflattering color for the former beauty who hung on to her youth by every means money could buy. She was so enraged she was speechless. She pushed her chair back and stood. "We don't have to listen to this."

Dan was more than angry. "Sit your bony lipo sucked ass back in that chair, Liz," he commanded in a menacing tone. "That is, unless you'd like me to raise my voice and embarrass you in the presence of all your *dear friends*. I'm not finished."

"Now see here, old man...," Lyle began.

"Tell me, Lyle, where did that phony British accent of yours come from? You were born in Pittsburgh, right? Or was it Cleveland?"

"How dare you!" Liz hissed.

"How dare I?" Rage roared inside Daniel. "How dare I? You people amaze me. You're the parents of a beautiful, intelligent, and talented woman, and you've spent a lifetime making her feel unloved and never quite good enough for you."

A smiling waiter approached the table. "Go away," Dan ordered. Like a wavelet in the surf, he quickly dissolved into the frothy edges of the crowded dining room.

"Who the hell do you think..." Lyle tried once again to assert his manhood.

"Who am I? I'm the man who loves Caroline, the man who wants to marry her and have a life with her. You think she's overly emotional? You don't even know her. You've made her afraid to show any emotion, to risk loving anyone. You weren't even on her side when she was jilted by that cheating comes-from-a-good-family bastard you tried to marry her off to."

"You keep your voice down, you crude boor." Liz's voice dripped with venom. "Our family is none of your business."

"Save your theatrics for someone else. You think your inherited, correction, married-into wealth, entitles you to special privilege and respect? I clean up messes for pretentious jerks like you for a living. A very good living, I might add."

Lyle straightened, his face flushed. "I'm horrified my daughter ever took up with a man like you."

"Took up with me? You mean fucking me for the past three years." That crudity felt real good rolling off his tongue.

Liz paled and fell back in her chair.

Daniel dipped a finger in his ice water and flicked it in her face. "Don't faint, Lizzie. You'll embarrass me." He was on a roll. She had it coming.

Lyle stood abruptly. "That's enough, young man. I think you'd better leave." He finally found his balls, and he meant business this time.

Smiling his slickest lawyer smile, Daniel stood and reached for his hand. "Might as well make it look cordial. For appearances, right?" He clutched Lyle's hand, quickly dropped it, and made a point of wiping his on a napkin.

Smiling sincerely this time, Dan waved and nodded to Wolfie as he left.

The cool California night air braced him. He clenched and unclenched his fists while waiting for the valet to bring the car.

Once inside, he punched Care's icon on his cell phone.

"Hello, Danny." Her voice sounded tired, defeated.

"I'm on my way over. I left your folks with their friends." He began to regret losing his cool with them in spite of how good it felt. He hadn't helped her cause by telling them off.

"Go on home, Danny," she replied wearily. "I have a monster headache. I'm going to take a bath and go to bed."

"My briefcase is there." No way would he leave her alone.

"Okay. Well, use your key. When you get here, I'll probably be in the tub."

"All right, sweetheart. Take something for that headache."

Daniel pulled into the late-night traffic and maneuvered around slower cars. It seemed to take longer than usual to reach Care's neighborhood. He was concerned about her.

∽

The sound of running water greeted him when he entered her front door. He dropped his keys next to his briefcase and removed his jacket and shoes.

As he opened the bathroom door, she looked up, sighed, put her head back, and closed her eyes.

"You okay, babe? That was brutal."

"I've survived them this long. I guess I'll survive them again." She sighed and rolled her head from side to side. Tears brimmed on her lower lids. She swiped them away.

Dan knelt behind her and massaged her shoulders and neck. "I'm sorry you had to go through that." He felt her tension as she trembled. At last, he thought. In the three years they'd been together, he'd never seen her cry.

"Go ahead, babe. Let it all come out." He leaned in and kissed her on the shoulder, rested his head against hers.

She stiffened, slapped at the water, and stopped crying. "You don't know anything about it, Danny! Please, just go on home."

That hurt. It felt like she'd socked him right in the gut. He lifted his hands off her and stood. "Sure. Fine."

She could go right ahead and sit in her bathtub, building that little fortress around her heart. He'd had it up to here with Caroline and her pinhead parents.

He slumped on the sofa to put on his shoes. Rubbing a hand across the luxurious fabric of the seat cushion calmed him. He remembered teasing her about the money she spent for the sofa and had never told her how much he liked it. He loved everything about the room, just as he loved everything about her. It wasn't him she was lashing out against. It was them.

Bone tired, he flopped back, dropped his head on the back of her sofa. Staring at the ceiling, he wondered what was next for them. Was there a *next* for them?

CHAPTER 26
Caroline

I'd spent enough time in the tub bawling and feeling sorry for myself, and I deeply regretted taking it out on Danny. Sometimes I'm a real nincompoop. The water was cooling, and I had to get out of the tub and take something stronger than aspirin.

I decided to make a cup of tea and stare at the boob tube for a while, then go to bed. I was shocked to see Danny sitting there watching me when I walked into the living room.

"Danny?" We stared at each other across the room.

"That's me, babe, good old dependable Danny." He seemed defeated. His shirt was open at the collar and his tie was all loose and lopsided. "Come here."

"Danny, I..."

"Just shut up and come here." He held his hand out to me. "Please."

Those couldn't be tears in his eyes.

I crossed the room and stood before him. He pulled me onto his lap. I tensed a little as he put his hand on the back of my head and pushed it onto his shoulder.

"Relax, Caroline. It's me, Dan." He rubbed his hand up and down my back and kissed me on the forehead. "Oh, babe," he croaked.

His sympathy flowed into me. I clutched his arm and sobbed. I didn't want to cry anymore. For a split-second, I hated him for making me cry again. I pushed against him and tried to stand, but he held on tight.

"No, sit still," he whispered. "It'll be fine."

"Danny, please let me go." I sobbed. "This is stupid."

I wasn't sure whether I was angrier at my parents for being who they were or at Danny for loving me. I didn't feel lovable. I had a good look at myself in the bathroom mirror when I put on my robe. I didn't look lovable.

"Go ahead and cry, babe. You won't feel better until you finish it. I have nothing but time." He rocked me side-to-side, rubbing his hand over my back, bottom, and leg. I melted against his chest, helpless to hold back the tears. He made comforting little sounds and squeezed me hard.

Finally, I began to breathe normally. Danny was quiet. He kept holding me and rested his head against mine. I felt his heart beating, strong, steady, reliable. Danny's heart, beating not just for him, but for me. I loved him, and I didn't deserve him. Why should he have to go through all my crap?

I was all wrong for Danny. He'd be better off with someone like Flynn's wife, Claire. Someone kind and gentle, someone who wanted a big family, and enjoyed being a full-time homemaker. Anybody but me.

"Don't start that now," he whispered.

"Start what?"

"Over analyzing yourself." He gave me another squeeze.

"How do you...?"

"It's okay to feel what you're feeling right now, Care. Can't you trust me? This is between us. There's nobody else here, just you and me." He tilted my head up.

"I look hideous."

"You look beautiful."

"Don't tease me."

"Can you imagine how much I love this raggedy old robe, and the woman in it?" He smiled then and slid his hand inside, stroking my hip. "You could put on a few pounds, though."

I smiled back and rested my head on his shoulder again. "Why do you put up with me?"

"Damned if I know. You're a real big pain in the neck." He continued rubbing that big hand up and down. It felt so good, so warm, so right.

"I got tears and snot all over your shirt and tie."

"Yeah, pretty gross."

"My headache's gone."

"Good."

I twisted against him and rubbed my hand on his chest. "Do you want to go to bed?"

"Nope."

"What do you want to do?"

"This."

"Okay."

CHAPTER 27

Matthew

Ah, yes. That's better. They shouldn't be angry with each other. It was the circumstances of the meeting with her parents that had upset them.

While I am delighted in how they've mended their breach, I have the odd sensation I'm indulging in voyeurism. Of course, that is nonsense. I am merely doing my job. It is strange how taking on mortal form has affected my thought processes.

In all my being as the Kavanaugh family companion, I don't ever recall feeling uncomfortable while being present in the most intimate situations. I've been with my charges every moment of their lives.

I will discuss my feelings with some of my more experienced colleagues.

CHAPTER 28

Daniel

Dan had the coffee going and was about to whip up a batch of Danny's Famous French Toast when he spotted Caroline leaning against her kitchen doorway. He poured coffee for them and carried the cups to the table.

She opened the fridge and pulled out the creamer. "It's barely six o'clock." She sat down.

"Yep."

"I have huge bags under my eyes."

"Yep."

"Is that all you have to say? Yep?"

"Yep."

She grinned big. Her smile would light up any room.

God, she is beautiful.

"You bastard." She blew on her coffee and continued to smile.

"You don't know the half of it." He was about to tell her what had transpired between him and her parents. "Hungry?"

"I could eat a mountain of your French toast. I hope that's what you were about to fix. You did say you wanted to fatten me up." She leaned back and took a sip of coffee. "Mmm, good, vanilla bean, reminds me of Seattle."

"The time you were with *me*, I hope." He couldn't help it. Even though he'd managed to break Angeli's nose, and it didn't make sense anymore, he was still jealous.

She blew on her coffee. "Let's talk about something else."

"Claire had a baby girl yesterday. Ten pounds, red hair, blue eyes." He was so proud you'd have thought it was his kid. "They named her Danielle Claire."

She stopped sipping, "Danielle?" Her eyes grew wide with astonishment. "They named their baby after you?"

"Yeah, well, Flynn loves his baby brother. I know it seems like all he ever wants to do is pound on me, but that's his way of showing his brotherly love."

"Wow, finally a girl. Do you think they'll quit now?"

"I suspect they might, but you never know." He flashed a stage wink in her direction. "They love making babies."

"Can we go see them at the hospital?"

That surprised him. It was the first time Care had shown much interest in any of the infants. She liked all the kids, but Flynn's Ryan was the only one special to her.

"They're home. We can go there later if you want." He beat the eggs, had already laid out thick slices of cinnamon bread.

"Have a baby on Friday and home on Saturday? Woo." She went to the refrigerator and took out a bowl of strawberries and pulled a bottle of maple syrup from the cupboard. "I'll set the table. Get a move on, lover boy. I'm starved."

∼

Danny watched in awe. She packed away as much food as he and still wouldn't gain an ounce. She was the only woman he'd ever known who wasn't obsessed about dieting and 'Do I look fat in this?'

He cleared his throat. "Not that I want to introduce an unpleasant subject on top of this—if I may say so myself—great breakfast, but after you left the restaurant last night, I went back inside and talked to Lizzie and Lyle for a few minutes. I don't think I did your cause any good." He tried for a contrite expression.

"And what?" She stared at him and made little circles with her fork.

"Suffice it to say—they didn't like me before—and they like me even less now." He swallowed some coffee.

"Are you going to tell me, or are we going to play twenty questions?" She picked up their plates and carried them to the sink.

Dan held his cup for a refill. "I told them they were a couple of jerks, and they didn't appreciate or deserve you."

He was still holding out his cup, but she stopped in her tracks and held the coffee pot suspended in midair.

"You told them they were jerks." She winced.

"Yeah...sorry." He failed at the contrite face again.

"Sorry you said it, or sorry they're jerks?"

He still held his cup in front of her. "Both. Are you going to pour that?"

"No." She walked back to the coffeemaker and set the pot on the hot plate. Her back was turned, both her hands rested on the countertop. She lowered her head, and her shoulders shook, accompanied by choking sounds.

He jumped up and went to her. "I'm sorry." He gathered her into his arms. "I'll apologize to them."

"Oh, no you won't!" She turned and faced him.

Her smile was a mile wide and what he thought were tears, was laughter. "I owe you an apology for leaving you alone with them. I wish I'd been there when you told them off. It would have been priceless."

"You're not mad at me?"

"How could I be mad at somebody who makes such great French toast?"

CHAPTER 29

Caroline

Flynn answered the door when Dan knocked. He looked like he hadn't had much sleep, which I suspected was true. A smattering of gray at the temples gave him a sexy, debonair look. Liam and Mary had produced a crop of fine-looking sons. Flynn was forty-two, I think, and a bit shy of Danny in height, but every bit as powerful looking. They embraced in a bear hug and pounded each other on the back.

Danny gave him a big kiss on the cheek. "You done good, big brother. Now show us my namesake and the happy mama."

"She's not your namesake," Flynn said. "We liked the name."

Landing a playful punch in his brother's midsection, Danny said, "Like hell."

"Hey!" Flynn smacked Danny on the cheek. "Go easy there, squirt, I haven't slept for two days."

"So what? Claire did all the work. You're a guilty bystander." Danny danced around Flynn like a boxer, feinting jabs at his face. "You think you can take me? Come on, old man."

I watched the two of them, remembering when I had first observed Danny and his brothers in action. I'd had the impression they hated each other. Roughhousing was foreign to me then. Now, I was pretty much used to it.

I pushed myself between them. "Can't you two behave? Come on, Flynn. Where's the baby?"

He swept me up in a crushing hug. "Hello, sexy woman. Gimme a kiss. I deserve it." He picked me up and started for the bedroom. "This is the best-looking kid we've made yet."

"Put me down. It might be catching!" I tried to sound annoyed, but it came out as laughter instead.

He made growling sounds while chomping at my neck. The whole damn bunch of Kavanaugh brothers were clowns.

Claire watched us from the open door at the end of the hallway. Flynn carried me through to their bedroom and unceremoniously dumped me at the foot of the big king bed. She merely smiled while stroking a tiny, fuzzy red head. Raucous scenes were nothing new in this household.

"You want to hold her?" Claire asked me. "She's not asleep, I just finished feeding her." She held the baby out to me.

I stopped breathing for a couple of seconds.

"I want to hold her," Danny said, intercepting the infant. He held her in his big hands, supporting her head, a broad smile growing on his face. "Hey, beautiful girl, I'm your Uncle Dan." He nuzzled her downy cheek, then expertly rested her on his shoulder and gently patted her back. She burped.

"A true Kavanaugh." I stood and walked around Danny to get a better look at her. The thought of holding her terrified me. Babies and I are from two different planets. I'm not comfortable around kids until they were two years old, *at least.*

"She looks a lot like Ryan," I said, unable to think of anything else to say. She was all pink and doughy, like if you pushed your finger into her fat little arm, it would leave a dent.

Danielle had fallen instantly asleep on Danny's shoulder. Her tiny mouth was open, and she drooled. He rested his cheek on her head and sat on the bed next to Claire. "She's beautiful, Claire. Perfect," he said.

God, Danny would make such a good daddy, the way he held the baby, so confident, so natural.

"Yes, she is," Claire whispered, reaching out to take her.

Danny carefully placed the infant in her mother's arms, then stroked Claire's cheek with his finger.

"You're amazing," he murmured. He kissed her and stood. Reaching for my hand, he pulled me to his side and put his arm around my shoulders.

All I could think at that moment was that Danny would probably be a father by now if he were with anyone other than me. I was cheating him. He deserved someone who fit better into the lifestyle he was born into. Family was essential to him. What could I possibly offer him that would be so lasting? To my horror, the tears started.

Claire gazed at me with a serene Madonna smile. "I want to cry, too, when I look at her," she said. "An infant is such a beautiful, awesome thing. She's a miracle." She cuddled little Danielle to her breast.

Flynn stroked his wife's hair. It was such a simple gesture but said everything about the depth of their love for each other. I put my hand to my mouth to stifle a sob. I felt like such an idiot. I looked at Danny in desperation.

He rescued me. "We have to get going. Mom and Dad are expecting us about now. I promised we'd give them a hand with your other three miscreants this afternoon."

He pulled me in the direction of the doorway. "Get some sleep, big brother. I have a feeling little Danielle will be awake and lively around three in the morning."

Flynn crawled onto the bed next to Claire and the baby, lowering his head onto the pillow with an exhausted sigh. "You got that right."

Claire patted his arm and beamed at us. "He's so tired. I think we'll all take a nap now. Thanks for coming."

When we got back into the car, I said, "I'm turning into a real blubber puss. I don't know what's the matter with me."

He squeezed my knee. "I love you."

"Yeah?"

"Yeah, you're a real softy, babe. You have a great mind and a great heart. It's a dangerous combination."

That was a frightening thought, me, a heart? For reasons which I couldn't fathom, I *had* been a lot nicer lately. Scary.

∼

Ryan was skateboarding on the sidewalk in front of Mom and Dad's house. The two younger boys were nowhere to be seen. He spotted us and made a beeline in our direction. Danny parked the car.

"Hi, Caroline," he puffed, turning red from the neck up.

"Hey, good lookin', you going to give me another skateboard lesson today?"

"Sure!" The blush faded as Danny joined us. They exchanged a few playful jabs, the Kavanaugh male ritual.

"My woman gets hurt, and you're going to pay, little man," Danny warned. He towered over Ryan menacingly.

"Ah, she won't get hurt." There went the blush again. "She's a natural."

"Go away, Danny. Ryan and I have things to do." I gave him a shove.

The front door flew open, and Ryan's little brothers came exploding down the front walk, hurling themselves at Danny. They squealed in delight as he grabbed one of them in each arm and spun them around like a carnival ride.

Mary stood in the doorway, arms crossed, shaking her head. "Thank goodness you're here. Those boys have worn your father to a frazzle. Come on in," she called to me, "I'm putting the finishing touches on dinner."

"Ryan's going to give me my next skateboard lesson," I answered. "Call if you want us to help with something."

"You two have fun. I'll put Daniel to work. Looks like he has some excess energy to burn." She looked at her *baby*. "Don't you, dear?"

"Yes, ma'am." Danny kissed his mother on the cheek and carried the two squealing boys into the house.

"That was close," I said to Ryan. "Let's move on down the block before they find some work for us to do."

"Totally." He laughed and trotted ahead of me, the big skateboard tucked under his arm.

I had the urge to ruffle my fingers through his sweaty red hair, but didn't. He'd die if I treated him like one of the littler kids. He was my boyfriend, after all, we were soulmates.

Dropping the skateboard on the sidewalk, he hopped on and turned to look back at me grinning that great Kavanaugh grin.

"Come on, slowpoke." He raced ahead of me.

I laughed and jogged along behind him, glad I'd put on my sneakers that morning. He slowed as we got to the corner and flipped the skateboard expertly into the air, catching it neatly. Time to head back home.

"Show off." I was breathless when I caught up to him.

"Nah, you can do it, Caroline. I'll show you how."

For the next fifteen minutes or so, Ryan patiently demonstrated how to jump on and off the board while it rolled along the sidewalk beside him. I'd always mounted while it was stopped, then pushed off with one foot to get it rolling.

"Okay, you try it now," he said. "It's easy once you get the hang of it."

"That's what you say." My answer oozed skepticism.

"Give it a little shove. When it's rolling fast enough, hop on." He made it sound so simple and safe. He looked at me eagerly. He was convinced I could do it as easily as he had. How could I disappoint him?

"Okay, here goes." I pushed the board with my toe, clenched my teeth and hopped on. I screeched gleefully as I cruised ahead without falling. Ryan ran along beside me, laughing and cheering.

I looked up and noticed Mary standing on the sidewalk, gesturing for us to come to the house. I waved back and gave myself a little push for more speed. Looking down, I saw a big crack in the sidewalk looming ahead and quickly jumped off the board, sending it flying down the pavement.

Ryan spurted after it. A neighbor's car backed out of their long driveway ahead of him. He didn't see it.

Mary shouted, "Ryan!"

"I'm coming, Gramma," he yelled, eyes on the skateboard.

The car kept backing out.

My heart caught in my throat. "Ryan, stop!"

"It's okay, I got it." Breathless, he ran straight into the path of the car.

I froze. Ryan and the car were on a certain collision course, and I was helpless to stop him. For a split-second, everything went into slow motion as if I was looking through water. Then, I swear to God, Matthew stood on the sidewalk in front of Ryan, between him and the car. He put out his foot and stopped the board. Ryan reached down and swept it up. I squeezed my eyes shut, clutched my chest, and shook.

"Got it!" Ryan shouted. "Come on, Caroline, Gramma made my favorite thing today, cheeseburgers."

I opened my eyes to see him dodging expertly around the front of the car, waving at the startled neighbor.

I couldn't breathe. Grateful tears spurted into my eyes. I whipped around, looking for Matthew. He wasn't there. The neighbors' car moved down the street and Ryan had almost reached Mary. He turned around, skipping backwards, gestured for me to hurry.

Holy shit! Now I'm seeing things. "Dammit, Caroline, get a grip," I muttered out loud and dashed the tears away. I'll never, ever have children. How could anyone possibly survive if something happened to their child? Here I am hallucinating and crying, and he isn't even my kid.

CHAPTER 30

Matthew

Caroline was not supposed to see me. She's overly sensitive to my presence. Her distrust of me is based on this acute perceptiveness. She's convinced there's more to me than the obvious. It puzzles and unnerves her.

The question she asked herself about losing a child is an important one. Yet parents do manage to survive somehow. Don't they? Caroline needn't worry. She may choose whether or not to be a mother. What she doesn't understand, however, is that one does not have to be the parent of children to care desperately for them, to worry about them, and to suffer when something bad happens to one of them.

Caroline has an affinity with children. Her former G.A., oh, did I mention Caroline has been transferred to me? No? Well, she has, and her old G.A. told me that her childhood experiences have made her extremely sensitive to the tender psyche of a child.

He related an endearing story about a ballet recital in which she was a featured dancer when she was seven. Her father promised her that he would be in the audience when she made her debut as a little ballerina. Overjoyed, she could barely stand still from the excitement. Her grandmother fussed with her costume and hair when the phone rang.

"Hello? Yes, Lyle, are you on your way? We're about to leave for the school. What? Hold on a moment. Caroline, dear, would you go into my room and look for that nice pink ribbon I bought yesterday? I think it's on my dressing table."

Caroline skipped out of the room and stopped outside the door when she heard her grandmother's voice rise in anger.

"Lyle, I swear by all that's holy if you do not attend this recital, I shall disinherit you! Oh, yes, I do mean it, son. You will *not* disappoint this child again. Do I make myself clear? Good. Be on time. It starts at seven sharp."

Caroline was puzzled. She couldn't understand how her daddy could be disinterred when he wasn't even dead. She knew from watching Perry Mason re-runs with Gramma, that sometimes dead people had to be dug up so that the police could find out which bad person had killed them. She must have misunderstood what her grandmother said. She shrugged and skipped down the long hallway to her grandmother's room.

When she returned with the ribbon, she stood patiently as Gramma wove it through her French braid. When they left for the recital, Gramma admonished her to sit still in the car, such was her excitement. It would be one of the happiest days of her life when her parents appeared backstage after the performance with a sweet little bouquet of flowers. Her mother didn't hug her but kissed her on the cheek. Daddy picked her up and smiled proudly. It really takes so little for a parent to make a child happy, to feel worthy and important.

CHAPTER 31

Caroline

All during Mary's tasty dinner, I studied Ryan and his two brothers. When did it happen? When had I begun to care so much about Flynn's and Claire's children? Now that I thought of it, I cared for all of Danny's nieces and nephews.

Danny watched me curiously, probably wondering what was going on in my head, while he and his dad chatted about golf, the Lakers and debated points of law.

Ryan piped up. "Grampa's teaching me how to golf. He bought a big bag of Whiffle balls and a net for the backyard." He looked at me expectantly. "Want to come out and hit some with us after we eat?"

"I think I should help your grandmother do the dishes first."

"Gramma says you're not very handy around a kitchen."

"Ryan!" Mary's head shot up, the flush of embarrassment blooming on her cheeks.

"Well, you did," he said, probably wondering why she had corrected him.

Liam and Danny were all ears and silly smiles.

I laughed. "And she's absolutely right, too." I winked at Mary. "Your Uncle Danny does most of the kitchen duties around my place."

Ryan wasn't finished. "Are you going to marry Uncle Danny?"

The other adults sat silently, looks passing between them. The two younger boys gazed at me with expectant faces.

Ryan's question gave me a pause, and I punted. "Gee, I thought I'd wait until you were old enough so I could marry you."

"You're teasing me," Ryan said with a little pout. "Daddy said you were never going to marry Uncle Danny. He said you weren't marriage material. Is that true?"

"Well," Liam interrupted heartily, and stood. "I think it's time we went out and practiced that golf swing. Ryan, how about it?"

He and Danny picked up their plates and headed for the kitchen.

"Okay," Ryan answered with a questioning shrug. He picked up his dish and followed them. "Adults always change the subject."

"Go ahead, Ryan," I said after him. "I'll be there in a few minutes. I'm going to show your Gramma that I know my way around a kitchen."

I smiled at Mary, who hastily cleared the table, a look of mortification on her face. Alone in the kitchen, she shook her head in dismay. "Caroline, I'm so embarrassed. You never know what will come out of the mouth of a child."

She put leftovers into plastic bags and containers.

"Don't worry about it, Mom." I opened the dishwasher and began scraping and rinsing dishes.

She explained further, "What I actually said was, some women were handy in a kitchen and some women had other kinds of jobs. I said you had a job that a lot of women couldn't do."

"Mom, you don't need to explain. You don't. He's a sweet kid."

I loaded the dishwasher while she returned to the dining room to retrieve the remains on the table.

When Mary came back to the kitchen, I stopped what I was doing and turned around to face her. "Do you wonder if I'll ever marry Danny?"

"Yes, dear, I do," she answered candidly. "I often think about his happiness and yours. I know he loves you very much." She touched my arm briefly and gave it a little squeeze.

My chest hurt. "I love Danny so much."

"I know you do." She opened the refrigerator and put the leftovers inside.

"Why am I so afraid to marry him then?"

"That's a question I can't answer for you." She closed the refrigerator and studied me. "You should never marry until you're certain in your heart it's right. Even if you know it's utterly right, it's never easy."

"I look at your family, your daughters-in-law, your grandchildren, and I think I'm so different. I can't be like them."

She brushed off her hands. "Yes, you are different. That's precisely why Daniel chose you. Don't you know that?" She tilted her head and a wry smile played across her lips.

"I don't want to be a mother," I confessed, "and Danny would make a wonderful father. I feel I'm cheating him. You should have seen him this morning with little Danielle. I cried when I saw the way he held her." The memory of it made my eyes water.

"You know, dear, you don't have to be a parent to love and enjoy children. Daniel has so many little nieces and nephews, I'm not sure he'd miss being a father all that much." She gazed at me, then reached out and touched my cheek. "Have you talked about this with him?"

"Yes. He says he doesn't care about having children, but I don't believe him." I sighed with dismay.

"You have such a soft heart under all that self-assuredness."

"That's what Danny said."

"My baby's very perceptive." She opened her arms and reached out to me.

"Oh, Mom," I cried as she embraced me. "What should I do?"

"I wish I could answer that," she whispered. "Now," she straightened and became all business, "Ryan is waiting. Go hit some golf balls."

"Yeah, okay." I gave her a wobbly smile and dried my hands. As I turned to leave, she smacked my bottom. That little gesture of affection nearly did me in.

It was pretty late by the time Danny and Mary had the two younger boys bathed and in bed. I sat in the study with Ryan and Liam, watching Dirty Jobs. We laughed and cringed when Mike Rowe crawled out of the sewer pipe covered with sludge and a big smile on his face. The episode ended right at the top of the hour.

Liam ruffled Ryan's hair and suggested it was time for him to go to bed.

Ryan got up from the sofa reluctantly, grumbling that he should be allowed to stay up much later than his two baby brothers.

"Good night, Caroline," he mumbled. His head hung in defeat.

"Good night, handsome."

He grinned and blushed. "Good night, Grandpa."

"Good night, son. Send your Uncle Dan in here. I think Caroline is ready to go home." He looked at me and I nodded in the affirmative. I was tired and glad tomorrow wasn't a work day. I loved sleeping in with Danny on weekends.

On the way to Danny's apartment, I was quiet in the car. Thoughts buzzed in my head like a busy beehive. Danny didn't try to make conversation. A couple of times, he reached out and stroked my hair or squeezed my hand, but he left me to my thoughts.

When we were inside his apartment, he turned and put his arms around me. I rested my head on his chest.

"Want to take a shower before we go to bed?"

I glanced at him. I must have looked beat.

He raised his hands. "Just a shower, nothing else."

I smiled. "Okay."

CHAPTER 32

Caroline

It wasn't what I'd planned, but I spent the next afternoon cleaning Danny's apartment. He kept apologizing, following me around, picking up things, and generally driving me nutty. I told him to go play with his computer or something.

"Get out of my hair, okay?" I thrust a week's worth of newspapers into his hands. "Get rid of this."

"Yes, ma'am." He slunk away.

I grinned behind his back. Let him feel guilty. It's good for him. How he ever got any work done in that disaster of a den of his, while all this chaos surrounded him, is a mystery to me. He needed a personal servant to follow him around with a laundry hamper and a waste basket.

While I was busy grousing to myself about what a slob he was, it dawned on me that I actually enjoyed picking up after him, trying to civilize him. Good God! This was information that Danny must never have. Never!

Tomorrow I will go back to Wilshire Bank about my business loan. Were they going to reconsider? Reynolds had called and said he needed a little more information from me. I didn't understand. Tiffany and I were so ready to start. Yesterday wouldn't have been soon enough.

This train of thought was getting me nowhere fast, so I took the cleanser and headed for the bathroom. Nothing takes the mind off worries better than a good ring in the toilet bowl.

CHAPTER 33

Daniel

Danny loved it when Caroline fussed and fumed around his place like a housewife. He thought she probably liked it a little bit, but he'd keep that to himself. He knew a good thing when he saw one. When she got into one of her cleaning frenzies, it meant one of two things: either she was mad as hell at him, or she was crazy about him and feeling really domestic. He preferred to believe the latter.

She was antsy about the bank. He couldn't wait to see her face when she found out she'd get the money. She'd be one happy lady. Tiffany and Caroline were on the starting block, waiting for that pistol shot. They already knew of a bargain priced commercial space on a side street in North Hollywood. Caroline said it would fit their needs perfectly to begin with.

She also said they didn't need anything fancy. She didn't care what it looked like from the outside. It had loads of room for the furniture and fixtures they'd need. If a potential customer wanted a consultation, she'd take her portfolio and meet at the customer's place. Fancy offices were way down on her priority list.

Matthew's suggestion to contact the bank manager privately and sign a confidential loan guarantee for Caroline's funding was a winner. Dan thought perhaps he should give Matthew a break; he wasn't all bad.

CHAPTER 34

Matthew

Let us pray.

Now that Caroline's business loan is arranged, all seems to be on the right track. She and Daniel have achieved a new level of trust. I can no longer justify my physical presence. Any mopping up can be done from my usual distance.

My first priority tonight is to find the right words with Tiffany. I had almost rather be roasted over hot coals, but there's no putting it off.

She decided we should go to Riccio's for a romantic dinner for two. I'm meeting her there at seven. I brought a small bouquet with me to Riccio's, and Gina kindly offered to place it in a glass. I positioned the flowers on the table between the candles. A bottle of Tiffany's favorite Pinot Noir sat breathing contentedly on a side table, the empty glasses winked in the candlelight. Reaching into my pocket, I retrieved a turquoise jeweler's box, with a white bow, and placed it next to the flowers. Then I waited.

I sensed her approach. Unseen, I soared down the street to follow her. I loved to shadow her, watch her walk. Her hair fluttered in the breeze, and she had a happy spring in her step. She turned around once, walked backwards, and peered down the sidewalk, looking for me. Swinging around full circle, she shook her head and chuckled.

When she entered the door of Riccio's, I rose from my chair and smiled. Opening my arms, I welcomed her into my embrace.

She hugged me tightly and rested her head on my chest before she looked up and smiled. "Hi. I thought I'd be here first. I swear you were behind me on the sidewalk, but when I looked back you weren't."

"I was here, waiting for you." That wasn't really a fib. I pulled out her chair and took her jacket. As she sat, I leaned close and kissed her on the head, then took my own seat. "You're looking lovely this evening, my darling."

"Thank you." She noticed the flowers. "For me?"

"Who else?" I raised the wine bottle and poured a glass for each of us. "I saw them at the corner flower vendor. I thought you'd like them."

"I love them. What's the occasion?" Her smile dazzled me.

"You are the occasion," I answered, raising my glass. "To you, my one true love for all time."

A smile fluttered across her lips, briefly. The tiniest spark of fear darkened her fawn's eyes. Shaking it off, she lifted her glass and sipped. "Mmm, my favorite."

Her brief unease took me by surprise, and for a moment I was at a loss for words. I reached to place my hand over hers. "Yes, it is excellent. My Papa used to make delicious wine."

I could think of nothing else to say, so I sipped some more. When the silence stretched into awkwardness, I was saved by the approach of Gina. She carried a basket of fresh baked bread and a bowl of seasoned olive oil, which she placed on the table.

"Shall I pour more wine for you?" Gina asked.

"Yes, please," Tiffany answered, "What are the specials this evening, Gina?"

Tiffany's hand trembled slightly when Gina took her glass. She folded her hands together and hurriedly placed them out of my sight on her lap.

"Tonight, we have tender veal piccata, served with a medley of fresh grilled garden squashes and a Caesar salad. We also have Mama's wonderful homemade meatballs and spaghetti. Shall I bring a menu?"

"Not just yet," I said. "We'll enjoy the wine and bread for a while."

"Yes," echoed Tiffany. "We'll enjoy the wine." After Gina left the table, Tiffany leaned forward and whispered, "And each other." Her smile faltered, ever so slightly, as she squeezed my hand.

I sat mute, my well thought out speech forgotten. My human heart squeezed painfully in my chest. This was not going well. In desperation,

I gazed at the jeweler's box and mentally nudged it from the side of the vase, ever so slightly. The flames of the candles fluttered and flared.

She startled, almost spilling over her wine. "Did you see that?"

"See what?" My maneuver was intended to go unnoticed, not appear as a flamboyant magician's trick. I cursed myself silently for my ineptness. I couldn't meet her eyes.

"What's going on here, Matthew?"

I shrugged. "Perhaps it was an air current. Someone probably opened a door in the back. Here," I said clumsily, "I brought this for you." I pushed the box toward her with the end of my finger.

"What is this?" She drew back from the box as if it were a poisonous spider. When she looked up, her eyes were wary.

"It's a gift." I felt panic at her reaction. Somehow, she was able to tune in to my thinking.

"Why?" She stared at the box.

"Why?" I slid it a little closer to her. "I saw it and thought you'd like it." I worked to clear my mind. "Open it."

Hands trembling, she put down her wineglass. Tentatively, she touched the box, as if she expected it to burn her. Slowly picking it up, she turned it in her hand.

"Tiffany's." She spoke the name as if it were an unkind joke, not the signature box from the well-known jeweler.

The irony seemed unexpectedly cruel and thoughtless of me. I murmured a clearly inadequate response.

"What is it?" she asked, unwilling to open the box.

"A small gift, that's all. It made me think of you." By now I was almost as reluctant for her to open the box as she. "If you don't like it, I'll return it." I reached for it. "Would you like me to take it back?"

"No, I'm being silly." Her smile never reached her eyes. She looked away from me and tugged at the white bow. The ribbon slid away. She slowly lifted the box lid, then reached to remove the square of cotton.

I hadn't drawn a breath.

She stared at the contents in silence. I couldn't see her eyes, but I did see the tear that slipped silently down her cheek.

I reached for her hand.

"Oh, Matthew," she whispered on a quiet sob, "you're leaving me, aren't you?" She continued to gaze at the contents of the little box.

It was the truth. "Yes." It was all I could say. Both our hearts were breaking.

"But...why?" She gazed at me with tear-filled eyes. "I don't understand. I thought we loved each other."

I looked into her sweet face and searched for the words that would ease her pain. Somehow, I knew I searched in vain. I cursed myself for allowing this to happen in the first place. I'd known better. I had been warned, but I became so consumed with her I ignored those cautions.

It may seem hard to comprehend, but *angels* also have a good measure of free will. Our life, or existence, doesn't consist of sitting around on puffy clouds, strumming harps, polishing our halos, and preening. We have responsibilities. We are constant companions to our charges and often feel a deep form of love and obligation to them. It's complicated. I don't completely understand it myself.

I squeezed her hand. "I don't know how I can explain it to you."

"Try." Her eyes beseeched me. "I have to know."

"What I'm about to say to you is the truth. I love you, body and soul. I would gladly stay with you, but I cannot. I have to go."

No punishment would be severe enough for what I was doing to her.

Her back stiffened. "That's not good enough." She withdrew her hand. "You give me these beautiful diamond and pearl earrings, then you leave? Am I some child you can mollify with a trinket? What's going on here?" She pushed the box toward me.

I studied the exquisite little earrings made in the popular image of angels. I would attempt to get nearest to the truth as possible, for her sake as well as mine.

"Look at these for a moment." I slid the little box back to her.

"I don't want them." Her voice was cold. "I'm leaving." She started to stand, and I quickly reached out, grasping her wrist.

"Please, Tiffany, stay. I'm trying to explain. Look at the box." She sat again, and I nudged the box yet closer to her. Her stare was cold, her soft brown eyes, usually lively and mischievous, were flat and icy. My chest clutched in pain. Her eyes should never look that way. I'd done that to her. I swallowed. "Look at them, please."

She reluctantly tilted her head down and trained her eyes on the little box. "What am I supposed to see?" Her voice flat, emotionless.

Suddenly, she jerked back. "Oh, God, what was that? How did you do that? This is not funny, Matthew, make it stop!"

As quickly as it had begun, the little angel wings stopped fluttering. The earrings once again were nothing more than inanimate gold and precious stones.

"I hate you, Matthew."

Her glare was a knife in my heart.

"No, my darling, you don't hate me. I'm sorry, Tiffany. Please listen, I'll try to explain myself to you. I owe you that."

I reached for her hand, but she withdrew it from the table and shook her head in a sharp, silent no.

"Explain that," she demanded, pointing to the box.

"It was a cheap trick, which I now regret. It will never happen again. Please take the earrings. I want you to have them. Perhaps you'll understand in time why I selected them for you."

"I'm tired of this. You'd better start making some sense." She folded her arms across her chest and glared at me. Her rage gave me hope.

"All right, I'll try." Searching for the words, I clasped my hands together and lowered my forehead to them with a moan. I rolled my head from side to side.

"Praying again?" Her uncharacteristic tone sharp and nasty.

Ignoring her bitterness, I answered, "Yes, I think it's appropriate."

She snorted, "You'll have to do better than that."

"Yes." I raised my eyes to hers. "Here goes, then." Drawing a deep breath, I said, "I have to go back to my Father. I've been called home."

"You told me your father died a long time ago."

"Yes."

"He's dead, but he called you and you have to go to him?" She looked at me as if I'd taken leave of my senses.

"My earthly father is dead. I was referring to the Father of us all."

"God?" A look of astonishment washed over her. "You're talking about God?"

"Yes." I kept my expression solemn.

"You're going to go visit God." Her head turned slowly from side to side.

"Yes. No, not exactly. It's not a visit." I raised both my hands palms up in frustration. "This is so difficult."

A look of horror came over her face. Her mouth flew open, and she gasped, "Dear God! You're sick? Are you going to die?"

"No. That's the thing, you see. I can't die."

She shook her head as if to clear her mind. Her hands flew to her face, and she covered her eyes and moaned. I began to speak again, but she put out one hand to stop me, then placed it back on her face.

"No." Her voice was muffled behind her fingers. "Don't—just don't—say anything for a minute. Let me think. I have to think." Her breath came rapid and shallow.

I sat silent. Gina approached us from across the now crowded dining room. When had all these people come in? I caught Gina's eye and shook my head, indicating we wanted privacy. She smiled and turned her attention to another table. I perceived glimmerings of Tiffany's thought processes. She weighed my answers and discarded her conclusions. A little war raged in her mind between logic and fantasy.

I leaned toward her. "Tiffany."

She shook her head. "Hush, I'm thinking."

"I can see that. Perhaps I can answer some of those questions."

Her head jerked upright. "What does that mean? You're reading my mind now?"

"I confess." My attempt at a reassuring smile fell short.

"That is so rude! Move away from me then." She flicked her fingers toward the bar. Her spark of annoyance gave me more hope.

"It won't help, I'm afraid. There's no place far enough away to prevent that. I'm sorry."

"Wait a minute. Just wait a minute." She shook her head to clear it of fog and fluttered her hands in frustration. "This is all too weird. You can read my mind. You're not going to die, but you're going to see God. You can make jewelry come alive. You can make candles flare. I *know* you were behind me on the sidewalk." She stared intently into my eyes. "You were, weren't you?"

I nodded silently and reached for her hand again. This time, she didn't snatch it away.

"Oh, Lord. Oh, good heavens. You are not a...an..."

"Um-hmm." I nodded slowly, seriously.

"No." Total astonishment took hold of her. She continued to shake her head in denial. "No, you're not. I know you're not, because an ange...those things, they don't do what you've done–we've done." She shook her head with resolve, which quickly crumbled. "Do they?"

"I'm afraid so. Sometimes. I did." More confession on my part, and more to come, I was sure of it.

"You don't look like one. You don't have any wi...wi..."

"I don't usually look like this. I chose to appear this way so I could be here in person to do my job. I hadn't planned on meeting you." I took her hand and brushed a kiss on her palm. "I didn't plan on falling in love with a mortal, with you."

"If you love me, can't you resign or something? Can't you stay?" Tears sprang to her eyes again. Her lovely lips trembled with sorrow. "I don't want to lose you." She gasped for air.

I kissed her hand again. "You can't lose me, my sweetheart. Not really. I'll always be with you to the end of your life and beyond." I placed her hand against my cheek and leaned into it. My eyes grew moist. "I can't stay here any longer. I'm interfering with all your wonderful possibilities."

"I thought you were *my wonderful possibility*. I don't know whether to scream, cry, or laugh." She took a gasping breath. "This is a nightmare. I want to get out of here so I can scream. I need to scream."

"You can go ahead and scream." I looked around the dining room. "They won't hear you."

"Oh, sure. If I did that, in a few minutes I'd be taking a ride in the little padded van." She gave me a sour look, so out of place on her sweet face.

"No, they won't hear you." I insisted. "Trust me."

"Trust you? That's a laugh." She sat back in her chair and looked around at the other tables. The noise level had risen in the cozy room, which by now had diners at every table.

"Look, I'll prove it to you."

Leaning back, I took a deep breath and let out a loud roar. She gasped, placed her hands over her ears and ducked her head in embarrassment. When there was no response from anyone in the room, she slowly raised her head. Her face flushed and her eyes went big as she stared around us, astonished. Nobody in the room except us had heard my outburst.

"Oh, my," she whispered. "Oh, boy, oh, boy, oh, boy." She drank her wine down in two gulps and poured another glass. "Are we invisible?" She drank that glassful also.

"Certainly not." I raised my hand and signaled Gina. "I'll show you."

She made her way across the room to our table. "Are you ready to order?"

"It seems neither of us is very hungry this evening. Would you be so kind as to bring us two small Caesar salads?" I cast a mental question at Tiffany, and she nodded in the affirmative.

"My pleasure," Gina answered. She picked up the bread basket and peeked under the napkin. "This is cold. I'll bring you some fresh, hot bread with the salads."

"That would be very kind," I said with a smile. As Gina left our table, I turned to Tiffany. "Sorry, my darling."

"I don't think you should call me that anymore." She pouted. "You can quit showing off now, too. I believe you."

I chuckled softly at her resilience. What a remarkable woman. Was it any wonder that I loved her so completely?

"Where do we go from here?" she demanded. "Are you going to go poof like a puff of smoke?" Her hand gesture reminded me of a stage magician.

"Something like that."

"Just don't stick me with the tab," she warned. "I'm ordering another bottle of wine when Gina comes back, and you're paying for it."

"Absolutely."

"Why did you come here in the first place? Other than to break my heart, that is." Her undisguised anger was good.

"I had a particular job to do, and in my flawed judgment, I thought I would have better results as a mortal. I'd already been frustrated with trying to accomplish my task with my other powers."

"What job?" She'd polished off another glass of wine, and it was having an effect on her speech.

"I'm not at liberty to discuss it with you. One thing I *can* tell you is that you're going to be instrumental in helping me resolve it."

"Me? That's rich. Me, an assistant angel. I am so *not* an angel. I don't even have the wardrobe for it."

That thought, mixed with the wine, tickled her funny bone, and she giggled. "I have to go to the girl's room," she said. "Will you still be here when I get back?"

"Of course."

"Of course," she mimicked. "Of course."

She stood unsteadily and turned in the direction of the restroom. I lent her a bit of assistance walking. She turned and frowned. "Don't do that. I'm jus' fine."

"Yes, I can see that." I grinned. "Hurry back."

∽

Somehow, we made it through the salads, a basket of bread, and yet another bottle of Pinot Noir without Tiffany toppling from her chair. There were no more tears, no more sarcasm. A quiet melancholy settled over her, a resignation.

We left Riccio's late. Gina called a taxi for us, and we waited in the cool air. The fragrance of night-blooming jasmine surrounded us. Tiffany shivered, and I put my arm around her to warm her. The cab arrived, and I opened the door.

She hesitated, looking at me with a sad smile. "Are you coming?"

"I shouldn't."

"Please, I want you to," she beseeched softly, soberly.

A few blocks from her place she fell asleep across my lap. When the taxi stopped, I paid the driver and gently lifted her out.

The driver winked. "Looks like you're in luck, pal."

I ignored him, carried her into the bungalow and to her bedroom. I placed her gently on the bed, settled next to her, and put my arm around her. She would sleep soundly. I would be gone when she awakened.

CHAPTER 35

Caroline

I called Tiffany before I left the apartment to let her know the bank had contacted me. I needed to meet with the loan officer right away. I wanted her to cover for me when I made the excuse to leave the office for an hour or so. I was hopeful the call meant they were going to give me the loan.

"Hello," she answered, sounding vague and fuzzy. Not like her at all. For a second, I thought I dialed the wrong number.

"Tiffany?"

"Hi, Caroline." She was definitely down or sick.

"What's the matter? You don't sound like your usual bubbly self. Did I wake you?"

"No, I've been up for a couple of hours. I'm kind of bummed. I was thinking of taking the day off. I'm still in my bathrobe."

"Are you sick?"

"No, heart-broken." Her voice cracked, and it sounded as if she was about to cry. "Matthew and I are, uh, we're not together anymore." She drew a ragged breath.

"What?" I couldn't believe it. They were made for each other. "What did he do?"

"It's a long and complicated story. I don't feel like trying to explain it right now. Maybe later when I've had a chance to think about it." She gave a big sigh. "Anyway, it stinks and I'm having a good cry. I'm going to stay home and wallow in my misery."

Now what? I sympathized with her, mostly, but right now, all I could think about was getting over to the bank.

"Jeez, Tiffany, you're really putting this best girlfriend thing to the test."

"I am?"

"The bank loan officer wants me to come back and meet with him first thing this morning. I'm feeling a glimmer of hope that they're going to reconsider and lend us the money. I hoped you could cover for me while I was out of the office."

"Gosh!" she answered with excitement. "I'll jump right in the shower, take two Alka Seltzer, and put on a happy face. I'll be at the office in thirty minutes, how's that?"

"Are you sure?" The last thing I wanted to do was talk her out of it, but she was my best girlfriend, right? I'd find a way to make it up to her.

"Yes, the show must go on." Decision ruled her voice. "I'm on my way."

I was nervous, returning to the scene of my last harrowing visit to the Wilshire Bank Loan Department. Mister—I couldn't remember his first name—Reynolds was on the phone, but he gestured for me to come in and take a seat by his desk. I almost wished I'd waited outside because he was explaining to some poor customer why his loan hadn't been approved. It sounded too familiar. I know it was only a couple of minutes, but it seemed like an eternity. It was all I could do to keep from glancing at my watch.

Reynolds smiled and indicated he wouldn't be much longer. He looked skyward and shrugged as he listened to the response, then continued. "Yes, I understand completely. It *is* disappointing, but my hands are tied, you see. I'm merely passing on the decision of the loan committee. Yes, sir, that's right. Thank you for thinking of Wilshire Bank. I hope we have the opportunity to serve your needs in the future."

He set the phone down with a regretful sigh and the face of a sad old Basset hound. I imagined him on the phone all day long, the bearer of bad news for all the hopeful loan applicants.

Shaking himself, he took a deep breath and smiled at me. The smile changed him dramatically. "I hate having to do that."

With sympathy, I said, "It must be a real downer to be the one to break the bad news." There was no point in not being as friendly as possible. Even if they still weren't going to lend me the money, I might need them in the future. My hands were sweating, and all I wanted to do was scream, *do I get the money or not!*

"Well, Ms. Clayton, this time I have the pleasure of being the bearer of good news." He smiled, and my heart skipped a couple of beats. "The loan committee has taken another look at your application and your references and has decided to make the business loan after all."

His smile grew bigger. All of a sudden, he reminded me of Santa Claus reaching for a manila folder and placing it on the desk. My excitement grew as he opened the folder and began to leaf through the pages. He glanced at me and smiled. I think I smiled foolishly in return. I may have even giggled. It's all a blur now.

∽

I was hellbent to keep a straight face when I walked into L.E.H. I did okay until I looked at Tiffany, and then there was no way to hold back the big grin that had been tugging at my lips since I'd entered the work room.

She knew immediately I had the loan and ran over. I reached in my bag and pulled out the checkbook Reynolds had handed to me. Holding each end, I waved it up and down like a picket sign.

Tiffany bounced. She grabbed my wrists, and we jumped up and down like two high school girls who'd been noticed by the football team captain. I couldn't help it. I laughed out loud because we were both in such high spirits.

Moody stared balefully from his office in the back of the room. I turned and wrinkled my nose at him. Juvenile, I know, but it felt so good. He leaped from his desk and came charging across the office. Eight pairs of eyes followed him. He approached us with his head down like a Pamplona bull.

"That's the last straw, Clayton. Who in hell do you think you are? You come waltzing in here two hours late and don't even give me the courtesy of coming up with some faintly plausible excuse. I have half a mind to——"

"Fire me?" I was still grinning.

"Yes, fire you," he snarled. "Do you know any reason why I shouldn't?"

"I can think of several, but I'll save you the trouble. I quit."

A murmur built among the troops. I turned and made a smart curtsey to my soon-to-be former co-workers.

"Get back to your work station, Gaines," he snapped at Tiffany. "Clayton and I are going to have a little chat."

"No, we're not," I said. "She quits, too."

A collective intake of breath as everyone reacted, agog at the little drama.

Before Moody could get his mouth closed, I took Tiffany by the elbow and guided her toward our desks. She hadn't said a thing. She went to her station, pulled open the drawer and tossed her things into a canvas bag. I was doing likewise. In no time, we were packed up and on our way to the lobby.

Moody, sputtering, stood with hands on hips, blindsided, stunned. He hadn't moved from the spot where he'd descended on us. Tiffany and I turned at the door and waved to the serfs. They raised a faint cheer.

As we were about to leave, Tiffany said, "Wait." She trotted across the lobby to the break room. Sandra Russell, the receptionist, stared, mystified. When Tiffany came back, she was holding our coffee mugs aloft.

"We'll need these, girlfriend." We waved goodbye to Sandra and strolled out of the office arm-in-arm, laughing all the way to the ground floor.

"Let's go right now and make a deposit on that office we looked at," I said.

"I'll meet you there. I don't want to leave my car here. I don't ever want to see this place again."

Once in my car, I pulled out my cell phone and poked the number for Danny's office. As soon as he came on the line I took a deep breath. "Can you meet me for lunch?" I was determined not to tell him over the phone.

"Sorry, babe, I can't. I'm on my way out to meet with a client, and then I'm going to the airport. I have to fly up to Frisco. I won't be back till tomorrow morning. I left a message on your phone." He sounded genuinely disappointed.

"Phooey," I said. "Oh, well, it'll wait till tomorrow."

"What?"

"Never mind." I maneuvered my car out onto the boulevard and saw Tiffany right behind me. "I have to be somewhere in a few minutes. What time will you be back?"

"Around eleven, I think." I heard him flipping through some papers. "Yeah, here it is, my flight gets into Burbank at ten fifty-five."

"Okay, call me when you get back. I gotta go."

"Love you, Care," he said.

"I know, Danny. Love you, too." I disconnected before he could add anything.

CHAPTER 36

Matthew

Now, at last, we were making progress.

The two women had the time of their lives running from their new office suite to the office supply store, the printer, and the cable company.

My darling Tiffany bravely hid her wounded heart and jumped enthusiastically into the project. Caroline, usually so controlled, was excited as she went this way and that, but Tiffany kept her corralled. By three o'clock, they accomplished all they could for one day and headed back to Caroline's apartment.

Once inside, they dropped their bags, kicked off their shoes, and ambled to the kitchen, exhausted. Caroline opened the refrigerator, reached way in the back, and pulled out a bottle of champagne.

"I've been saving this since last New Year's Eve." She twisted the wires at the bottleneck. "I can't think of a more appropriate occasion for opening it."

"That's good stuff. Don't you want to wait till you and Dan can celebrate together?" Tiffany asked, flexing her tired feet.

"Nope, this is just for you and me. The four of us can get together tomorrow night and share another one." She poured and smiled at Tiffany. Caroline's smile vanished. "Dang it, Tiffany, I'm sorry. I'm such an insensitive witch. I forgot about you and Matthew. About..."

Tiffany held up her hand and shook her head. "No, it's okay." Her artificially bright smile didn't quite reach her shimmering eyes. She reached for one of the glasses. "Really, I'm fine. Really." Her tears belied her words.

"Oh, honey." Caroline embraced her. "It'll be all right." She patted Tiffany on the back and rocked her back and forth. "All men are bastards."

"No," Tiffany protested into Caroline's shoulder, "Not Matthew. Matthew's an angel. Really, he is." She sighed deeply and pulled back. Wiping the tears from her eyes, she streaked mascara across her cheeks. Looking like a wounded raccoon, she attempted another smile. "Really."

"If you say so." Caroline hugged her and sighed. "Let's get plastered, and you can tell me what an angel he is." She led the way to the living room, and they sank back into the sofa cushions with a mutual sigh.

I was heartened to see Caroline take Tiffany's hand in hers.

They didn't get plastered as Caroline had suggested. Instead, they stopped at two glasses. Not ready to talk about me, Tiffany steered the conversation to their business plans.

"How much did we spend today?"

Caroline grimaced. "About eleven thousand dollars, I think. Tomorrow, we'll go furniture shopping and get the bare necessities, a couple of desks, some file cabinets, and a drafting table. The communications consultant will be there first thing in the morning to start on the phone installation and computer hookup. Good thing FedEx is just down the street. I don't even want to think how much a blueprint-copier costs."

"I don't remember when they said the business cards would be ready. Do you? And the announcements? We need to do a snail-mail and an email campaign right away." Tiffany sat back. "And, I hate to mention it, but how much am I being paid?"

Depression being foreign to her nature, Tiffany was feeling less blue. The project was now foremost in her mind, and she was all business. My brave trooper.

"You've only worked for me one day and already you want to get paid?" Caroline was only partly jesting. "What was L.E.H. paying you?"

Tiffany huffed. "Not enough." She wrinkled her nose at Caroline. "I need to know if I can pay my rent and afford to eat for the next few months. Then we'll negotiate."

"I had no idea you were such a rapacious little bully."

"Hey, I told you I minored in business. This *is* going to be a business arrangement, isn't it?" She cocked her head, and a little smile quirked the corner of her mouth.

"I suppose next you'll want stock in the corporation." Caroline downed the last of her glass of champagne.

"You're catchin' on, girlfriend."

They sized each other up and laughed, relaxed and satisfied. I felt *I* could relax a bit now too, until her phone rang.

"Hello...Yes, this is Caroline Clayton...You want Mr. Kavanaugh?...Which Mr. Kavanaugh?...Oh, this isn't his number....Would you like his office number?"

She raised her eyebrows and shrugged at the question on Tiffany's face.

"He needs to what...Sign what paper?...I'm confused. What does Daniel Kavanaugh have to do with my business loan?" She stood abruptly and paced as she listened. "I think you're mistaken. Let me talk to Mr. Reynolds...When will he be back?" She gestured in frustration. "Okay, I'll be there when you open tomorrow. Tell him to expect me."

Tiffany bolted upright, concerned. "What's going on?"

"I'm not sure, but the bank said that Danny needs to come and sign one more form they overlooked when he was there a couple days ago. I don't know what they're talking about. Why would he need to sign anything? It's *my* loan."

With alarm, I sensed the wheels turning in her head as she put two and two together. I experienced a rush of dismay. Something had gone haywire. On my advice, Daniel had gone to see Reynolds and was assured that his involvement would be held in strictest confidence, even though the transaction was outside the normal lending policy guidelines. Daniel's promissory note to the bank was what swayed the loan committee to grant Caroline's business loan. Somehow, I had to warn Reynolds before she got to the bank. My goodness! This project was once again going from bad to worse.

CHAPTER 37

Daniel

Dan couldn't wait to get to Care's place. The afternoon dragged by, and he was anxious to get out of the office. He would have gone straight to her apartment from the airport, but she hadn't answered her cell phone all morning. Tiffany wasn't at work or home either. There was nothing to do but wait till quitting time. He was pretty sure Caroline asked him to meet her for lunch yesterday to tell him her loan had been approved. She'd be on cloud nine. There'd be a celebration tonight.

Wouldn't you know the client he had lunch with yesterday called at ten to five and just had to meet with him to go over a couple of clauses in her contract? It took the patience of Job to deal with those showbiz prima donnas. Dan huffed with frustration after arranging the meeting.

He thought it would probably take a quart of red wine to calm her down. Hers was one of the best contracts he had ever negotiated, but somehow, she wasn't comfortable with something in it. More than likely, she didn't understand it. Dan asked her to meet him at Riccio's. At least then he'd be near Caroline's apartment by the time he rushed her through the meeting.

He called Caroline to let her know he would be late. She wasn't home so he left a voice mail message. "Hey, Babe, it's me. I have to meet with a client as soon as I leave here, so I'm going to be a little late."

He added an obnoxious kissing sound before he disconnected. She hated that. Dan grinned as he visualized the sour expression on her face before she punched the delete button.

By six-thirty, he was afraid he was going to blow his cool with the starlet. One TV deal and they thought they could ask for the moon. Daniel patiently explained all the provisions of the contract to her. He made clear the very sound reasons why she would be better off to wait for the series to premier before she demanded more money. The pilot had just aired. There was no guarantee the series would be picked up after the first couple of episodes. He pointed out that producers were much more likely to hire her again if she made nice on this contract. Dan emphasized how much wiser it was for her to be making friends at this point, rather than enemies.

"Oh, Daniel, may I call you Daniel?" she said in her breathless *Marilyn* voice. "It's just that I'm so nervous and excited. My agent said you were the best. I should trust her judgment. I know you're looking after my interests."

She fluttered her overly darkened eyelashes and took a dainty sip of wine. She held the stem of her glass in both hands, the long fingers intertwined. Her professionally done nails, wickedly long were the same color as the Bordeaux in the glass she caressed.

She leaned toward him and smiled. Her dress was cut practically to her navel. He was fascinated, expecting her hooters to spill right out onto the table. She took in his gaze with a satisfied smile, sliding her fingers up and down the stem of the glass.

Dan cleared his throat. "Of course, we're looking after your best interests. Our firm focuses on building long-lasting and trusting relationships with our valued clients."

"Oh, I agree," she purred. "They're the very best kind."

The little vamp was making a play for him, and she had to be all of twenty. He was flattered and irked at the same time.

"Well, ah, good. Yes, uh, yes." He signaled Gina to bring the check. "I'll be happy to call you a cab." He glanced at his watch. "I hate to be rude, but I'm running late for another meeting."

She made a tiny sound of protest and pursed her bee-stung lips into a sexy pout. "I was hoping we could have dinner."

"I'm sorry. Perhaps another time?" He was anxious to get to Caroline. "As I said, I have another meeting tonight. Feel free to call me if you have any other questions or concerns about your contract." He laid two twenties on the table and stood.

She wriggled out of her chair and snatched her evening bag. "I'll walk out with you. The studio has a car and driver waiting for me."

She took his arm in a proprietary way as they made for the entrance. The head of every guy in the room swiveled as they walked past. She knew exactly the reaction she was getting.

Once outside, he sucked in a big breath of fresh air.

The limo spotted her and pulled smoothly to the curb. She turned and kissed Daniel lightly on the cheek. "Call me later if you'd like to drop by for a nightcap," she whispered. "You've got my number."

He had her number all right. The driver hopped out and held her door open. She melted onto the back seat, her skirt sliding up endless silky legs in blatant invitation. When he glanced at her face, she smiled and tugged demurely on the hem of her dress, right where he'd been gaping.

"Goodnight, Daniel." It was an invitation.

He answered formally. "Goodnight, Ms. Rayce."

Daniel rolled his eyes and breathed a sigh of relief when the big stretch limo pulled away from the curb. He jogged to his car. He couldn't get to Care's place fast enough.

∽

The only light on in her apartment when he unlocked the door was coming from the kitchen. She usually had all the lights blazing. He put down his stuff and called out to her. "I'm here, babe."

Tossing his jacket on the coat tree, he headed to the kitchen. She hadn't answered his greeting. He heard the clattering of plates and the muted sounds of the stereo. He stepped to the door and observed her washing dishes. He didn't want to startle her, so he tapped on the door frame.

She spun around. From the look on her face, he had either jolted her or she was sorely pissed. He stepped forward. She put her hands out like a traffic cop, stopping him dead in his tracks.

"What?"

"I'd like my key, please." Her voice was pure ice.

"Your key?"

She put out her hand, her face stony. "Yes, my key."

For a couple of seconds, he couldn't figure out what she was so upset about then it suddenly hit him. "Oh, wait a minute. You don't think...no. She's a client...I wouldn't..."

"You're a liar, Daniel Kavanaugh. I want my key, and I want you out of here."

"Come on, Care. Jessica Rayce is a client. We were discussing her contract. I have absolutely zero interest in the little bimbo."

Didn't it figure she would see them at Riccio's? He wanted to kick himself for not picking a different place to meet with Rayce.

"I don't know what you're talking about." She wiped her hands on the towel and tossed it viciously on the counter. "I want my key." She put her hand out again.

"Do you mind telling me what the hell is wrong?" He was stumped. "Help me out here."

"Give me the key," she demanded for the fourth time. Then she pointed. "That's the way out."

He pulled his keys out of his pocket, twisted hers off the ring, and tossed it to her. "Happy now?"

"No!" Her lips trembled slightly. "Get out, and you can inform your parents that I won't be able to attend Thanksgiving dinner."

Dan thought she was about to cry. She turned her back on him.

"Babe, what is it?"

He stepped over and put his hands on her shoulders. She immediately threw her elbows back and shook him off.

"Okay, okay, I won't touch you, but you have to tell me what's wrong."

She shook her head silently and leaned on the counter. He stood there, completely baffled. He felt as if he touched her again, she'd shatter into a zillion pieces.

"Caroline, please tell me. We can fix it." He was about ready to cry too. He didn't know whether he was more scared or more frustrated at her refusal to talk. "We can fix it, babe."

"No, we can't." She said it barely above a whisper.

"Why can't we?"

"You're just like them."

"Like them? Who?"

"My parents, they don't respect me. You don't respect me."

"That's crap! I'm not like them."

Her accusation was pure bull.

"You went behind my back, Danny. You know what you did." Her tone was flat, beaten.

Still baffled, he shook his head. Then the light bulb lit. She knew about the loan. Somebody at the bank had spilled the beans. "Jesus! The promissory note." He smacked his forehead. "How did you find out?"

"Does it matter? I found out."

"Look, I'm sorry. What's the freakin' big deal? I love you. I did it to help you." He turned and pounded his fist on the door frame. "Damn it, I'd like to kill somebody!"

"How could you do that? How could you patronize me like I'm a child?" She turned on him, anger flaring. "All my life, everyone's treated me as if I were a halfwit. Nobody believes in me. Not even you!"

She was shrill, close to screaming. "How could you?"

"For crying out loud, Care. *I* believe in you! That's why I did it! You deserved a break, and I wanted to help you. That's what married people and couples do. They help each other. They work as a team."

He knew he'd made a mistake, but her intractable touchiness bugged him.

"We're not married. As of now, we're not a couple. Please get out of my house." She brushed past him.

"What the hell do you want from me?" he shouted. Without thinking, he reached out and spun her around. "Don't turn your back on me, dammit! Look at me when I'm talking to you!"

He gave her a little shake. She stared, expressionless. He dropped his hands and paced.

"You know, Babe, I'm up to here with your insecurities." Dan swiped a finger across his throat. "Your attitude is totally inflexible. You won't accept my help, but you weren't too proud to ask Liz and Lyle for the money. You say you love me, but you won't live with me, and you won't marry me. What? Were we supposed to go on like this indefinitely?"

She didn't answer, just stood there, cold, remote.

"Okay, okay, I give up." He raised his hands in surrender and backed away from her. "I've wasted three years of my life with you, Caroline Clayton." The venom in his voice surprised him. He was hurt. "See you around."

He slammed the door so hard he was surprised the hardware didn't fly off. Still seething when he reached his car, he nearly ripped the door off the hinges. He sat, slamming his hands against the steering wheel, and then peeled out, without even looking. She said he was like her parents!

She's like her parents—those jerks!

CHAPTER 38

Matthew

My brilliant conversation with Daniel about going behind Caroline's back to help her with the financing could not have been more idiotic. What was I thinking? I should have known what her reaction would be if she found out. I do possess extraordinary powers. What good are they if I don't use them?

My passion for Tiffany turned my brain to mush. Well, there's nothing for it but to go see the Boss and face the music.

CHAPTER 39

Caroline

How I hated him. No. I didn't hate him. I hated myself for falling in love with him, and his parents, and his brothers and sisters-in-law, and all those kids, especially Ryan. I'd sworn I would never fall in love again because that's when you leave yourself wide open to get your heart broken. Why is that? You should be able to trust the people who love you, right?

I'm going back to the bank first thing in the morning and see what I have to do to get the loan cancelled, or get Danny's name off it, or re-negotiate it, or whatever. Tiffany and I have already spent a pile of the money. I'm not sure what arrangements I can make, but if I have to give them every penny of my savings to get it paid off, that's what I'll do.

Tiffany stared at me. "I don't understand why you're so upset with him. He wants to help you get started. At times like this, I wonder if you're as smart as you seem. Wake up. The man loves you."

I answered her stubbornly. "He manipulated me. Anyway, it's none of your business." Why was my private life everybody else's business, my parents, my boss, Danny, and now her?

"Manipulate you? What crap!" She disgustedly picked through the loan file, looking for the contract. "Sometimes you amaze me."

"I said it's none of your business."

Why was I taking it out on Tiffany?

"Oh, get off your high horse and shut up," Tiffany ordered. "Here.

This is the contract you signed. It probably wouldn't be a bad idea if you read it through before you go back to the bank."

She thrust it at me. I didn't like that she'd told me to shut up, but I *had* been storming around the empty office like a madwoman the past half hour. We were waiting for the furniture delivery, which I had to sign for otherwise I'd be sitting on the bank's doorstep waiting for them to open.

"Don't you have something to do?" I asked.

"Don't take out your paranoia on me. I'm on your side, remember? Or do you think I'm trying to manipulate you, too?" She sniffed with disgust.

"What is it with you and your big nose in my personal life, huh? I should fire you."

I had my hands on my hips, and we were nose to nose.

"Caroline Clayton, you're a damn fool! You have a terrific man who's in love with you. He puts up with all your wacky insecurities and your bitchiness. He even signs his name on the dotted line at the bank so you can get the money you need to go into business."

"I'm warning you, Tiffany."

"Go ahead and warn me all you want. I'm telling you what you need to hear. What has he done that's so unforgivable? He wants to help you, and he wants to marry you. Ooh, he's a nasty one all right." She shook her head and threw up her hands.

This was a side of her I'd never seen. The unsinkable Tiffany Gaines had a dark streak. It unnerved me. I thought she was the one person left I could trust. I'd been wrong before, hadn't I?

"You're fired."

"You can't fire me."

"Who says I can't? You're fired!"

"Give it a rest, will you? I have work to do and here comes the delivery truck. Get out of my way or get busy directing them where to put things." She took out her cell phone and walked over to the card table in the corner, which served as a temporary desk.

I was about to fire her again when two guys showed up at the door with the furniture delivery forms and started asking questions about where everything was to be placed. I was still furious with her.

The men took about forty-five minutes to get all the stuff up the stairs. Then I had a big argument with them about hauling away the packing boxes. They were planning to leave them behind, and *we* were supposed to figure out how to break them all down and dispose of them. They put them on the truck, grumbling all the while about how the boss was going to give them hell for bringing them back to the warehouse, like I gave a damn.

I looked around the office after they left and concluded that it would not be such a good idea to have any customers showing up there. They might think this was an example of how we designed office suites. Definitely a make-do arrangement.

By the time I was ready to sit down and study the loan documents, the communications guy showed up to do the wiring for our phones and computers. I had already sketched out the plan for the wiring, and with the furniture in place, it would be a pretty straightforward job. He carried in all his tools and got to work.

Tiffany was on the phone, so I'd have to wait to fire her until after I returned from the bank. Who was I kidding? I wasn't going to fire her, and she knew it, the little smartass. I picked up the loan papers again and began to read through them. My cell phone rang.

"Caroline Clayton," I said, all business.

"Care, it's me. We need to talk," Danny said.

My heart wrenched. "No. We don't." I hung up and looked guiltily across the room to see if Tiffany heard me. She had. I got that pinch-mouthed, little disgusted look from her again. I sent her a glare. The phone rang once more.

"I don't want to talk to you," I shouted into the phone.

"Clayton?" a man's puzzled voice answered me.

"Yes," I answered meekly. *Now what?*

"Peter Langley here. I called your office, and they said you didn't work there anymore. It's a good thing I have your mobile number. What's the story?"

"I...uh," I stumbled through my response. "I decided to go out on my own. This is our first morning at the new office. I haven't had a chance to send out any notices or contact any of my accounts."

I'd forgotten that many of the accounts I had been working with knew my cell phone number. "It's nice to hear from you, Peter. Is there a problem with the job?"

"No, it's about finished. I have a referral for you. Al Guerrero was hired for what was supposed to be an ordinary remodel job that's turned into a bigger project. He's convinced them they need to consult with a designer before they go any further. Are you interested?"

"Are you kidding? Of course, I am. Hold on a second while I find something to write on. It's a mess around here." I put the phone down and fast walked over to Tiffany's table. She was in the process of moving all her stuff to one of the desks. "Give me something to write on, quick."

"Who is it?" She shoved the papers around and came up with a sticky-note pad.

"It's Langley in Seattle, says he has a referral for us." I went back to the other side of the room.

She gave me a thumbs up. "That's great!" Her smile was back, not that I'd earned it.

I took all the information from Langley, and we talked for a few minutes about the progress on the two jobs we'd worked on together, jobs he was wrapping up. The new customer wanted a call right away, so Peter let me go and said I should get my phone number and address to him as soon as the cards and stationery were available. He would be coming to L.A. soon and would probably have some more referrals for me since he had no love lost for L.E.H. and dear old Moody.

I should have felt good about getting a referral on my first day in business, but my insides were hollow. Something was missing. What Danny had done had taken all the enthusiasm and joy out of me. Tiffany had been no help, coming down on me like some kind of avenging angel. I looked across the room. She was watching. I swiveled my chair around and punched in the number Langley had given me.

The customer owned a medical clinic in downtown Tacoma. They hired Al to enlarge and spiff up their reception area, then decided they wanted a bigger room for their files and medical transcription workspace. The supervising physician wanted his office redone while they were at it. Al was getting in deeper than he cared to and told them they needed to consult with a good designer before he knocked out any more walls. They asked me to come up right away. I told them I'd fly there this evening and meet with them in the morning. The price I quoted included my travel costs, hotel and fee. They didn't even flinch.

I put down the phone and turned to face Tiffany. "We got what could be a profitable job. Langley referred a medical clinic in Tacoma.

They're pressed for space and need to update their offices. I'm going to fly there tonight and meet with them in the morning."

"That's great! I'll make your reservations while you go to the bank. Should I schedule your return for tomorrow about midday?"

"No, make it late afternoon," I answered. "I'll make a few courtesy calls in Seattle while I'm there." I wasn't going to miss the opportunity to schmooze existing and possible new business.

"Good idea, especially since they're paying for the ticket. I'll book you a car."

"Get the smallest cheapest one and a Super 8 or something by the airport."

"It's a little different when it's your nickel, isn't it?" she said with a laugh.

I couldn't stay mad at her. "Look, Tiffany, about earlier. You're not fired."

The cable guy pretended he wasn't listening, but the smirk on his face told me otherwise. I had to smile.

"I know." She flashed her familiar, big grin. "Go duke it out with the bank. I'll hold down the fort, girlfriend."

"Okay, wish me luck. Call and leave the travel information on my home phone voicemail." I was already on my way out the door. "I'll keep you posted."

When I arrived at Wilshire Bank, I learned Reynolds was going to be out for the next couple of days. Not liking the looks of his little Harry Potter clone, weenie, assistant, I made an appointment to see Reynolds in two days. I'd take care of the loan mess later. I had to get myself to SeaTac and secure the new customer.

My phone rang when I got inside my apartment door, and I grabbed it, thinking it was Tiffany with my travel info. My chest hurt when I heard Danny's voice.

"Care, don't hang up."

I didn't say anything. I gritted my teeth and held back the tears that threatened.

"Are you there?"

"Mmm," was all I could manage.

"This is nuts, babe. We have to talk and get this thing worked out."

"It's too late," I mumbled.

"No, it's not. I'll find a way. I was wrong. I know I shouldn't have done that without your permission. It was a bonehead thing to do. I'm sorry. It was Matthew's idea, but I should have known better. He's not responsible. I am."

Matthew's idea? I didn't know what he was talking about, but I didn't have time to discuss it. Anyway, just talking to him made my stomach ache. My grip on the phone was so tight my hand was bloodless.

"I can't talk now. I'm on my way to the airport. I have a flight to SeaTac in a couple of hours. I'll think about it. I'll be home in a couple of days."

"Where are you staying?" I detected hope in his voice.

"Gotta go." I hung up. If I stayed on the phone with him one more second, I'd be bawling. I loved Danny. Being in love is the quickest way to brain meltdown. I did want to see him. I did and didn't want to talk to him. I did and didn't want to think about him.

I could think of little else.

CHAPTER 40

Daniel

Without too much trouble, Dan managed to get Tiffany to reveal Caroline's return flight number. He got to Burbank airport in plenty of time to meet her when she arrived. The only way he would get to her was to be there when she entered the terminal. He figured she'd be too shocked to make a scene but was prepared to tackle her if necessary.

~

When Tiffany told Caroline Matthew had left her, Dan was angry and now had another reason to wring the guy's neck. How he ever let Matthew talk him into going behind Caroline's back was still a mystery. For an educated man of above average intelligence, he marveled over how his life had spun out of his control.

Standing a little back from the gate so she would be through the door before she saw him, he waited. She exited the aircraft and stepped down the stairs. No matter how often he watched her from a distance, he still got that rush. Hair prickled on the back of his neck just enjoying her special walk.

His view was temporarily blocked by a flurry of movement and murmuring in the crowd around him. He lost sight of Caroline and stretched up on tiptoes to see above the commotion. Then he heard the shrill squeal of a female voice.

"Daniel! Darling, you came to meet me!"

Whoever it was must have been talking to someone else, because the voice wasn't Care's, and she was the only woman he'd come to meet.

He heard a shout, "There she is!" and a camera's flash went off about six inches from his face. All he could see was a freakin' big, blue spot. He put his hands to his face and rubbed his eyes, trying to see what the hell was going on when a woman's body landed against his and arms flew around his waist.

"Daniel, how sweet," she cooed.

That definitely wasn't Caroline's voice in his ear. It sounded eerily familiar, though. The woman kissed him on the cheek as the crowd jostled. He instinctively put his arms around her to keep her from falling.

By then, he could focus through the spots in his eyes. Jessica Rayce twisted against him and smiled lovingly into his eyes...and there was Caroline standing stock still a few feet away, disgust cloaking her shocked expression.

He went to call out to Caroline when Jessica's hand turned his face toward hers. She kissed him full on the mouth. Camera flashes flared all around them. When Dan extricated himself from Jessica's death grip, Caroline stalked away.

Ah, hell!!

"Daniel, you should have told me you were coming to meet me, darling. I would have had my manager keep my flight secret from the paparazzi, but I'm so glad to see you!" She pressed so tight against his leg he was afraid the keys in his pocket would leave a permanent imprint on his thigh.

He groped for an answer as Caroline disappeared from the arrival hall through a side exit to the parking lot.

"Ms. Rayce, Ms. Rayce!" someone shouted, and the shoving match started all over again. "Ms. Rayce, would you make a statement to the press about your role on *Ordinary Lives*?"

"Ms. Rayce, who's the guy?"

Jessica fluttered her lashes, and answered, "He's someone *very* special." Looking like a lioness that had just made a kill, she added, "That's all I'm going to say." She gave Daniel the Nancy Reagan *gaze*.

Some obnoxious jerk put a camera right in Dan's face and yelled, "What's your name, dude? You boinking the lady?"

That did it. Dan grabbed the jackass by the neck and shoved him back into the crowd. He went down on his butt, and the hatchet-faced hag who'd been standing next to him belted Dan in the eye with her microphone, the same eye which had collided with Angeli's elbow.

Next thing Dan knew, he was on his butt with Jessica Rayce on her knees, hovering across his chest like a guardian angel, screaming, "Help! Call the police!" Flashbulbs popped all over the place.

CHAPTER 41

Caroline

"That two-timing jerk! That lower than pond scum, lying, creep bastard!" I slammed the door so hard all the windows in the office rattled. I smacked my briefcase on the desk and glared at Tiffany.

"Who?" She jumped up and came across the office to where I paced back and forth in a fury. "What happened?"

"Who else? Daniel Kavanaugh, that's who. The snake! The two-timing worm!" I threw my purse clear across the room.

Tiffany cringed, then stared.

"What are you staring at?" I yelled.

"I'm not sure. I thought it was Caroline Clayton who came through that door, but now, I don't know." She calmly stepped across the carpet and picked up my purse. "I think you dropped this."

"I don't need your attitude right now, Tiffany." My arms flailed, and I howled like a wounded coyote. "I got off the flight from hell and walked right smack into Danny Dickhead!" I threw the purse on the floor again, and the contents went flying.

"For Pete's sake, Caroline, are you going to tell me what happened, or should I call nine-one-one and order up the nut wagon?" She stood with her arms folded across her chest waiting for an answer.

I paced back and forth, continuing to fume. "All men are slime. You should know."

"Oh, for goodness sake. What did he do? My crystal ball is in the shop this week. Be specific."

She knelt and began picking up my stuff and shoving it back into my bag.

"Stop that, I clean up my own messes." I knelt beside her and nudged her away. The phone rang, and she went to answer it. By the time she'd hung up, I'd cooled off some and flopped into my chair.

She took a seat across my desk from me, folded her arms again and sat still, patiently waiting.

"I hate him." My lips trembled. I put my hand up to cover my mouth. I didn't want to cry over the big, rat bastard.

"I don't think so."

I answered bitterly. "What do you know?"

"I know he loves you, and I'm pretty sure you love him. Otherwise, whatever it is he did wouldn't matter so much. Would it?"

I sobbed. I wanted to crawl into a corner and hide my head. "Love stinks. You might as well paint a big target on your chest that says, I love you, go ahead and break my heart." Tears slid down my cheeks.

Tiffany sighed and came around to my side of the desk. She went behind my chair and put her hands on my shoulders and massaged gently. "I wonder if anyone besides me and Matthew know what a scaredy-cat you are, big tough girlfriend."

I made a little snort of disgust, but she continued kneading my shoulders. "Matthew," I spat out. "Another slime-ball in lamb's clothing."

"No," she answered with a sigh.

"Sure, you go right on believing that, and in the meantime, where is he?"

"I told you, he's an angel, and he couldn't stay here any longer."

"Sounds like *I* need to call for the nut wagon and make reservations for both of us." My remark was half-laugh, half-sob.

She smacked me on the shoulder and laughed sadly. "When are you going to tell me what Dan did?"

I got up and went to the coffee pot, the contents so strong smelling it would keep me awake for hours. I held the pot up to the light and squinted at it.

"When was this made, last week?" I took a tentative sip. "Yummy," I grimaced. "Want some?"

"Sure, it's about six hours old. Should be aged to perfection." She sat back down, and I carried the two cups back to the desk and slid one toward her, secretly grateful for her loyal presence.

I proceeded to tell her the whole sordid story of walking into the terminal to see Danny kissing that little starlet skank. I was sure to emphasize how she was rubbing herself up and down his leg, while he stood there gawking at me.

"I was the last person he expected to see. He was stunned when I caught him red-handed. I wonder how long that's been going on." I took a big sip of the vile coffee and swallowed with a shudder.

"An hour, at least," Tiffany said, an ironic smile playing on her lips.

"An hour, what?"

"I suspect his affair's been going on at least an hour. He called and pleaded with me to tell him your flight number. He wanted to meet you, to patch things up with you. I have no idea how *the little starlet skank* got in the picture. He went there to meet you."

She put her cup down and stared at her nails.

"You told him when my flight was arriving? How could you?"

She gave me a stern look and said the words slowly as if she were speaking to a moron. "I could because I care about both of you, and this whole thing is completely stupid and blown out of all proportion. You're throwing away a terrific man because he made the unforgivable mistake of helping you."

I lashed out nastily. "Stay out of my private life, kiddo. I noticed *your* boyfriend is no longer on the scene. You're a fine one to be interfering and giving advice."

"I'd crawl on my knees through fire to get Matthew back. I'll love him till the day I die. I've said it before, and I'll say it again. You are a fool." She stood and leaned across my desk, glaring at me.

I was about to take her on when the phone rang. She reached over and picked it up.

"Clayton and Gaines," she answered sweetly, making a nasty face at me.

"Clayton and Gaines, my patootie," I muttered. "You're fired."

She thrust the phone toward me. "Give it a rest."

"Who is it?"

"Daniel."

I crossed my arms refusing to take the phone from her. "Tell him I'm not here."

"She says she's not here, Dan." She listened for a second and looked at me. "It's important, an emergency."

I grabbed the phone and shouted into the mouthpiece, "Get lost, creep!" I slammed it down so hard coffee splashed out of my cup onto my desk. "Crap!" I grabbed a handful of tissues and dabbed at it.

The phone rang again, and Tiffany snatched it before I had a chance. "Clayton and Gaines." She listened for a moment then looked at me. "I think you should talk to him."

I reached over, took the phone from her hand and hung it up. She shrugged and walked to her desk. She picked up her purse.

My head throbbed. My hands shook. "Where are you going?" I demanded.

"Out. I need to get away from you for a while. You answer the phone when it rings." She went through the door and closed it quietly.

In seconds, the phone rang. Not sure whether it was Danny again, I answered in my professional voice and was surprised when Ryan spoke. "Caroline? Is that you? It's me, Ryan. Uncle Danny asked me to..."

"You tell your rotten Uncle Danny that I think he's stooped to a new level of low to have you call me for him." I shook my head in disbelief and hung up. It rang almost instantly. I let it ring about four times then picked it up in frustration.

"Caroline? Don't hang up, please." It was Ryan's voice again.

"Ryan," I tried to sound nice, "tell your Uncle Danny that I don't wish to speak to him, now or ever."

Interrupting me, he said, "Grampa fainted or something, Uncle Dan and Gramma went in the ambulance with him to the hospital. I'm scared." His voice wavered, and I was too taken aback to answer him. "Caroline? Are you there? Hello?"

I leapt from my chair. My pulse pounded in my throat, my ears. "Yes, I'm here, what happened, Ryan? Tell me what happened."

"Well, uh..." he cleared his throat, "I was at Grampa's house playing cards with Gramma when Uncle Danny came in. He had a big Band-aid on his eyebrow, and he was telling Grampa something about—something that happened when he went to the airport to get you. Grampa laughed then he started choking, and he fell over, and we thought he was kidding around, but his face was turning blue, and he couldn't breathe, and Gramma yelled for me to call nine-one-one, and I did, and Uncle Danny gave Grampa CPR, and Gramma was crying and then the ambulance got here and then they left, and Uncle Danny told me to call you and tell you." He took a big, ragged breath. Like he was trying not to cry. "They went to Cedars hospital."

Liam? Oh, my God, Dad.

My hands trembled. I made my voice as calm as I could. "Ryan, it's going to be okay. Stay right there. I'm coming now. Call your dad at work and tell him what happened, okay? Tell him I'm coming to get you." He didn't answer for several seconds. "Ryan?"

He choked out, "Yeah?"

"Did you understand what I said?"

His answer was faint and shaky. "Yeah."

"Okay, I'll be there in about fifteen minutes. Stay by the phone."

"Please hurry, Aunt Caroline. I'm scared."

Aunt Caroline. He'd never called me that before. I could barely speak when I said, "Okay, sweetie. I'll hurry."

I quickly put the phones on the answer mode and scribbled a quick note to Tiffany. I knelt down on the floor and crawled around looking for my car keys. It seemed an eternity before I found them. Ryan was waiting for me. He was alone. He was scared.

I rushed through the front door of the building and heard the hideous scream of brakes and a loud crash. Metal on metal screeched and groaned. I looked out to the street, and my heart nearly stopped beating, my limbs went cold. Tiffany had driven out of our parking lot into the path of a big delivery truck.

Forgetting everything, I ran toward the awful scene like the hounds of hell were nipping at my heels. The stench of burning rubber and gasoline filled the air. I reached Tiffany's car and looked inside. She was slumped across the driver's seat, covered with blood.

"Tiffany!" I screamed. "Tiffany, are you okay?" She didn't respond. I turned and yelled to everyone, anyone. "Call an ambulance!"

I struggled with the door. It was crushed so badly I knew I'd never get it open. I pulled and yanked anyway. The truck was on its side a few feet away. Someone was helping the driver climb out through a shattered window.

Sirens screamed in the distance. Brakes screeching, an LAPD black-and-white pulled into the middle of the street. Onlookers scattered out of his way. The officer spoke into a radio on his shoulder as he stepped out of the vehicle. I hoped he was calling for an ambulance. Tiffany was unconscious, I was terrified for her.

The officer reached me. "Stand back, ma'am."

I didn't let go of the car door. "Help her. You have to help her." Frantic, sobbing, I shouted, "Tiffany, dammit. Wake up!"

The officer placed his hands on my shoulders and firmly pulled me away. He put his head in the broken window and reached through the glass. Gingerly he touched Tiffany's hip. He stepped back and put the radio to his face.

"We need jaws to get a vic free of her vehicle...I don't know. There's no response. A young woman, maybe twenties, I can't tell if she's breathing or not, and I can't reach in far enough to get a pulse."

Numb, I stared at the twisted heap of metal that had been Tiffany's car. Through a veil of tears, I peered at her, shaking so bad I could barely stand, my head a buzzing wasp's nest.

This is my fault! She left the office to get away from me.

The officer turned toward me. He grabbed as I sank to my knees and gently lowered me to the curb. "Do you know the driver of this car?"

I nodded mutely, unable to speak, drowning in shock and devastation. Gasping, I said, "Is she alive? Will she be okay?"

"I don't know, ma'am. The EMTs are on the way. Who is she?" He pulled a small notebook from his breast pocket.

"Tiffany Gaines." I didn't recognize my own voice. It came from a hollow distance. The world around me spun into obscene slow motion. "Tiffany Gaines. She's, she's my business partner." I pointed back to the building. "We work...our office...it's in there."

"Who is her next of kin?" He made small, crabbed notes on his pad.

"I don't know."

I should know. She's my best friend. I should know this.

I put my head between my knees and gagged. My skirt was hiked nearly to my waist, but I didn't care. I didn't care about anything, except Tiffany.

I staggered to my feet when I heard the ambulance. It pulled to a stop and the back doors flew open. A man and woman dressed in dark blue uniforms jumped out, dragging a gurney with them. They went to the driver of the truck and bent down to see what condition he was in.

Frantic, I yelled, "Come here, over here!"

The officer took my arm. "They can't help your friend until we get her out of the wreck. The rescue crew is on the way. We need to move over here. "Step back, people! Give them room!"

Like the living dead, I backed into the parking lot, never taking my eyes off Tiffany's car. I labored to breathe and went down on my knees.

A bystander peered in my face. "You okay, lady?"

"No." I fell over sideways and passed out.

∽

Loud tearing, scraping and screeching noise penetrated my brain. I opened my eyes and realized it was real.

A woman from the leasing office waved a magazine in front of my face, her expression anxious. "Ms. Clayton?"

I pushed myself up on my elbows. Someone had put a large towel or piece of drapery under me on the parking lot surface. "Tiffany!"

"Don't get up, Ms. Clayton." She put her hand on my shoulder and gently pushed me back. I reached to see what was under my head and found my purse. The woman continued to fan the magazine in my face.

"Stop, please, I have to get up. What's happening?" She didn't push me back this time. "Please, what's happening?"

"The fire department crew is wrenching off the driver's side door so they can get Ms. Gaines out. They got here about five minutes ago." She took my hand and pulled me to my feet.

Tears spilled from my eyes, and I shook. The woman put her arm around my waist, made comforting sounds, while supporting me.

"Tiffany...is she...is she...?" I could barely get the words past my lips, strangling with every labored breath. I couldn't face the prospect of losing her. It wasn't possible.

"They don't know yet. Come over here and sit, please. We'll know something soon." She led me to a folding chair in the shade in front of the building.

I resisted, then allowed her to lead me to the chair. The moment I sat, I slumped forward and would have fallen flat on my face if she hadn't been right there to support me. As she pushed me upright in the chair one of the EMTs walked over to us, carrying a medical bag. He knelt, opened it and pulled out a packet, ripped it open and wiped it gently across my knee. I jerked back with the sting and was jolted wide awake.

"What? Ow!"

"You cut your knee when you fell. This will prevent infection. I'll bandage it. Let me look at your head." He stood and gently probed through my hair, pulling it this way and that. "A big bump, that's all. You may want to check with your family doctor later."

He put a butterfly bandage on my cut, patted my shoulder and turned to leave.

"Wait! I don't care about me, what about...?" My hand shaking, I pointed at Tiffany's car surrounded by men and equipment working furiously to extract her from the wreckage.

"All I can tell you right now is she's breathing. We can't assess the extent of her injuries until they get her out. It shouldn't be long now. I'll let you know as soon as I know."

He headed toward the crew working to get Tiffany out. Her car was precariously wobbling and tipping.

"Thank God, thank God. She's breathing," I sobbed a laugh, and leaned against the woman. Someone came out of the building with a box of tissues and a bottle of water and handed them to me. I took them and numbly held them in my lap as if I didn't know what they were for. Tears and mucus ran down my face.

Bystanders gaped in macabre silence while the rescue crew worked. Office workers peered from the building across the street. Breathing came easier. I felt a glimmer of hope that all the blood on Tiffany was not as bad as it looked. Head wounds always bleed excessively, even small ones. She'll be okay. She'll be fine.

Another ambulance drove up while the first one to arrive pulled away.

"Why are they leaving?" I reached out my arm as if I could stop them.

"They're taking the driver of the truck to emergency. He was able to walk with help away from the wreck. This other one is for Ms. Gaines."

"Oh sure, that's it. It's for Tiffany." I stood, surprised that my head was clear and the wobbliness of my legs barely noticeable. I swabbed my face with a handful of tissues and turned to the woman whose name I couldn't remember. "I'm okay. Thank you for your help."

She took my hand, "Sure thing, honey. Everything will be fine. Let's just wait here till they pull her out." She had no intention of leaving me on my own yet.

A murmur rose from the crowd, and we watched the crew reach into what was left of the car. They placed a brace to stabilize Tiffany's neck and gently lifted her out on a plastic board and onto a gurney. Completely limp and covered with blood, one of her legs twisted obscenely in the wrong direction. My hand flew to my throat. My knees shook again. "Oh, God!"

They covered her with a blanket and placed an oxygen mask over her face, all the while pushing the gurney to the back doors of the ambulance. I started forward only to be held back by the woman at my side.

"Wait." Her hand tightened on my arm. "Let them do their job. Don't get in their way."

"I have to know where they're taking her." I tried to pull away. She increased the pressure on my arm.

The officer who'd arrived on the scene first, came over to us. He took off his hat and mopped sweat from his forehead with his shirt-sleeve. I stepped forward. He extended his hand out to stop me. "Stay here, ma'am. They're taking her to Cedars Sinai. I'll drive you there in the patrol car as soon as they clear out."

"Is she...?"

"She's breathing. That's all I know."

CHAPTER 42

Matthew

I was at the home office, trying to mend fences, when everything unraveled.

Sitting with an advisor, I shook my head. "Just when I thought I could step back—everything is bollixed up. I'm thinking I should request reassignment."

"Listen to yourself, Matthew. You sound like Heaven's biggest whiner." The voice was teasing but tinged with disgust.

That was Raphael. Yes, I had an archangel breathing down my neck, because my immediate supervisor had thrown up her hands in despair and called in help.

I was unable to keep the petulance from my voice. "I know. I apologize, but I feel incapable and ineffective."

He shook his magnificent head. "Are you listening to yourself? Pity our poor colleague who had the Charles Manson assignment. He had legitimate grounds for despair. You know that we cannot pick and choose our humans."

I slapped my hands on my knees. "I know. I know. It's been a bad few weeks. I'll get right back to work."

"This time you must go strictly by *The Book*. Do I make myself clear on that point?" He waggled those great bushy eyebrows. I squelched a smile. He resembles Andy Rooney, one of our distinguished residents.

"Yes, very clear, sir. I doubt I would be so frustrated at this point if I had followed normal procedure all along. Although, I must confess, I still have strong feelings of human love for Ms. Gaines, Tiffany."

"That's to be expected, considering how much time you spent down there. Remember, Matthew, we never stop learning from our experiences, either here or down there." He gave me a pat of encouragement, then said, "Now I suggest you get back to work immediately."

I nodded and left his presence. I chided myself while making my way back to the archives, and by the time I replaced everything, I had a new sense of determination.

First things first.

The immediate problem was Ryan, left standing on the front steps of his grandparent's home, waiting vainly for Caroline to come for him. To expedite the matter, I appeared at the house in a taxi and whisked him to the hospital.

He didn't know me, of course, and at first was reluctant to get in the taxi. I introduced myself, explaining that I was a friend of Caroline, and his Uncle Daniel, and that Caroline had asked me to stand in for her following Tiffany's automobile accident outside their office.

That seemed to satisfy him, and he settled back against the seat, fidgeting all the way across town. "What happened, Matthew? Was Aunt Caroline hurt?"

"No, my boy, she's fine. Her friend Tiffany was injured. They are on their way to emergency as we speak." I patted his shoulder to reassure him.

When we pulled up to the entrance of Cedars Sinai, he thanked me, hopped out, and ran through the door to look for his family.

It being no longer necessary for me to remain in an earthly body, I paid off the cab driver and resumed my accepted form.

Upon reaching the trauma unit, I immediately noticed that Tiffany's G.A. stood post next to the doctors and nurses working frantically to save her. Tiffany's lovely, broken body would not be mended, no matter the heroic efforts of these experts.

~

"Greetings, Miriam." I acknowledged her and continued, "A traumatic day for our charges."

She sighed with compassion, but no sadness. "Yes, Matthew. Caroline and Tiffany's family will suffer greatly today."

Death is merely a transition. We do not view it the way our human charges do.

"Will they have a moment to speak, to say goodbye?" Even though my human nature is dissolving rapidly, I felt a soft spot of tender-heartedness for Caroline's ordeal.

"Yes, Tiffany will briefly regain consciousness before I accompany her home." Miriam smiled. "She has fulfilled her destiny. Many humans have benefited by her brief presence. I am blessed to be her guardian." Miriam reached out and placed her hand on Tiffany's head.

"May I?" I asked Miriam as I reached to hold Tiffany's hand.

"Certainly, Matthew, I know all that has passed between you."

"She's responding!" one of the doctors shouted. "We have a pulse!" A flurry of activity surrounded the table.

Color appeared in Tiffany's sweet face, and her eyes fluttered. She looked at me and smiled. "Matthew," she muffled into the oxygen mask, "I thought I might see you today."

"I am so happy to see you too, my sweetheart."

"How did I do?"

"You were magnificent, my darling." I stroked her broken fingers. Soon her body will be restored to perfection. She smiled again.

"What's she saying?" a nurse asked.

A technician answered, "She's hallucinating."

"Okay, people, let's get her stabilized and to surgery," the resident doctor directed. They knew their jobs so well his words were a mere formality.

I kept my hand in Tiffany's. Miriam's hand caressed her head. We murmured soft reassurances, as her pain lessened with the help of powerful drugs.

"Do I know you?" Tiffany's eyes looked upward into Miriam's face. Miriam merely smiled her beatific, angelic smile.

"I'm Dr. James," the physician answered, assuming Tiffany was speaking to him. "We're going to take good care of you."

"I need to talk to Caroline," Tiffany said. "May I talk to her before I go?"

"Anybody here know who Caroline is?"

"Patient's hallucinating. She came in alone," one of the E.R. nurses answered.

An attendant spoke up. "There's a cop outside the doors with a distraught woman at his side. Maybe that's who she's talking about. I'll go see."

The doctor said, "No, she's ready to go. We'll find out when we get outside the doors."

They pushed the gurney across the room and through the double doors. Miriam and I followed.

"Tiffany, oh God, Tiffany," Caroline cried. "Is she going to be all right?"

"Are you Caroline?" the doctor asked.

"Yes, is she going to be all right?" Caroline put her hand on Tiffany's shoulder, nearly trampling through me.

"She wants to talk to you. I can only give you a minute. We're on our way to surgery." The doctors and nurses took a step back.

"Tiffany, honey, it's my fault. I'm so sorry."

"Caroline, I need you to promise me something. Say you promise."

"Anything, I promise. We're best girlfriends, aren't we?" She gently placed her hand on Tiffany's cheek. "What is it?"

"Promise me you'll trust Danny. He loves you so much. You might be hurt, but you have to try and live your life completely. Promise?"

"Tiffany, what are you...? Don't worry about me. You just get through this, and we'll have a long gabfest, okay? You can boss me around, and we'll argue about it." Tears streamed down Caroline's cheeks.

"No, Caroline, you have to promise now! Do you promise?"

"Yes, I promise. Tiffany, don't..."

The doctor stepped forward. "Okay, gotta go now. Step aside, ma'am. Hold those elevator doors open, Charlie. We're code blue here."

They pushed swiftly and silently into the elevator. The doors whooshed closed behind them.

"I know she's going to be fine." Caroline nodded to the police officer. "Yes. Fine."

CHAPTER 43

Caroline

After a virtual eternity, the doctor came into the waiting room, his expression grim. "Ms. Clayton, I'm so sorry. We did everything we could. Her internal injuries were so massive there was no way to save her." He sat next to me. "Will you be okay?"

I didn't answer, I couldn't. I attempted to process what he said. How was it possible Tiffany died? She was the most *alive* person I had ever known. She was my friend, my best friend. She saw through my problems and loved me for my real self. She would never abandon me—except—now she had.

"Ms. Clayton?" The doctor touched my arm. "We need to notify Ms. Gaines' next of kin. When the social worker comes from the office, will you be able to give her that information?"

"I...no, I can't. I don't know their names or where they live." I closed my eyes and even though I didn't think it possible, there could be any more tears, a wave of devastation swept me.

"Perhaps her employer would have that information in their personnel records. Do you know where she worked?"

"We...she and I, we started a business together a few days ago. We were setting up our office today, when she decided to go out for a while. I'm sorry. I should know, but I don't."

I reached for a large box of tissues on the table next to the sofa and mopped my eyes and nose.

"Perhaps you know her previous employer?"

"Oh, yes, of course. I'm not thinking. She worked for Leebow Elvey Honnet. They're just off Wilshire. They would know."

He stood and touched my shoulder. "Is there someone we may call for you, someone to come take you home?"

I shook my head. I couldn't remember how I had come to the hospital, or where I had left my car. Through the window I saw that it was night. "What time is it?"

"It's just after nine. Perhaps I should call a cab for you?" He had a kind face, a weary and sad face. He had to be about the same age as Ryan's dad, Flynn, young, forties.

"No. I need to sit here for a while. Don't be concerned with me, doctor. I have to think, decide what to do."

He patted my shoulder. "All right then. Take your time. Go to the nurse's station if you need anything. Okay?" He pointed down the hall to my right.

I nodded. My head throbbed, and I wasn't aware of how much time had passed when a bumpy rattling sound jolted me. A white-haired old lady pushed a cart through the waiting lounge. She stopped and smiled when she reached me.

"Would you like coffee, tea, or a magazine, dear?" The skin on her face was marshmallow soft and rosy pink. Her wispy hair formed a halo about her face and head, her smile kind and comforting. She could have been an angel. Straight from Central Casting.

An automatic smile trembled on my lips. That I could smile so soon after what had happened, mystified me. All around me, people went to and fro, talking, studying charts, carrying supplies. *Their* lives hadn't changed, only Tiffany's. And mine.

"Tea would be nice," I heard myself say, fighting tears again. Where were all the tears coming from?

She poured tea into a Styrofoam cup and held it out to me. When I reached for it, my hand shook so badly she placed it on the table instead.

"I'll just put it here, dear. It's too hot to drink right now anyway. Why don't we let it cool off for a few minutes?"

"Yes, thank you." I leaned back on the soft, broken-down sofa and rested my head on the back cushion. I must have closed my eyes. Time held no meaning.

Someone sat next to me. I woke with a start, stared at Dan's mother,

Mary, and suddenly remembered Ryan's telephone call, Liam's emergency, the ambulance. Please, God, please not him too.

"Mom!" My throat so tight the words choked me. "Is Dad okay? What happened? Oh no, I forgot about Ryan!" My frantic sobs were barely intelligible.

Mary embraced me. "Liam will be fine, Caroline. He aspirated a bit of food. They'll keep him overnight, for observation." She rocked me back and forth. "The nurse told me about your friend, Tiffany. We're so terribly sorry."

Her caring and sincere sympathy unraveled me. I collapsed into her, and the tears began afresh. She tightened her arms around my shoulders and made soothing sounds while she rubbed my back and arms.

"I didn't know," I bawled, "I didn't know it was possible to feel so much pain." I pressed my fist to my chest. My entire body shook. "It really hurt when my grandma died, but she was old and had been ill for over a year. Tiffany? Why?" My chest racked with sobs.

"I know it hurts," Mary said. "You will get through it, Caroline. We'll help you. We love you."

When Mary said *we*, I glanced up to see Ryan standing in the doorway. He seemed afraid to come any closer. I extended my arm, and he approached shyly, to sit beside me.

I grabbed his hand. "Ryan, I'm sorry I forgot you."

"That's okay, Aunt Caroline." He squeezed my fingers.

"How did you get here?" I smeared tears off my cheeks with my free hand.

"Your friend, Matthew, came to the house and brought me to the hospital in a taxi cab because he doesn't know how to drive." He studied my face. "Your nose is red."

A sound resembling a sob more than a laugh erupted from my throat. I kept laughing and sobbing and couldn't stop. Surprised, I hadn't thought I could ever laugh again. *Matthew!* Would I be hearing his name for the rest of my life? I took a deep breath, accompanied by a hiccup and a sob.

"Would you like me to go relieve Daniel?" Mary asked me. "He's with his father, just down the hall."

There was nothing I wanted or needed more at that moment than Danny, but I said, "No." I'm not sure why. "I have to go close my office.

I have to look through Tiffany's desk and see if I can find her parents' phone number. I should call them."

Just saying Tiffany's name was a knife in my heart. I hugged Mary and Ryan and stood, picked up my bag, and sped for the exit. They waved sadly as I left.

The parking attendant whistled up a cab for me.

I raised my hand. "Oh, I forgot to pay that nice old lady for the tea."

She cocked her head with confusion. "Old lady? I'm not sure who you mean."

"The lady pushing the tea cart."

"Someone in the cafeteria?"

My hair prickled. A hollow feeling filled me. Some force gnawed my insides. "No. Forget it. It was probably a dream." I turned and made my way to the taxi on shaky legs.

I dreaded every mile that got me closer to the new office.

The building was mostly dark and the parking lot near empty. After I paid the cab driver, I noticed broken glass and other bits of debris that hadn't been cleaned up after the wreck. My stomach gave a wrench, and I felt lightheaded again.

"There was a horrible wreck here this afternoon." I quailed at the voice from the darkness and gasped with surprise and alarm.

"I'm sorry, lady, I thought you saw me," the man said. "I drive a delivery route through this neighborhood." He was middle-aged and well-groomed in a dark blue uniform. He didn't look as if he posed any threat.

"Yes," I answered in a croaky voice. "I saw it earlier."

"Sure hope it wasn't anyone you knew," he said, shaking his head sorrowfully.

"Uh...no," was all I managed before my throat closed and tears threatened.

"I wouldn't spend too much time out here on the street, miss. Neighborhood's not safe for a woman alone at night."

"No, I...uh...I'm going inside," I gestured to the building and turned toward the entrance. "Thank you. Goodnight."

"You take care now," he said, and continued on the way to his truck.

∼

Slumped at Tiffany's desk, I was unable to open her drawer or files. Paralysis overcame me, and tears streamed down my cheeks once again. I folded my arms, lowered my head, and gave myself up to the pain and grief. The sense of loss overpowered me. Too much, too much. Wrenching sobs tore at my stomach and chest.

Why Tiffany? Why? I'm sorry, I'm so sorry.

Unaware that hours had passed, I noticed the rosy-gray color of the sky and realized it would soon be light outside. Another day of my life. Tiffany's ended yesterday. It wouldn't sink in; I was disconnected from reality in a way completely foreign to my experience. This world was a place I'd never been, was unfamiliar with.

I rose and went into the bathroom. After using the toilet and splashing water on my face, I looked into the mirror. Except for the ravages of tears and lack of sleep, it was the same face I had seen in the mirror for thirty years. I had expected to look different.

How could I look the same? The events of the past twenty-four hours had changed me inside, but outside I was the same as before.

I went through the motions of making coffee. Such a mundane task seemed obscene to me. The telephone answering machine blinked. I had no interest in checking messages. They were of no importance to me, and I wasn't sure I could take any action the calls might require.

With the steaming fresh cup of coffee placed on Tiffany's desk, I reached for her center drawer. Unable to bring myself to open it, I picked up the cup instead. The heat and fragrance of the coffee had a clarifying effect on my brain, which was unwelcome. I was ashamed that I could even notice the smell and taste of the coffee.

Setting the cup down, I placed my hand on the drawer again and pulled it tentatively toward my waist. I stared at the neat, organized contents, the pens, pencils, and paperclips. Sticky notes and Scotch tape. I reached for a photo with a couple of pinholes in the top border. A Mouseketeer's cast grouping. Tiffany, at about ten years, stood smiling in the center of the first row. The same smile I'd seen a few hours ago in this room. My gut twisted when I burped sour coffee.

As I opened the drawer farther, I found her day planner and a blue jewelry box. I should have reached for the planner, but it was the box that found its way into my hand.

A small stiff card had been folded and slipped beneath the white bow. I pulled it free and read the note.

To Tiffany, my Angel and my Sweetheart for now and for all time. Matthew.

Sliding the ribbon from the box, I slowly opened it. Inside were two diamond and pearl earrings designed in the image of angels. The stones were brilliant and perfect, the gold glowing with warmth. I touched one of them with the tip of my finger and felt a rush of love for Tiffany. My best girlfriend, my partner, the woman who ignored her broken heart to go to work and cover for me the morning after the man she loved deserted her.

The same woman who put up with my temper and insecurities with good sense and lively humor. The friend who packed up her desk and walked away from a secure job to help me without looking back, because she trusted me and cared for me. How had I deserved such a friend? A friend I'd known for such a short, significant time in my life.

"Caroline?"

I screamed, and the box flew from my hands and skittered across Tiffany's desk. I nearly knocked over the coffee cup but steadied it as I looked to the entrance door. My father stood there, alone.

"Dad? What? How?" I pressed my hand against my chest in a futile attempt to calm my heartbeat.

He raised his hands helplessly. "I need you," he said, as if ashamed of the words. He looked older to me, older and very tired.

CHAPTER 44

Daniel

When Lyle Clayton called Dan after midnight, he'd just come in the door of his apartment, dead tired and worried sick over Caroline. He should have gone to her immediately when Mary and Ryan told him what happened to Tiffany. Something held him back. She needed to ask for him. If she didn't want him with her now, she never would.

He jumped when the phone rang and grabbed the handset. "Care?"

A man's voice answered, "Hello? Is this Daniel Kavanaugh?"

Panic lodged in his throat. Oh my God, what now? "Yes, who is this?" A pulse throbbed in Dan's neck, sweat slicked his palms.

"It's Lyle." The man cleared his throat. "Lyle Clayton, Caroline's father."

Was the man nuts? Dan knew Lyle Clayton was Caroline's father. "What's happened? Is she all right?" What else could have gone wrong?

"She's fine, I'm sure. I thought she might be with you. I couldn't locate her at her place."

Daniel paced, took a breath, tried to relax his neck. "If she isn't home, she might be at her new office." Hearing no reply, he said, "Hello? Are you there?"

"Yes, her new office?"

"Lyle, why in hell are you looking for her at this time of the night? Has something happened?"

"I just got into LAX," he said. "I was hoping she could pick me up."

"Jesus! You people are clueless. Why in God's name don't you hire a car! I can't believe you'd expect her to pick you up in the middle of the night." Dan was ready to hang up on him. "I gotta go."

"Wait!" Lyle said. "You're right, I know you're right. I'll call her in the morning. Do you have the address of her office, the phone number?"

Dan gave him the information. Clueless didn't cover it. All Care needed right now was her parents. What else would be dumped in her lap?

CHAPTER 45
Matthew

Regretfully, during her crisis, Caroline will now be called upon by her father. She is strong, stronger than she knows. She will feel overpowered and helpless but will find her deep well of strength.

What she should do now is answer her telephone or at least turn on her cell. Things are happening that she should know of.

I shall try to remain calm and have faith. I'm crossing my fingers even though I know that's piffle.

CHAPTER 46

Caroline

Uncomprehending, I stared at my father. "You need me for what?" I don't know where it came from, but a bitter laugh erupted from my throat. "On the worst day of my life you show up, and *you* need *me*?"

"I have no one else, Caroline." He dropped into the chair across from me. "Only you."

I studied his beseeching, helpless expression. *This man is my father, lucky me.* I shook my head. "Where's Beth? Why are you here?"

Instead of answering, he dropped his chin to his chest and drew a shaky breath. I was astonished to see that he was crying. At first, I couldn't believe it, but the teardrops on his shirt were proof enough.

I pushed a box of tissues toward him. "Dad, what's happened to Mother? Why did you say you have only me?" No response. "Dad, talk to me, please." I rose because I'd intended to go to him and put a comforting hand on his shoulder. Instead, I stood rooted to the floor.

He raised his tearstained face. He'd aged at least ten years in the few weeks since I'd been with them. He tried to talk, stopped, swallowed, and cleared his throat.

"Elizabeth left me."

"She left you where? Here?"

I went behind Tiffany's desk to the coffeepot and poured a cup for him. "Here, Dad. Have some coffee, and then maybe you'll make sense." The cheap new desk chair emitted a squeak of protest as I flopped back down.

Dad wiped at his eyes with the cuff of his shirt and raised the coffee cup to his lips. His hand shook. I was afraid he would spill it before he managed to take a swallow. My heart ached when I saw his lips trembling like those of a very old man.

He carefully took a small sip. The thought that he wouldn't always be around came as a revelation to me. How old was Dad? Right then, I couldn't bear to think of losing anyone else from my life.

He set the cup down and looked me squarely in the eye. "Caroline, your mother has left me. She's divorcing me. I've lost her."

"She's left you?" I parroted the words stupidly. "She's divorcing you? No, no, Dad." I thought if I just stood, shook myself, took a few deep breaths and opened my eyes again, he'd be gone. I'd be alone and waking from a gloomy, confusing dream. I squeezed my eyes closed and opened them.

He was still there.

I folded my arms on the desk and dropped my forehead to my wrists and groaned. I felt his fingers gently touch my hair.

"It's true," he choked out on a sob. "Elizabeth left me for another man."

The choking sob became more of a laugh. "The man—arrogant, old snot— is an obscure Italian count with piles and piles of old money and no heirs." He stopped to take a breath. "They've already drawn up a binding co-habitation and pre-nuptial agreement."

He laughed and gulped great gobs of air. "She's going to be filthy rich!"

I raised my head. Staring at him, giddy laughter welled up. Dropping against the back of my chair, I took a deep breath and put my hand on my mouth, trying stop it. There was no stopping it. Hysterical guffaws poured from me until tears streamed down my face once again. "Dad, I... Dad, I don't..."

"My mother warned me," he said with a guffaw of his own.

We hee-hawed like a couple of plastered drunks, unable to exercise the tiniest control over what we said or did. I reached across the desk, and he grabbed my hand, squeezed it hard.

The laughter subsided as quickly as it came. We gazed soberly at each other through tear washed eyes. I let go of his hand and walked around to his side of the desk. He rose at the same time as me, and we embraced in a long overdue and desperate hug.

The door clicked open, and a woman's voice said, "I'm sorry. I didn't mean—" Sandra Russell, the receptionist at L.E.H. waited, awkward, embarrassed.

Dad and I parted. I wiped at my eyes. "Sandra? What is it? What are you doing here?"

"Mr. Moody's been trying to find you. You haven't been answering your phone here or at your apartment. He's worried, and he sent me to see if I could find you."

She opened the flap of her shoulder bag and pulled out an envelope. "Here, he wanted me to give you this." She held it out to me.

Moody, worried about me? I must have heard wrong. The last thing in the world would be that Moody would even think about me, much less worry. "What is this?" I held the envelope in my hand.

Sandra looked uncomfortably at Dad.

"It's information about Tiffany's..." She choked on the words and cleared her throat, "Tiffany's funeral."

I found my manners. "Dad, this is Sandra Russell from L.E.H., Sandra, my father, Lyle Clayton."

I ripped open the envelope. "Funeral? She just died a few hours ago."

The note was written in Moody's distinctive scrawl.

Caroline,

Tiffany's funeral is this afternoon at three o'clock, at Temple Beth Shalom in Burbank. Her parents have been trying to find you. They would like you to attend. Mr. Kavanaugh will be at your apartment around one-thirty to accompany you. L.E.H. is closing this afternoon so that our staff may be in attendance. We're deeply shocked and terribly sorry. Hopefully, we'll see you there. Arthur

Arthur. Moody had never used his first name with me. "I don't understand. Why are they having her funeral today? It's so soon," I wondered aloud.

"They're Jewish," Sandra answered. "Jews have to be buried within twenty-four hours of death. We're all going, everyone from the office."

Tiffany was Jewish? Another thing I had not known about *my best girlfriend*. It was all about you, wasn't it, Caroline? I didn't even know the most basic facts about her. Shame engulfed me like a furnace blast. I sat in the chair Dad had vacated.

"I have to go back to work," Sandra said, backing toward the door. "Are you coming to the funeral?"

"Yes, of course. Yes, I'll be there." I gave her a limp wave as she left the office.

Dad put his hand on my shoulder and asked me what had happened. I told him about my tantrum, how Tiffany had left the office to take a break from me and her awful accident. He groaned with sympathy and apologized for burdening me with his crisis.

I patted his hand. "I guess I better close the office and go home, make some phone calls, and get ready. The note from my old boss says Danny's going to pick me up at one-thirty."

"What can I do to be of help?" Dad asked.

I shook my head, still unable to put together a clear thought. "Nothing, Dad, go on to the Bel Air, and I'll call you this evening."

"I'm not registered at the Bel Air. I'll be at Mother's house in Hancock Park." He took a scrap of paper from Tiffany's desk, wrote something, and handed it to me. "Here's my cell number."

"You never stay there, not in years." I was further confused. "Dad, only caretakers have been in that house since Gramma died. I went there when she was very sick and stayed with her for a few days, but you and Beth always used the hotel when you were in town."

He shrugged. "I know. Elizabeth refused to stay in Mother's house. I always loved that great, old place. Come over later. I'll wait supper for you."

I shook my head, tried to clear my muddled brain. "I have to lock up here before I go home. I'll call you later."

"No. You go home and do what you have to do. Leave me the keys. I'll pick up your phone calls and messages and lock up when I leave. If you need me, I'll be here, then at Mother's."

It was probably my imagination, but he seemed younger than he had when he first walked through my office door. I couldn't think of anything to say except, "Okay, thanks, Dad."

He put his hand on my back and walked me out. "When you come to Mother's this evening, there are some things I need to tell you about her house, but it will wait. Go."

CHAPTER 47

Matthew

In case you were wondering—of course I knew. We all knew Tiffany and her family were of the Hebrew faith. We make no such distinctions here. Those are human contrivances to which we pay little attention. Like it or not, the fact is, we're all in this together.

CHAPTER 48

Caroline

I paced, waiting for Danny to arrive to take me to Tiffany's funeral. While driving home from my office, I remembered the diamond earrings I'd found in her desk. I should have brought them with me and given them to her mother. I figured it was unlikely I would see Tiffany's parents after today. I'd package them up and mail them.

In my heart, I knew it was my responsibility to take them and not mail them. I hated the thought of having to go through another wrenching experience, but I had to do it. That was all.

I'd showered, then rested for a couple of hours but couldn't sleep. I tried to get my mind around all that had happened in the past twenty-four hours from my tantrum to my childish refusal to talk to Danny—Liam's emergency trip to the hospital—Tiffany's horrible death—forgetting to pick up Ryan. And the topper of my dad showing up to tell me he and my mother were divorcing.

At least Dan was being his adult, dependable self, coming to accompany me to the funeral. He was so good, always there for me. I couldn't remember a time since we'd met that he had ever let me down. I was ashamed I couldn't say the same for myself. I have to find a way to make it up to him and quit behaving like a spoiled child.

When the doorbell rang, I wondered, for an instant, why he didn't use his key. Then I remembered the asinine scene I'd created when I demanded he return the key to me and leave. I opened the door and stopped short.

"Flynn?" I couldn't understand why Dan's big brother was standing on my doorstep.

He smiled sadly. "Hello, Caroline."

"What are you doing here?"

Puzzled, he cocked his head. "I came to accompany you to Tiffany's funeral. Didn't they tell you? I asked your old boss to let you know."

"Uh, yes, they told me, but I assumed they meant Danny. The note said Mr. Kavanaugh. I assumed——"

"I'm sorry. I specifically gave them my first name."

"There's no need to apologize. It was a mix-up." I took my jacket and purse from the hall table. "Thank you for coming. We should go."

The sickening fear that I'd lost Danny for good grew like a shard of ice in my heart. Being the decent man he was, he'd sent Flynn to make sure I wouldn't be alone at the funeral. It was probably for the best, as far as Danny was concerned. He should move on with his life now and find a woman who deserved him. I certainly didn't. What should have surprised me was that it took him three years to get completely fed up. The sense of loss I felt was doubled.

You did it to yourself, Caroline.

Flynn put his arm around my shoulders on the way out to his car, and I had to grit my teeth and swallow to keep from crying. Any show of sympathy or compassion would destroy me. I had to keep it together for the sake of Tiffany's family.

CHAPTER 49

Matthew

Miriam and I attended Tiffany's service. As you should remember, Miriam, Tiffany's G.A., was present at the hospital while those valiant doctors and nurses attempted to save her.

Miriam would now concentrate more on Melody, Jake, Avi, and their parents. My Kavanaugh clan is much larger than the Gaines family, but we both have our work cut out for us. We're eternally devoted to our charges.

Human beings are often comforted greatly by rituals of funerals and wakes. It is their way to ponder their common loss, reminisce, and reflect. I expect that Caroline, especially, will benefit from the day. She will come to realize that loss, even sudden tragic loss, is not fatal. One can soldier on with life, learning from all events, happy or wretched.

In my experience, it is often tragic events which come to be such valuable lessons, enabling those brave enough to reach for and treasure every moment of joy their earthly lives have to offer.

CHAPTER 50

Caroline

Temple Beth Shalom is in a quiet Burbank neighborhood. The street was packed with cars parked on both sides for at least two blocks in either direction. It was useless to even think of entering the temple parking lot. "Looks like we're going to have a hike," Flynn said as he parked his beautiful new Lexus a few blocks away. He came around to my side to open the door to help me out. That's what all the Kavanaugh men did.

Two tall, blond, young men stood at the door greeting mourners as they arrived. The older one cocked his head when he reached for my hand. "You're Caroline, aren't you?" He squeezed my hand. "I'm Avi. Thank you for coming. My mother will be so glad."

"How did you...I don't believe we've met."

"Tiff had a picture of the two of you on her refrigerator door, a snapshot someone had taken during a birthday party at the office. You look exactly like your photo."

The younger blond man handed Flynn a small cap, which he placed on his head. I was confused and would ask Flynn about that later.

"I'm Jake," the young man said. "We're Tiffany's brothers. Mom, Dad, and Melody are inside. Thank you for coming."

I was stunned at the number of people in the large auditorium. There must have been two hundred mourners milling about. I recognized many Hollywood celebrities. Flynn leaned close and whispered,

"That's Michael Eisner talking to those two people near the podium. The elderly gentleman at the end of the first row is Roy Disney."

How could all these people have assembled on such short notice? On the far side of the room, Sandra Russell saw me and waved. Moody acknowledged me with a somber nod.

A small woman in a dark suit approached. "Caroline? Thank you for coming, dear. Tiffany talked about you so much. She was so fond of you. She said you were her best friend. I'm Sarah, her mother." She turned and extended her arm to a man and young girl. "This is my husband David and Tiffany's sister, Melody."

Speechless, I couldn't understand how these people could be so calm, so civilized. I tried to smile, but it was useless. Instead, I turned and said, "This is Flynn Kavanaugh, Danny's brother. We're so sorry for your loss. I don't know what else to say."

Flynn shook hands with David Gaines who said, "Our Tiffany was a special person to many." He stepped forward and offered his elbow to me. "We'd like you to sit with our family, Caroline."

Flynn followed, Sarah on his arm with Melody, the image of Tiffany, following close behind. Once seated beside the Gaines family, I choked back tears and grasped Flynn's hand. He held on tightly.

During the heart-wrenching service, the rabbi spoke lovingly of Tiffany. He'd known her since her birth and had presided at her Bat Mitzvah. Later, remembrances spoken by friends were sprinkled with humor and love. A cantor sang traditional Hebrew prayers throughout the service. At the end he sang "You Light up my Life," in his beautiful baritone voice. My heart ached.

The rabbi stepped forward and said, "We wish shalom for Tiffany's soul, as her true spirit lives on in all those gathered here today and beyond. Truly, she lives forever as long as she is remembered and spoken of by those whose lives she touched with her grace and beauty."

Many tears flowed among the mourners. Mine, too.

At the conclusion, we stood for a final prayer, then exited row by row. Mourners filed past Tiffany's casket with heads bowed in respect. Everyone was to follow the hearse and the family to the new Mount Sanai cemetery in Simi Valley.

The sun shone bright in the early evening sky, the temperature in the high sixties, no cloud in sight. We completed the long, winding road off the Ronald Reagan freeway to the burial site. We noticed many others walking in the same direction. Flynn parked, and we got out of his car.

"Look at all these people," I heard Tiffany's mother exclaim when she stepped out of the limousine. "Isn't it wonderful, David?"

The graveside ceremony was brief as the sun would soon set over the western hills, embracing the valley. At least a hundred more people were present for the burial than had attended the temple service. My heart jolted when I saw Danny standing at the rear of the crowd in the shade of an ancient California live oak. He didn't indicate that he'd seen me. When I glanced in that direction again, he was walking away.

Mourners drifted off. Sarah told me they were having a gathering at the temple activity hall and would love Flynn and I to attend. There was no polite way to refuse. When we arrived back at Temple Beth Shalom, several young people stood by the door with pitchers of water, bowls, and disposable towels for each person entering.

Avi noted my confusion. "It's to wash off the sadness and grief and to signify a new beginning of a different life without Tiffany."

I understood how incredibly lucky I was to have had Tiffany as my friend. I was a better person because of her.

CHAPTER 51
Daniel

Dan watched the burial service from the fringe of the crowd, keeping his eyes on Caroline. He was surprised when she looked in the distance and glimpsed him. He thought she would be too distressed to notice who was at the cemetery, considering the impressive size of the crowd.

Flynn had agreed immediately when Daniel asked him if he would escort her and stay with her. Wayne, Grant, Stewart, and Liam had also volunteered, but Dan didn't wish to overwhelm her, just lend support.

Caroline had no one else.

He'd hurt deeply when she hadn't called him. He would have been by her side in an instant, and he had no doubt she knew it. Whatever held her back was something she'd have to work out for herself.

CHAPTER 52

Caroline

Flynn took me back to my apartment. I thanked him again and asked him to pass on my love to the other Kavanaughs. As soon as he left, I went directly to my car and headed for Gramma's house in Hancock Park. Dad said he'd wait supper for me, and I supposed I might as well get one more unpleasant chore out of the way before the end of this dreadful day.

Hancock Park is a wealthy old neighborhood of L.A. Development began in the early 1900's. It was once considered the most exclusive residential neighborhood in the city and still very high-end. When I lived at Gramma's house, our next-door neighbor was the British Ambassador. His two young daughters and I attended the same school, and we often made tea parties and played Princess together. Hancock Park was originally a large producing oil field with hundreds of wells pumping day and night.

Today, the neighborhood surrounds Wilshire Country Club. The homes are large, worth millions and set well back from the street. Fences were considered gauche, but many of the more recent owners had added them. These days, there exists a very real liability issue if one has a swimming pool. It's almost as necessary to have as much pool security as you'd find at a minimum security prison. Soon, I expect, California residents will have to raise their hands to ask permission from the state legislature to pee or eat a Snickers bar.

California backyards are treated as another room. Elaborate gardens were developed to create privacy without need of fences and walls. I loved Gramma's patio and garden.

The house looked just as elegant as the last time I'd been there. The lawns and gardens were well tended. Christmas lights twinkled from the large pine tree in the front. I had no idea how much money my parents spent to keep the place looking so great. I often wondered why they didn't sell it instead of letting it sit empty year after year.

The long narrow driveway from the street went past the house and turned left into a wide parking area in front of a four-car garage. A Honda Accord sat parked in front of one of the roll down doors, and I assumed it was Dad's rental. If it was, what a dramatic come down. For years he'd kept a sleek green Jaguar here in the garage, and for all I knew it was still there. Maybe the Honda belonged to a visitor or a caretaker.

I pulled forward and parked next to the Honda. The gate from the patio to the back terrace was ajar, and I let myself in through the French doors which led to the sunroom. "Dad?" I walked through to the sunroom. "Dad? You here?"

Conversation drifted toward me from dining room. My Dad and another man were speaking. I walked in that direction, enjoying the lovely old furniture and draperies from my childhood. The shelves in the butler's pantry gleamed with sparkling crystal. It seemed as if it had been used daily for the past four years. Nothing had changed except, of course, Gramma wasn't here anymore.

"Dad?" I called out once again.

"In here, Caroline. I'm in the library." He peeked around the doorway just as I stepped into the hall. "Come in here, I'm just going over opening the house with Rodney and Marta."

Rodney had been chief cook and bottle washer of Gramma's house since before I was born, but I didn't know Marta.

Rodney flashed me a big smile when I entered. "Ms. Caroline, how wonderful to see you after so long." He opened his arms, and I stepped into his familiar bear-like embrace. I'd enjoyed more hugs from Rodney than my father during my childhood. Memories flooded me with his familiar scent of Aqua Velva. I was surprised they still sold it.

As soon as I felt his big chest against my cheek, the tears started. Rodney rubbed my back, saying over and over how sorry he was to hear about my friend's death. He reached into his pocket and pulled out a huge white handkerchief, which he put into my hand. Nothing had changed. I was a child again, and Rodney had always been there to comfort me. I wiped my eyes and looked into his beautiful, battered face with his mashed boxer's nose and cauliflower ears. Rodney was a professional prize fighter in his teens. He wore the marks of that time with dignity.

He turned and gestured toward a sweet-faced, round little woman. "This is my wife, Marta. Marta this is my little girl, Caroline."

"Your wife?" I was pleased and surprised. "Marta, I'm so happy to meet you. I'm sorry to cry all over your husband."

Marta smiled and placed her hand in the crook of Rodney's elbow. At least twenty years his junior, her love for him lit up her face. She looked down shyly and murmured something that I didn't hear.

"Marta's my little shy one." Rodney patted her hand. "We were married last week at City Hall."

"Congratulations!" I surprised myself by embracing both of them.

"You remember Judge Tanzman, don't you? She lived across the street for many years while you were growing up. She married us."

"Yes, I remember her. I thought she retired."

"She still performs marriages, and she was happy to do it for Marta and me." He placed his arm around Marta. His little wife's head barely reached his shoulder. They were an odd pair.

"Dad, did you know Rodney's great news?" I poked Rodney with my elbow. "I thought you were a bachelor for life. What happened?"

My father had observed our conversation with obvious pleasure. He stood with hands in his pants pockets and grinned. "No, I didn't know until today, but I couldn't be happier. We were just discussing which rooms to open, and which part of the house Rodney and Marta would like to call their own."

This was a shock because it always seemed to me that my parents treated Rodney and the other servants as if they were invisible. Gramma favored the expression "Wonders never cease," and this was certainly one of those wonders.

Rodney spoke up, "We can decide later, Marta has dinner ready for you. You should enjoy it while it's hot and fresh. She's a wonderful cook." He smiled at Marta. She dipped her head shyly and walked quickly to the kitchen, her round bottom bouncing under her starched uniform skirt.

"I'll set up service in the dining room," Rodney said.

I stopped him. "No, please. I'd rather eat in the kitchen. Is that okay with you, Dad?"

"Fine, it will be just like old times."

Old times?

Dad put his hand on my shoulder. "You've had a bad day. Why not go up to your old suite and freshen up? We'll meet in the kitchen in say, ten minutes? We have a lot to talk about tonight."

His comment put a damper on my psyche. I sighed and headed upstairs.

CHAPTER 53

Daniel

Flynn called when he got home to let Dan know that Caroline was going straight to meet her dad, and she probably wouldn't be back to her apartment till late.

Daniel figured that if she hadn't called him by the time she got back to her apartment, she probably wasn't going to call at all.

He sighed. She was one hard-headed female, and he was still on her shit list.

He had half a mind to call the little vamp, Jessica Rayce, and ask her out. That would serve Caroline right.

Half a mind is right, Dan-o.

He'd sit tight and stick by the phone, just in case.

CHAPTER 54
Matthew

I think it would be an excellent idea if I just minded some other business for a while. Let them work it out without my interference.

CHAPTER 55
Caroline

Dad sat at the kitchen table waiting for me when I came downstairs. I was surprised to see it set for four. Dad poured water, and Rodney carried a platter to the table. Marta stood by the sink, wiping her hands on her apron, a look of uncertainty on her round, little face.

"I thought it would be a good idea for all of us to sit together for dinner," Dad said. "There's a lot of business to discuss, regarding this house." He gestured for me to sit and turned to invite Marta to the table. "Please, Marta, sit with us."

I was beyond astonished. Dad sitting down with servants? I had the feeling I'd entered The Twilight Zone. Who was this man masquerading as my father? What was I doing here? Still, like a programmed robot, I took a seat.

Dad picked up the platter. "Doesn't this look delicious? I don't remember the last time I had homemade Mexican food."

My eyes had to be lying. Could that be my father, Lyle Clayton, dishing up tamales, quesadillas, taquitos, and carnitas? I thought it best not to say anything and picked up the bowl of black beans to put a small helping on my plate.

"My Marta loves to cook." Rodney beamed.

From the looks of the kitchen, new pots and pans, and the clay pots of fresh herbs on the windowsill above the sink, I concluded that Marta had been cooking here for Rodney for a while.

Well, good for them.

Dad raised his glass, "Here's to this magnificent old house." He smiled, inviting everyone to drink.

Now that was something I could toast. "Yes, here's to Gramma's house. It's a very special place for us." I turned to Marta. "Congratulations on your marriage to a wonderful man."

"Hear, hear," Dad said.

I smiled at Marta's shy blush. "You know what would taste good with this food? A bottle of Corona or Pacifico."

She jumped up as if she had springs on her seat and went to the refrigerator. "How many?" Four hands, including hers, shot up, and we all laughed. She pulled four frosty bottles of Corona from the fridge and brought them to the table, then went back and retrieved a small bowl of lime wedges.

"Now you're talking." I was beginning to feel like myself again. Maybe I would be able to think straight once more, to face whatever came next.

We stuffed ourselves while my father and Rodney discussed the management of the house and grounds. Dad was alert and animated. It had been a long time since I had seen him take over a conversation, to speak with such self-assurance. Now that I thought about it, I couldn't remember the last occasion. Maybe it was a good thing Mother had left him.

Dad suggested Rodney and Marta take over the two-bedroom cottage behind the greenhouse as their residence. Rodney had always lived in the small apartment above the garage, what snooty old-timers called the Carriage house. Rodney told Dad the cottage hadn't been lived in for several years and would need renovations to make it livable. Father told him to go ahead and do whatever updating, decorating, painting or repairs were necessary to make it their own. He'd pay for everything; Rodney had been a member of the family since he, Lyle, was a teenager. It would be his wedding gift to them.

Eyes shining with unshed tears, Marta stood to clear the table.

Despite the early hour, I began to nod. I usually never went to bed before eleven, but I was drowning in exhaustion.

Dad said he had a lot more to talk to me about, but I told him I had to get home and get to bed, that I had to open my office at nine in the morning. I still wasn't sure how I was going to handle it alone but was much too tired to give it coherent thought tonight.

When the alarm went off at seven, I rolled over and tapped the shut-off button, stretched and smiled at the bright sun's rays fighting to get through my bedroom drapes. In the next instant, I remembered Tiffany and got that huge cement lump in my chest.

"No, no more tears. Take a breath. Get in the shower. Go to work," I said out loud.

I went to the kitchen and started the coffee maker, pressed the delete button on my flashing answer machine, and went straight into the bathroom. Wrapping a towel around my head, I stepped into the shower. I didn't even wait for the water to reach a comfortable temperature. It was cold, and I hate the feel of cold water on my skin, but I stood there and punished myself with it before it finally warmed up.

By the time I got out and dried myself, I was fully awake. One big cup of coffee and maybe I'd be able to think clearly. I had a big investment and big obligations in my business. I wasn't about to let it go down the tubes while I sat around and felt sorry for myself.

The parking lot at my office in North Hollywood was empty except for a small delivery van and my father's green Jaguar. Thank goodness he was there. I realized he had my only set of keys.

He stepped out of the car when I parked beside him. He carried a brief case and a small, insulated cooler.

"Dad, I'm so glad you brought my keys. I thought I'd have to call a locksmith." I looked at what he was carrying. "What's all this? I have so much to do, and I don't even know how I'm going to manage it alone." I was afraid he'd brought a lot of paperwork concerning the divorce.

He shrugged and smiled. "I came to help you. Let's get to work." He walked to the entrance of the building and left me standing there. "Come on. We open at nine, right?" He held up the cooler. "Marta packed our lunch."

Now I knew I was in a parallel universe. Who was this man? What happened to my life?

The first thing Dad did was get the coffee maker going. I had no idea he even knew how to boil water, let alone make coffee.

I sat at my desk and began the chore of picking up all the phone messages since yesterday, making notes, and prioritizing the call-backs. Dad picked up incoming calls and took more messages for me.

The father imposter brought me coffee, accepted a package from the UPS guy, broke down some empty packing cartons, and carried them to the dumpster in the alley. When he came back upstairs, I asked him to open Tiffany's desk and gather all her personal belongings to put in a banker's box, except for the little blue Tiffany's box.

I pretty much had a handle on how I would proceed for the rest of the day. I made a couple of appointments with clients for the following week and touched base with the two nearly completed jobs in Seattle that belonged to L.E.H. My intention was not to steal them, but to let them know I was available if any problems came up that I could help with.

"Let's put the answering machine on and break for lunch," the impersonator said. "Looks like you could use a square meal before we attack the rest of the day."

"We?" I leaned back in my chair and studied him. "Look, Dad, if that's who you really are, what is going on here? Yesterday you showed up on my doorstep devastated and alone, after the Mother person's wild peccadillo, begging me to help you. I'm confused."

Dad sighed and sat across the desk from me. He rubbed the bridge of his aristocratic nose with his thumb and forefinger and closed his eyes briefly. "I realized something after you left for your friend's funeral yesterday. It may be too little, too late, but I had some sharp insight on our relationship."

"Look, Dad——"

"No, Caroline, let me finish what I have to say. Please?"

I raised my hands in surrender and settled back for what I expected to be the usual excuses and clueless self-justifications.

"For the past thirty-odd years, I allowed Elizabeth to set the tone of our marriage, to make major decisions about finances, investments, residences, and even select our so-called friends. It makes perfect sense that she'd eventually walk out on me. What a complete bore I must have been all those years."

He couldn't have missed my shocked expression. He gave me a weak smile.

Dad nodded. "At the risk of being crude, there's a colorful expression I'm sure you've heard, which described me, it ends with whipped." He smiled more broadly and said, "Go ahead, laugh. It's so pathetic it's funny, even to me. I've made a royal mess, haven't I?"

He leaned back and shook his head. "I'm a pitiful excuse for a man. I admit it."

I leaned my elbows on the desk and covered my face with both hands. I wanted to laugh, and I didn't want to laugh, so I sighed deeply and lowered my hands to look him in the eyes. My elegant, aristocratic father—*True Confessions*—who would have guessed?

"Dad, I only wish Gramma was here to listen to this."

He continued. "I was a great disappointment to Mother, I know. She didn't deserve a thoughtless son like me. Believe me when I tell you that *you* more than made up for it. With you, Mother got the child of her dreams."

"For heaven's sake, Dad!" I rolled my eyes. "This isn't Dr. Phil."

"Agreed, but I needed to say it. I realized last night that I had no business asking you to help me. I'm the one who should be helping you. By allowing Elizabeth to run my life, I sacrificed a very precious thing, a full, loving relationship with my daughter."

He wasn't finished. "Daniel hit the nail on the head that night he came back in the restaurant after you stormed out. He told us exactly what he thought of us. He was absolutely right. I thought twice about Daniel after that. Elizabeth and I had unpleasant words about him later that night at our hotel. I have a great deal of respect for him, and you are a lucky woman to have found him. Believe me, I've been around the block, and men like Daniel are rare."

It was nice of Dad to point that out now that I'd completely screwed up my relationship with Danny.

He retrieved the picnic Marta had prepared for us and set out napkins and plates on my desk. He asked me to get us a fresh cup of coffee while he arranged the covered containers and utensils.

"Look, Dad, I uh...I'm not hungry, I don't think I..."

He said nothing, just pointed at the cups and the coffee maker and continued with what he was doing.

What the heck, I might as well eat. What's the worst thing that can happen? Never mind. I take that back.

I got the fresh coffee, took it back to my desk, and sat like an obedient Daddy's Girl. I was rewarded with a genuine smile from his handsome face. His eyes, however, still seemed lost and sad.

"Thank you, Caroline."

"For what?"

"Just, thank you. Here, which salad would you prefer, tuna or chicken?"

"Can't I have some of each?" I dared ask.

"Anything for my brilliant and beautiful daughter."

Finally, we relaxed in each other's company and enjoyed a delicious lunch and some genuine laughter.

CHAPTER 56

Matthew

How sad that so many years of their lives have been wasted. I'm heartened to see them connect emotionally, however tenuous. Parents and children. Believe me, I was no exception. I'm sure I caused my earthly father many a sleepless night.

I truly love my job at times like this.

CHAPTER 57

Daniel

Dan had a conversation with Mary this morning. He was supposed to be working on a contract deadline but took the time to talk to her just the same. He put a higher priority on his own life than on that damn contract. Anyway, he could probably bang it out in his sleep if he had to.

He closed his door and buzzed Billie, asked her to hold all calls and make plausible excuses for him while he called his mother.

"You take your time, hon. Nobody will get past me."

Billie is a gem, he thought. I gotta remember to order her some flowers.

Talking with his mother had a way of giving him the ability to step away from the moment and get some perspective. He was so good at helping clients do that very thing, but when it was for himself, he liked a conversation with his mother.

"You know how much I hate to give advice, Daniel." The fact was, she was solicited for and gave advice all the time. Dan figured she just didn't like that label.

"Yeah, I know, Ma. I'm not really expecting you to have the answers I want to hear. It just helps to talk about it."

It would be nice though, if she could tell him what to do and presto, problem solved.

"Go right ahead, honey. I'm glad to listen."

"Okay, here goes. Caroline is dragging out this situation for no good reason, and she knows it. She's just too damn stubborn to call me. I'm pissed with her because now, especially now, after Tiffany got killed. She knows she needs me to be with her. I should be with her."

"Sounds to me as if you're in a stalemate."

"Well, yeah." Danny detected a soft chortle from her end of the line and couldn't help smiling.

"Dan, you're probably thinking that you're in danger of losing her, and you don't know how to fix things, or even if it's up to you to try. Am I getting close?"

"Very."

"Look, son, I don't think Caroline's going anywhere. I happen to know she loves you very much, and that's probably why she's so upset with you. If she didn't love you, she wouldn't be so angry. Have you thought about that?"

Dan had on a headset and was about to wear a permanent path across the new carpeting in his office.

"Yes, I've thought about that, but she's blown everything out of proportion. You'd think I committed a third-degree felony instead of what I did do, co-sign a loan so she could get a start on her business. I'd like to take her by the throat and give her a good shaking."

"Since you asked for my advice, I wouldn't advise that."

"How do I undo the mess I've made of things? I knew when I signed on that dotted line that she'd go ballistic if she ever found out. What a dunce I am for listening to that meddlesome jerk, Matthew!"

"My goodness, who is this Matthew I keep hearing about? Is he the same man who got hurt in that riot in Seattle? He seems to be around an awful lot. He picked up Ryan in a taxi and took him to the hospital the other night. Is he a friend of yours or Caroline's?"

Dan waved his hands, stirring the air in his office. "No! He's no friend of mine. He seemed to come out of nowhere several weeks ago. Next thing I know, he's Tiffany's boyfriend. I don't even like the guy. He almost got me killed playing a game of golf."

He shook his head when he heard her snickering as she remembered the golf fiasco and his big, black eye.

"Don't laugh, Ma. It isn't funny."

"I'm afraid it is, dear."

"You're supposed to be on my side, remember?" He flopped into the client chair and put his feet up on the front edge of his desk. "Christ! I've made a mess of things."

"Don't be too hard on yourself, honey. You were only trying to help the woman you love. You used poor judgment is all."

"That's a nice way of saying I have shit for brains!" He yanked off his tie.

"I would never say or even think such a thing. Keep a civil tongue in your head if you wish to continue this conversation."

"I know, I'm sorry."

"I know you are. Now here's my advice. Give her more time and get on with your own life. Whatever is going to happen will happen. Send her a sincere note. Let her know how sorry you are about Tiffany and tell her you're available to her if she needs anything or wishes to talk with you. What else can you do?"

"Thanks, Ma. Love you."

"Love you too, my baby boy."

If anyone ever put a tap on his phone, they could use that declaration of Mary's to blackmail him. He loved to hear it, though.

CHAPTER 58
Matthew

Meddlesome jerk, eh? I expect I deserve that one.

CHAPTER 59
Caroline

A couple of times during the afternoon at my office, I cried when I thought of Tiffany or looked at that little blue box on my desk. So many tears and from where? I must have been saving them all my life. I was also teary thinking of Danny. In my heart, the one Danny claimed I had, I knew he went behind my back to help me because I was too stubborn to allow him to do it openly. What did I think was going to happen if I agreed to let him loan me the money? That I'd lose myself somehow? Lose my integrity? Make me dependent on him?

I should see a shrink.

Dad passed my desk and picked up the cup of cold coffee. He patted me on the shoulder as he went by, and that got me started again.

"It will get easier, Caroline. I know."

"I know too, Dad. It's just so hard right now." I warmed to a sense of love and gratitude toward my father. He was here because he loved me and needed me. We needed each other.

"It's none of my business, but where *is* Daniel Kavanaugh?" He rinsed out the cups in the small sink and commenced cleaning the coffeepot.

I sighed and crossed my arms. "I've messed up my life, Dad. It's not Danny's fault. I might have lost him for good. I'm a fool. Tiffany told me so, and she was right."

"Seems to be going around." He knocked the coffee grounds into a wastebasket.

"You think it runs in the family?" I tried to make a joke, but it was a pretty lame attempt at humor.

To my surprise, Dad turned around and smiled. "Quite possibly, daughter, quite possibly."

With Dad's unexpected help, I actually did get a handle on things. We got the office organized and returned all the calls. I even made a consultation appointment for the next day to meet with a potential customer in Santa Monica. Dad went to the printer's and picked up the stationery and business cards. I laughed and then cried again when I saw that Tiffany had the chutzpah to order them with the name "Clayton & Gaines. Experts in Commercial Office Design."

I will never change the title, and I'll miss that brassy little schemer. I hadn't fully appreciated what a gem she was. Looking at those business cards and stationery would be my daily reminder.

Thanks, girlfriend.

I held them up and showed them to my father. "Have a look at what Tiffany ordered from the printer."

His smile widened. "I wish I'd known her."

Dad suggested I get a website up and running as soon as possible. I didn't know a thing about computers that didn't involve email or design drafting. An old schoolmate of Dad's had a son who designed websites for a living. He quickly got on the phone and called his friend to get the name of the son's company.

Dad fired up Tiffany's computer, pulled up the man's website, and sent an email inquiry. I had no clue that he knew one side of a computer from the other. We made an appointment to meet the guy that evening for dinner at a restaurant near his office in Van Nuys.

I was astonished what I did *not* know about my father. All those years, I assumed the only thing he knew how to do was travel around the world, following Beth like a puppy, while she squandered his inheritance.

He'd graduated from Wharton with a degree in business and finance. As far as I could remember, he'd never had a real job. My Gramma had hoped he'd take over the family business, which she'd run since my grandfather died. They manufactured and held the patent on some sort of high-tech concrete pumping equipment, which was used all over the world in the construction of roads, bridges, and highways. When Dad became totally besotted by dear old Mom, he demonstrated no further interest in the company. Gramma reluctantly took it public. Dad remained the majority stockholder, maybe, but I didn't know that for sure. It was something we should talk about one of these days. Especially now that Mother is divorcing him for her little old Italian gazillionaire, and I'm the heir apparent to whatever is left.

Things were moving right along, at least in the business side of my life. My personal side, a big fat question mark.

CHAPTER 60

Matthew

My supervisor just informed me that I made the right move by arranging for Caroline and Lyle to be thrown together in a working situation. Truthfully, she used the word "meddling", rather than arranging, but I got it right for a change.

My intuition is improving. Even she admits it. I do fret about humans who have guardian angels like me. On-the-job-training is not that beneficial to our charges.

We less experienced G.A. s are often redeemed by the excellent oversight system in place here. The tether may be yanked back quickly, on short notice. I speak from experience.

It also helps a great deal when one's human charges are intelligent and resourceful.

CHAPTER 61

Caroline

After dinner and drinks at a nice little hole-in-the-wall in Van Nuys, I contracted with Sean Cronin to begin construction on my website, Clayton & Gaines, the following week. The price was right, and he brought his laptop to show samples of his work.

One more thing out of the way.

Lingering after Sean left, Dad and I polished off the last of the wine. "Tell me what's happening with you and Mother."

"If you tell me what's happening with you and Daniel."

"I asked first."

He sat back in his chair and crossed his arms. His thoughtful expression indicated he had to consider what he would to say to me. He cleared his throat. "First, I think I should explain further why we refused your request to release part of your trust fund."

He blushed. Either that or he'd had too much to drink, which I knew wasn't the case.

My chest constricted at the memory of that evening. "That might be a good place to start."

"I'll just say it. There is no trust fund."

That was a slap in the kisser. "What? But Gramma said-she told me-I saw the paperwork on it. I have it in my bank safe deposit box."

"I didn't say there never was a trust fund. What I meant to say is there's no money left in it." He leaned forward with his elbows on the table and shook his head. "I'm terribly ashamed to admit this to you."

He linked his fingers and twisted his hands.

"Just what are you admitting?" Talk about blindsided. This was one for the books.

"I need to assure you that you have an inheritance. The trust fund no longer exists, though." He shifted uncomfortably and continued. "I make no excuses for my actions. I want you to understand that. Elizabeth and I were the trustees of the fund and had total control. Mother didn't trust Elizabeth and put safeguards in the terms of the fund, one of which was that no moneys could be withdrawn without both Elizabeth and me signing off on it. I allowed Elizabeth to pressure me into using the money from your fund, which amounted to about three million dollars, for the purchase of the land on Portovenere."

My head buzzed. "Three million dollars! I had three million dollars? And you…"

He grimaced and continued, "Elizabeth rationalized that you were heir to the property, which would eventually increase your assets."

He couldn't even look me in the face. Still in shock, I asked him, "Are you insane? You could end up in jail for doing something like that. I knew that you let her lead you around as if you had a ring in your nose, but this I cannot believe."

Dad raised his hands and nodded. "You're absolutely right. I make no excuse for my behavior. I knew at the time it was the wrong thing to do, but I went right ahead and signed off on it. Allowing Elizabeth to do anything and everything she ever wanted, without so much as a piddling protest, has been the pattern of my adult life." He finally looked me in the eye. "I'm terribly ashamed and sorry."

"Ashamed and sorry? You stole my future." I pushed my chair back, prepared to leave.

He reached out and put his hand on my arm. "No, wait, there's more."

I sank back into the chair. "More? Oh, please tell me. I can hardly wait to hear it." Sarcasm I'd perfected over many years dripped from my lips.

"When I fully realized what I'd allowed to happen, I tried to cancel the real estate deal and recover the funds. Elizabeth and I had the first of several long and bitter rows. The contract was not cancelable. That was the beginning of the end for me and your mother. Actually, it was probably the end of the end. I was far too dense and giddy with love for Elizabeth. I was too befuddled to recognize it."

I shook my head in disgust. "I really don't care what happened with you and Mother. She was never a mother to me, and you were the poorest excuse for a father. If I hadn't had Gramma—"

"I know, Caroline. There is no way for me to make up for all those years that you and I have lost, but you need to know—"

Deep hurt and anger burned my stomach and chest. I glared at him. "I don't need to know anything else from you. I'm not interested in what you have to say, and I don't care if I ever see you or hear from you again. Danny was so right about you."

His chin trembled, and his eyes grew watery. "Yes, he was. I admit it, but I did my best to set things right. I sold a large block of my stock in the company and set up a retirement account for you. I also deeded the Hancock Park house into your name. That was the final straw for Elizabeth. That's when she left me."

Overwhelmed at trying to take in everything he'd told me, I sat silent and stunned. How Gramma had produced a son with so little backbone was a mystery, or else Beth must have powers for which I have no understanding. My father had given control of his entire adult life over to her. A woman so shallow I couldn't comprehend the hold she had over him. In my book, that's another very good reason not to fall head-over-heels in love and hand your life over to someone, anyone.

"I can't take this in. What were you thinking when you deeded the house to me? There is no way in hell I can afford the taxes and upkeep on that place. The annual property taxes alone must be in the five digits. I'll have to sell it immediately or it will be seized for property tax default. My future credit could be ruined. My God, I just started a business with money that Danny signed a guarantee for and have no ability to repay. Now you've dropped the burden of Gramma's house in my lap."

He sat upright. "I thought of all that. I have a plan."

My response was sarcastic. "I can't wait to hear it."

Dad patted his hands in the air. "Okay, just listen and think about it. Then we'll discuss all our options when you've had a chance to digest everything. That's all I ask."

I shook my head with wonder. "I'm listening. I don't know why but go ahead."

"I have money, not as much as I did, but I still own a substantial majority of shares in the company. If you consent to me living in *your* house, I'll pay all the taxes, upkeep, salaries and any other costs associated with it. I've been doing that ever since Mother died."

Hair on my neck prickled. "Go on."

"It's not apparent, but I do have a good head for business, otherwise Elizabeth would have gone through every cent in the past thirty years. I'm going to look for a position, perhaps with the company board of directors. If not there, I will find one. I'm only fifty-eight and have many productive years left. You know I have excellent contacts. I'd like to make up for lost time."

"Dad..." I raised my hands, then dropped them in my lap.

"Just be quiet for another moment, please. I need to say everything I have to say. You can pick it apart later. You're good at that. You take after my mother."

He raised his hand again to stop me from speaking and continued. "I'd like to help you get your business off the ground. It will be a sound investment for me. I propose to be your silent partner. I'll pay off your bank loan in full. You'll have complete control of every aspect of the firm. We'll set up a corporation. I'll be a minority stockholder. Just allow me to continue to assist you as I have been for the past couple of days, until things are rolling along, and you can afford to hire help. Then I'll back away. I want to do this for you, Caroline. I owe you."

CHAPTER 62

Matthew

Well, my goodness. Even I didn't anticipate that turn of events. So much for my superior angelic powers. I do admit, though, I am enjoying the show.

CHAPTER 63

Daniel

The week after Thanksgiving, Wayne and Grace, in their vast wisdom, probably feeling sorry for Dan because he hadn't heard from Caroline in weeks, invited him to dinner. They told him they were also inviting a couple, friends of theirs. What they failed to tell him was the *couple* consisted of two single women friends.

As soon as he walked through their door, he saw the setup and so did the ladies.

He smiled at Betts, his old high school girlfriend, now a divorced mother with three small kids. She and Dan peered at each other and shook their heads, quickly detecting Wayne and Grace's conspiracy. The reason she *was* an old girlfriend was because there never had been any sexual chemistry between them. They were pals. They'd enjoyed being together for a couple of semesters. That was it.

The other lady, and Dan used the term cautiously—was a criminal defense lawyer with a reputation for having very sharp teeth and a merciless sarcastic wit. She also saw the setup, didn't like being trotted out like a prize heifer, and she and Daniel had hated each other from the get-go.

What a lovely evening they had. Dan was seated between the two women at the dining table. The defense lawyer's conversation consisted of a diatribe against men in general, lawyers who wasted their law school education doing business with wealthy and corporate clients, instead of defending scumbags—Dan's words, not hers—against a flawed justice system, and women who marry dallying dunces then get dumped along with their small children.

Dan's old girlfriend kicked him under the table a couple of times when she sensed he was about to let the bitch have a piece of his mind. Betts had a lot more equanimity about the situation than he did. She and Dan peered at each other and shared a quiet chuckle now and then, giving Grace the impression that she'd been successful as their matchmaker.

He popped her bubble instantly when he saw her give Wayne a satisfied, sidelong look. Dan commenced five minutes of non-stop praise for Caroline, and his happiness for the launch of her new business, in the face of the Tiffany tragedy. He spoke of her superior intelligence, fortitude, and the fact that, in his opinion, she was the most beautiful and desirable woman in the world. He concluded by adding that he hoped they'd be married before long.

The defense lawyer made a hasty retreat the moment dinner concluded. Her excuse that her cell, set on vibrate, had received an urgent message from one of her less-than-sterling clients, rang hollow. She had to leave immediately to take care of the crisis. She thanked Wayne and Grace for the invitation to dinner in a tone of voice that clearly indicated she would never set foot in their home again.

There were a few moments of icy silence when she closed the front door—too bad it didn't smack her in the ass—as they sat staring at one another. Betts and Daniel burst into simultaneous laughter.

She threw her arms around his neck. "Good show, Danny." She giggled and then added, "You struck a solid blow for those of us fed up with militant feminism. You would have made a great defense lawyer, by the way."

"I considered it once." He gave her a hard hug. "How are you doing, by the way? I heard about what good old Barry did to you and the kids."

She exhaled with a resigned smile. "I was devastated at first and then slowly came to the realization we were better off without him. The kids aren't quite sure yet, and I don't bad-mouth their dad. They'll figure it out on their own."

Dan faced Grace. "I told Betts at her wedding reception that Barry was a class A turd. She didn't like it much." He turned to her again, "Did you, hon?"

"Your timing was a little off, don't you think? Why didn't you say something sooner?" She placed her napkin on the table and stood, prepared to help Grace clear the dishes.

Dan leaned back in his chair. "Seriously now, would you have paid any attention to me if I had?"

"Hardly," she answered over her shoulder on the way to the kitchen with a stack of plates, Grace following close behind.

Dan put his chin on his fist and glared at Wayne. "Should I kick your ass now or later?"

"I'd prefer later."

"What were you thinking? Don't blame it on Grace."

"It *was* her suggestion, but I went along with it. It seemed like a good idea at the time." He stood, picked up the serving dishes, and stacked them to one side. "Have another glass of wine. I'm not going near that kitchen. Let's go to the living room." He picked up the bottle and his glass.

"Capital idea, brother."

An abashed Grace served dessert and coffee in the living room about thirty minutes later. Dan sat next to Betts. She showed him pictures of her cute kids, twin girls and a three-year-old boy, named Barry, Jr. When he raised his eyebrows at the mention of the kid's name, Betts shrugged and gave him an ironic *oh well* look. "His initials are BJ, but I would never hang that around his neck."

Grace wrinkled her brow. Daniel and Wayne burst into laughter.

Betts told them she'd been rehired as a teacher at the Montessori school, and little Barry could go with her each day. Leaving him with a babysitter had been hard for her to contemplate. The two girls were in first grade at the same school. Betts was thrilled to have been offered her old teaching position as well as greatly reduced tuition for her kids.

Dan asked her if she would like him to take her and the kids to Disneyland the following weekend, and she readily accepted with a happy smile.

When he left Grace at the front door, he whispered in her ear, "I know you love me, Gracie, but don't ever do that again. Please."

She went dark red and gave him a fierce hug. "Sorry, Danny."

Wayne and Dan stood outside, leaning on the side of Wayne's van for a while. He was about to leave for their parents' home to pick up his kids.

"Wayne, what's the best thing Mom and Dad ever taught us?" When he gave Dan his famous Thoughtful Wayne expression, Dan continued, "Fidelity."

Wayne nodded his head. "Um hum."

"You can pass on to Stewart, Grant, and Flynn that if any of you ever try to set me up with another woman, I'll kick your asses from here to Sunday and back. I love Caroline, and I'm not interested in any other woman. Got it?"

Lips pressed together, Wayne nodded. "Got it."

CHAPTER 64

Caroline

Surprise! I was very pleased with the way things were going in my business and with my father. He'd been a real help getting me over a rough beginning. We'd drawn up a business partnership contract, his silent partner minority shareholder position, in return for the payoff of my loan at Wilshire Bank.

I retained total control in every aspect of the business, which was developing better than I had hoped. Old contacts paid off. I had half a dozen projects going already. When Dad got sick of being my *administrative assistant*, I would definitely have to hire someone to replace him.

We also had a lease agreement on *my* house, spelling out the terms and conditions. He would continue to pay all taxes and upkeep associated with the property for as long as I consented to him living there. He suggested I give up my apartment and come live in the big house, but I wasn't nearly ready for that level of intimacy. He was deeply involved with his team of divorce lawyers and actually apologized to me for the amount of time he spent making personal calls while at work. That made me smile.

I got two unexpected phone calls yesterday. One was from Moody, of all people. He told me he had hired a very promising junior designer so as not to lose him to a competitor, but L.E.H. was a bit top-heavy. If I would need anyone in the near future, he'd rather see the guy come to work for me than someone else. I was so shocked I nearly choked. He also invited me to have lunch with him the following week, which I politely declined on the basis of being too short-handed to leave the office except for appointments with clients. He took it well, I thought. When I hung up, I shook my head in wonder.

The other phone call was from Ryan. "Hi, Caroline." I recognized his voice immediately.

"Hi, good-lookin'. How you doing?" I was shocked and warmly pleased to hear his voice.

"I...um...was...ah," he cleared his throat. "I had my birthday yesterday. I'm thirteen now."

"Well, congratulations and happy birthday, Ryan. I wish I'd known before. I would have sent you a card, or we could have gone out on a date or something." I smiled at the memory of his freckled face.

"A date? That would be great because...uh...it would be fun, and anyway I think Uncle Danny has a new girlfriend now."

My heart stopped for an instant. I was sure of it. I couldn't think of a darn thing to say and sat holding the phone against my shoulder with my chin, my hands suddenly stilled on top of the mail I'd been sorting. The letter opener was pointed at my chest and for a moment I considered impaling myself.

I finally found my voice. "A new girlfriend?" Very thirsty, I twisted frantically at the top of the water bottle on the corner of my desk, unable to open it. Dad peered across the room curiously, and when he saw what I was trying to do, he stepped over, took the bottle from my hands, and removed the cap.

He raised his eyebrows in concern, and I shook my head quickly while trying to drink and hold the phone at the same time. The phone shot out from under my chin and flew across my desk. It bounced and took some of the paperwork with it as it sailed toward the floor.

"Dammit!" I choked on the water I was swallowing, almost knocked Dad over as I stood to make a grab for it while rounding the corner of my desk.

"What?" Dad crinkled his forehead with alarm.

"In a minute." I retrieved the phone and shouted into it, "Ryan? Are you still there?"

"Yeah, what happened?"

I took a couple of deep breaths. "You said, I, um, thought you said Dan has a new girlfriend. Is that what you said?"

"I think it's more like a new old girlfriend. Dad told Mom last night that he took her and her kids to Disneyland yesterday. They used to go out on dates and stuff when they were in high school. Dad said she's a real nice lady. Everybody likes her. Her name is Betts."

I wondered what in the heck *stuff* Danny and this woman had done when they were in high school.

"I'm sure she is nice." I turned to face Dad and made an evil, mean face. "Danny has a new girlfriend, great. That's great." I hoped the look on my face hadn't been conveyed in my voice.

Dad made a funny mouth, shrugged, turned, and went back to Tiffany's desk.

The rest of my conversation with Ryan was somewhat of a blur, but we agreed to meet at the mall a few blocks from his house the next afternoon for pizza and a movie. I did look forward to it. I missed the kid, but, Danny, a new girlfriend? I didn't like that one bit.

CHAPTER 65

Matthew

What an interesting development. I was so enjoying this turn of events that I invited Tiffany away from her mentors to come and observe with me. We greeted each other like old friends. I no longer had any intimate desire for her, but I will love her for eternity. She's in the early stages of letting go of her lingering human emotions. Our embrace was warm and satisfying for both of us.

"Matthew, sweetheart, I'm so glad to see you. How did you ever get me out of class?" Her smile brought back stirring memories. I admit it.

"You'll be pleased to know that things are happening with our project, events that I'm sure you'll enjoy." We found a soft, comfortable place to recline and look upon my earthly charges.

Billie buzzed Daniel's office to tell him there was a woman on the phone demanding to talk to him. She thought it might be Caroline but wouldn't swear to it.

"Put her on, Billie." A click, some silence. "This is Daniel Kavanaugh, may I help you?"

"I don't think so, you cheating skunk!"

"Excuse me, but who is this, please?"

"You know darn well who this is. What are you up to, Kavanaugh?"

His smile warmed up to megawatts. "Up to?"

"Don't play the innocent with me. Ryan told me you had a new girlfriend. What is that all about? What new girlfriend?"

"I don't know what Ryan told you, Care, but—"

"He wouldn't lie to me, Danny. The only liar in the entire Kavanaugh family is you!"

"Dammit, babe, you are enough to drive a sane man crazy. What do you care whether I have another girlfriend or not? You don't want me. You made that crystal clear." Danny paced in his usual spot, back and forth in front of his desk.

Tiffany grabbed my hand, and we exchanged smiles.

Caroline sat in her car in the parking lot in front of her office, fuming, fuming because Danny was so darn dense, and because she had to leave her nice cool office to have a private phone conversation. "What are you talking about, Dan? I never said any such thing. All I did was ask for my key back. You haven't called me in almost two months. I'm really mad at you."

He stopped, put his hands on his hips. "You're mad at me. Well, that's unusual. I'm shocked, so shocked I have to sit down. Could you hold on while I get hold of myself?"

"Don't be a smartass!" She opened her car door, stepped out onto the concrete and matched Daniel's pacing step for step.

"What the hell do you want from me, Care? Am I supposed to sit around twiddling my thumbs while you take an eternity to get your act together?" He flopped on one of the client chairs in front of his desk.

Caroline sounded angry now. "Me? Me get my act together?"

"Yes, you, babe. I know what I want. You're the one with the problem."

"You...you...Danny, you make me crazy!" She turned and kicked her car door shut with such force she hurt her toes.

He sat forward, alert. "What was that?"

"It was nothing." Caroline gritted her teeth and flailed her arm. "It was my car door if you must know."

"I certainly hope you're not driving in the state you're in." A wide smile grew on Daniel's face.

I glanced at Tiffany. She smiled back at me and gave me a thumbs up. I whispered, "We might be getting somewhere."

She winked. "You think?"

Caroline stopped pacing, put both arms straight to her sides and fisted her hands, nearly mashing her phone. She looked skyward. "Dammit, Tiffany Gaines, where are you when I need you?"

FOR HEAVEN'S SAKE, MARRY THE MAN

Tiffany leaned forward and whispered, *"I'm right here, girlfriend. Remember your promise? Don't blow it!"*

Caroline's eyes flew open, and she staggered back against her car. She barely heard Daniel calling to her from the phone she'd pressed against her heart. She slowly raised the phone to her ear. "What?"

"Care? Babe? Are you okay? I was joking." He stood and resumed pacing. "Care, we need to talk."

She took a deep breath. "You bet we do, Buster. You be at my place by seven this evening, and you'd better be armed with a believable story, because if you ever had any idea of marrying me, the explanation has to be iron clad!"

"I'll be there. Seven. I'll be there." He threw a fist in the air and grinned.

"I mean it, Danny."

"You love me, don't you, Care? Say it."

She groaned, then sighed, dropped her head back, staring at the sky where she thought she'd heard Tiffany's voice. "Yes, I love you, okay? I have to get back to work." She hit End on the phone and returned to her office.

Danny buzzed Billie. "Where's the new law clerk?"

"I think Marty's in the law library. He went there straight from your office about an hour ago. Do you need him?"

"Yeah, I do. Send him in please."

When the young intern arrived, Dan handed him several bills. "I have an important errand for you. You only have an hour to get it accomplished. Head over to Macy's and buy me the ugliest Christmas sweater you can find. My size. The ugliest. You got it?"

Marty stared wide-eyed and nodded. He took the money his boss handed him. "I'm on it, boss."

Danny yanked off his headset, opened his office door to the reception area, grabbed an astonished Billie and danced her around the shiny marble floor while singing Sweet Caroline. The three executive secretaries exchanged glances and burst into laughter.

Bill Knight poked his head out his office door. "What the...?"

Danny dipped Billie low, like a romantic lover. "She loves me, Billie girl!"

"She'd be a fool not to, Danny boy."

Tiffany and I laughed and mimicked Daniel and Billie by dancing around our own little piece of Heaven.

Danny stood outside Caroline's door at seven on the dot. He knocked.

Caroline pulled the door open and gasped. "What in heaven's name are you wearing?"

"Christmas wrap." He twirled around. "You like?"

"It's abominable, Danny." She grinned.

"Don't judge the gift by the wrapping, babe."

She grabbed the front of the sweater and pulled him inside. "Wouldn't think of it."

Epilogue

New Year's Day

When Flynn's wife Claire placed the short veil on Caroline's unruly auburn curls, Caroline heard, "Good going, girlfriend."

"What did you say, Claire?" You'd never know she'd recently had a baby girl. Let alone those three boys.

"I didn't say anything but see how beautiful you look, soon-to-be sister-in-law." She held up the hand mirror.

Caroline heard the words again and smiled when she recognized Tiffany's voice. Caroline nodded at her reflection. "Do you like my dress?" She smoothed down the front of her emerald green silk sheath.

Claire and Tiffany both answered, "I love it."

She took one more turn in front of the triple mirrors. "Let's do it then."

Right hand in the crook of her father's elbow, Caroline peeked around the corner of the house. Under the ivy, white tulle, and flower decorated, trellis she admired Danny and his Best Man, Ryan, standing at the front, handsome in their tuxedos. Behind Danny, his four brothers were lined up waiting. On the other side, her four sisters-in-law were beautiful in their red silk dresses, holding tiny bouquets of white lily of the valley. Everyone in the wedding party, including Caroline and her dad, wore red sneakers.

The wide backyard of Mary and Liam Kavanaugh's house overflowed with large vases of white freesia and yellow roses. The weather was perfect for their wedding, and the Rose Parade earlier this morning.

The audience, even though large, were just family members. Caroline insisted Rodney and Marta be included. They were her only family except for her father.

Any minute now, the deejay would play the traditional Wedding March. She turned to Lyle Clayton with a nervous but happy smile on her face. The music began and they stepped out on the white cloth path. The Kavanaugh smile immediately bloomed on the faces of all the males at the altar, including the Justice of the Peace who suspiciously resembled Matthew. No, couldn't be. Her imagination was running wild.

The ceremony was brief and beautiful. When called upon, Danny and Caroline spoke their vows in unison. Ten simple words. "I will love you until the end of my life." They exchanged plain gold wedding bands, and then Danny kissed his bride. At last.

Amen.

The End

∼

Don't miss out on your next favorite book!

Join the Satin Romance mailing list
www.satinromance.com/mail.html

THANK YOU FOR READING

Did you enjoy this book?

We invite you to leave a review at the website of your choice, such as Goodreads, Amazon, Barnes & Noble, etc.

∽

DID YOU KNOW THAT LEAVING A REVIEW...

- Helps other readers find books they may enjoy.
- Gives you a chance to let your voice be heard.
- Gives authors recognition for their hard work.
- Doesn't have to be long. A sentence or two about why you liked the book will do.

About the Author

I wrote my first novel at the age of six. It was titled "The Mouse," and was two pages long—including illustrations! My mother saved that *first edition* and every now and then, I take it out and smile over it. When my beloved husband of many years suddenly died, I'd come home after a long day of work and write. Writing allowed me to pour out all my sadness. Then, the more I wrote, the more I realized I would go on. I would be happy, I had a lot of living to do, and love stories to tell. I'm published now in Romance novels and an anthology of short stories. But my first two manuscripts still reside on a CD somewhere in my house. I can't bear to erase them because they're mine, they're loved, and like a crazy relative one hides in the attic, they reside in a quiet, safe place.

pattycampbell.com
pattycampbellauthor.blogspot.com

facebook.com/Patty-Campbell-Author-536855299661241
goodreads.com/goodreadscomuser_PattyCampbell

Also by Patty Campbell

Wounded Warriors Series
Heart of a Marine
Love of a Marine
Soul of a Marine
Always a Marine

Novels
Risky Business
Forever Amber
Once a Marine
Jelly's Big Night Out (Coming Soon!)

Made in the USA
Columbia, SC
21 March 2022